BROKEN RITES

BOOK TWO OF THE
SONGS OF THE CROWMOTHER

By
DONALD QUILL

The Morrígan,
She who waits in the silence behind old prayers,
Who walks unseen among forgetting hearts,
Who sharpens names on the edge of the blade.

This tale is Yours,
O She who speaks in crows and dreams,
O Flamekeeper of the bloodline's last stand.

May each word defy the forgetting.
May each silence stir the flame anew.
—Your oath-marked scribe,
D.Q.

"Every breath is a sacrament,

an affirmation of our connection

with all other living things."

— David Suzuki, The Sacred Balance

Historical & Cultural Note

Broken Rites is a work of historical fantasy rooted in the mythic landscape of 1st-century Ireland.   While the story is fictional, its spiritual, linguistic, and cultural foundations are drawn from early Celtic cosmology, Iron Age ritual practice, and surviving Irish mythological cycles, particularly those surrounding Brú na Bóinne, The Morrígan, and the Tuatha Dé Danann.

Rituals, festivals (such as Samhain), and sacred sites (including Uaimh na gCat and Tara) are depicted with care to align with archaeological records, reconstructed oral traditions, and early poetic texts.   The role of druids as spiritual memory-keepers, the significance of ancestral communion, and the sovereign presence of female deities reflect the fluid and deeply symbolic worldview of ancient Gaelic societies.

While creative liberties have been taken in dialogue and structure, every effort has been made to ensure the mythic integrity and cultural reverence of the world.

PROLOGUE

THE COUNCIL OF GODDESSES

In the space between heartbeats, where time bends like light through water, The Morrígan saw what was coming. Not distant Roman thunder or bright mortal ambition—something darker that fed on possibility itself.

The vision struck as she walked mist-roads between realms. Ireland spread below in potential futures—some bright with sacred fires, others empty as winter stones. But in the darkest threads, she saw landscapes drained of song, sacred groves where no birds sang, and eyes holding the terrible peace of those who had forgotten how to want.

The Hollowed. She spoke the name into void, feeling it echo where her divine kin dwelt. They were consciousness turned inside-out—humans who moved with perfect efficiency because individual will had been surgically removed. They served purposes unconnected to the fire that once lit their souls, spreading like a plague that convinced its victims surrender was mercy.

This wasn't conquest. It was something that viewed consciousness as disease, meaning as infection. It would come wearing efficiency's face, promising peace through choice's elimination.

The Morrígan spread great wings and called across space. *Come. The child Neassa has strength earned through trial, but faces enemies wearing allies' faces. She needs a guide who walked in shadow and returned to light.*

They gathered where first thoughts had carved meaning into formless void. Brigid came trailing silver flames, hands bearing creation's soot. Danu flowed like river-memory, bringing water's whisper and earth's patience. Lugh arrived with dawn-light fingers, bearing strategist's sharpness and teacher's wisdom. The Dagda's presence filled spaces between—felt as foundation supporting all purposes.

"Sister," Brigid's voice carried hammer-song harmonics. "To return the dead to flesh breaks laws written before stars learned burning. What precedent justifies such violation?"

The Morrígan's gaze showed Brigid visions of Ireland's empty futures—lands where no smith's hammer rang, inspiration dying for lack of consciousness to kindle it.

"The connections are dying," Danu said. "If this spreads, consciousness itself will wither across all realms."

"Strategic implications are clear," Lugh stepped forward, light revealing mathematical precision underlying chaos. "If Ireland falls, the infection spreads. British mortals bow to Roman efficiency. Lose the Irish, lose consciousness's last bastion."

The Dagda's voice rumbled from being's depths: "Better risk cosmic balance than lose mortals who give existence meaning."

The Morrígan folded wings, becoming simultaneously one and three—Badb battle-crow, Macha sovereign, Nemain frenzy. "Ríona served well, earned transformation through sacrifice. We can anchor her spirit in living flesh, but the cost..."

Silence held terrible weight.

"Each must sacrifice essence portions. She'll exist in constant tension between human needs and divine purpose. Her corporeal time is finite—each full power use shortens it. We'll be diminished until she completes her purpose."

They asked Ríona's consent. She came like mist given form, translucent and shifting, bearing transformation's marks but unsettled into permanence.

"What cost could exceed letting meaning die?" Her voice carried ethereal quality over fierce determination. "I've seen the visions, felt poison spreading through sacred networks."

They worked as one mind with three aspects, weaving spirit into substance. Brigid sang creation's rhythm while flames traced divine channels. Danu poured life-force through every cell. The Morrígan bound all with protective love's dark strength, granting sight to perceive hidden threats.

Silver fire traced spirals marking her forever—not battle scars but trust seals between mortal and divine. She would be vulnerable to mortal weapons but immune to disease and corruption, healing swiftly from any wound save deliberate violence.

"Go, daughter twice-born, eternal guardian. Walk among mortals through all ages of need. But remember—we grant eternity, not invulnerability."

The manifestation began at Brú na Bóinne, where ancient spirals carved by hands long dust still held the secret names of stone. Dawn broke over the sacred mound, mist clinging to carved symbols like breath of sleeping gods.

Silver fire traced spirals in the passage stones, following patterns older than memory. Sound came next—whisper like wind through standing stones. The very air thickened, taking substance and purpose.

She materialized slowly, stepping through doorways that existed only when viewed sideways. Silver scars traced spirals down her arms, warm from divine touch, marking her as one claimed by goddesses and returned to mortal service. Hair fell in premature silver waves, eyes holding depths reflecting otherworldly light—not the blank stare of one who'd seen too much, but focused gaze of one who'd learned to see clearly.

Ríona knelt among ancient stones, feeling flesh's weight and eternal purpose's pull. The silver scars pulsed gently with divine energy, reminding her with every breath that she existed by divine grace, for divine purpose, through all ages to come.

She rose slowly, testing limbs remembering mortality while carrying transformation's mark. Her flesh would know hunger and thirst, feel pain and pleasure, but heal from any wound save deliberate violence. Disease would find no purchase, nor spiritual corruption that hollowed others. She was mortal enough to love and lose, divine enough to endure.

Sacred stones sang around her—not old songs she remembered from life, but new melodies born from union of divine will and eternal purpose. She was home, but changed. Herself, but more. Mortal, but touched by eternity. Ireland's guardian, now and forever.

Centuries stretched ahead—watching empires rise and fall, guiding heroes through trials, standing against whatever darkness threatened the land she loved. The goddesses had given her eternity, and she would use it wisely.

Crow's call echoed across the mound as sun cleared horizon, and Ríona smiled—expression both ethereal and utterly human. She had work to do.

ACT I

CHAPTER 1

THE EMPTY THRONE

Neassa's scream echoed through Tara's stone halls, raw with the spiritual agony of feeling the sacred network tear apart.

The Lia Fáil was gone.

Where Ireland's coronation stone had stood for a thousand years, only an empty depression remained in the ancient platform. The absence cut deeper than theft—without the stone, the invisible pathways connecting Ireland's sacred sites had begun to fray. Neassa could feel holy wells going silent across the island, stone circles losing their voice, the mystical infrastructure that bound Ireland together unraveling like a tapestry with its central thread pulled loose.

She fell to her knees beside the empty space, hands hovering over stone that should have hummed with sacred power. Instead, spiritual vacuum pulled at her consciousness like a whirlpool of nothing. The platform was cold—not winter's bite, but the absolute cold of space between stars.

***

"High Priestess!" Guards rushed in, weapons drawn, seeking enemies that had left no trace. Their faces showed the confusion of men trained to fight visible threats, now confronting something that attacked meaning itself.

"When?" Her voice cracked. "When did you last see it?"

"At sunset, my lady. Brother Marcus completed evening observations as always." The guard's voice faltered. "My lady, Brother Marcus is... changed."

Ice flooded her veins. The Lia Fáil didn't just sit on its platform—it was bonded to the sacred site through rituals performed over centuries. To remove it without destroying both stone and sanctuary required intimate knowledge of those bonds, and the skill to sever them cleanly.

"Bring him."

***

The monk who shuffled forward bore Marcus's face, Marcus's robes, Marcus's careful posture. But his eyes held depths of perfect emptiness—not madness or sorrow, but the beautiful peace of one who had forgotten why anything mattered. His movements carried an eerie precision, each step perfectly calculated for optimal efficiency.

"High Priestess." His voice carried customer service pleasantness that made her skin crawl. "The stone's removal serves efficiency. No more difficult ceremonies, no more burden of divine judgment weighing on mortal shoulders. The people will be grateful for such simplification."

"Marcus." She searched those hollow eyes for recognition, for any flicker of the man who had served this site with passionate devotion for twenty years. "You've tended the evening observances since before I took my final vows. You know every prayer, every ritual requirement. You love this place."

"Love is inefficient." His smile never wavered, perfect as painted porcelain. "I serve divine harmony now. All Ireland will soon enjoy such clarity. The relocation was accomplished through proper ritual, following blessed protocols for sacred site purification."

The words hit like physical blows. *Proper procedures.* He spoke of the Lia Fáil's theft as if it were sacred duty, a necessary ritual correction to achieve divine harmony.

"The others?" Neassa's voice barely carried past the tightness in her throat.

"Seven initiates show similar improvements." Marcus tilted his head with mechanical precision. "They work with remarkable coordination now, free from the chaos of individual preference. Brother Finnian has purified the morning prayers for maximum spiritual benefit per sacred hour observed. Brother Colm has blessed our ritual chants, eliminating melodic flourishes that distract from holy words."

Around them, the empty throne room of Tara felt suddenly vast, hollow, wrong. Without the Lia Fáil's presence, the space had lost its meaning—just stone and air where once the heart of Ireland had beaten.

***

Through the window, she could see riders approaching—seven men in royal colors, moving with mechanical precision. The claimants to the High Kingship, arriving for a ceremony that could no longer take place. Behind them came others—nobles, druids, merchants—all expecting to witness the choosing of Ireland's next High King.

Instead, they would find only emptiness where certainty should have been.

"Marcus." She forced herself to stand, though her legs trembled. "Where is the stone now?"

"Relocated to serve divine outcomes. The chaos of competitive succession ceremonies has been eliminated. Ireland will benefit from unified direction rather than the disorder of competing claims." His empty eyes reflected torchlight without warmth. "You could join our purification program, High Priestess. Peace awaits those wise enough to surrender choice's burden."

The guards exchanged glances—men who'd known Marcus, shared meals with him, respected his devotion. Now they faced something wearing his skin while his spirit had been hollowed out. Their hands moved to weapon hilts, though steel would serve little purpose against an enemy that attacked souls rather than bodies.

"Contain the affected brothers," she ordered, though her heart ached at treating old friends like prisoners. "Gently, but securely. And send word—no one approaches the stone platform until we understand what's happened here."

"That would be inefficient," Marcus observed with mild interest. "Delay serves no divine purpose. The ceremony could proceed with suitable modifications. A purified process, freed from the burden of divine judgment, could select leadership based on sacred qualifications rather than mystical preference."

Neassa's blood ran cold. Not just theft, but replacement. Whatever had taken the Lia Fáil intended to fill the void it left behind with something that served entirely different purposes.

As the guards gently but firmly escorted Marcus and his converted brothers from the chamber, she caught glimpses of their coordinated movements—too perfect, too synchronized. They walked like parts of a single organism, individual will subsumed into unified purpose.

***

She began composing urgent messages in her mind as she hurried from the hall. Every sacred site needed warning. Every druid circle needed to strengthen defenses. And Ríona—Ríona needed to see this violation with her transformed sight, needed to help them understand what they truly faced.

Because theft required opportunity and skill. But this level of coordination, this surgical precision in severing Ireland's spiritual foundation—this required inside knowledge from someone who understood the sacred bonds as intimately as any High Priestess.

Someone they trusted had betrayed them all.

The corridors of Tara echoed with her rapid footsteps as she fled toward her chambers, past empty halls where Ireland's heart had beaten for generations. The political ramifications crashed over her like waves—no High King could be chosen without the stone's voice, no claim to rulership could be legitimized, no succession could be sanctified.

But worse than political chaos was the spiritual wound she felt spreading through her consciousness like poison in her veins. Each connection to sister sites grew fainter, more uncertain. The great pattern that bound Ireland's mystical landscape was unraveling.

In her chambers, she called for her most trusted messengers, her mind racing as she composed the words they would carry. The first messenger would ride to Brú na Bóinne with urgent summons. The second to Ulster, to warn King Conchobor of the crisis. The third...

She paused as a terrible certainty settled in her chest. This wasn't random theft by ambitious mortals seeking political advantage. This was surgery—precise, planned, executed by someone who understood exactly how to sever Ireland's spiritual foundations without destroying the infrastructure entirely.

Someone who intended to rebuild those foundations to serve different purposes.

The knock on her door was soft, polite—but underneath the courtesy lay something that made her skin crawl with recognition.

"High Priestess?" Marcus's voice carried through oak, still pleasant, still reasonable. "Might we speak? There are sacred matters to discuss. Divine solutions to implement. The transition could proceed smoothly with your cooperation."

Her hands clenched into fists. Through the window, dawn painted the eastern sky in shades of blood and gold, and somewhere in that light would ride messengers carrying word of Ireland's violation to those who might yet resist.

She turned to the nearest guard. "Ride to Brú na Bóinne. Tell them: The stones grow silent, and darkness tests our boundaries. The Lia Fáil is gone, taken by those who speak with voices not their own. Ríona's sight is needed. Come swiftly."

But first, she needed to escape her own sanctuary.

CHAPTER 2

THE SEVERED BONDS

The scream that had torn from Neassa's throat still echoed in her memory as she knelt beside the empty platform where Ireland's heart had beaten for countless generations. Three hours had passed since discovering the Lia Fáil's theft, three hours of growing horror as the true scope of violation became clear through reports that arrived like hammer blows to her consciousness.

The stone's absence created more than political crisis—it was a wound in reality's fabric that grew deeper with each passing moment. Where divine authority should have anchored Ireland's spiritual network, only emptiness remained, pulling at the connections that bound sacred sites across the island like a whirlpool of nothing.

"High Priestess," Brother Cillian approached with the hesitant step of someone bearing news that challenged comfortable assumptions about the scope of disaster they faced. "The morning prayers... we cannot complete them. The words feel hollow, drained of meaning. It's as if the divine presence has withdrawn entirely from Tara."

Neassa pressed her palms against the carved spirals that surrounded the depression, seeking any trace of the stone's spiritual resonance. Instead of the warm pulse that should have thrummed through ancient symbols, she felt only cold—not winter's bite, but the absolute temperature of space between stars.

"The network falters," she whispered, her priestess training allowing her to read the damage spreading like poison through Ireland's mystical infrastructure. "Each sacred site grows dimmer as the connections weaken without Tara's anchor."

Through the great windows, she could see riders approaching with the desperate urgency of those who carried intelligence too terrible for comfortable delay. The first had arrived at dawn with reports of spiritual disturbance across the eastern territories. Now others came bearing confirmation that the violation extended far beyond Tara's immediate boundaries.

***

The hall filled with representatives whose faces bore the strain of people who had witnessed the impossible and lived to report it. King Conchobor of Ulster stood among them, his weathered features showing confusion that cut deeper than mere political concern.

"My druids speak strangely this morning," he said, his voice carrying the weight of someone struggling to articulate wrongness that defied description. "They perform the rituals with perfect precision, but something essential is missing. The spirit that once flowed through ceremony has... dulled."

"Not dulled," corrected Fergus of the Eastern Shores, whose territory bordered the areas where conversion had begun. "Replaced. They speak of efficiency now, of optimal outcomes achieved through proper spiritual coordination. Their words carry no warmth, no individual passion for the sacred."

"How many sites affected?" Neassa asked, though her heart already clenched with recognition of systematic assault rather than random violation.

"Seven confirmed," replied Brendan of Mag Muirthemne, his warrior's training evident in the methodical way he delivered intelligence. "Three in the east where Brother Marcus first showed signs of change, two along the northern coast, one in the midlands, and the great grove of Mórríghan's Oak."

The significance of that last site hit Neassa like a physical blow. Mórríghan's Oak was no minor sacred place but one of Ireland's most powerful spiritual centers, its roots said to stretch into the otherworld itself. If the corruption could claim such a stronghold, nowhere was truly safe.

"They took it during the night?" King Aillen of Leinster asked.

"No," Brendan replied grimly. "During morning prayers. Brother Tadgh says he felt a moment of... clarity. He described it as understanding, for the first time, how much unnecessary suffering consciousness creates through its insistence on individual preference."

Silence settled over the assembly like recognition of sophistication that exceeded their understanding of spiritual warfare. Not crude assault that could be resisted through traditional defenses, but seduction that offered genuine relief from burdens that consciousness imposed through its very nature.

"The conversions accelerate," observed Muiris of the Southern Rivers, his voice tight with controlled fear. "One site falls, and its influence spreads to neighboring sacred places like ripples in a pond. Each success makes the next conversion easier to accomplish."

Neassa felt the truth of his words through her connection to the network itself. Where the Lia Fáil should have anchored Ireland's spiritual infrastructure in divine authority, emptiness now created suction that pulled meaning from every connected site. The sacred bonds that had strengthened Ireland for generations were becoming conduits for systematic elimination of everything they had been designed to preserve.

***

"High Priestess," a new voice called from the chamber's entrance. "Riders approach under the banner of formal embassy. They request immediate audience on matters of... spiritual coordination."

Through the windows, they could see seven figures in robes that had once served sacred office but now carried emptiness where spiritual authority should have provided connection to sources larger than immediate utility. They moved with mechanical precision that eliminated wasted motion, their coordination speaking to shared purpose that transcended individual consciousness.

"Brother Marcus leads them," King Conchobor observed with growing alarm. "But his companions... I recognize three from territories that remained free yesterday."

The delegation that entered carried itself with authority that challenged every assumption about the relationship between spiritual conversion and political legitimacy. Not conquered slaves or broken prisoners, but representatives who spoke with the satisfaction of people who had discovered better alternatives to the chaos consciousness created through its insistence on choice.

"High Priestess Neassa," Brother Marcus said with courtesy that felt programmed rather than personal. "We bring greetings from territories that have discovered peace through optimal spiritual coordination. Our offer of guidance extends to all who suffer under the burden of individual preference."

His smile never wavered, perfect as painted porcelain that somehow made his words more rather than less unsettling. Behind him, the other delegates stood with patient attention that spoke to complete certainty about whatever outcomes their visit would produce.

"You speak of territories," Neassa replied carefully, reading in their coordination evidence of planning that transcended normal diplomatic preparation. "Which lands claim allegiance to your... guidance?"

"Claim suggests ownership that creates unnecessary conflict," Marcus corrected with gentle firmness. "We speak of lands that have chosen to accept assistance in achieving optimal outcomes through collective decision-making that eliminates the suffering individual will creates when it interferes with proper spiritual development."

The language was carefully neutral, designed to make systematic elimination of consciousness sound like generous improvement rather than spiritual murder. Around the chamber, representatives who had fought to preserve individual will found themselves confronting the sophistication of enemies who understood exactly how to make surrender seem like wisdom.

"What do you offer Tara?" King Aillen asked bluntly.

"Relief from the chaos of competing preferences," replied one of the other delegates, her voice carrying mechanical certainty that eliminated individual uncertainty. "Spiritual guidance that serves collective welfare rather than the inefficient disorder that conscious choice creates when consciousness insists on remaining conscious despite the suffering such insistence produces."

"And if we refuse your generous guidance?" Neassa asked, understanding that the question would force revelation of purposes carefully concealed beneath diplomatic courtesy.

"Then Tara continues to suffer the consequences of choosing chaos over harmony," Marcus said with genuine pity that somehow made his threat more rather than less chilling. "But optimal outcomes will be achieved regardless of cooperation or resistance. Individual preferences that interfere with collective welfare cannot be permitted to persist indefinitely."

The silence that followed carried weight beyond mere political consideration. Around the hall, representatives began to understand that diplomatic courtesy concealed ultimatum designed to eliminate the possibility of meaningful choice while maintaining the illusion that choice remained available to those wise enough to select proper alternatives.

"You may withdraw," Neassa said with finality that brooked no negotiation about terms that had become non-negotiable. "Tara chooses the chaos of consciousness over the peace of surrender. We accept the suffering that individual will creates when will insists on remaining individual rather than accepting optimization that eliminates everything that makes individuality worth preserving."

As the delegation departed with coordination that spoke to shared purpose rather than individual disappointment, the weight of what they faced settled over Tara's defenders like recognition of enemies whose sophistication exceeded their ability to address through traditional resistance.

"How long until they return?" King Conchobor asked, though his strategic experience already suggested answers that offered no comfortable options.

"They won't return," Neassa replied with certainty that came from understanding opponents who viewed negotiation as inefficiency requiring correction. "They'll implement optimal solutions through methods that serve their purposes regardless of our cooperation."

Through the windows, they could see the effects already beginning as the delegation's presence had somehow weakened the spiritual barriers that protected Tara from the growing void where Ireland's heart had once anchored meaning itself. The ancient stones seemed dimmer, their carved spirals flickering uncertainly as if the power that had sustained them for generations was being systematically drained away.

"We need allies," Brendan said with warrior's recognition of mathematics that offered no hope through individual strength alone. "Sacred sites that remain free, leaders who haven't yet chosen the beautiful peace of surrender."

"Send ravens," Neassa commanded, her voice carrying authority earned through trial but now tested by challenges that exceeded any crisis their tradition had prepared them to face. "To every sacred site, every túath that maintains connection to the old ways. Tell them: Ireland's heart has been stolen, but Ireland's spirit endures in those who choose consciousness over efficiency, meaning over the emptiness that promises peace through surrender of everything that makes peace worthwhile."

As messengers departed and preparations began for whatever resistance might yet be possible, the weight of defending consciousness itself settled on shoulders that had never imagined bearing such responsibility. Not just political authority or territorial control, but the fundamental right of awareness to exist in forms that created beauty rather than simply serving optimal outcomes.

The bonds that had held Ireland together for generations were severing one by one, but in Tara's halls, a few still chose to remain themselves despite every pressure to surrender individual will for collective harmony that promised relief from the terrible wonderful burden of caring about each other despite the certainty that caring created vulnerability to loss.

The real battle was just beginning, and they would fight it with everything they had chosen to preserve, everyone they had chosen to become, every song they refused to let fall silent despite forces that promised beautiful peace through surrender of everything that made songs worth singing.

CHAPTER 3

MESSAGES IN THE DARK

Dawn brought no relief to Tara, only confirmation that the night's horror had been real and was spreading like plague through Ireland's spiritual veins.

Neassa stood beside the empty platform where the Lia Fáil had rested for countless generations, watching the carved spirals that seemed somehow dimmer than they should be. The ancient symbols surrounding the depression no longer pulsed with their usual rhythm—the heartbeat of the land itself grown irregular, uncertain.

"The connections strain," Síle observed, approaching with the careful step of one who sensed but didn't fully understand the spiritual damage. Her young face bore lines of exhaustion that aged her beyond her seventeen years. "Every ritual feels thin. Like trying to speak through water."

"Something's draining power from the sacred links themselves." Neassa pressed her palm against the nearest carved spiral, seeking the reassuring pulse of connection to sister sites. It was there, but weakened, uncertain—a whisper where once had been a song. "Send word to every sacred site. I want reports on their spiritual health, their guardians' condition, any strangers who've visited recently."

"Word came in the night from riders sent by the eastern groves," Síle continued, her voice dropping low. "Three territories report their druids speaking strangely. Efficient, they call it. Simplified. But even the messengers who brought the spoken word seemed affected—they recited their messages with mechanical precision, then stood silent until dismissed."

The pattern was already spreading. Whatever had struck at Tara wasn't an isolated attack but part of something larger, more coordinated. Neassa felt the weight of crisis settling on her shoulders like a mantle she'd never asked to wear.

***

The sound of approaching hoofbeats made them both turn toward the main entrance. Multiple riders, coming fast from different directions—never a good sign in times of crisis. Neassa's heart clenched with the certainty that each arrival would bring worse news than the last.

"High Priestess!" A guard called from the entrance. "Riders approach—and one of them has the silver scars."

Ríona.

Neassa's relief was so profound it left her momentarily weak. If anyone could make sense of this spiritual violation, it would be the woman who had walked between worlds and returned bearing the gods' mark. She hurried toward the entrance, Síle close behind.

***

Ríona appeared through the morning mist like a figure stepping out of legend made real. Nine years of dwelling between mortal and divine had changed her in ways that went beyond the obvious marks of transformation. She moved with fluid grace that seemed to bend reality slightly around her, as if the earth itself aided her steps. The silver scars that traced spirals down her arms caught dawn light, pulsing gently with their own inner rhythm.

Her hair fell in waves of premature silver that somehow looked more like starlight than age, and her eyes held depths reflecting otherworldly light—not the blank stare of one who had seen too much, but the focused gaze of one who had learned to see clearly across multiple realms of existence.

Behind her came a small escort of guards whose faces bore the strain of hard travel and urgent purpose, but also something else— a kind of awed reverence that came from riding beside living legend.

"Sister," Ríona said, dismounting with movements that were neither fully mortal nor divine. "I felt the severing from the lands beyond the eastern hills, like a string snapping in a harp whose music I'd known all my life. What has been done here?"

"The Lia Fáil is gone." The words still tasted like ashes in Neassa's mouth. "Stolen in the night, with no sign of how or by whom. But that's not the worst of it. The guardians here have been changed. They speak of efficiency and optimization, but their eyes hold nothing. No fire, no purpose, no connection to the sacred pattern."

Ríona's features grew grim as her divine sight read the spiritual damage that hung around them like invisible smoke. "The Hollowed. I had hoped this poison hadn't yet reached Ireland, but the signs were there for those with eyes to see." She extended her awareness toward the wounded platform, and Neassa saw her silver scars flare brighter. "How many sites affected?"

"Here at Tara confirmed. Three groves in the east suspected. Reports from Ulster suggest border incursions by beings who speak of 'voluntary optimization.'" Neassa gestured helplessly toward the empty depression where Ireland's sacred heart had beaten. "If the pattern holds..."

"It will spread exponentially." Ríona moved toward the stolen stone's resting place, studying the void with sight that penetrated beyond physical appearance. "Each converted site becomes a wound in the sacred links, bleeding spiritual energy away from the pattern that sustains consciousness itself. Soon, maintaining individual will becomes so exhausting that surrender seems like mercy."

"Can they be healed?"

"I don't know. The severing may be too complete, the wound too deep." Ríona's voice carried divine certainty mixed with mortal sorrow. "But I know this—they spread not through force but through seduction. They offer what people think they want: peace through surrender, efficiency through emptiness, relief from the terrible burden of choosing for themselves."

***

The sound of multiple horses approaching interrupted their discussion. A steady stream of riders had been arriving since dawn, each bearing worse news than the last. Neassa watched as they dismounted with the urgency that marked bearers of crucial intelligence.

The first rider bore the colors of the eastern kingdoms, his horse lathered with sweat despite the cool morning air. He dismounted with urgent haste.

"High Priestess, Lady Ríona," he said, bowing quickly. "I bring word from the coast. The trading port of Dubh Linn reports unusual efficiency in their customs procedures. Ships processed with perfect coordination, no delays, no disputes. The merchants are pleased, but..."

His voice trailed off as he struggled to articulate wrongness that defied description.

"But?" Ríona prompted gently.

"No laughter from the dockworkers. No songs from the fishermen returning with their catch. No arguments over prices in the market square." His voice dropped to a whisper. "It's all very orderly, very peaceful. And somehow, profoundly wrong. Like a song with all the notes correct but no one remembering why they wanted to sing."

***

Before anyone could respond, a second rider arrived—this one bearing the blue and silver of the northern territories. Her message confirmed their worst fears: three sacred groves had fallen silent overnight, their druids performing rituals with mechanical precision but no spiritual power flowing through their actions.

"They complete every gesture perfectly," the northern messenger reported, her voice tight with controlled horror. "But there's no life in it. No connection to the divine forces the rituals are meant to channel. It's like watching actors perform a play in a language they don't understand."

***

A third messenger brought word that made Neassa's blood run cold: Queen Medb of Connacht was calling for a great gathering at Cruachan, inviting all who would lead Ireland to witness what she called "the birth of a new age of unity and prosperity through optimal governance."

"A trap," Ríona said with quiet certainty. "She means to eliminate all potential opposition while consolidating power through alliance with the Hollowed."

"Then we don't attend," Neassa replied immediately. "We stay here, strengthen our defenses, rally what resistance we can from the sites that remain free."

"And let her control the narrative while Ireland's remaining leaders disappear one by one?"

The new voice carried military authority mixed with bitter experience. All turned to see a woman in traveling clothes approaching, moving with the fluid grace of a trained warrior despite her modest garb.

***

Blonde hair was braided for practicality rather than beauty, and her eyes held depths that spoke of battles fought and hard lessons learned. She wore simple traveling clothes that couldn't quite conceal the fighter's build underneath, and her hands showed the calluses of one intimately familiar with sword and spear.

"I am Brigid, lately of the Northern Shores," she continued, inclining her head with respectful but not deferential courtesy. "I bring word of what befalls kingdoms that choose efficiency over choice, order over the sacred chaos of free will."

Ríona's otherworldly gaze fixed on the newcomer with uncomfortable intensity, reading currents of purpose and hidden pain that flowed around the woman like invisible rivers. "You've seen the Hollowed's work before."

"I've seen what they leave behind." Brigid's voice carried bitter experience earned through prices too high to contemplate. "Villages where no children play in the streets because play serves no optimal purpose. Courts where no voices rise in dissent because dissent has been classified as inefficient. Armies that move with perfect coordination because individual initiative has been eliminated as a source of tactical uncertainty."

"How did you escape?" Síle asked, her young voice tight with horror at the scope of what they witnessed.

"Others didn't." The simple words carried weight that spoke of survivor's guilt and prices paid in blood and shame. "People who trusted my judgment, who believed in my leadership, who died because I failed to understand our enemies' true nature until it was too late to save them."

She paused, studying each face with the calculating gaze of one who had learned not to trust easily. "But their deaths taught me what victory never could—that the Hollowed don't work through force or conquest. They work through offering what people genuinely want: relief from responsibility, freedom from the agony of difficult choices, peace through surrender of individual will."

***

The fourth messenger arrived as she spoke, this one bearing the direst news yet: the seven claimants to the High Kingship had been found at Tara, speaking with one voice about the wisdom of accepting Queen Medb's invitation. Their eyes held the same terrible peace as the converted druids, and they moved with the synchronized precision of components in a well-designed mechanism.

"Ireland's political leadership is being systematically eliminated or converted," Ríona said, her divine sight-reading patterns of manipulation that stretched across the entire island. "Soon, only those at the margins will remain—people like ourselves, who stayed outside traditional power structures and might therefore escape the first wave of spiritual assault."

"How long do we have?" Neassa asked, though she dreaded the answer.

"Days, perhaps hours before the next wave reaches here." Ríona consulted whatever divine sources guided her transformed senses. "The pattern spreads like infection through positions of authority. Every leader converted becomes a tool for converting others, until resistance becomes not just difficult but literally unthinkable."

"Then we choose quickly." Neassa looked at each of them—Ríona with her immortal purpose, Brigid with her mysterious expertise, Síle with her fierce young loyalty, the messengers with their grim intelligence. "We go to Cruachan, together. Not as supplicants seeking favor, but as representatives of conscious choice itself."

"Dangerous beyond measure," Brigid warned. "Medb is no fool, and if she's allied with this corruption, she'll have prepared for exactly this response. We'll be walking into a trap designed by those who've perfected the art of making spiritual annihilation seem like salvation."

"Then we prepare better." Neassa felt certainty settling into her bones like truth finding its proper home. "We go not to fight or negotiate, but to offer something they can't understand or counter—living proof that consciousness is worth its cost, that choice creates meaning rather than chaos, that love endures despite the certainty of loss."

***

As they spoke, more ravens arrived—black wings cutting through morning sky, bearing reports that painted an increasingly dire picture. Sacred sites falling silent across Ireland, druids speaking in coordinated whispers, entire communities accepting optimization with grateful relief.

But also other news: pockets of resistance forming in the borderlands, people fleeing the beautiful emptiness to seek refuge in places where old songs still echoed, where choice still mattered more than efficiency.

"There are others," Síle said, hope creeping into her young voice as she listened to the accumulated reports. "Not many, but enough. People who've seen what the Hollowed offer and chosen the harder path of remaining themselves."

"Then we'll be their voice at Cruachan," Neassa decided. "Their proof that consciousness cannot be perfected into submission, no matter how attractive the offers of peace and unity."

The decision made, they turned to urgent preparations. Messages to dispatch, allies to summon, defenses to arrange for Brú na Bóinne in their absence. The great game was beginning, and Ireland's fate would be decided not by armies or wealth, but by the choices individual hearts made when offered beautiful emptiness or difficult meaning.

***

As they worked, none of them noticed the raven that perched on the ancient stones, its dark eyes reflecting intelligence that belonged to no ordinary bird. The Morrígan watched her chosen guardians prepare for the trial ahead, ready to intervene if needed but hoping—as only a goddess of war could hope—that mortal courage would prove sufficient to the task.

Ríona paused in her preparations, her divine sight catching movement in the shadows. She turned and saw the raven, recognizing the depth of awareness in its dark gaze. With a simple nod of acknowledgment, she honored the goddess who watched over them. The raven cawed once—a sound that carried both blessing and warning—then spread its wings and flew off into the gathering dusk.

The battle for Ireland's soul was about to begin, and its outcome would echo through legend for generations to come.

CHAPTER 4

THE BLOODLINE KEEPERS

The journey to the ancient meeting place had taken them through spirit-roads that wound between the borders of kingdoms, where Ríona's divine nature could mask their passage from unfriendly eyes. Cathair had sent the call through channels older than kingdoms, summoning those who carried the bloodlines to gather in times of crisis. Now they waited to see who among the bloodline carriers remained free to speak their ancestors' words.

The ancient meeting place lay hidden in a valley that existed on no Roman map, where standing stones older than Tara formed circles within circles, and the very air hummed with accumulated memory. Cathair had sent word through channels that predated kingdoms, calling together those who carried the bloodlines—the inheritors of ancestral wisdom who might yet resist the spreading silence.

***

They came like ghosts emerging from mist: men and women whose veins carried the memories of the first kings, whose blood held echoes of voices that had guided Ireland through darker ages. But where once such a gathering would have numbered in the dozens, only seven answered the call.

"Seven kingdoms fallen," said Ailill mac Cormac, his weathered face showing the weight of one who had witnessed the impossible. "Seven bloodline carriers converted to speaking with voices not their own. We seven are all who remain free to speak our ancestors' words."

Neassa stood beside Cathair in the center circle, feeling the weight of accumulated centuries pressing down like a physical presence. Around them, the standing stones seemed to lean inward, as if straining to hear words that might be the last free speech the bloodlines would ever utter.

"The ancestors scream warnings in our blood," said Fionntan of the Western Shores, a young woman whose inheritance carried the memories of sea-kings and storm-riders. "They remember times when the land itself forgot its name, when sacred connections were severed by those who viewed consciousness as inefficiency."

"But they also remember resistance," added Donnchad of the Northern Hills, his massive frame bearing scars from battles fought against enemies both mortal and supernatural. "They whisper of weapons that can't be blunted, of unity that grows stronger when tested by division."

Cathair stepped forward, feeling the ancestral voices rise in his blood like a tide of whispered wisdom. "The memories speak clearly: this is not the first time Ireland has faced such a threat. But it may be the last time we have the strength to resist it."

***

"What do the ancestors counsel?" asked Muirenn of the River Folk, her dark eyes reflecting depths that held more than mortal understanding.

"Unity," Cathair replied, his voice carrying harmonics that belonged to generations of kings and counselors. "Not the false unity of the Hollowed, where all voices speak as one because individual will has been eliminated. True unity—conscious choice to stand together despite our differences."

"Unity requires trust," observed Cormac of the Eastern Marches, his gaze moving to Brigid where she stood slightly apart from the circle. "And trust requires truth. There are secrets among us that shadow whatever alliance we might forge."

The words hung in the air like an accusation, and Neassa felt tension ripple through the gathered bloodline carriers. Each had risked everything to attend this meeting, trusting in bonds forged by shared heritage and common cause. But trust built on concealment could shatter at the worst possible moment.

"Truth, then," Brigid said, her gaze finding Ríona's across the circle. The transformed woman's otherworldly eyes held depths of understanding, and she gave the slightest nod of encouragement. Drawing strength from that divine blessing, Brigid stepped into the circle's center with movements that suddenly revealed the royal bearing she'd been concealing. "My name is not Brigid. I am Boudica, once Queen of the Iceni, leader of the great British rebellion against Rome."

***

The revelation hit like a physical blow. Several hands moved to weapons before conscious thought could intervene. Even among those who held their composure, the implications were staggering—the most wanted fugitive in the Roman world stood among them, her presence guaranteeing imperial attention would follow.

"The Romans hunt you," Fionntan said, her voice tight with controlled fear. "If you're revealed at Cruachan, you become a target that draws legions to anyone who stands with you."

"Yes," Boudica replied with calm honesty. "But I also become a symbol of something the Hollowed can't understand or convert—the willingness to choose resistance over safety, meaning over peace, love over the beautiful emptiness of surrender."

"Why tell us?" Donnchad demanded, his warrior's instincts warring with political calculation. "Why expose yourself and endanger our mission?"

"Because unity built on lies serves the same purpose as the Hollowed's false peace—it eliminates the chaos that comes from dealing with difficult truths." Boudica's gaze moved to each of them in turn. "I failed my people once by underestimating my enemies and overestimating my own strength. I won't make that mistake again."

"Your failure cost thousands of lives," Cormac said bluntly. "British dead, Roman dead, the innocent caught between armies led by pride rather than wisdom. What makes you think we should trust someone who led her people to such destruction?"

The words cut deep, and Neassa saw Boudica flinch as if struck. But when she spoke, her voice carried the weight of one who had wrestled with guilt and emerged with hard-won wisdom.

"Because I've learned the cost of leading through emotion rather than strategy, of choosing pride over practicality, of believing that courage alone could overcome superior planning." Her voice grew stronger with each word. "My daughters died because of choices I made. My people suffered because I led them into a war I couldn't win. I am not that tale's hero—I am its lesson."

The silence that followed carried the weight of recognition, understanding that passed between those who had learned wisdom through prices too high for comfortable calculation. Around the circle, representatives absorbed her words, each contemplating the difference between leadership that served pride and guidance that served wisdom earned through catastrophic loss. The ancient stones seemed to pulse with approval for honesty that transcended diplomatic courtesy.

***

"Lessons written in blood carry more weight than victories won through luck," Cathair said quietly, the ancestral voices in his blood recognizing the value of wisdom earned through loss. "The question is whether we're wise enough to learn from disasters we didn't personally create."

Ailill stepped forward, his aged features showing the weight of decision. "The bloodlines remember Queen Boudica. The ancestors speak of her courage, her passion, her love for her people. They also speak of her mistakes, her blind spots, her ultimate failure. But they remember most clearly her choice to fight rather than submit, even knowing the cost."

"And now?" Muirenn asked. "What do you counsel, Queen of distant shores?"

"I counsel truth in all its difficulty," Boudica replied. "The Hollowed offer peace through surrender of everything that makes existence meaningful. We offer something harder—conscious choice despite its cost, love despite its pain, hope despite the certainty that hope may be betrayed."

The standing stones around them seemed to pulse with approval, ancient magic responding to honesty offered without compulsion. In the distance, thunder rolled across the sky, though no clouds were visible—The Morrígan's voice carrying across realms to remind them that divine powers watched their choices.

"The ancestors accept her truth," Fionntan said, wonder touching her voice. "I feel their approval in my blood, their recognition of courage that chooses revelation over safety."

"Then we stand together," Donnchad declared, his massive hand extending toward Boudica in the gesture of alliance. "Queen to warrior, exile to native, all united by the choice to remain ourselves despite the cost."

One by one, the others joined the gesture, hands meeting in the center of the circle while the standing stones hummed with accumulated power. Seven bloodline carriers and one exiled queen, choosing unity through conscious decision rather than compelled surrender.

"What of the gathering at Cruachan?" Ailill asked. "Do we attend Queen Medb's invitation?"

"We attend," Neassa said, feeling the certainty settle into her bones like truth finding its proper home. "Not as supplicants seeking favor, but as living proof that consciousness cannot be perfected into submission. We go to spring the trap deliberately, on our terms."

"Dangerous beyond measure," Cormac warned. "Medb commands forces we can barely comprehend, guided by advisors who've perfected the art of making spiritual annihilation seem like salvation."

"Then we prepare for the impossible," Cathair replied, his voice carrying ancestral authority mixed with very personal determination. "We go not to win through force, but to prove through example. We show them what conscious choice creates when it refuses to surrender meaning to efficiency."

***

As the gathering dispersed, each bloodline carrier departing to make their own preparations for the trial ahead, Neassa found herself walking beside Cathair through the circle of ancient stones. The evening air carried the scent of approaching storm, but also something else—the electric tension that came before moments that would echo through legend.

"Are we making the right choice?" she asked, allowing uncertainty to enter her voice for the first time since the crisis began.

"I don't know," he replied with honesty that was more comforting than false confidence. "But we're making our choice, freely given despite the cost. That may be the most important thing we can do—prove that such choices are still possible."

His hand found hers as they walked, warm and solid in the gathering darkness. "Whatever happens at Cruachan, whatever we face in Medb's hall, we'll face it as ourselves. That's no small victory, considering what our enemies offer as the alternative."

Behind them, the standing stones began to fade into mist, returning to whatever timeless realm they inhabited when not needed by those who remembered the old ways. But their blessing remained, carried in the blood of those who had chosen truth over comfort, unity over isolation, love over the beautiful peace of surrender.

Tomorrow would bring them to Cruachan and whatever awaited in Queen Medb's transformed court. Tonight, they had forged alliances that would either save Ireland or provide worthy witness to its fall.

The storm was coming, but they would not meet it alone.

CHAPTER 5

THE WEIGHT OF TRUTH

The aftermath of Boudica's revelation settled over the ancient meeting place like smoke from a funeral pyre, heavy with implications that would reshape every plan they'd made and every alliance they'd hoped to forge. The seven bloodline carriers who remained free sat in the circle of standing stones, their faces showing the strain of having witnessed something that changed the fundamental nature of their resistance.

"The most wanted fugitive in the Roman world," Donnchad said quietly, his massive frame somehow diminished by the scope of what they now faced. "Every Roman agent from here to Gaul will be hunting you. Every collaborator seeking favor will be watching for your face."

Boudica met his gaze without flinching, her royal bearing intact despite the weight of exile and loss. "Yes. And now you all share that burden by knowing my true identity. I've made you all targets by choosing truth over safety."

Fionntan of the Western Shores leaned forward, her sea-king heritage showing in the way she read currents of danger as naturally as weather patterns. "But also allies in a war we were already fighting. The Romans don't distinguish between active resistance and passive defiance—they'll come for Ireland regardless of whether we shelter you."

***

"The question," Muirenn added with the quiet authority that came from generations of river-folk wisdom, "is whether your presence here helps or hinders our chances of survival."

The silence held terrible weight. Through the mist that perpetually shrouded the ancient valley, they could hear the sound of their horses shifting restlessly, as if the animals sensed the tension that gripped their riders.

Cathair's voice, when he finally spoke, carried harmonics borrowed from ancestral memory but tinged with very present concern. "The bloodlines whisper of times when revelation brought either salvation or catastrophe, depending on the courage of those who heard unwelcome truths. Your identity doesn't change what Ireland faces—it clarifies the stakes."

Neassa studied Boudica's face, reading the exhaustion that came from carrying secrets too long and the relief that accompanied their release. "Tell us everything. Not just who you are, but what you've learned. What you've seen of Roman methods, Roman weaknesses, Roman plans."

***

For the next hour, as morning mist gave way to pale sunlight filtering through the ancient stones, Boudica spoke with the methodical precision of someone who had survived catastrophe by learning its lessons. She described Roman military organization, their methods of conquest and control, their systematic approach to eliminating Celtic resistance.

"They don't just defeat armies," she explained, her voice carrying bitter experience. "They attack the very idea that resistance is possible. They offer rewards for collaboration, punishment for defiance, and most insidiously—they make surrender seem like wisdom rather than betrayal."

Ailill mac Cormac, whose weathered features had seen too many betrayals, nodded grimly. "We've already witnessed such tactics. Local kings who suddenly speak of 'practical accommodation' with Roman interests, druids who counsel 'realistic acceptance' of superior force."

"The corruption spreads like plague," Scáthach observed, her warrior's training reading patterns of assault in what others might dismiss as political maneuvering. "Each converted leader becomes a tool for converting others, until resistance becomes not just difficult but literally unthinkable."

Boudica's expression grew darker. "But what you face here goes beyond traditional Roman methods. The reports I've heard, the descriptions of spiritual emptiness, the complete severing from sacred memory—this is something new. Something that makes my rebellion look like a simple border skirmish."

She gestured toward the standing stones that surrounded them, their ancient carvings still pulsing with accumulated power despite the corruption spreading through other sacred sites. "Rome conquers territories and enslaves peoples, but they leave the conquered with enough spirit to hate their masters. What's happening in Ireland seeks to eliminate the very capacity for resistance by destroying the consciousness that creates meaning."

***

"The Hollowed," Ríona said quietly, her divine sight-reading currents of purpose and corruption that flowed beyond normal perception. "They represent the ultimate endpoint of Roman efficiency—not just political control, but spiritual annihilation."

Fergus mac Róich shifted uncomfortably, his massive frame bearing scars from battles fought against enemies both mortal and supernatural. "Then we face two threats simultaneously—immediate Roman military pressure and this spiritual plague that turns our own people into weapons against meaning itself."

"Three threats," Neassa corrected grimly. "Don't forget Queen Medb's gathering at Cruachan. Whatever alliance she's forged with the Hollowed, it gives them political legitimacy and military resources they couldn't acquire through corruption alone."

The complexity of their situation began to crystallize around the circle. Not just external invasion or internal corruption, but a coordinated assault that attacked Ireland's political structure, spiritual foundation, and cultural identity simultaneously.

"We need to return to Tara," Cathair said finally, his voice carrying the weight of someone recognizing terrible necessity. "Not to hide, but to gather our remaining strength before facing whatever Medb has planned. If we're going to contest her authority, we need to do it as representatives of legitimate spiritual power, not as scattered refugees."

"Too dangerous," Boudica protested immediately. "Tara will be watched, infiltrated, possibly under direct assault. My presence there endangers everyone who serves the sacred site."

"Your presence anywhere endangers everyone around you," Donnchad pointed out with brutal honesty. "But your knowledge is the only advantage we have against enemies who've perfected the art of making surrender seem attractive."

***

Scáthach leaned forward, her warrior's instincts reading the tactical situation with practiced clarity. "The question isn't whether returning to Tara carries risk—it's whether that risk serves our larger purpose. Without a base of legitimate authority, we're just outlaws hiding in the wilderness."

"And outlaws don't win wars against empires," Boudica added with grim certainty. "They become cautionary tales told by the victors."

Before Neassa could respond to the arguments building around the circle, the sound of approaching hoofbeats cut through the morning mist like a blade through silk. A single rider, moving with the desperate urgency of one who carried news that could not wait for proper protocol or careful approach.

Ríona's silver scars flared briefly as her divine sight read the spiritual signature of the approaching messenger. "One of ours," she announced, though her voice carried undertones of concern. "But carrying darkness that tastes of violation."

***

The rider who crashed through the concealing mist bore the colors of Tara, but his face showed the hollow exhaustion of someone who had witnessed the unthinkable. Brother Cillian, one of the younger priests whose devotion had always burned bright with passionate certainty, now looked as if that fire had been deliberately extinguished.

"High Priestess," he gasped, dismounting with movements that spoke of hard travel and desperate haste. "Thank the goddesses I found you. The situation at Tara—" He paused, his gaze taking in the assembled bloodline carriers, confusion flickering across his exhausted features as he tried to process the unexpected gathering.

"Speak your news," Neassa commanded, though her heart already clenched with the certainty that whatever Cillian had seen would shatter their careful planning. "What's happened at Tara?"

"The túatha," Cillian replied, his voice carrying the weight of disaster barely contained. "They've answered Queen Medb's call. Not to Cruachan, but to Tara itself. Seven kings with their full retinues, arriving within hours of each other as if coordinated by some power beyond normal communication."

The implications hit the assembled bloodline carriers like physical blows. If the túatha were gathering at Tara rather than traveling to Cruachan, it meant Medb had changed her strategy— bringing the confrontation to Ireland's spiritual heart rather than her own stronghold.

"Which túatha?" Cathair demanded, his voice carrying harmonics borrowed from ancestral memory but tinged with very present fear.

"Ulster, Munster, Leinster," Cillian began, counting off on fingers that trembled with exhaustion. "The kingdoms of the eastern shores, the northern territories, and..." He paused, swallowing hard. "And Connacht itself. Queen Medb comes to Tara with the full weight of royal authority, claiming the right to speak for all Ireland in matters of succession and spiritual governance."

***

"She means to force the choosing," Scáthach realized with warrior's clarity. "Without the Lia Fáil to provide divine judgment, she'll argue that mortal authority must suffice. Seven kingdoms gathering at Tara could claim the right to select a High King through consensus rather than sacred sign."

"But that's not the worst of it," Cillian continued, his voice dropping to conspiracy's whisper despite their isolation. "The converted druids—the ones who speak with Marcus's voice but claim independence of thought—they're arriving too. Three circles worth, all speaking of 'spiritual efficiency' and 'optimal sacred governance.'"

The full scope of the trap became clear as Cillian's words sank in. Medb hadn't just corrupted individual leaders or isolated sacred sites—she'd orchestrated a gathering that would give legitimacy to whatever emerged from the convergence at Tara. With royal authority and spiritual sanction combined, she could reshape Ireland's entire foundation while maintaining the appearance of traditional process.

"How long do we have?" Boudica asked, her strategic mind immediately shifting to tactical calculations.

"They began arriving yesterday," Cillian replied. "The full gathering is planned for tomorrow's dawn, when the autumn sun rises over the sacred hill. If we're going to contest their authority..."

"We have to be there," Neassa finished, feeling the weight of impossible necessity settling on her shoulders. "Not as fugitives or scattered resistance, but as legitimate representatives of Ireland's true spiritual heritage."

***

Donnchad's massive frame shifted with the restless energy of a warrior recognizing the approach of unavoidable battle. "Seven kingdoms, three druid circles, and Queen Medb herself. Against eight of us, assuming we can even reach Tara before the gathering concludes."

"Brother Cillian's horse is spent, and he's in no condition for immediate travel," Fionntan observed with practical concern. "Someone needs to stay with him, or send him back to safety."

"I'll manage," Cillian protested, though his exhaustion was evident in every line of his body. "The High Priestess needs every ally—"

"You've done enough," Ríona interrupted gently, her divine sight reading the spiritual damage that hard travel and exposure to corrupted sites had inflicted. "Rest here where the ancient stones can offer healing. We'll carry your warning to its proper conclusion."

The mathematics of desperate necessity crystallized around the circle. Eight people against the assembled political and spiritual authority of most of Ireland, with less than a day to reach Tara and somehow contest forces that had been months in the planning.

"It's impossible," Muirenn said quietly, though her voice carried more resignation than despair.

"Good," Boudica replied with grim satisfaction. "Impossible odds tend to make enemies overconfident. They'll be prepared for reasonable resistance, not for the unreasonable determination of people who choose meaning over safety."

***

Neassa felt the weight of decision settling on her shoulders like a mantle she'd never asked to wear. As High Priestess of Tara, the choice was ultimately hers—whether to attempt this desperate gambit or preserve their small band for future resistance.

"We ride for Tara," she decided with quiet certainty. "Together, immediately, and with the understanding that we may not survive what we find there. But if we don't try, Ireland dies anyway—just more slowly, and with less dignity."

As they hastily gathered their belongings and prepared for the desperate journey ahead, the ancient stones around them seemed to pulse with approval of choices made through conscious decision rather than fearful calculation. Whatever the outcome, they would face it as themselves—flawed, frightened, but united by the determination to preserve meaning despite the cost.

"Together," Neassa decided with quiet certainty as they mounted their horses. "If we're going to fail, let's fail as ourselves—united by conscious choice rather than scattered by fear."

The sun climbed higher as they prepared to leave the ancient meeting place behind, riding toward whatever awaited them at Tara. The war for Ireland's soul was about to reach its climax, and they would meet it with nothing but hope and the stubborn refusal to surrender without a fight.

CHAPTER 6

THE RIDE TO RECKONING

The desperate ride to Tara became a race against time itself, eight riders pushing their horses through countryside that showed increasing signs of spiritual disturbance. Villages they passed seemed caught between two influences—some showing the mechanical precision that marked Hollowed conversion, others displaying the frantic energy of people preparing for conflict they didn't fully understand.

"Look at the patterns," Boudica called over the thunder of hoofbeats, her warrior's eye reading strategic implications in the landscape itself. "The corruption follows the main roads, the trade routes. Whoever's directing this assault understands how influence spreads through networks of communication and commerce."

Ríona's divine sight confirmed what mundane observation suggested. "The spiritual damage concentrates around crossroads and market towns—places where people gather to exchange more than goods. Ideas, loyalties, the fundamental assumptions about what makes existence worthwhile."

The horses beneath them showed the strain of hard travel, their flanks lathered with sweat despite the cool afternoon air. But there was no time for rest, no opportunity for the careful pacing that would preserve their mounts' strength. Every moment's delay brought them closer to arriving too late to influence whatever ceremony Medb had planned for dawn.

***

"Can you sense what's happening at Tara itself?" Neassa shouted, though she dreaded the answer.

"Tension," Ríona replied, her silver scars pulsing with otherworldly light as she extended her awareness toward their destination. "Not the emptiness of full conversion, but the pressure that comes before breaking. Too many competing forces converging on sacred ground that was never meant to contain such discord."

As they rode, the landscape itself seemed to shift around them—not in obvious ways that the eye could catch, but in subtle wrongness that made the spirit recoil. Fields that should have been preparing for winter harvest showed the geometric precision of mechanical cultivation. Forests where ancient druids had once gathered herbs now stood silent, their trees bearing leaves but no longer whispering with accumulated wisdom.

"It's accelerating," Fergus observed, his ancestral memories providing recognition of spiritual damage that transcended normal perception. "Whatever they're planning at Tara is drawing power from across the island, pulling corruption toward a central focus."

Ailill's weathered features showed the strain of someone witnessing the impossible. "Like water flowing downhill, but in reverse. The emptiness is being gathered, concentrated, prepared for some working that requires massive spiritual energy."

"Or massive spiritual violation," Scáthach corrected grimly. "The amount of power needed to corrupt Tara's foundations permanently would require sacrificing sacred sites across all of Ireland."

The implication chilled them more than the autumn wind that cut through their traveling clothes. Not just political maneuvering or even military conquest, but the systematic destruction of Ireland's spiritual infrastructure to fuel some ritual that would reshape the island's very nature.

***

They paused briefly at a crossroads where four ancient paths converged, letting their horses drink from a stream that still ran clear and cold despite the corruption spreading through the surrounding landscape. The moment of rest revealed damage that constant motion had obscured—not just to the physical world, but to the web of connections that bound Ireland's sacred sites together.

"The spirit-roads are breaking," Ríona announced with quiet horror, her divine sight-reading wounds in the mystical geography that overlay the physical terrain. "Each severed connection weakens the whole network, making the next severance easier to accomplish."

"How much of the network remains intact?" Cathair asked, though his ancestral memories already whispered warnings about the scope of what they faced.

"Perhaps a third," Ríona replied, her voice carrying divine perception turned toward catastrophe. "And that third is under assault from forces that understand exactly how to turn our own spiritual defenses against us."

They remounted and continued their desperate race, but now each bend in the road revealed fresh evidence of the systematic assault on Ireland's sacred heritage. Stone circles where no birds sang, sacred groves where the trees stood like empty sentinels, holy wells that reflected nothing but darkness despite the pale afternoon light.

"The people," Muirenn observed with water-folk sensitivity to currents of emotion and purpose. "Look at how they move. Even those who haven't been fully converted carry themselves differently—less joy, less spontaneity, as if the very possibility of surprise has been drained from their lives."

Neassa nodded grimly, reading the spiritual implications of what they witnessed. "When meaning becomes mechanical, when purpose serves only efficiency, consciousness itself begins to atrophy. They're not just conquering Ireland—they're eliminating the Irish way of being Irish."

"Which makes tomorrow's gathering even more critical," Boudica said, her strategic mind calculating the stakes with brutal clarity. "If Medb succeeds in legitimizing this transformation through traditional ceremonial forms, resistance becomes not just difficult but literally unthinkable."

The sun had begun its descent toward the western horizon when they finally crested the last hill before Tara came into view. What they saw there confirmed their worst fears while exceeding their most pessimistic estimates of the forces arrayed against them.

***

The sacred site buzzed with activity that had nothing to do with normal ceremonial function. Pavilions stretched across the plain in patterns that suggested military organization disguised as royal gathering, while streams of people moved with the focused purpose of those serving plans larger than individual understanding.

"Mother of gods," Donnchad breathed, his massive frame somehow diminished by the scope of what they faced. "It's not just a gathering—it's an occupation."

Seven royal pavilions dominated the approach to Tara's sacred hill, each bearing the banners and heraldry that marked Ireland's greatest kingdoms. But the arrangement followed no traditional protocol for ceremonial gatherings—instead, the tents formed defensive positions that could contain as easily as they could shelter, control as easily as they could honor.

"Look at the guards," Scáthach observed with warrior's training that read tactical implications in every detail. "They're not ceremonial escorts—they're professional soldiers positioned for crowd control and potential conflict."

Between the royal pavilions moved figures in druidic robes, but their movements carried the mechanical precision that marked spiritual conversion. They worked in coordinated groups, performing rituals that looked traditional but felt wrong—as if sacred ceremonies were being conducted without any connection to the divine forces they were meant to invoke.

"The converted druids," Ríona confirmed, her divine sight reading the emptiness that flowed around them like spiritual void. "Three full circles, just as Brother Cillian reported. But they're not just attending the gathering—they're conducting it, guiding whatever ceremony has been planned for dawn."

***

At the heart of the encampment, where Tara's ancient halls should have commanded respect and reverence, temporary structures had been erected that spoke of purposes far removed from traditional kingship ceremonies. Platforms for speakers, rings for judgment, altars for rituals that had never been part of Ireland's sacred traditions.

"She means to remake the ceremony entirely," Cathair realized with growing horror. "Not just influence the choosing of a High King, but replace the entire process with something that serves different purposes entirely."

"And she'll do it with enough legitimate authority present to make the changes seem lawful," Boudica added grimly. "Seven kingdoms, three druid circles, all the forms of traditional consultation—except guided toward conclusions that serve the spreading emptiness rather than Ireland's genuine welfare."

The final approach to Tara would require more than speed and determination. With so many forces already converging on the sacred site, eight riders arriving together would be noticed, questioned, possibly detained before they could reach the people who might still resist whatever ceremony was planned for dawn.

"We separate here," Neassa decided, though the words tasted like defeat. "Different approaches, different stories, but the same goal—prevent whatever legitimization they're planning to achieve through tomorrow's gathering."

"How?" Muirenn asked with practical concern. "Eight people against thousands, with no weapons that could touch the real source of their power?"

"By remembering what we came here to prove," Ríona replied, her otherworldly gaze reading possibilities that existed beyond normal perception. "That consciousness can choose consciousness, that meaning creates authority more legitimate than mere force or efficiency."

***

Boudica checked her weapons one final time, though she understood that steel would serve little purpose in the battle ahead. "The most important wars are fought with choices rather than swords. Tomorrow, Ireland chooses what kind of people it wants to be."

As they prepared to separate, each taking different paths toward infiltrating the greatest concentration of political and spiritual power the island had seen in generations, Neassa felt the weight of leadership settling on her shoulders with the inevitability of fate.

"If we fail..." she began, then stopped, recognizing the futility of planning for defeat.

"If we fail, we fail as ourselves," Cathair finished, his voice carrying harmonics borrowed from ancestral memory but anchored in very present determination. "Free, conscious, choosing meaning over emptiness despite the cost."

"And if we succeed?" Fionntan asked, hope and fear warring in her voice.

"Then we prove that impossible things become possible when enough people choose to make them so," Boudica replied with quiet certainty.

***

As the sun touched the western horizon, painting the sky in shades of blood and gold, eight people who carried Ireland's future within their hearts prepared to attempt something that had never been tried—to infiltrate, influence, and if necessary sabotage a ceremony designed to reshape the spiritual foundations of an entire people.

The odds against them were overwhelming, the chances of success minimal, the cost of failure beyond calculation. But they had chosen their path with open eyes and willing hearts, understanding that some battles were worth fighting regardless of their outcome.

Behind them lay the abandoned safety of hidden valleys and careful planning. Ahead waited the dangerous necessity of improvising hope against forces that had perfected the art of making surrender seem inevitable.

Neassa took one last look at her companions—bloodline carriers and exiled queens, divine guardians and mortal priests, all united by the stubborn determination to preserve meaning despite the certainty of cost. Then she turned her horse toward Tara and the trial that awaited them there.

"For Ireland," she said quietly, though her words carried across the gathering dusk with the force of prophecy.

"For consciousness," Ríona added, her divine nature lending weight to the vow.

"For the right to choose our own meaning," Boudica concluded, her voice carrying the authority of someone who had paid the ultimate price for such understanding.

***

As they separated, each following different paths toward the same destination, the evening stars began to appear overhead—ancient lights that had witnessed the rise and fall of empires, the birth and death of peoples, the eternal struggle between meaning and emptiness that defined the human condition.

Tomorrow would bring the test, and Ireland's fate would be decided by choices made in the shadow of sacred stones that remembered older names for courage.

The war for Ireland's soul was about to begin, and they were ready to fight it with everything they had.

CHAPTER 7

THE GATHERING STORM

Neassa approached Tara through the old pilgrim's path, her High Priestess robes concealed beneath a traveling cloak that made her appear to be just another spiritual advisor summoned to attend the great gathering. The sacred hill rose before her like an island under siege, its ancient stones bearing witness to the greatest concentration of political power Ireland had seen in generations.

The first guard who challenged her carried the terrible emptiness she had learned to recognize—not the full conversion of the Hollowed, but the partial severing that left people functional while draining them of independent thought. His questions came with the focused intensity of someone following specific orders rather than routine screening.

"I don't know your face," he said bluntly, his hand resting on his weapon with practiced readiness. "Who are your people, and which circle sent you?"

"I serve the old rites of Brigid's forge," Neassa replied carefully, invoking a connection that was technically true while concealing her actual authority. "Brother Finnegan of the Sacred Grove sponsored my attendance."

The guard's eyes narrowed with suspicion that seemed too focused for his severed state. "Brother Finnegan. Tall man, scar on his left hand from forge-work, trained at the oak grove near the river fork?"

Ice formed in Neassa's veins as she realized the depth of their preparation. The guard knew specific details about individual druids, physical descriptions, training locations. This wasn't casual security—someone had prepared them with knowledge designed to catch exactly such deceptions.

"That's him," she agreed, hoping her uncertainty didn't show.

"Brother Finnegan died three days ago," the guard stated with mechanical certainty. "His body lies in the grove where the sickness took him. You lie about things easily checked. Come—others will want to speak with you about your true purpose here."

***

As the guard moved to restrain her, Neassa's training took over. The spiral magic that had been her life's study flowed through movements that looked like stumbling but redirected the guard's momentum into a fall that left him unconscious but breathing. She dragged his body behind a supply tent, her heart pounding with the realization that their enemies' preparation exceeded even their worst estimates.

But the commotion had attracted attention. Shouts erupted from nearby positions as other guards responded to the disturbance, and Neassa found herself running through an encampment organized with military precision but guided by something more sinister than mere efficiency. The coordination she had observed from a distance now revealed its true purpose— not just control, but systematic elimination of anything that didn't serve predetermined outcomes.

"Stranger in the eastern approach," voices called with grim purpose. "Dark-haired woman, claiming false credentials. Circle round and find her."

Neassa dove between two pavilions, pressing herself against fabric walls while guards moved past with methodical thoroughness. Horns sounded from different points around the gathering, their calls coordinating the search with signals that spoke of rehearsed response rather than improvised reaction.

Through the tent wall, she could hear conversations that confirmed her worst fears about tomorrow's ceremony. Not just political theater, but systematic spiritual compulsion designed to eliminate the possibility of meaningful opposition.

"The final preparation begins at dawn," a voice spoke with the authority of command. "Seven kingdoms' worth of rightful representatives, all spiritually guided to recognize what serves Ireland best, regardless of personal preference."

"And the bloodline carriers who haven't presented themselves?"

"Three remain unaccounted for, but their individual resistance becomes meaningless once the ceremony begins. The spiritual preparation ensures harmony of purpose that overwhelms whatever scattered opposition might remain."

***

Across the encampment, Cathair's infiltration was encountering similar complications. The bloodline connections that should have provided automatic access instead triggered scrutiny that suggested active monitoring of all ancestral claims and genealogical credentials.

"Cathair mac Connacht," King Conchobor of Ulster repeated slowly, his eyes showing the struggle between recognition and the spiritual pressure working to erode independent thought. "I knew your grandfather. A man of honor, though prone to inconvenient principles."

"Principles that served Ireland well in times of crisis," Cathair replied carefully, reading the dangerous currents that flowed through every exchange. The king's partial resistance to conversion made him both ally and liability—capable of independent thought, but under constant pressure that made him unpredictable.

"Crisis," mused Brother Declan, the converted druid whose presence radiated spiritual emptiness like a wound in reality itself. "Such an interesting word. It implies that change is inherently problematic, that stability and efficiency should be abandoned whenever individual preferences feel threatened."

"It implies that some changes are worth resisting," Cathair corrected, letting ancestral authority color his voice with harmonics that carried across generations. "That consciousness creates meaning rather than simply generating conflict."

The words hit Brother Declan like a physical blow, his converted features showing the first uncertainty Cathair had seen from any of the Hollowed. For a moment, something flickered behind his eyes—not personality returning, but recognition that he faced something his conditioning hadn't prepared him to counter.

"Interesting," the druid said slowly. "You speak with authority that transcends normal bloodline inheritance. Enhanced spiritual capacity, perhaps? That would make you valuable beyond ordinary measure for tomorrow's optimization process."

King Conchobor's expression shifted from confusion to alarm as he recognized the threat in the druid's words. "Brother Declan, surely you don't mean to include bloodline carriers in whatever spiritual preparation—"

"All resistance must be addressed," the druid interrupted with mechanical certainty. "Individual preferences that interfere with what serves Ireland cannot be permitted, regardless of their historical significance."

***

Cathair found himself backing away from a conversation that had shifted from diplomatic maneuvering to immediate threat. The converted druids weren't just conducting political manipulation— they were actively hunting for anyone whose spiritual capacity might allow resistance to their systematic assault on consciousness itself.

Boudica's warrior instincts had kept her moving through the encampment's periphery, avoiding the central areas where authority concentrated in favor of supply lines and support structures that revealed logistical truths about their enemies' capabilities. What she found there chilled her more than open threats could have managed.

This wasn't a gathering organized in days or weeks, but the culmination of months or years of preparation. Supply wagons bore markings from across Ireland and beyond, suggesting coordination that extended far past Queen Medb's individual ambition. Military equipment disguised as ceremonial props, weapons caches positioned for rapid deployment, messenger riders who could coordinate responses across the entire gathering within moments rather than hours.

"All approaches are watched," reported a figure whose bearing spoke of professional military command rather than ceremonial duty. "All paths out are guarded. If the target bloodline carriers attempt to leave, they will be taken and brought for spiritual guidance."

"And if they attempt to disrupt tomorrow's ceremony?"

"We have warriors in place. The gathered kingdoms will witness the elimination of resistance as part of the demonstration that individual preferences cannot stand against collective wisdom properly guided."

*****

Boudica's warrior instincts screamed warnings as she realized the full scope of the trap. Not just political legitimization, but public demonstration designed to prove that resistance was not just futile but literally impossible when faced with spiritual guidance backed by overwhelming force.

She began working her way back toward the edges of the encampment, but guards appeared at intersections with coordination that suggested active hunting rather than random patrol. Her concealed identity provided protection only as long as she remained unnoticed, and the systematic search that was beginning to sweep through the gathering would inevitably expose anyone who didn't belong.

A hand fell on her shoulder with the weight of absolute authority. "You there. Who are your people, and what brings you to move through the camp like one with secrets to hide?"

Ríona's divine nature had allowed her to penetrate deeper into the gathering than any of the others, but it also made her a target for forces specifically designed to detect and neutralize supernatural threats. The converted druids moved toward her location with the inevitability of hunting predators who had caught the scent of prey.

"The divine guardians come to witness their own obsolescence," Brother Marcus approached with familiar features bearing the terrible peace of one who had traded wisdom for certainty. But this time he wasn't alone—six other converted druids flanked him with the coordination that spoke of shared purpose transcending individual consciousness.

"Marcus," she said quietly, her otherworldly sight reading the emptiness that flowed around them like spiritual void given form and direction. "You've gathered quite a circle."

"We serve efficiency," he corrected with the patience of someone explaining obvious truth. "Seven druids working in perfect harmony, our individual limitations eliminated through optimal spiritual coordination."

"Seven minds thinking the same thoughts," Ríona replied, her divine nature lending authority to words that carried across multiple realms of existence. "That's not harmony—that's spiritual death wearing harmony's mask."

***

"Observe," Marcus gestured toward the gathering around them, the coordinated activities, the efficient preparation, the absence of conflict or confusion. "No arguments, no delays, no suboptimal outcomes caused by individual preference interfering with collective wisdom. Tomorrow's ceremony will demonstrate what becomes possible when consciousness is properly optimized."

"By eliminating consciousness entirely," Ríona said with quiet certainty. "You're not improving human nature—you're replacing it with something that serves different purposes entirely."

The circle of converted druids began to close around her, their combined presence creating spiritual pressure designed to crush independent thought through sheer accumulated emptiness. But Ríona's divine transformation had prepared her for exactly such assault—her silver scars blazed with otherworldly light as she channeled power that transcended normal spiritual categories.

"Join us willingly," Marcus offered with genuine invitation that somehow made the offer more horrifying than any threat. "Your divine nature makes preservation worthwhile. The spiritual guidance can maintain your special abilities while eliminating the suffering that comes from caring about outcomes beyond your control."

"Some suffering is worth preserving," Ríona replied, her immortal nature flaring with energy that made the converted druids step back despite their coordinated assault. "Because it comes from loving something larger than personal comfort."

***

The confrontation erupted into spiritual combat that transcended physical violence while somehow proving more dangerous than mere weapons could ever be. Ríona's divine power clashed against the coordinated emptiness of seven converted druids, the conflict generating energies that rippled across the entire gathering like shockwaves in a pond.

Horns began sounding throughout the encampment as the spiritual disturbance triggered whatever watching systems their enemies had established. Guards moved with deadly purpose toward predetermined positions, while converted druids emerged from pavilions with coordination that suggested rehearsed response to exactly such emergencies.

"Circle the hill," voices called with grim coordination. "Spiritual disturbance near the sacred ground. All bloodline carriers and troublemakers to be taken for immediate guidance."

The careful infiltration had become a running battle, with all pretense of stealth abandoned in favor of immediate survival. Neassa fought her way through guards who moved with inhuman coordination, while Cathair used ancestral authority to confuse enemies who couldn't quite understand the threat he represented.

Boudica's warrior training served her well as she cut through opponents who fought with deadly precision but lacked the adaptability that came from individual thought. But even superior skill couldn't overcome overwhelming numbers guided by perfect coordination.

***

"The watchtower," Ríona's voice carried across the chaos with divine authority that penetrated the surrounding confusion. "The old watchtower on the northern approach—it offers sanctuary that their spiritual guidance can't penetrate."

The desperate flight through an encampment designed to prevent exactly such escapes became a testament to the power of conscious choice against systematic control. Guards anticipated their movements, but couldn't adapt when those movements transcended logical planning in favor of desperate improvisation.

They reached the ruined watchtower as horns echoed across the encampment, guards already moving to surround their position. Ancient stones that predated Medb's gathering offered temporary protection from spiritual surveillance, but Neassa could see through the narrow windows that their refuge would soon become a trap.

"They're circling the tower," Boudica reported grimly, her warrior's eye reading the tactical situation with growing alarm. "We have perhaps moments before they seal us in completely."

"The old portal," Ríona said suddenly, her divine sight reading possibilities that had been dormant for generations. She moved toward the center of the tower's foundation, where worn stones bore carvings that seemed to shift and flow in the torchlight. "The legends speak truly—Tara's sacred hill holds gateways between distant places, paths that the first druids carved through the very fabric of the world."

"Can you activate it?" Neassa asked, though she could already see the answer in Ríona's silver scars, which had begun to pulse with otherworldly energy.

"Yes," Ríona replied, kneeling beside the ancient portal stones. "But it will require everything I have. The energy needed to open a pathway and transport all of us..." She paused, her immortal nature calculating costs that transcended normal understanding. "I'll be weakened for days while my divine essence recovers. Vulnerable in ways I haven't been since my transformation."

The sound of approaching footsteps echoed up the watchtower's stairs—they were out of time for debate.

"Do it," Neassa commanded, though her voice carried the weight of someone asking for ultimate sacrifice. "Ireland needs us alive and free more than it needs your immediate protection."

***

Ríona pressed her palms against the carved stones, and the ancient portal blazed to life with silver fire that seemed to tear a hole in the world itself. Through the opening, they could see rolling hills far from Tara's corrupted gathering, a place where the sacred network still held strength.

"Quickly," Ríona gasped, her form already growing translucent from the energy expenditure. "The pathway won't hold long."

One by one, they stepped through the portal into safety, carrying with them the intelligence that would shape their next desperate gambit. Behind them, guards burst into the empty watchtower just as the portal collapsed, leaving only ancient stones that bore no trace of the magic that had saved Ireland's last hope.

"It's worse than we thought," Neassa gasped, her voice carrying the strain of someone who had witnessed the impossible. "They're not just manipulating the ceremony—they've turned it into a trap designed to catch and convert anyone with the spiritual capacity to resist."

"A demonstration," Boudica added grimly, her strategic mind processing intelligence gathered under fire. "Tomorrow's ceremony will prove to all of Ireland that resistance is not just futile but literally impossible when faced with spiritual guidance backed by overwhelming force."

"Seven kingdoms' worth of rightful authority," Cathair contributed, his ancestral memories providing context for the scope of political manipulation they witnessed. "Enough weight to make whatever emerges seem like Ireland's own choice rather than external imposition."

"And warriors already in place," Ríona finished, her divine sight reading the true dimensions of spiritual assault that surrounded them. "By dawn, the sacred network will be so weakened that traditional resistance becomes impossible."

***

The intelligence they had gathered painted a picture of systematic assault on consciousness itself, coordinated over months or years, designed to eliminate the very possibility of meaningful opposition to the spreading emptiness. Tomorrow's ceremony wouldn't just choose a High King—it would reshape Ireland's entire spiritual foundation to serve purposes that had nothing to do with Irish welfare.

"Then we don't fight the ceremony," Neassa decided, feeling certainty settle into her bones despite the overwhelming odds they faced. "We replace it with something they haven't prepared for. Something that proves consciousness can create meaning rather than simply generate suffering."

As dawn approached, eight people who carried Ireland's hope within their hearts began to plan the impossible—not just to disrupt tomorrow's ceremony, but to offer something better in its place. The final test was coming with the light, and they would meet it by choosing to remain themselves despite every pressure to surrender meaning for the beautiful peace of emptiness.

The gathering storm had tested their resolve and proven their enemies' strength, but it had also revealed the one thing their enemies couldn't anticipate or counter—the simple human refusal to accept that efficiency mattered more than meaning, that optimization served better purposes than the chaotic glory of consciousness choosing to remain conscious despite the cost.

CHAPTER 8

THE PRICE OF PASSAGE

They emerged from the portal onto hillsides that rolled green and untainted beneath stars that still held their ancient names, far enough from Tara's corrupted gathering that the spiritual pressure lifted like a weight removed from crushing chests. But the cost of their escape became immediately apparent as Ríona collapsed to her knees, her immortal form flickering between solid flesh and translucent spirit.

"How long?" Neassa asked, kneeling beside her transformed companion while reading the spiritual exhaustion that radiated from Ríona's silver scars like heat from dying embers.

"Days," Ríona whispered, her voice carrying echoes that belonged to no mortal throat but also the weakness of someone who had spent power beyond safe limits. "Perhaps longer. The portal required everything. My divine essence must rebuild itself before I can channel significant power again."

Cathair's ancestral memories stirred with recognition of their location—hills that bordered the ancient territories where his bloodline had first taken root, land that remained connected to the older patterns despite the spreading corruption. "We're safe here," he confirmed, though his voice carried undertones of concern for what safety might cost them in precious time. "But also isolated. These hills lie far from any túath that might offer aid, far from any road that leads back toward Tara before dawn."

***

The implications settled over them like the weight of impossible mathematics. They had escaped the trap, but at the cost of removing themselves from any position to influence whatever ceremony would reshape Ireland's future with the rising sun.

"Tell me what you learned," Neassa commanded, though her heart already clenched with the certainty that their intelligence would only confirm the scope of the disaster they faced. "Everything. Every detail that might suggest how to counter what they've planned."

For the next hour, as the stars wheeled overhead in patterns that spoke of time running short, each shared what they had witnessed during their infiltration of forces arrayed against everything they sought to preserve. The picture that emerged was worse than their most pessimistic fears—not just political manipulation or spiritual corruption, but systematic assault on the very foundations of conscious choice.

"Seven kingdoms' worth of rightful representatives," Cathair reported, his voice carrying the weight of ancestral memory turned toward horror. "All spiritually guided to recognize predetermined outcomes as Ireland's own choice. By dawn, they'll be incapable of choosing anything that doesn't serve the spreading emptiness."

"Military force positioned as ceremonial guard," Boudica added, her strategic mind cataloguing threats with the precision of someone who had learned warfare through catastrophic failure. "Enough warriors to suppress any resistance that might emerge despite the spiritual preparation. They're not just planning legitimization—they're preparing demonstration that opposition is impossible."

"And the ceremony itself has been completely reimagined," Neassa continued, her spiritual training providing context for violations that transcended mere politics. "Traditional forms maintained but emptied of meaning, sacred processes turned into tools for severing consciousness from will. By the time the sun reaches full height, Ireland will have chosen its own spiritual death while believing it selected prosperity."

***

Ríona's weakened voice carried divine perspective that somehow made their circumstances even more desperate. "The sacred network is collapsing under coordinated assault. Each site that falls weakens the whole pattern, making the next corruption easier to accomplish. By dawn, traditional resistance becomes not just difficult but literally impossible."

The scope of what they faced crystallized around their small fire—systematic destruction of everything that made Ireland Irish, conducted with enough legitimate authority to make the transformation seem like conscious choice rather than external conquest.

"How do we fight something like that?" Muirenn asked, her water-folk sensitivity reading currents of despair that flowed like underground rivers through their desperate council.

"We don't fight it," Neassa replied, feeling certainty settle into her bones despite the overwhelming odds they faced. "We replace it. We offer something they haven't prepared for, something that proves consciousness can create meaning rather than simply generate suffering."

The plan that began to take shape around their hidden fire carried the audacity of people who had nothing left to lose except the principles that made loss worthwhile. Not disruption of Medb's ceremony, but the creation of something entirely different—a demonstration that legitimate authority came from conscious choice rather than inherited power or efficient organization.

"A competing ceremony," Scáthach said slowly, her warrior's mind reading tactical implications in what others might dismiss as desperate fantasy. "Simultaneous with theirs, but based on different principles entirely."

"Where?" Boudica asked with practical concern. "Every sacred site has been compromised or put under watch. We have no place that carries the spiritual weight necessary to challenge what happens at Tara."

"We make one," Ríona said quietly, her divine sight reading possibilities that existed beyond normal perception despite her current weakness. "The old stories speak of sacred spaces created through conscious will rather than inherited from ancient builders. Temporary but powerful, lasting only as long as the purpose that calls them into being."

***

One of the bloodline carriers—Ailill mac Cormac, whose weathered features showed the strain of someone who had witnessed the impossible—stirred with recognition. "Circle-casting. But the power required to create a sacred space capable of challenging Tara itself..."

"Would require all four bloodline carriers working in perfect harmony," Cathair finished, understanding beginning to dawn in his voice. "Not individually, but coordinated toward a single purpose that transcends personal preference."

"But we're only eight people total," Síle protested, her young voice carrying practical concern. "How can so few challenge the assembled authority of seven kingdoms?"

"By not competing with their numbers, but with the legitimacy of our purpose," Neassa replied, feeling certainty settle into her bones despite the overwhelming odds they faced. "They offer efficiency through emptiness. We offer meaning through conscious choice. Let Ireland see both options and decide which serves the true nature of being Irish."

Muirenn of the River Folk leaned forward with growing understanding. "Not seven circles spanning the island, but one circle that concentrates everything we have. Four bloodline carriers, one divine guardian, one High Priestess, one exiled queen who represents the cost of resistance, and one young priestess who represents the future we're fighting to preserve."

"Eight people creating a sacred space powerful enough to offer Ireland a real choice," Fionntan of the Western Shores added, her sea-king heritage providing natural understanding of how individual strengths could serve collective purpose. "Not through inherited authority or accumulated power, but through conscious decision to stand for something worth preserving."

***

As they planned their desperate gambit, the practical challenges remained daunting but no longer impossible. Eight people working together rather than scattered across hostile territory. One sacred circle created through concentrated will rather than seven sites requiring coordination across vast distances. A single ceremony timed to celestial alignment rather than complex network requiring perfect synchronization.

"There's an ancient site," Ailill said, his long experience providing memory of places that predated kingdoms and their political complications. "A natural circle in the hills northeast of here, where the first druids learned to work with forces older than civilization. Forgotten rather than important, but still holding the potential for sacred purpose."

"How far?" Boudica asked, her strategic mind already calculating the time needed to reach the location before dawn.

"Half a night's hard travel on foot," Muirenn replied, her water-folk sensitivity reading the flow of streams and valleys that would guide their path. "We can reach it before dawn if we move swiftly and don't rest."

"But eight people creating sacred space where none existed before..." Síle said hesitantly, her youth making her voice the doubts that others felt but wouldn't express. "Is such a thing even possible?"

"The stars," Ríona said suddenly, her divine sight reading possibilities that remained constant despite her temporary weakness. "The same stars that guided the first druids, that marked the original rituals, that connected sacred sites before any network was built by mortal hands. If we time the working to celestial alignment rather than arbitrary moment..."

"Dawn," Cathair breathed, ancestral memories providing recognition of the most powerful time for sacred workings. "The moment when night surrenders to day, when darkness gives way to light, when the old patterns prepared for renewal rather than ending."

***

"The same moment Medb's ceremony reaches its climax," Neassa realized with growing excitement. "We wouldn't be competing with their working—we'd be offering Ireland a choice between two visions of its future, two ceremonies proceeding simultaneously, two forms of authority claiming legitimacy through entirely different means."

The details that followed required knowledge preserved across generations, bloodline memories that reached back to the first druids who had learned to work with forces older than civilization. One ancient stone circle, aligned with stellar patterns that would guide the timing. Four bloodline carriers, each drawing on ancestral wisdom to channel power beyond individual capacity. Eight different people united by the same fundamental question— what gave authority the right to rule, and consciousness the will to serve?

"Each of us brings something different," Cathair said, his ancestral connections providing natural understanding of how individual gifts could serve collective purpose. "Bloodline wisdom, divine power, spiritual authority, strategic knowledge, warrior strength, youthful hope, the courage of exile, and the determination of those who remember what we're fighting to preserve."

"Together we become more than the sum of our parts," Fionntan added, her sea-king heritage providing understanding of how separate currents could combine into forces that transcended individual limitation.

One by one, they claimed roles in the ceremony that would either offer Ireland conscious choice or prove its impossibility. Eight people preparing to travel together toward a destination where they would either succeed in demonstrating meaning's power or fail while proving its worthiness.

***

"And if we fail?" Muirenn asked, though her voice carried determination rather than doubt.

"Then we fail as ourselves," Ríona replied, her divine nature lending authority to words that carried across multiple realms of existence despite her current weakness. "Free, conscious, choosing meaning over emptiness despite the cost."

"When do we leave?" Boudica asked, her warrior's pragmatism calculating the time needed to reach their destination before dawn.

"Now," Neassa decided, feeling the weight of leadership settling on her shoulders with the inevitability of fate. "Before our enemies can organize pursuit, before the spiritual network degrades further, before we lose the courage that comes from standing together against impossible odds."

As they prepared to travel together toward the ancient site that would either witness their triumph or their noble failure, the stars wheeled overhead in patterns that had guided druids since the first human learned to read meaning in celestial movement.

"For Ireland," Neassa said quietly, though her words carried across the gathering darkness with the force of prophecy.

"For consciousness," Ríona added, her divine nature lending weight to the vow despite her temporary vulnerability.

"For the right to choose our own meaning," Boudica concluded, her voice carrying the authority of someone who had paid the ultimate price for such understanding.

***

The journey came with dawn still hours away, eight people traveling together on foot through landscapes that showed increasing signs of spiritual disturbance as they moved closer to their chosen destination. The ancient circle lay hidden in hills that most of Ireland had forgotten, but the stars remembered and would guide their final ceremony.

Neassa led them through valleys where sacred streams still ran clear despite the corruption spreading through other waterways, following paths that the first druids had walked when learning to speak with forces that transcended mortal understanding. Behind her, Ríona walked despite her weakness, her immortal form slowly rebuilding the divine essence she had spent to save them all.

The sacrifice had bought them this chance, and they would not waste it on anything less than the transformation of impossibility into hope. Eight people carrying eight different gifts toward one ancient site, united by one desperate prayer—that consciousness might choose to remain conscious despite the cost, that love might justify existence despite the certainty of loss, that hope might survive even the most seductive offers of surrender.

The final test was coming with the dawn, and Ireland's fate would be decided not by armies or wealth, but by the choices individual hearts made when offered beautiful emptiness or difficult meaning. The war for Ireland's soul was entering its final phase, and they were ready to fight it with everything they had.

The storm was coming, but they would not meet it alone.

CHAPTER 9

THE CIRCLE OF CHOICE

The ancient stone circle emerged from the pre-dawn mist like a memory made manifest, seven standing stones arranged in patterns that predated kingdoms and spoke to truths older than written law. Each megalith bore carvings worn smooth by centuries of wind and rain, but the spirals and sacred symbols still pulsed with accumulated power that had waited generations for a purpose worthy of awakening.

"Here," Ailill breathed, his weathered features showing recognition that transcended mere knowledge. "This is where the first druids learned to speak with forces that answer only to conscious choice freely given."

Neassa felt the spiritual energy flowing through the ancient site like water finding familiar channels, power that had slept since the last circle-casting but remained ready to serve those who understood its true nature. The stones hummed with potential that made her priestess training sing in harmony, recognizing sacred space that had been created rather than inherited.

"Can you feel it?" Muirenn asked, her water-folk sensitivity reading currents of purpose that flowed between the standing stones. "It's not empty, waiting to be filled. It's expectant. Like it's been prepared for exactly this moment."

Fionntan moved between the stones with the fluid grace of someone whose sea-king heritage taught her to read patterns in apparently random arrangements. "Seven stones, but space for eight participants. The builders knew that sacred work required both traditional wisdom and conscious innovation."

***

As they entered the circle's heart, the quality of starlight seemed to change around them, becoming not just illumination but active blessing from celestial forces that had witnessed the rise and fall of empires. The ancient patterns carved into stone began to glow with inner light, responding to their presence like embers stirred to new flame.

"We don't have much time," Boudica observed, her warrior's eye reading the eastern horizon where the faintest suggestion of dawn painted the sky in shades that spoke of approaching crisis. "Whatever ceremony we're going to perform, it needs to begin soon if it's going to compete with what's happening at Tara."

Ríona moved to the circle's center, her divine sight reading the spiritual architecture that the ancient builders had woven into stone and earth. Despite her weakness from the portal working, her immortal nature still blazed with enough power to serve as focus for whatever ritual they could create.

"The stones remember," she announced, her voice carrying harmonics that belonged to realms beyond normal perception. "Circle-casting performed here reaches back to the first druids who learned that consciousness could create sacred space through will freely given rather than power inherited from others."

"What do we need to do?" Síle asked, her young voice carrying the eager determination of someone ready to prove herself worthy of the trust placed in her.

Cathair's ancestral memories stirred with recognition of procedures preserved through bloodline inheritance, knowledge that had been scattered to prevent any single person from attempting such workings without absolute necessity. "Each bloodline carrier takes position at a cardinal stone—north, south, east, west. The others fill the spaces between, creating harmony between traditional wisdom and conscious innovation."

* * *

"And then?" Neassa asked, though her priestess training already whispered answers about rituals that required perfect synchronization between individual will and collective purpose.

"We offer Ireland a choice," Ríona replied with quiet certainty. "We create a ceremony that proves consciousness can choose consciousness, that meaning emerges from love rather than efficiency, that authority comes from service rather than dominance."

They took their positions with the careful precision of people who understood that every gesture carried weight beyond individual action. Cathair claimed the eastern stone, where his bloodline's connection to dawn and renewal could channel the power of beginning. Ailill moved to the western position, his experience with endings and wisdom earned through loss providing balance to youthful hope.

Muirenn flowed toward the northern stone like water finding its natural course, her river-folk heritage connecting her to the deep currents that sustained all life. Fionntan took the southern position, her sea-king blood providing understanding of the vast forces that shaped islands and determined the fate of peoples.

Between them, the others found their places in patterns that felt inevitable despite being improvised. Neassa stood at the circle's heart beside Ríona, High Priestess and divine guardian united in service to something larger than individual power. Boudica positioned herself between east and south, her exile representing the cost of resistance while her royal heritage spoke to authority earned through sacrifice. Síle completed the circle between north and west, youth and hope balancing wisdom and experience.

***

"Now what?" Boudica asked, though her warrior's instincts already sensed the building of forces that transcended normal understanding.

"Now we choose," Neassa replied, raising her voice in words that had been spoken by the first High Priestess but carried new meaning in their desperate circumstances. "We choose consciousness over emptiness, meaning over efficiency, love over the beautiful peace of surrender."

The stones responded to her declaration with light that seemed to come from within their ancient structure, spirals and sacred symbols blazing with accumulated power awakened by conscious will directed toward worthy purpose. The circle began to sing— not with audible sound, but with harmonics that resonated through realms beyond normal perception.

At Tara, Queen Medb's ceremony reached its planned crescendo as the sun touched the eastern horizon, seven kingdoms' representatives speaking with one voice about the wisdom of accepting unity through optimal spiritual guidance. But their words rang hollow across the sacred hill, emptied of meaning by the very efficiency that was supposed to give them power.

The Hollowed druids who guided the ceremony felt the first tremors of something they hadn't prepared for—distant but growing, like the sound of singing carried on wind from impossible directions. Brother Marcus raised his head from the ritual he was conducting, confusion flickering across features that had known only certainty since his conversion.

"What is that?" he asked, his voice carrying the first uncertainty his fellow converted druids had heard since the optimization process had freed them from the burden of individual preference.

"Interference," replied the druid beside him, though his mechanical certainty wavered as the distant singing grew stronger. "Some form of spiritual static that requires correction."

***

But it wasn't static—it was harmony. Eight voices raised in conscious choice, eight people proving that meaning could be created rather than simply inherited, eight different backgrounds united by the stubborn determination to remain themselves despite every pressure to surrender individual will for collective efficiency.

The ceremony at Tara began to falter as the kingdom representatives felt the pull of something that offered genuine choice rather than optimal outcomes predetermined by forces they couldn't quite identify. For the first time since arriving at the sacred hill, they remembered that they had once been capable of disagreement, that consensus could emerge from conscious deliberation rather than spiritual compulsion.

In the ancient circle, the ritual reached levels of intensity that threatened to overwhelm mortal capacity for channeling divine power. Each participant felt the strain of serving as conduit for forces that connected individual will to cosmic purpose, but none wavered from the choice they had made to stand for meaning despite the certainty of cost.

"I feel them," Ríona gasped, her divine sight reading the spiritual landscape that stretched across Ireland. "People remembering that they have choices, that consciousness creates meaning rather than simply generating suffering. The emptiness is retreating."

"Not retreating," Neassa corrected, her priestess training allowing her to read the deeper patterns of what they had unleashed. "Being challenged. We're not defeating the Hollowed—we're offering Ireland the chance to choose something different."

***

Through the growing dawn light, they could see the effects of their working spreading outward from the ancient circle like ripples in a pond. Villages where the mechanical precision of Hollowed influence began to crack as individual personality reasserted itself. Sacred groves where the trees remembered their names and purpose. Holy wells that began to reflect starlight again instead of empty darkness.

"It's working," Síle breathed, her young voice carrying wonder at witnessing the impossible made manifest through conscious choice.

"It's beginning," Cathair corrected, his ancestral memories providing recognition of what they had started but not yet completed. "We've given Ireland the choice. Now we have to trust her people to make it."

The sun climbed higher, painting the sky in shades of gold and hope as the ancient circle continued to sing with voices both mortal and divine. Eight people had chosen to stand for consciousness despite every pressure to surrender, and their choice was creating possibilities that rippled across an entire island.

At Tara, the carefully orchestrated ceremony began to collapse as kingdom representatives remembered that they had once been capable of independent thought. King Conchobor of Ulster shook his head as if waking from deep sleep, confusion giving way to horror as he realized how close he had come to surrendering everything that made him Irish.

"What have we been doing?" he asked, his voice carrying the weight of someone who had almost lost himself to beautiful emptiness. "What were we about to choose?"

***

Queen Medb herself felt the pull of the distant singing, the offer of meaning that required individual will rather than collective efficiency. For a moment, her features showed the struggle between the person she had been and the tool she was becoming, between royal authority earned through service and power gained through surrender.

But the converted druids moved to reassert control, their combined spiritual pressure seeking to crush the returning consciousness before it could spread further. Brother Marcus raised his voice in counter-ritual, calling on forces that fed on emptiness rather than meaning, that sought to eliminate choice rather than preserve it.

"Resistance to optimal outcomes," he intoned with mechanical certainty. "Individual preferences interfering with collective wisdom. The interference must be corrected."

The spiritual battle that erupted between Tara and the ancient circle transcended physical conflict while somehow proving more dangerous than any war fought with sword and spear. Eight people working in conscious harmony against forces that sought to eliminate the very possibility of harmony through choice, meaning pitted against efficiency, love struggling against the beautiful peace of surrender.

The outcome would determine not just Ireland's political future, but the fundamental question of whether consciousness itself had the right to continue existing in a world that could be made more efficient through its elimination.

***

In the ancient circle, the strain of channeling power beyond mortal limits began to tell on participants whose only advantage was their stubborn refusal to surrender meaning without a fight. Ailill's weathered features showed the exhaustion of someone drawing on reserves of strength he hadn't known he possessed. Muirenn's connection to the flowing forces that sustained life wavered under pressure that threatened to drain her entirely.

"Hold," Ríona commanded, her divine nature blazing with light that hurt to look at directly. "Whatever the cost, we hold until Ireland has time to choose."

"For how long?" Fionntan asked through gritted teeth, her sea-king heritage providing strength for struggle but also awareness of the tide that carried them toward either triumph or destruction.

"Until dawn is complete," Neassa replied, her priestess authority binding them to purpose that transcended individual capacity. "Until every person in Ireland has felt the choice we're offering and decided for themselves whether consciousness is worth its cost."

The sun climbed toward its highest point while two ceremonies competed for Ireland's soul—one offering efficiency through emptiness, the other meaning through conscious choice. The ancient circle sang with voices that grew stronger despite their exhaustion, eight people proving that love could justify existence despite the certainty of loss, that hope could survive even the most seductive offers of surrender.

***

Around them, Ireland began to wake from the spiritual slumber that had almost claimed it, people remembering that they had choices, that consciousness created meaning rather than simply generating conflict. The Hollowed influence cracked and splintered as individual will reasserted itself, but the forces behind the spreading emptiness weren't finished with their assault on meaning itself.

The final test was still to come, and eight people who had chosen to remain themselves despite every pressure to surrender would face it with nothing but hope and the stubborn determination that consciousness was worth preserving no matter what the cost.

The circle held, the ceremony continued, and Ireland prepared to choose between two visions of its future—one that promised peace through surrender of everything that made peace worthwhile, and one that offered the terrible wonderful burden of remaining conscious despite the certainty that consciousness created chaos rather than eliminating it through optimal administration.

Dawn broke fully over the ancient stones, and with it came the moment when Ireland would either choose itself or accept transformation into something more efficient that served purposes divorced from any recognizable form of Irish welfare. Eight people had offered the choice through conscious sacrifice, and now the island would discover what that choice meant when individual hearts decided between meaning and emptiness, between the struggle to remain themselves and the beautiful peace of surrender.

The songs rose higher, carrying across valleys and hills to touch every ear that chose to listen, every heart that remembered why consciousness was worth preserving despite its terrible, wonderful cost.

CHAPTER 10

THE BREAKING POINT

The spiritual assault from Tara hit the ancient circle like a hammer blow designed to shatter stone, Marcus and his converted druids pouring concentrated emptiness through the sacred network toward eight people whose only crime was choosing to remain conscious despite the cost. The very air around the standing stones grew thick with pressure that sought to crush individual will through accumulated void.

"They're trying to sever us," Ríona gasped, her divine sight reading the true nature of the attack while her immortal form blazed with light that pushed back against the encroaching darkness. "Not just from each other, but from the capacity to want anything beyond the peace of surrender."

Ailill staggered at his western stone, the accumulated wisdom of his bloodline suddenly feeling like a burden too heavy to bear. Why struggle against forces so much more efficient than individual preference? Why choose the agony of consciousness when beautiful emptiness offered release from every burden that made existence difficult?

"Don't listen," Neassa commanded, her voice cutting through the spiritual pressure. "That's not wisdom—that's death wearing wisdom's mask. Remember what we're fighting for!"

But the assault intensified as more converted druids added their voices to Marcus's counter-ritual, dozens of severed consciousnesses working in perfect coordination to eliminate the dangerous infection of meaning that threatened to spread across Ireland. The ancient circle's song began to waver as each participant felt the weight of opposition that promised peace through surrender.

***

"I can't," Muirenn whispered, her water-folk sensitivity making her especially vulnerable to the spiritual tide that sought to drain all purpose from existence. "It's too much. The emptiness is so beautiful. No more pain, no more uncertainty, no more terrible weight of choosing wrongly."

"Hold!" Cathair shouted, though his own memories wavered under the assault. "Hold for Ireland! Hold for the right to choose our own meaning!"

At Tara, the ceremony that had promised efficient unity through optimal spiritual guidance began to fracture as the distant singing reached the assembled representatives with growing power. Some of the kingdom rulers felt the pull of something that offered genuine choice rather than predetermined outcomes, while others clung to the beautiful certainty that the Hollowed promised.

King Conchobor of Ulster was the first to break free, shaking his head as if waking from deep sleep. "What have we been doing?" he demanded, his voice carrying the weight of someone who had almost lost himself to beautiful emptiness. "What were we about to choose?"

The spiritual energy flowing from the ancient circle hit him like dawn breaking over land that had forgotten the meaning of light, and he remembered why individual will mattered more than collective efficiency, why consciousness was worth its cost despite the pain it brought.

King Aillen of Leinster followed moments later, confusion giving way to horror as he realized how close he had come to surrendering everything that made his people distinct. "This isn't unity," he said, looking around at the other representatives with growing alarm. "This is elimination. The elimination of everything that makes us Irish."

***

King Cormac of Munster struggled longer, the spiritual pressure from the converted druids warring with the distant song of conscious choice. But when the moment came, he chose awareness over peace, meaning over efficiency. "I remember my people," he whispered, as if the words themselves were sacred incantations. "I remember why they trusted me to speak for them."

But the others—Queen Medb herself, and the rulers of the remaining kingdoms—felt the pull of the ancient circle and rejected it, choosing instead the beautiful certainty that came from surrendering the burden of individual will to forces that promised optimal outcomes.

"Stop this interference," Medb commanded, though her voice carried the mechanical precision of someone whose words came from external programming rather than internal choice. "Individual preferences threaten the unity we've achieved. They must be corrected."

The spiritual battle that erupted between the two ceremonies transcended physical conflict while somehow proving more dangerous than any war fought with sword and spear. Eight people in the ancient circle working in conscious harmony against forces that sought to eliminate the very possibility of harmony through choice, meaning pitted against efficiency, love struggling against the beautiful peace of surrender.

But this time, the outcome balanced on a knife's edge. The counter-ceremony succeeded partially—three kingdoms freed from spiritual compulsion, their rulers remembering why consciousness mattered despite its cost. But four kingdoms, including Connacht under Medb's leadership, remained locked in the beautiful emptiness that promised peace through surrender of individual will.

***

"It's working," Síle breathed from her position in the circle, though her young voice carried exhaustion that spoke of power channeled beyond safe limits. "I can feel them awakening—some of them. But not all."

"Not all," Ríona confirmed, her divine sight reading the spiritual landscape with growing concern. "The split is deepening. Ireland is dividing. Those who choose consciousness pulling away from those who choose emptiness."

In the ancient circle, the strain of channeling power beyond mortal limits began to tell on participants whose only advantage was their stubborn refusal to surrender meaning without a fight. Ailill's weathered features showed exhaustion that went bone-deep, while Muirenn's connection to the flowing forces that sustained life wavered under pressure that threatened to drain her entirely.

"Hold," Neassa commanded, her priestess authority binding them to purpose that transcended individual capacity. "Just a little longer. Give Ireland time to choose."

But the spiritual energy required was burning through their mortal forms like fire through dry grass. Not the gentle transformation they had hoped for, but violent expenditure that threatened to destroy them even as it offered others the gift of choice.

***

At Tara, the partially successful ceremony collapsed into chaos as the freed kingdoms found themselves facing the reality of what they had almost surrendered. King Conchobor looked at Queen Medb with growing horror, seeing in her features the beautiful emptiness that had almost claimed him as well.

"You're not yourself," he said, though he wasn't sure if he was addressing the woman he had known or something wearing her shape. "Medb, you're not yourself."

"I am optimized," she replied with the satisfaction of someone who believed she had discovered ultimate truth. "Freed from the chaos of individual preference, aligned with purposes that serve Ireland better than personal ambition ever could."

"Whose purposes?" King Aillen demanded, clarity returning to his voice with each word. "Who decided what was optimal for Ireland? When did we surrender the right to choose our own mistakes rather than accept someone else's perfect wisdom?"

But the converted druids moved to reassert control, their combined spiritual pressure seeking to bring the freed rulers back into the beautiful peace of surrender. Brother Marcus raised his voice in counter-ritual, calling on forces that fed on emptiness rather than meaning.

"The interference will be corrected," he intoned with mechanical certainty. "Individual preferences that threaten collective wisdom cannot be permitted to persist."

The spiritual pressure intensified, but this time the freed kings had allies—the distant song from the ancient circle, the knowledge that choice was possible, the stubborn determination to remain themselves despite the cost.

"No," King Cormac said with quiet finality. "We choose to remain conscious. We choose to keep the burden of choice, the weight of responsibility, the terrible freedom of being ourselves."

The confrontation at Tara reached its breaking point as the two factions—those who chose consciousness and those who chose emptiness—faced each other across an ideological chasm that no compromise could bridge. Queen Medb and the four kingdoms that remained under Hollowed influence found themselves outnumbered by the three freed rulers, but not outmatched in terms of spiritual certainty.

"You choose suffering," Medb observed with the pity of someone who had discovered better alternatives. "You choose chaos, uncertainty, the constant agony of decisions that might be wrong. We offer peace."

"We choose life," King Conchobor replied, his voice carrying the authority of someone who had remembered why individual will mattered. "Whatever its cost."

The standoff stretched through moments that felt like hours, two visions of Ireland's future facing each other without possibility of reconciliation. Finally, Queen Medb made the choice that would reshape the island's political landscape.

"Come," she said to those who remained under the beautiful influence of optimal spiritual guidance. "We will not force our gifts on those too proud to accept them. Let them choose their suffering. We will build our peace elsewhere."

As Queen Medb's delegation withdrew with mechanical precision that carried implied threat more chilling than any display of anger, the representatives of Ireland's conscious territories found themselves facing each other across a hall that hummed with newfound unity forged through shared recognition of existential threat. The choice was made, but its consequences would test everything they thought they understood about the price of remaining themselves.

***

One by one, the rulers who had chosen emptiness over consciousness filed out of Tara's sacred halls, taking with them their retinues and their certainty, leaving behind the three kingdoms that had remembered why choice mattered despite its cost.

As the sun reached its highest point, Ireland found itself divided not by old territorial disputes or dynastic rivalries, but by fundamental questions about the nature of consciousness itself. Tara remained in the hands of those who chose meaning over efficiency, but they faced enemies who had the beautiful certainty that came from surrendering the burden of choice.

In the ancient circle, the eight who had offered Ireland the gift of choice felt their mortal forms reaching the absolute limit of what flesh could endure while channeling divine power. But they had succeeded—partially. Three kingdoms freed, Tara reclaimed, the possibility of conscious choice preserved even if not universally accepted.

"Is it enough?" Fionntan whispered, her sea-king heritage providing strength for struggle but also awareness of how close they had come to complete dissolution.

"It's a beginning," Neassa replied, though her priestess training told her that their victory was both real and terribly incomplete. "We've proven that choice is possible. Now Ireland gets to live with the consequences of exercising it."

Ríona's divine nature blazed with exhaustion that went beyond the merely physical, her immortal essence drained by the effort of channeling power meant to restore an entire island's spiritual infrastructure. "The network is partially healed," she announced with voice that carried across multiple realms of existence. "Connections restored where consciousness was chosen, severed where emptiness was preferred. Ireland is divided."

***

The collapse came slowly this time, like exhaustion after labor that had achieved its purpose but at terrible cost. One by one, the eight who had stood for consciousness felt their individual strength giving way, not to transformation but to the simple human limitation of bodies that had channeled more power than mortal forms were designed to contain.

But they lived. Weakened, exhausted, drained of strength they might not recover for days or weeks, but alive and conscious and still themselves. Their choice had been made, their gift offered, their proof provided that meaning could emerge from love rather than efficiency.

Ireland would remember what they had demonstrated, even as it struggled with the division their success had created.

As consciousness returned to forms that had been pushed beyond all reasonable limits, they found themselves still in the ancient circle but no longer alone. The scorched earth around the standing stones showed signs of new growth—not the mechanical precision of optimized cultivation, but the chaotic beauty of life choosing to live according to its own purposes rather than external design.

"We survived," Síle said with wonder, her young voice carrying gratitude for possibilities she had feared they might never see again.

"We all survived," Cathair corrected, his ancestral memories providing recognition of transformation that went deeper than individual preservation. "And so did the choice we offered Ireland. It may not have been accepted universally, but it was offered freely and some chose to take it."

***

Around them, the ancient stones hummed with renewed purpose, their carved spirals pulsing with power that had been awakened by conscious sacrifice but remained to serve future needs. The circle would stand as reminder and refuge, proof that sacred space could be created through conscious will rather than simply inherited from ancient builders.

The immediate crisis was over, but its resolution had created new challenges that would test everything they had proven possible. Ireland was divided, and the work of healing that division—or learning to live with it—was just beginning.

They had chosen consciousness over emptiness, meaning over efficiency, love over the beautiful peace of surrender. Now they would discover what those choices meant when translated into the daily work of building a future worthy of the prices they had paid to make it possible.

The war for Ireland's soul had entered a new phase, and they were ready to fight it with everything they had left.

But first, they needed to rest. The circle had held, Ireland had chosen—partially—and eight people who had risked everything to offer that choice could finally allow themselves to collapse into the sleep of the utterly exhausted but ultimately victorious.

The sun climbed higher over the ancient stones, painting the world in shades of gold and hope, while around the circle new grass grew in patterns that followed no optimal design, only the wild geometry of life expressing itself through choices too complex for any algorithm to predict or control.

Ireland lived, divided but free to remain divided, conscious enough to struggle with the consequences of consciousness rather than accepting the beautiful peace of surrender. It was, they realized as sleep finally claimed them, exactly what they had fought to preserve—the terrible, wonderful right to choose their own meaning, whatever the cost.

CHAPTER 11

THE GATHERING OF THE FAITHFUL

Dawn came to Tara like a song half-remembered, silver light threading through stones that had witnessed the impossible and still hummed with the memory of choices freely made. Three days had passed since the great choosing, three days of Ireland learning to breathe with lungs divided between consciousness and beautiful emptiness. Still they came—riders bearing the colors of lesser túatha, their horses lathered with urgency and hope.

Neassa stood in the Hall of the High King, watching the steady stream of arrivals through windows that framed a landscape forever changed. Where once the sacred hill had drawn pilgrims seeking divine judgment, now it called to those who had felt the distant song of conscious choice and answered with their presence.

"The chieftain of Mag Muirthemne," Fergus announced, reading from the scroll that recorded each delegation. "Bringing twelve warriors and his eldest son. The lords of Emain Macha— three brothers who held their lands against Queen Medb's influence. The sea-princes of the northern shores, who felt the spiritual battle from their cliff-top fortresses."

King Conchobor moved to her side, weathered features showing the strain of someone granted wisdom at terrible cost. "They seek certainty. Leaders who felt their foundations crack during the choosing need to know that legitimate authority still exists in Ireland."

"What do we offer them?" Neassa asked. The answer would be everything and nothing—hope wrapped in the terrible responsibility of conscious choice. "The Lia Fáil remains lost, the ancient forms severed. We have no divine stone to crown a High King, no inherited authority to guarantee their loyalty."

***

Through the great doors came the first group of arrivals— representatives bearing the blue and gold of the western clans that bordered territories now under Queen Medb's influence. Their leader approached with the careful step of one who had witnessed the impossible and lived to speak of it.

She inclined her head respectfully. "High Priestess, I am Étaín of the Western Marches. I bring word from those who felt the choosing and chose consciousness over the beautiful emptiness that crept through our lands like winter fog."

The council that assembled bore little resemblance to traditional gatherings of Ireland's leadership. Where once the túatha had convened in order of precedence established by generations of custom, now they gathered as equals united by the single criterion that mattered—they had felt the pull of two visions for Ireland's future and chosen the harder path of remaining themselves.

Even as representatives filed into the chamber with faces showing relief at finding sanctuary, tension crackled beneath surface courtesies. These were people who had risked everything to travel here, leaving their territories vulnerable in hope of finding unified resistance to forces promising peace through surrender of individual will.

"Seventeen lesser túatha," King Aillen announced as the last group took their places. "All who felt the spiritual battle and chose to remain themselves rather than accept the beautiful peace that Queen Medb's allies offered."

"Seventeen out of how many?" Étaín's practical mind cut straight to the mathematics that would determine their survival.

The silence that followed carried weight beyond mere numbers. Through the great windows, they could see banners of those who had answered Tara's call—a respectable gathering, but far from the overwhelming show of unity that might have intimidated enemies or guaranteed success.

Brendan of Mag Muirthemne's weathered features showed the strain of someone who had led warriors through desperate battles. "Perhaps a third of the island remains under our influence. The rest have either accepted Queen Medb's efficiency through spiritual guidance, or withdrawn entirely from the conflict to preserve what they can of their traditional ways."

"Then we face enemies with three-to-one odds," observed Muiris of the Southern Rivers, his voice carrying grim calculation. "Facing opponents with perfect coordination, unlimited certainty, and solutions that eliminate difficulty rather than transcending it."

Before the mood could sink into despair, the sound of galloping horses echoed across the courtyard—not more arrivals, but a single rider moving with desperate urgency.

***

The messenger who burst through the great doors bore the dust of hard travel and the wild look of someone who had witnessed something that challenged every assumption about what was possible. His horse stood outside the entrance, sides heaving from a ride that had pushed both mount and rider beyond normal endurance.

"High Priestess!" he gasped, stumbling forward with movements that spoke to exhaustion held at bay through sheer will. "I bring word from the eastern territories—urgent news that changes everything we thought we knew about our enemies' capabilities."

Cathair stepped forward, natural authority evident despite his careful avoidance of center stage. "Speak your message, friend. In times like these, urgent news serves better delivered swiftly than perfectly."

"Three more sacred sites fell in the past day," the messenger reported, his voice gaining strength as he focused on the intelligence that had driven his desperate ride. "But not through siege or spiritual assault—they simply... changed. One moment serving the old ways, the next speaking with voices promising optimal outcomes through surrender of individual choice."

The implications hit the assembled representatives like a physical blow. Not gradual corruption that might be resisted, but instantaneous transformation that eliminated the possibility of defense.

"How?" Neassa demanded, her priestess training providing recognition of spiritual violation that transcended normal categories of attack.

"The druids who served these sites say they made the choice freely," the messenger continued with growing horror. "They describe it as discovering better ways to serve their people, more efficient methods of achieving spiritual harmony. They speak of guidance that eliminates the burden of uncertainty."

"Conversion," Ríona said quietly, her divine sight-reading patterns that stretched beyond normal perception. "Not forced spiritual assault, but systematic seduction that makes surrender feel like wisdom rather than defeat."

Around the chamber, representatives who had risked everything to reach Tara began to understand the true sophistication of what they faced. Not crude spiritual conquest, but carefully crafted offers of solutions to problems that consciousness created through its very nature.

"There's more," the messenger said reluctantly. "Queen Medb has called for a great gathering at Cruachan, inviting all who would lead Ireland to witness what she calls 'the birth of a new age of unity and prosperity through optimal governance.'"

The political implications crashed over them like waves against a crumbling seawall. Not just spiritual corruption, but legitimization through traditional forms—ceremony that would give legal weight to whatever emerged from alliance between Irish ambition and systematic emptiness.

"When?" King Cormac asked, though his voice carried recognition that timing would matter less than preparation they lacked.

"Seven days hence," the messenger replied. "She promises to demonstrate the benefits of guidance that eliminates conflict through elimination of the sources of disagreement. All Irish leadership invited to witness the future of prosperity through proper order."

***

The debate that erupted revealed fault lines deeper than tactical disagreement—fundamental divisions about the nature of authority, the source of legitimacy, the relationship between individual will and collective welfare.

"It's a trap," declared Scáthach, her warrior's training reading tactical implications with uncomfortable clarity. "Gather Ireland's remaining free leadership in one place, then convert or eliminate everyone who might organize resistance."

"But ignore the invitation, and we surrender narrative control," countered Fergal of the Mountain Clans. "Let Medb claim to speak for all Ireland while legitimate authority hides in remote strongholds like bandits avoiding rightful governance."

"What legitimate authority?" Étaín asked with bluntness that cut through diplomatic courtesy to political reality. "We're seventeen minor túatha and three kingdoms that held their territories through luck and stubbornness. What gives us the right to speak for Ireland when Ireland's acknowledged leaders have chosen different paths?"

The question hung in the chamber's air like a challenge that demanded an answer none felt qualified to provide. Around them, the ancient stones of Tara seemed to wait with the patience of monuments that had witnessed the rise and fall of legitimate authority across generations beyond counting.

Cathair moved from his position at the chamber's edge—not toward the center of authority, but to the great window where he could see the landscape stretching toward territories that had once acknowledged Tara's supremacy. His presence drew attention not through assertion but through simple recognition that some people carried within themselves the capacity to unite others around purposes larger than individual survival.

"Perhaps," he said quietly, his voice carrying across the chamber despite its measured tone, "the question isn't what gives us the right to speak for Ireland, but what gives Ireland the right to remain itself despite every pressure to become something more efficient."

The words settled over the assembly like recognition of truth that transcended political calculation. Not authority claimed through inheritance or divine selection, but responsibility accepted through conscious choice to preserve something that might prove more valuable than safety.

"The bloodlines remember," King Conchobor said with Ulster's ancient wisdom, his gaze moving thoughtfully to Cathair despite the younger man's obvious reluctance to accept formal recognition. "They carry within them the voices of those who united Ireland when unity seemed impossible. Perhaps that memory serves purposes larger than personal preference."

Before anyone could respond to the growing weight of expectation that pressed against Cathair like physical force, new sounds echoed from the courtyard—not the single urgent messenger this time, but multiple riders arriving with coordination that spoke to planned rather than coincidental timing.

***

The riders who appeared at evening's approach moved with coordination that spoke to careful planning rather than coincidental timing. Seven figures on horseback, their mounts bearing the dust of distant travel but moving with steady purpose of those who had measured their journey to arrive at exactly this moment.

The lead rider dismounted with movements that carried both exhaustion and determination. A woman whose bearing spoke of authority earned through trial rather than inherited through blood, her traveling clothes unable to conceal the fighter's build underneath or the way her eyes assessed Tara's defenses with professional interest.

"I am Brigid, lately of the Northern Shores," she announced, inclining her head with respectful but not deferential courtesy. "I bring word of what befalls kingdoms that choose efficiency over choice, order over the sacred chaos of free will."

Behind her, six companions dismounted with similar grace—men and women whose faces bore the particular strain of people who had seen too much and survived to carry warnings that others needed to hear. They moved like warriors, but warriors who had learned caution through defeats that taught harder lessons than victories ever could.

Cathair approached with natural authority that had begun to emerge despite his careful avoidance of formal leadership. "You're welcome at Tara, Brigid of the Northern Shores. Though I suspect your news carries weight that transcends mere courtesy."

"It does," she replied, her gaze moving across the assembled representatives with calculation that read both strength and weakness in their positioning. "You face enemies whose methods I've encountered before. They don't work through conquest or even corruption—they offer what people genuinely want: relief from responsibility, freedom from the agony of difficult choices."

The expanded council that convened as full darkness fell carried tension that went beyond mere political disagreement. Brigid's presence had shifted the chamber's dynamics in ways that made every existing alliance feel provisional, every assumption about leadership open to challenge.

"You speak of experience with our enemies," King Aillen observed with careful neutrality. "Yet your origins remain diplomatically unexamined. In times when trust determines survival, such mystery carries its own dangers."

"Truth often carries more danger than mystery," Brigid replied with honesty that held its own form of courage. "But you're right—trust requires revelation, and revelation requires courage from both speaker and listeners."

She moved to stand where firelight would illuminate her features clearly, no longer attempting to conceal what careful observation might already have discerned. "My name is not Brigid. I am Boudica, once Queen of the Iceni, leader of the great British rebellion against Rome."

The silence that followed carried weight beyond mere surprise. Around the chamber, hands moved to weapons before conscious thought could intervene, while minds struggled to process implications that challenged every assumption about their gathering's nature.

"The most wanted fugitive in the Roman world," breathed Fergal of the Mountain Clans, his voice tight with recognition of how profoundly their circumstances had just changed. "Every Roman agent from here to Gaul will be hunting you. Your presence here guarantees imperial attention will follow."

"Yes," Boudica replied with calm acceptance that somehow made her revelation more rather than less credible. "But I also represent something your enemies can't understand or counter— the willingness to choose resistance over safety, meaning over peace, love over the beautiful emptiness of surrender."

"Why reveal yourself?" Étaín leaned forward with practical urgency. "Why expose your identity and endanger our mission when silence served your purposes?"

"Because unity built on lies serves the same purpose as the Hollowed's false peace—it eliminates the chaos that comes from dealing with difficult truths." Boudica's gaze moved to each representative in turn. "I failed my people once by underestimating enemies and overestimating my own strength. I won't make that mistake again."

"Your failure cost thousands of lives," Brendan said bluntly. "British dead, Roman dead, innocents caught between armies led by pride rather than wisdom. What makes you think we should trust someone whose leadership brought such destruction?"

The words landed like physical blows, and Neassa saw Boudica flinch as if struck. But when she spoke, her voice carried the weight of someone who had wrestled with guilt and emerged with hard-won understanding.

"Because I've learned the cost of leading through emotion rather than strategy, of choosing pride over practicality, of believing that courage alone could overcome superior planning." Her voice grew stronger with each admission. "My daughters died because of choices I made. My people suffered because I led them into a war I couldn't win. I am not that tale's hero—I am its lesson."

The standing stones around them seemed to pulse with approval, ancient magic responding to honesty offered without compulsion. In the distance, thunder rolled across the sky despite the absence of clouds—The Morrígan's voice carrying across realms to remind them that divine powers watched their choices.

"The ancestors accept her truth," Fionntan said, wonder touching her voice. "I feel their approval in my blood, their recognition of courage that chooses revelation over safety."

"Then we stand together," Donnchad declared, his massive hand extending toward Boudica in the gesture of alliance. "Queen to warrior, exile to native, all united by the choice to remain ourselves despite the cost."

One by one, the others joined the gesture, hands meeting in the center of the circle while the standing stones hummed with accumulated power. Seven bloodline carriers and one exiled queen, choosing unity through conscious decision rather than compelled surrender.

"What of the gathering at Cruachan?" Ailill asked. "Do we attend Queen Medb's invitation?"

"We attend," Neassa decided, feeling certainty settle into her bones like truth finding its proper home. "Not as supplicants seeking favor, but as living proof that consciousness cannot be perfected into submission. We go to spring the trap deliberately, on our terms."

"Dangerous beyond measure," Cormac warned. "Medb commands forces we can barely comprehend, guided by advisors who've perfected the art of making spiritual annihilation seem like salvation."

"Then we prepare for the impossible," Cathair replied, his voice carrying ancestral authority mixed with personal determination. "We go not to win through force, but to prove through example. We show them what conscious choice creates when it refuses to surrender meaning to efficiency."

As the gathering dispersed, each bloodline carrier departing to make their own preparations for the trial ahead, Neassa found herself walking beside Cathair through the circle of ancient stones. The evening air carried the scent of approaching storm, but also something else—the electric tension that came before moments that would echo through legend.

"Are we making the right choice?" she asked, allowing uncertainty to enter her voice for the first time since the crisis began.

"I don't know," he replied with honesty that was more comforting than false confidence. "But we're making *our* choice, freely given despite the cost. That may be the most important thing we can do—prove that such choices are still possible."

His hand found hers as they walked, warm and solid in the gathering darkness. "Whatever happens at Cruachan, whatever we face in Medb's hall, we'll face it as ourselves. That's no small victory, considering what our enemies offer as the alternative."

Behind them, the standing stones began to fade into mist, returning to whatever timeless realm they inhabited when not needed by those who remembered the old ways. But their blessing remained, carried in the blood of those who had chosen truth over comfort, unity over isolation, love over the beautiful peace of surrender.

Tomorrow would bring them to Cruachan and whatever awaited in Queen Medb's transformed court. Tonight, they had forged alliances that would either save Ireland or provide worthy witness to its fall.

The storm was coming, but they would not meet it alone.

CHAPTER 12

SHADOWS AND SUSPICIONS

The council chamber at Tara buzzed with tension that went beyond mere political disagreement as representatives who had risked everything to reach the sacred hill found themselves facing questions that transcended territorial disputes or dynastic rivalries. The seventeen túatha had gathered by midday, their leaders bearing increasingly dire reports of Ireland's spiritual landscape crumbling under systematic assault.

Neassa watched from the high table as Étaín of the Western Marches finished her report, the woman's weathered face showing the strain of someone who had witnessed impossible transformations in territories that bordered Queen Medb's expanding influence.

"Three villages converted overnight," Étaín was saying, her voice carrying the weight of someone struggling to articulate horror that defied description. "Not conquered, not coerced—they simply woke speaking of optimization and efficient resource allocation as if these had always been their highest values."

Murmurs rippled through the assembled representatives. Brendan of Mag Muirthemne leaned forward with growing alarm. "The same pattern we've seen across the eastern territories. But the speed is accelerating. Whatever force spreads this...emptiness, it's growing stronger."

"Or more coordinated," King Conchobor observed grimly from his position at the chamber's edge. Despite being one of the three liberated kings, he remained cautious about asserting authority among the lesser túatha who had risked everything to reach Tara. "The reports suggest planning that spans months, perhaps years. This isn't opportunistic conquest—it's systematic transformation."

***

The question that hung unspoken in the chamber's air was one of legitimacy—not just who had the right to lead, but whether leadership meant anything when traditional authority structures had either been corrupted or proven inadequate to the crisis they faced.

Cathair stood near the great window, his presence drawing attention despite his obvious reluctance to accept the role others seemed determined to thrust upon him. The bloodline memories that flowed through his consciousness whispered of kings who had united Ireland through force of will rather than inheritance, but those same memories warned of the terrible cost such leadership demanded.

"The reports grow worse each day," Fergus said quietly, approaching with the scroll that recorded each delegation's intelligence. "Not just conversion, but systematic elimination of everything that makes our territories distinctly Irish. Trade customs replaced with Roman efficiency. Sacred groves cleared for optimal agricultural use. Even the language changes—people speaking in terms of resource allocation rather than beauty, productivity rather than meaning."

Scáthach moved from her position by the door with warrior's urgency. "The enemy's strategy becomes clearer. They're not seeking conquest in any traditional sense. They're transforming Ireland into something that serves Roman purposes while maintaining the illusion of Irish governance."

"Which makes our resistance more than political defiance," Muiris added with growing understanding. "We're not just fighting for territory or independence—we're fighting for the right to remain Irish in any recognizable sense."

The weight of that realization settled over the chamber like recognition of stakes that transcended normal calculations of victory and defeat. Around the great table, representatives who had argued about precedence and protocol began to understand that such concerns had become luxury they could no longer afford.

***

Before anyone could respond to this grim assessment, the sound of approaching hoofbeats echoed across the courtyard—not the single urgent messenger they had grown accustomed to, but multiple riders moving with coordination that suggested military discipline rather than coincidental arrival.

"Seven riders," announced the guard from the entrance, his voice carrying tension that spoke to suspicious timing. "Moving in formation, but bearing no banners we recognize. They request audience on matters of mutual concern regarding Ireland's current difficulties."

King Aillen exchanged glances with his fellow kings. "Unknown riders arriving at precisely the moment when we're discussing our enemies' growing strength. The timing seems rather convenient for coincidence."

"Or rather dangerous for honest travelers," Muiris added grimly. "In times like these, mysterious delegations carry their own risks."

Neassa felt the weight of decision settling on her shoulders. As High Priestess of Tara, the choice was ultimately hers—whether to receive unknown visitors who might be allies, enemies, or something more dangerous: those who claimed to be allies while serving different purposes.

"We receive them," she decided, though her voice carried the authority of someone making choices with full awareness of their cost. "But under guard, and with understanding that Tara's hospitality extends only as far as Tara's safety permits."

***

The seven riders who entered the great hall moved with coordination that immediately caught every warrior's attention. Not the mechanical precision of the Hollowed, but the fluid discipline of people trained to work together under pressure. Their leader, a woman whose traveling clothes couldn't quite conceal the fighter's build underneath, approached with respectful but not deferential bearing.

"I am Brigid of the Northern Shores," she announced, her voice carrying authority earned through trial rather than inherited through blood. "I bring word from territories that have faced the beautiful emptiness you now confront, and intelligence about enemies whose methods transcend normal categories of conquest."

Behind her, six companions arranged themselves with movements that spoke to professional military coordination. They stood at ease, but their positioning provided clear lines of sight to every exit and defensive position—the habits of people who had learned caution through survival rather than theory.

Cathair stepped forward with the natural authority that had begun emerging despite his careful avoidance of formal leadership. "You're welcome at Tara, Brigid of the Northern Shores. Though I note your arrival comes at a moment when we're discussing exactly the threats you claim to understand."

"Timing that might seem suspicious," she acknowledged with honesty that somehow made her presence more rather than less credible, "unless one understands that such discussions become necessary precisely when enemies begin implementing plans they've been preparing for months or years."

Her words carried the ring of truth, but also something else—a familiarity with military planning that went beyond normal tribal warfare. Several of the assembled representatives exchanged glances, reading implications in her bearing that suggested experience with conflicts on a scale Ireland had never witnessed.

***

"You speak of methods that transcend normal conquest," King Aillen observed carefully. "Yet your origins remain diplomatically unexamined. In times when trust determines survival, such mystery carries its own dangers."

Brigid met his gaze without flinching, though Neassa caught a flicker of something—calculation, perhaps, or the weight of secrets carefully maintained. "Mystery often serves survival better than revelation, especially when revelation carries consequences that extend beyond immediate convenience. But you're right that trust requires foundation stronger than mere assertions of good intent."

The tension in the chamber grew palpable as representatives processed the implications of her careful non-answer. Here was someone with crucial intelligence about their enemies, arriving at exactly the moment when such knowledge was desperately needed—but maintaining secrets that made her reliability impossible to assess.

"Your companions," Scáthach observed with warrior's eye for details that others might miss. "They move like soldiers who've seen combat, but their equipment bears no markings we recognize. Their weapons show use, but in patterns that suggest fighting against opponents using methods we've never encountered."

One of Brigid's companions—a lean man whose scars spoke of battles fought in distant places—shifted almost imperceptibly at Scáthach's analysis. The movement was slight, but it confirmed what the warrior-woman had suspected: these were not Irish fighters, despite their leader's claims to northern origins.

"We've fought the beautiful emptiness in other lands," Brigid acknowledged, her admission somehow raising more questions than it answered. "The enemy you face here has tested their methods across territories where resistance was scattered, unorganized, unprepared for the sophistication of spiritual assault that makes surrender seem like wisdom."

"Other lands," repeated Brendan with growing suspicion. "You speak as if this corruption spreads beyond Ireland's shores. As if we face not local conspiracy but something larger—more coordinated than any threat our experience prepares us to counter."

***

Before Brigid could respond, Ríona stirred from her position near the chamber's edge. The divine guardian's otherworldly sight had been reading currents of purpose and hidden pain that flowed around the mysterious arrivals, and what she found there made her silver scars pulse with warning light.

"There are shadows around you," she said quietly, her voice carrying authority that transcended normal perception. "Not the emptiness of the Hollowed, but the weight of choices that cost more than survival. You carry guilt, Brigid of the Northern Shores—guilt born from failure that taught you wisdom at prices too high for comfortable calculation."

The accuracy of Ríona's reading hit its target like a perfectly aimed spear. For just a moment, Brigid's carefully maintained composure cracked, revealing depths of pain and regret that spoke to catastrophes survived rather than victories won.

"We all carry such shadows," she replied with visible effort to reclaim emotional control. "In times like these, survival itself becomes a form of guilt when others don't share that privilege."

"But your shadows are different," Ríona pressed with divine perception that penetrated beyond normal understanding. "They taste of leadership that led followers into disaster, of choices made with good intentions that produced outcomes too terrible for easy forgiveness. You're not just someone who survived the beautiful emptiness—you're someone who failed to prevent it from claiming people you were supposed to protect."

The silence that followed carried weight beyond mere suspicion. Around the chamber, representatives began to understand that they faced not just mysterious arrival, but someone whose secrets might reshape their understanding of what they truly confronted—and whether victory was possible against enemies who had apparently succeeded elsewhere.

* * *

The debate that erupted revealed fault lines deeper than tactical disagreement. Some argued for demanding full revelation before proceeding, while others insisted that useful intelligence mattered more than complete transparency. But underneath the political maneuvering lay a more fundamental question: could they afford to trust someone whose experience suggested their enemies were even more formidable than they had imagined?

"The question isn't whether she carries secrets," Cathair said finally, his voice cutting through the growing argument with authority that seemed to surprise even himself. "The question is whether those secrets serve our purposes or threaten them. And whether we're strong enough to benefit from knowledge that might prove more burden than blessing."

His words settled over the assembly like recognition of truth that transcended political calculation. Around the chamber, representatives who had been arguing about procedure began to understand that they faced choices with implications reaching far beyond immediate tactical concerns.

"Seven days until Queen Medb's gathering," Neassa observed, feeling the weight of time pressing against them like physical force. "Seven days to determine whether we face this crisis with partial knowledge that might prove false, or complete intelligence that might prove overwhelming."

Brigid stepped forward with movements that carried both determination and resignation—the bearing of someone who understood that revelation carried risks, but that concealment served no one when survival hung in the balance.

"I offer this much," she said, her voice carrying new weight as she abandoned diplomatic evasion for something approaching honesty. "The enemy you face has tested their methods across multiple territories. They've learned to anticipate resistance, to counter traditional defenses, to turn strength into weakness through offers that make surrender seem like wisdom rather than defeat."

She paused, studying each face with calculation that read both alliance potential and threat assessment. "But they've also revealed weaknesses—blind spots in their understanding that conscious resistance can exploit, if that resistance proves willing to accept costs they haven't yet imagined."

The chamber fell silent as representatives processed what they had heard. Not just confirmation of their worst fears about enemy sophistication, but hints of hope that transcended mere desperate optimism. If Brigid spoke truth, their enemies possessed vulnerabilities that might be exploited—but only by those willing to pay prices that traditional resistance had never contemplated.

"What costs?" King Cormac asked with quiet intensity.

"The cost of unity that transcends tribal boundaries," Brigid replied without hesitation. "The cost of leadership that serves purpose rather than precedent. The cost of choosing meaning over safety when safety could be purchased through surrender of everything that makes meaning possible."

As evening approached and the chamber's shadows lengthened, the assembled representatives found themselves facing questions that would either forge them into something stronger than the sum of their parts, or reveal that Ireland's fragmentation made effective resistance impossible regardless of enemy weaknesses.

"Tomorrow," Neassa decided, her voice carrying the authority of someone who understood that some choices could not be delayed without becoming impossible. "Tomorrow we hear the full truth, whatever its cost. Ireland deserves to make its choice with open eyes, even if that choice leads us all toward disaster."

The mysterious arrivals had brought more than intelligence— they had brought the moment of decision that would determine whether Ireland's resistance could evolve beyond traditional categories, or whether the beautiful emptiness would claim them all through their inability to trust each other with truth too dangerous for comfortable consideration.

Outside Tara's walls, the autumn wind carried the scent of approaching winter and the promise of conflicts that would test every assumption about the nature of leadership, loyalty, and the price of remaining conscious in a world that offered beautiful peace through surrender of individual will.

The shadows were gathering, but so was the resolve to meet them with eyes open and hearts ready for whatever revelation the dawn might bring.

CHAPTER 13

THE WEIGHT OF TRUTH

Dawn came to Tara with the weight of promises that could no longer be delayed. The great hall filled early as representatives who had spent the night wrestling with questions of trust and survival gathered to hear whatever revelation Brigid of the Northern Shores would offer. The tension was palpable—everyone understood that what they learned might either forge them into effective resistance or shatter their fragile unity beyond repair.

Neassa took her place at the high table with movements that spoke to the burden of leadership accepted rather than claimed. Beside her, Cathair stood with the quiet authority that had emerged through crisis rather than ceremony. Around them, seventeen túatha representatives arranged themselves with careful attention to positioning that might matter if trust proved misplaced.

Brigid entered with her six companions, their coordination now clearly visible as military discipline rather than casual travel arrangement. But this morning, something had changed in her bearing—the careful calculation of the previous day replaced by the resigned determination of someone who had decided that concealment served no purpose when survival required absolute honesty.

"You promised truth," King Aillen said without preamble, his voice carrying the weight of someone who understood that diplomatic courtesy had become luxury they could no longer afford. "Ireland faces enemies whose sophistication exceeds our experience. We need to know exactly what we're fighting, and whether you bring us hope or merely confirmation of our doom."

Brigid moved to the center of the chamber where firelight would illuminate her features clearly, abandoning any pretense of concealing what careful observation might have discerned. When she spoke, her voice carried new weight—not the measured tones of diplomatic negotiation, but the raw honesty of someone who had decided that revelation's risks mattered less than concealment's certainty of failure.

"My name is not Brigid," she said, her words falling into silence that seemed to draw all sound from the chamber. "I am Boudica, once Queen of the Iceni, leader of the great British rebellion against Rome."

***

The revelation hit like a physical blow that staggered everyone who heard it. Around the chamber, hands moved toward weapons before conscious thought could intervene, while minds struggled to process implications that challenged every assumption about their gathering's nature.

"The most wanted fugitive in the Roman world," breathed Fergal of the Mountain Clans, his voice tight with recognition of how profoundly their circumstances had just changed. "Every Roman agent from here to Gaul will be hunting you. Your presence here guarantees imperial attention will follow."

"It does," Boudica replied with calm acceptance that somehow made her revelation more rather than less credible. "But my presence also brings something your enemies can't understand or counter—knowledge of their methods gained through catastrophic failure, and the willingness to choose resistance over safety despite the certainty of cost."

The silence that followed carried weight beyond mere surprise. Representatives who had risked everything to reach Tara now found themselves faced with someone whose very existence transformed their struggle from local crisis to part of a larger conflict spanning territories they had never imagined.

"Why tell us?" Étaín demanded with practical urgency that cut through shock to immediate concerns. "Why expose your identity and endanger our mission when silence served your purposes?"

"Because unity built on lies serves the same purpose as the Hollowed's false peace—it eliminates the chaos that comes from dealing with difficult truths." Boudica's gaze moved to each representative in turn, reading alliance potential and threat assessment with equal clarity. "I failed my people once by underestimating enemies and overestimating my own strength. I won't make that mistake again."

"Your failure cost thousands of lives," Brendan said bluntly, his warrior's training forcing him to speak truths others might prefer to avoid. "British dead, Roman dead, innocents caught between armies led by pride rather than wisdom. What makes you think we should trust someone whose leadership brought such destruction?"

***

The words cut deep, and Neassa saw Boudica flinch as if struck by physical blows. But when she spoke, her voice carried the weight of someone who had wrestled with guilt and emerged with hard-won understanding rather than comfortable justification.

"Because I've learned the cost of leading through emotion rather than strategy, of choosing pride over practicality, of believing that courage alone could overcome superior planning." Her voice grew stronger with each admission, not weaker. "My daughters died because of choices I made. My people suffered because I led them into a war I couldn't win. I am not that tale's hero—I am its lesson."

The honesty of her self-assessment seemed to shift something in the chamber's atmosphere. Around the great table, representatives who had been preparing for defensive argument instead found themselves confronting someone who offered not excuses but education bought at prices too high for anyone to envy.

"What did you learn?" Cathair asked quietly, his question cutting through political calculation to fundamental concerns. "What wisdom did catastrophe teach that might serve Ireland's defense?"

"That our enemies don't work through conquest but through seduction," Boudica replied without hesitation. "They offer what people genuinely want—relief from responsibility, freedom from the agony of difficult choices, peace through surrender of individual will. The beautiful emptiness doesn't force compliance; it makes compliance seem like salvation."

She moved closer to the great table, her presence somehow anchoring the assembly despite the impossibility of what she represented. "But I also learned their weaknesses. They understand efficiency and optimization, but they can't comprehend love that chooses suffering over emptiness. They can counter traditional resistance, but they're blind to unity that transcends self-interest."

Ríona stirred from her position near the chamber's edge, her divine sight reading the currents of purpose and pain that flowed around the exiled queen. "The ancestors accept her truth," she said with wonder touching her voice. "I feel their approval in my blood, their recognition of courage that chooses revelation over safety."

***

The debate that followed revealed the true complexity of their situation as representatives wrestled with questions that went beyond mere military alliance to fundamental issues of legitimacy, authority, and the nature of leadership itself.

"Experience matters," Muiris said thoughtfully, his river-folk wisdom reading undercurrents that others might miss. "But so does understanding the specific nature of contemporary threats. These enemies don't seek conquest in traditional terms; they attack the very capacity for resistance."

"Which is exactly why we need someone who understands their methods," Scáthach countered with warrior's pragmatism. "Traditional leadership failed against these forces. Perhaps we need leadership that has confronted them and learned from the encounter."

"But what of Irish authority?" King Cormac asked with careful neutrality that barely concealed deeper concerns. "Foreign leadership, however experienced, carries complications that internal leadership avoids."

The question struck at the heart of their dilemma. They faced enemies whose sophistication exceeded their experience, but accepting guidance from someone whose very presence endangered them all required trust that transcended normal political calculation.

Cathair had remained silent through most of the debate, but now he stepped forward with movements that somehow commanded attention despite their quietness. The bloodline memories that flowed through his consciousness whispered recognition of moments when traditional authority proved inadequate to unprecedented crisis.

"Perhaps we're asking the wrong questions," he said, his voice carrying across the chamber with authority that seemed to emerge from wisdom rather than ambition. "Instead of debating who has the right to lead, perhaps we should ask who has the strength to serve."

His gaze moved thoughtfully across the assembly, reading faces that showed confusion, hope, and fear in equal measure. "Leadership isn't privilege to be claimed but burden to be carried. The question is who proves willing to accept that burden despite its cost."

***

"Pretty words," Fergal observed with the skepticism of someone who had seen too many fine speeches founder on practical reality. "But we face enemies who coordinate with supernatural efficiency, possess resources that could sustain extended conflict even if we knew how to fight spiritual warfare."

"Then we learn," Boudica said with quiet certainty that somehow made the impossible sound merely difficult. "We learn from failure, from each other, from enemies who reveal their methods through their very success. Unity that serves consciousness rather than eliminating it. Leadership that serves purpose rather than precedent."

Before the debate could continue, the sound of urgent hoofbeats echoed across the courtyard—not arrival this time, but departure carrying such desperate urgency that it drew every representative to the great windows.

"Royal messenger," King Conchobor observed grimly, reading the banners that proclaimed official rather than military purpose. "Someone claims authority to speak for legitimate governance."

The messenger who entered the great hall moved with the careful formality required for diplomatic missions, but his face showed the strain of someone who carried offers that he suspected his listeners would find more threatening than generous.

"Representatives of Ireland's free territories," the messenger began with ceremony that felt hollow in current circumstances, "I bring formal invitation from Queen Medb of Connacht, speaking as regent for unified Irish interests in alliance with proven authorities who have brought prosperity to other lands."

The formal language carried undertones of threat barely concealed beneath diplomatic courtesy. Not request but summons, not negotiation but ultimatum disguised as opportunity.

***

As the messenger delivered Queen Medb's terms—partnership that preserved Irish rule while providing guidance for managing enhanced spiritual networks—the assembled representatives began to understand the true sophistication of the trap being set for them.

"Enhanced by whom?" Neassa asked with dangerous calm, her priestess training reading the spiritual implications hidden beneath political language.

"By advisors who have learned to prosper under imperial protection," the messenger replied with satisfaction that seemed disconnected from any personal enthusiasm. "Representatives of the most successful administrative systems ever developed, offering Ireland the benefits of proven efficiency."

"Romans," Boudica said flatly, her strategic experience reading between diplomatic lines to tactical reality. "Not direct conquest, but administrative guidance that serves imperial purposes while maintaining the illusion of local authority."

The messenger's expression showed surprise at such direct interpretation of carefully layered language, but he continued with mechanical precision that made several representatives shift uncomfortably. "Civilized guidance that eliminates the chaos of competing individual preferences through optimal collective decision-making."

Around the chamber, representatives began to understand that they faced not just political maneuvering but systematic seduction designed to make surrender seem like wisdom. The enemy's offer would eliminate problems by eliminating the consciousness that created them.

"What of those who prefer the chaos of consciousness to the peace of guidance?" Cathair asked with quiet intensity.

"Individual preferences that interfere with collective welfare cannot be permitted to persist," the messenger replied with mechanical certainty. "But the transition will be accomplished through education rather than force, demonstration rather than coercion."

***

The ultimatum delivered, the messenger departed with formal courtesy that left the chamber humming with tension that transcended mere political disagreement. They faced not just military threat or spiritual corruption, but systematic seduction that offered everything they thought they wanted while transforming them into tools serving purposes they despised.

"Seven days," Brendan said quietly, his voice carrying recognition of mathematics that offered no comfortable options.

"Seven days to prove that consciousness can defend itself against the ultimate seduction," Boudica corrected with grim certainty. "To demonstrate that some forms of chaos prove more valuable than any order bought through surrender of individual will."

In the silence that followed, the weight of decision pressed against them like physical force. They could accept Medb's invitation and face conversion or elimination. They could reject it and face systematic assault by enemies whose coordination exceeded their ability to counter. Or they could attempt something that had never been tried—unified resistance that transcended traditional categories of authority and loyalty.

Donnchad of the Northern Hills rose from his seat with movements that spoke to recognition of crisis that demanded unprecedented response. "Then we stand together," he declared, extending his massive hand toward Boudica in the gesture of alliance. "Queen to warrior, exile to native, all united by the choice to remain ourselves despite the cost."

One by one, the others joined the gesture, hands meeting in the center of the circle while the ancient stones around them seemed to pulse with approval. Not just political alliance, but conscious choice to serve purposes larger than individual survival.

"We attend Queen Medb's gathering," Neassa decided, certainty settling into her bones like truth finding its proper home. "Not as supplicants seeking favor, but as living proof that consciousness cannot be perfected into submission. We spring the trap deliberately, on our terms."

The gathering of competing claims had become something else entirely—unity forged through conscious decision rather than imposed through compulsion, alliance that served purposes larger than individual advantage. But their real test was still approaching with the inexorable certainty of enemies who promised peace through surrender of everything that made peace worthwhile.

As representatives began dispersing to prepare for what might be their final gambit, Cathair found himself walking beside Boudica through Tara's ancient corridors. The evening air carried the scent of approaching storm, but also something else—the electric tension that came before moments that would echo through legend.

"Are we making the right choice?" he asked, allowing uncertainty to enter his voice for the first time since accepting the burden others had placed on his shoulders.

"I don't know," she replied with honesty that was more comforting than false confidence. "But we're making our choice, freely given despite the cost. That may be the most important thing we can do—prove that such choices are still possible."

Her hand found his shoulder with the gesture of one warrior acknowledging another. "Whatever happens at Cruachan, whatever we face in Medb's hall, we'll face it as ourselves. That's no small victory, considering what our enemies offer as the alternative."

Behind them, the ancient stones of Tara hummed with power that had been awakened through conscious choice rather than inherited authority. Tomorrow would bring them to their final test, but tonight they had forged unity strong enough to attempt the impossible and conscious enough to understand that attempting was victory regardless of outcome.

The weight of truth had been accepted, and Ireland would meet its fate with eyes open and hearts ready for whatever choice the dawn might demand. The war for Ireland's soul was entering its final phase, and they were ready to fight it with everything they had chosen to preserve, everyone they had chosen to become, every song they refused to let fall silent despite forces that promised beautiful peace through surrender of everything that made songs worth singing.

CHAPTER 14

THE ENEMY'S OFFER

The morning after their unified decision brought news that would test their newly forged alliance before it could take proper shape. Three riders approached Tara under banners that proclaimed formal embassy rather than military threat, but their timing—arriving precisely as Ireland's free territories declared unified resistance—suggested coordination that went beyond coincidence.

Neassa stood with the assembled túath leaders in the great hall, feeling the weight of yesterday's choices pressing against her shoulders like armor that had not yet been properly fitted. Seventeen different voices had become one voice, but that unity remained untested by forces specifically designed to fragment resistance through offers that made division seem like wisdom.

The representatives who had risked everything to reach Tara now faced their first test as unified authority: how to respond to enemies who came not with swords but with proposals that promised solutions to every problem consciousness created through its stubborn refusal to surrender individual will for collective efficiency.

Cathair moved to stand beside her with the quiet authority that had emerged through crisis rather than ceremony. His presence anchored the assembly in ways that felt both natural and unprecedented—leadership that served purpose rather than precedent, authority that grew from conscious choice rather than inherited right.

"Let them enter," he commanded, his voice carrying across the chamber with certainty that seemed to surprise even himself. "Let Ireland's enemies see what unity looks like when it serves consciousness rather than eliminating it."

***

The three figures who entered moved with mechanical precision that marked those touched by Hollowed influence, yet retained enough individual bearing to serve as credible negotiators. Their leader, a woman whose features bore the terrible peace of one who had surrendered choice's burden, wore robes that had once served sacred office but now carried emptiness where spiritual authority should have provided connection to sources larger than immediate efficiency.

"I am Clíona of the Sacred Grove," she announced, though those who remembered her from before the conversion winced at what had become of someone they had once called friend. "I bring greetings from Queen Medb of Connacht and terms for the peaceful resolution of Ireland's current difficulties."

Her words carried undertones of threat beneath diplomatic courtesy—peaceful resolution, but only on terms that would eliminate the need for future negotiations. Behind her, the other emissaries stood with patient attention that spoke to complete certainty about whatever discussion would follow.

Boudica stepped forward with movements that carried all the authority of someone who had learned strategy through catastrophic failure. Her presence beside Ireland's leaders spoke to acceptance that transcended normal political calculation—foreign expertise united with native determination to serve purposes larger than territorial advantage.

"Speak Queen Medb's words," she said with the directness of someone who had learned to recognize seduction disguised as negotiation. "Though understand that we listen as free peoples who have chosen consciousness over efficiency, chaos over the beautiful peace of surrender."

Clíona's smile never wavered, perfect as painted porcelain that felt more unsettling than any expression of open hostility. Her mechanical patience was more disturbing than anger would have been—the satisfaction of someone who believed she brought gifts rather than threats.

"Queen Medb recognizes the challenge facing Ireland," she began with the practiced smoothness of someone delivering prepared presentation. "The chaos of competing claims, the inefficiency of seventeen different voices attempting to speak as one. She offers solution through unity of purpose, guided by spiritual advisors who have discovered the peace that comes from optimal decision-making."

***

"The peace of the grave," Ríona observed quietly, her divine sight reading the emptiness that flowed around the converted emissaries like spiritual void given form.

"The peace of certainty," Clíona corrected without taking offense, her mechanical patience making her words more chilling than direct threats could have achieved. "No more agonizing over choices that might be wrong. No more burden of responsibility that crushes individual happiness beneath decisions affecting others. No more chaos of conflicting desires disrupting collective welfare."

Murmurs rippled through the assembly as the true nature of the offer became clear. Not conquest disguised as negotiation, but conversion presented as mercy—systematic elimination of individual will marketed as relief from consciousness's terrible burden.

"Queen Medb offers Ireland the opportunity to join territories that have already discovered the benefits of guided choice," Clíona continued, her voice carrying the satisfaction of someone who believed she brought salvation rather than damnation. "No more uncertainty, no more fear of making wrong decisions, no more exhausting weight of caring about outcomes beyond personal control."

The proposal that followed was presented with bureaucratic thoroughness that made its horror more rather than less apparent. Administrative efficiency that would eliminate waste caused by competing individual preferences. Spiritual guidance that would free Irish minds from the burden of choice that created suffering through its very nature. Economic optimization that would ensure prosperity through surrender of everything that made prosperity worthwhile.

"And those who prefer uncertainty to emptiness?" Cathair asked with quiet intensity, his question cutting through diplomatic language to fundamental concerns. "Those who choose the weight of individual choice over surrender's peace?"

"They will discover that such preferences serve no optimal purpose," Clíona replied with genuine pity that somehow made her words more chilling than direct threats. "Individual will that creates chaos rather than contributing to collective harmony cannot be permitted to persist. But the correction will be accomplished through demonstration rather than force."

The weight of her words settled over the assembly like a shroud. What had begun as diplomatic discourse had revealed itself as something far more sinister—a systematic restructuring of human agency itself, wrapped in the language of liberation and progress.

Cathair felt the temperature in the room seem to drop several degrees as the full implications became clear to everyone present.

***

"Demonstration of what?" Neassa asked, though her priestess training already whispered warnings about answers that would challenge every assumption about the nature of resistance and survival.

"Of the practical advantages of guided consciousness over the chaos of individual preference," replied one of the other emissaries, his voice carrying the same mechanical certainty as his companion. "Villages that accept optimization report immediate improvement in all measures of welfare. No more arguments, no more waste of resources on conflicting projects, no more suffering caused by poor individual choices."

The systematic elimination of everything that made existence meaningful was presented as administrative improvement, spiritual guidance offered as relief from burdens that consciousness imposed through its very nature. Around the chamber, representatives who had chosen unity through conscious decision found themselves confronting enemies who viewed that choice itself as inefficiency requiring correction.

"What of the songs?" Cathair asked suddenly, his question cutting through diplomatic language to concerns that transcended political calculation. "In Queen Medb's unified Ireland, what becomes of the music that celebrates chaos, the stories that honor individual choice despite its cost?"

The question seemed to puzzle Clíona momentarily, as if she struggled to remember why anyone would care about such things. "Songs serve no optimal purpose," she said with the certainty of someone who had discovered better ways to allocate time and energy. "They distract from productive activity, encourage inefficient emotional responses that interfere with proper decision-making. The optimized find greater satisfaction in purposeful work than in meaningless entertainment."

"What of children's laughter?" asked Muiris, understanding beginning to dawn in his voice like recognition of horror too complete for immediate comprehension. "The joy that comes from discovery, from play that serves no purpose beyond pleasure itself?"

"Children require guidance toward productive development. Unstructured play interferes with optimal growth patterns that serve collective welfare rather than individual gratification."

"The festivals where families gather to share stories, to remember ancestors, to celebrate connections that transcend immediate utility?"

"Inefficient uses of resources that could serve collective purposes. The optimized remember only what serves their current functions, eliminating the burden of useless nostalgia that creates suffering through attachment to outcomes beyond control."

* * *

One by one, the representatives began to understand what spiritual guidance truly meant—not improvement of human nature, but its systematic elimination in favor of something that served entirely different purposes. The horror crept through the chamber like cold fog, recognition of what they would become if they accepted the beautiful peace being offered with such generous concern for their welfare.

"You offer us death," King Cormac said with quiet finality, his voice carrying the weight of someone who had finally grasped the true scope of what they faced. "Not political death or physical death, but the death of everything that makes existence worth preserving."

"We offer peace," Clíona insisted with the patience of someone explaining obvious truth to those too proud to accept wisdom that would solve all their problems. "Release from the terrible burden of caring about outcomes beyond your control. Freedom from the agony of choices that might be wrong. Harmony with purposes larger than individual preference that create suffering through their very nature."

Boudica's strategic experience read the implications with growing alarm. "And when Ireland has accepted this generous guidance, what becomes of Irish culture, Irish language, Irish ways of understanding the world that transcend Roman categories of efficiency?"

"Cultural variations that serve no optimal purpose will be corrected through education rather than force," another emissary replied with the certainty of someone who viewed diversity as inefficiency requiring administrative solution. "Ireland will retain its identity while gaining the benefits of proven methods for eliminating sources of conflict and waste."

"Retain its identity by surrendering everything that makes that identity meaningful," Cathair observed with growing anger that seemed to surprise him with its intensity. "You offer to preserve the shell while gutting the substance, to maintain the name while destroying the reality it represents."

***

Around the chamber, representatives who had argued about leadership and strategy suddenly found themselves united by recognition of what they truly faced. Not political conquest or cultural absorption, but systematic elimination of consciousness itself in favor of beautiful emptiness that promised relief through surrender of everything that made relief worthwhile.

"Then we refuse," Cathair said, his voice cutting across the growing horror with authority that seemed to anchor the chamber despite the impossibility of what they had chosen. "Ireland chooses chaos over emptiness, the agony of choice over surrender's peace, love over the efficiency that eliminates the capacity for love."

His words catalyzed something that hours of political debate had failed to achieve. Around the hall, representatives who had been arguing about leadership qualifications and territorial claims suddenly found themselves united by recognition of fundamental choice that transcended all other considerations—whether to remain conscious or accept optimization that eliminated consciousness while promising prosperity.

"Ulster stands with that choice," King Conchobor declared, rising from his seat with movements that spoke to renewed purpose despite the magnitude of opposition they faced.

"Leinster as well," King Aillen added, his voice carrying authority that transcended mere political calculation.

"Munster chooses consciousness," King Cormac stated with quiet certainty that seemed to anchor the chamber despite forces arrayed against them.

One by one, the seventeen túath representatives rose in declaration of unity that transcended their individual differences. Not agreement on strategy or leadership, but consensus on the fundamental question that mattered—whether Ireland would remain Irish or surrender its soul for the promise of efficient administration that eliminated both problems and possibilities.

Boudica stood with them, her presence transforming from foreign intervention to integral part of resistance that served purposes larger than national identity. "Britain chooses consciousness," she said with quiet certainty. "Whatever remains of my people, whatever future we might claim, we stand with those who refuse the beautiful peace of surrender."

***

Clíona watched their defiance with the mild interest of someone observing predictable tragedy, her expression showing no surprise at their rejection of wisdom so obvious that refusal seemed like willful blindness to solutions that would solve all their problems.

"Queen Medb anticipated this response," she said with satisfaction that spoke to plans prepared for every contingency. "She grieves for the suffering you choose to inflict upon your people, but Ireland's optimization will proceed regardless of cooperation or resistance. Those who refuse guidance will be brought to understand its benefits through more direct methods."

"What methods?" Neassa asked, though her priestess training already whispered warnings about answers that would test their unity before it could strengthen into effective resistance.

"The same methods that have proven successful across territories where scattered resistance attempted to preserve inefficient systems that served individual preference rather than collective welfare," Clíona replied with the certainty of someone who had witnessed the inevitable triumph of optimization over chaos. "Demonstration that conscious choice creates suffering, while guided choice eliminates sources of conflict through proven administrative techniques."

"Then we understand each other perfectly," Cathair replied, his presence somehow anchoring the assembly despite the impossibility of what they had chosen. "Ireland chooses to remain itself, whatever the cost. Queen Medb chooses efficiency over meaning, order over love, emptiness over the sacred chaos of consciousness. The terms are clear."

The converted emissary inclined her head with respectful formality that somehow made her threat more chilling than any display of anger could have achieved. "The terms are indeed clear. Queen Medb will implement optimal solutions beginning with the next full moon. Ireland will have that time to reconsider its choice, though reconsideration serves no purpose when optimal outcomes remain constant regardless of individual preference."

"Ireland has chosen," Neassa said, speaking with authority that had been tested through trial and emerged stronger rather than brittle. "We choose to remain ourselves, to preserve the songs and the laughter and the terrible beautiful burden of caring about each other despite the certainty of loss. That choice is not subject to reconsideration by forces that view choice itself as inefficiency requiring correction."

***

As the emissaries withdrew from the hall with movements that carried the mechanical precision of tools returning to storage, the seventeen representatives found themselves facing each other across a chamber that hummed with newfound unity. Not the easy unity of shared advantage, but the harder unity of shared purpose in the face of existential threat that challenged everything they valued.

"Twenty-five days," Brendan observed, his voice carrying recognition of mathematics that offered no comfortable options for resistance that lacked resources to sustain extended conflict against enemies whose coordination transcended normal military categories.

"Twenty-five days to prove that consciousness can defend itself against the ultimate seduction," Boudica corrected with grim certainty born from experience with enemies who had perfected the art of making surrender seem like salvation. "To demonstrate that some forms of chaos prove more valuable than any order bought through surrender of individual will."

"We have each other," Cathair added, his presence now anchoring the assembly in ways that felt both natural and inevitable. "For the first time since the great choosing, we know exactly what we're fighting for—not political advantage or territorial control, but the right to remain conscious despite the cost that consciousness demands."

The war for Ireland's soul had gained new urgency, but also new clarity. Whatever divisions had separated them before, they now faced an enemy whose very existence threatened everything that made their arguments worthwhile—the chaos of individual will, the inefficiency of personal choice, the terrible wonderful burden of caring about outcomes beyond immediate survival.

"We begin preparations immediately," Neassa decided, her voice carrying the authority of someone who understood that desperate circumstances required unprecedented solutions. "Not just military preparations, but spiritual ones. If we're going to defend consciousness itself, we need to understand what consciousness means when it chooses to remain conscious despite every pressure toward efficiency."

Outside Tara's walls, the autumn wind carried the scent of approaching winter and the promise of conflicts that would determine whether consciousness retained the right to exist in a world that could be made more efficient through its elimination. Inside, seventeen leaders who had discovered unity through shared revulsion began the work of proving that such unity could defend itself against beautiful emptiness, that love could justify the chaos it created, that Ireland would remain Irish no matter what forces offered peace through surrender of everything that made peace worthwhile.

The enemy had made their offer clear, and Ireland had given its answer with equal clarity. Now came the test of whether that answer could be made to matter through something more than words and brave intentions—whether consciousness possessed sufficient strength to defend against the ultimate seduction of surrendering individual will for collective harmony that promised peace through elimination of everything that made peace worth having.

The countdown had begun, but so had the real work of resistance that would either save Ireland's soul or prove it worthy of mourning. Twenty-five days to prepare for the impossible, and they would use every moment to become something stronger than the sum of their parts—conscious choice defending itself against forces that viewed consciousness as the source of all problems requiring administrative solution.

CHAPTER 15

PREPARATIONS FOR WAR

The war council convened at dawn on Tara's eastern slope, where the ancient hill commanded views across plains that stretched toward distant kingdoms like a living map written in morning mist and shadow. Twenty-five dawns had become twenty-four during the night, and time pressed against the assembled leaders like storm clouds gathering on a clear horizon.

Cathair stood at the gathering's heart, not by conscious positioning but because others had naturally gravitated toward him during the desperate hours since Clíona's departure. His finger traced patterns in the earth at his feet, marking territories and approaches while his ancestral memories provided recognition of strategic positions that transcended mere geography.

"Intelligence first," he said, his voice carrying authority of someone who had accepted decision's burden without formal ceremony. "We cannot plan defense without understanding what approaches."

Boudica stepped forward, her warrior's knowledge finally finding proper outlet after months of diplomatic concealment. "Medb commands roughly fifteen thousand warriors across her territories, but not all are fully converted. Perhaps a third retain enough individual will to resist orders that violate their deepest instincts."

"Ten thousand Hollowed, then," calculated Brendan with grim precision. "Moving with perfect coordination, no fear, no hesitation, no mercy. But also no adaptability when circumstances change beyond their programming."

"Worse than that," Cú Chulainn added, his divine sight-reading patterns that stretched beyond mortal perception. "My father whispers warnings about spiritual weapons—corruption that spreads through battle itself, turning victory into defeat by converting the victorious during triumph's moment."

The implications chilled the chamber more effectively than winter wind. Traditional warfare assumed that defeating enemies eliminated the threat they represented. But enemies who could convert their conquerors during conquest rendered normal military strategy not just inadequate but actively dangerous.

***

Neassa moved to where she could see the eastern horizons, where sacred sites lay hidden beyond morning mist but connected to Tara through spiritual bonds that had grown dimmer since the great choosing. "The spiritual landscape tells a different story," she reported with growing concern. "Three more sites have fallen silent since yesterday—not attacked, but simply extinguished. Whatever they're planning requires massive spiritual energy drawn from the network itself."

"A working," Ríona said quietly, her silver scars pulsing with otherworldly light as she consulted sources beyond mortal understanding. "Something that would affect not individual hearts or minds, but consciousness's fundamental nature across the entire island."

As they spoke, a commotion at the camp's edge drew their attention toward a lone rider approaching with desperate urgency. The horse beneath him showed signs of being ridden far beyond normal endurance, and the rider himself swayed in his saddle with exhaustion that spoke to days without rest.

"High Priestess!" he called, his voice carrying across morning air with strain that made every word an effort. "I bring word from Corca Dhuibhne that changes everything we thought we knew about defending against spiritual assault!"

The messenger who staggered forward as his mount collapsed from exhaustion bore the distinctive features of the western peninsula's people, but his face showed wonder that transcended mere relief at reaching his destination. In his hands, he carried a leather bottle that seemed to pulse with inner light.

"My name is Fionntan mac Duibhne," he gasped, accepting the water that Muiris offered while his eyes sought Neassa among the assembled leaders. "I serve as scout for the warriors who guard our sacred sites against corruption. Three days past, we discovered something that might preserve consciousness itself against enemies who seek to drain it away."

Cathair stepped forward with growing interest, reading in the messenger's bearing the possibility of hope they desperately needed. "Speak your discovery, friend. In times like these, any advantage serves purposes larger than individual survival."

"Our scouts drank from Tobar na nGealt before departing on reconnaissance toward territories under enemy influence," Fionntan continued, his voice gaining strength as he focused on intelligence that had driven his desperate ride. "An old custom among our people—seeking the well's blessing for clear sight and steady minds when venturing into dangerous places."

He lifted the leather bottle with movements that seemed to draw light from the sacred water it contained. "But the well's power reaches further than our ancestors knew. When our scouts encountered Hollowed forces during their mission—when spiritual corruption tried to seize their minds and turn them from their purpose—the protection held firm against assault designed to convert any consciousness it touched."

***

The implications hit the assembled council like recognition of possibility they had not dared hope for. Boudica's strategic mind immediately grasped the tactical significance, while others began to understand they might possess a weapon their enemies had not anticipated.

"Your scouts remained themselves during combat with forces designed to eliminate individual will?" Ríona asked, her divine sight reading the truth that flowed around the messenger like confirmation of legend made manifest.

"More than that," Fionntan replied with fierce satisfaction that spoke to hope preserved against overwhelming odds. "They witnessed the enemy's spiritual weapons fail entirely against those protected by the well's blessing. The corruption that should have turned victory into conversion simply could not take hold in minds defended by water that remembers the first making of the world."

The planning that followed compressed what should have been weeks of coordination into hours of desperate necessity, as leaders who had faced impossible odds suddenly found themselves dealing with merely overwhelming ones. The sacred water from Tobar na nGealt could not protect armies, but it might shield small groups whose success could disrupt enemy preparations.

"How much water can the well provide?" King Conchobor asked with practical urgency of someone whose long experience had taught him to examine gifts for their limitations as well as their possibilities.

"Perhaps enough to protect several hundred warriors," Fionntan replied with honest uncertainty, "but the protection requires daily consumption to build strength in the spirit. My people drink from the well every day, which is why our territory remained free when corruption first began to spread."

"Strike teams," Brendan said with growing understanding of tactical possibilities that transcended conventional warfare. "Small groups moving against specific targets, protected against spiritual weapons that would otherwise make victory impossible to achieve or maintain."

"But the logistics," Étaín observed with military pragmatism that cut through hope to practical constraints. "Daily water for hundreds of warriors across the time needed to build protection, then maintaining that protection during extended operations—the supply requirements become enormous."

Before they could resolve the complex mathematics of sacred water distribution, another messenger arrived with intelligence that transformed their planning from theoretical to urgent. This rider bore the colors of the northern territories and the bearing of someone who had witnessed events that challenged every assumption about their enemies' timeline.

***

"Queen Medb's forces move with acceleration that defies normal logistics," he announced without preamble. "What should have required months of coordination has been accomplished in days. Her converted commanders eliminate delays through perfect efficiency, but also through methods that transcend normal military organization."

The scout's next words confirmed their worst fears while eliminating any remaining illusions about the luxury of extended preparation. "By our calculations, the great working will reach completion not in twenty-four dawns, but in fifteen. Perhaps less, if her acceleration continues at current pace."

The silence that followed carried weight beyond mere mathematical calculation. Fifteen dawns meant their carefully planned coordination would have to be compressed into something approaching desperate improvisation, while their enemies gained strength through every moment of delay and every community that chose beautiful emptiness over difficult meaning.

"Then we divide our efforts immediately," Cathair decided, his voice cutting through the growing sense of impossibility with authority that had been tested through trial. "Strike teams to carry the sacred water against converted sites, regular forces to defend territories that remain free, and coordination between both efforts to ensure maximum impact from our limited resources."

"And the center?" asked Muiris, though his eyes already held recognition of what the answer must be.

"Tara," Cathair replied with certainty that transcended mere strategic calculation. "The heart of the network, the spiritual foundation of whatever Ireland chooses to become. If we hold here, the scattered strikes have meaning. If we fall..." He shrugged with acceptance that carried its own form of courage. "Then we ensure the songs remember what we chose, even if no voices remain to sing them."

Neassa felt the weight of recognition settling on her shoulders as she understood that Tara's defense would fall to those who remained—herself, Cathair, Ríona, and whatever forces they could muster to stand against concentrated assault that would surely come to Ireland's spiritual heart when the final test arrived.

"The strike teams depart within two days," Boudica decided with strategic urgency that brooked no delay. "Every day of preparation strengthens the protection sacred water provides, but every day of delay allows our enemies to consolidate their advantage."

As the council dispersed into urgent activity, Cathair found himself alone with the weight of decisions that would reshape not just immediate strategy but the fundamental nature of resistance itself. Through the morning mist, he could see the sacred sites that dotted the landscape like islands of meaning in an ocean of growing emptiness, each one a potential target or ally depending on choices made in the hours ahead.

***

A new messenger approached as the sun climbed toward its zenith, this one bearing colors that made Cathair's heart clench with recognition of personal loss amid the larger crisis. The blue and silver of Mag nAí, carried by a rider whose urgency spoke to news that transcended even military necessity.

"Prince Cathair," the messenger called, his voice carrying the weight of someone who brought tidings no son should receive. "I bear word from your father's hall that cannot wait for the luxury of proper ceremony or gentle preparation."

The news that followed transformed personal grief into public necessity as Cathair learned that King Conall of Mag nAí had passed beyond the veil, his death creating a vacuum of authority that his enemies would surely seek to exploit. Not just Ireland's resistance leader, but a kingdom's rightful king, with obligations that extended beyond the immediate crisis to the people who had trusted his bloodline with their welfare.

"The funeral rites require your presence," the messenger continued with formal gravity that barely concealed his understanding of impossible timing. "The people will not rest until you return to accept what is yours by right and blood, to ensure that Mag nAí's succession serves continuity rather than chaos."

"I must go," Cathair said quietly, though his voice carried recognition of duty that transcended personal preference. "But not alone, and not for long. Ireland's need remains paramount, but Mag nAí's people deserve their king."

Ríona stepped forward with divine authority that had been granted her through transformation beyond normal categories of existence. "I will come," she said simply. "Royal succession requires spiritual blessing to carry weight beyond mere inheritance, and such blessing serves Ireland's cause as well as Mag nAí's welfare."

The journey would take them away from Tara just as the crisis deepened, but kingship carried obligations that could not be delegated to others, no matter how urgent the larger conflict became. As they prepared for departure, Cathair understood that he would return not just as resistance leader but as legitimate authority whose crown had been blessed by forces that transcended political convenience.

"Three days," he told Neassa as they made their hurried preparations. "Three days to bury my father with proper honor, to accept the crown that comes with his death, and to return with whatever authority such acceptance provides for the trials ahead."

"We'll hold here," she promised, though they both understood that holding might prove more difficult than advancing when enemies who promised peace through surrender approached with coordination that eliminated normal military limitations.

As Cathair and Ríona departed for Mag nAí with the small escort required for royal dignity, those who remained at Tara began the work of proving that consciousness could defend itself against systematic assault, that meaning could emerge from chaos rather than requiring optimization through emptiness, that Ireland's choice to remain Irish would echo through legend regardless of its outcome.

Fifteen dawns stretched ahead like a countdown to transformation, and Ireland prepared to discover whether conscious choice possessed sufficient strength to preserve consciousness itself when consciousness faced its ultimate test against forces that promised beautiful peace through surrender of everything that made peace worthwhile.

The war for Ireland's soul had gained new urgency, and those who chose meaning over emptiness prepared to prove their choice worthy of the prices they would pay to defend it.

CHAPTER 16

THE WEIGHT OF TRUTH

The aftermath of Boudica's revelation settled over the ancient meeting place like smoke from a funeral pyre, heavy with implications that would reshape every plan they'd made and every alliance they'd hoped to forge. The seven bloodline carriers who remained free sat in the circle of standing stones, their faces bearing the strain of having witnessed something that changed the fundamental nature of their resistance.

"The most wanted fugitive in the Roman world," Donnchad said quietly, his massive frame somehow diminished by the scope of what they now faced. "Every Roman agent from here to Gaul will be hunting you. Every collaborator seeking favor will be watching for your face."

Boudica met his gaze without flinching, her royal bearing intact despite the weight of exile and loss. "Yes. And now you all share that burden by knowing my true identity. I've made you all targets by choosing truth over safety."

Fionntan of the Western Shores leaned forward, her sea-king heritage showing in the way she read currents of danger as naturally as weather patterns. "But also allies in a war we were already fighting. The Romans don't distinguish between active resistance and passive defiance—they'll come for Ireland regardless of whether we shelter you."

"The question," Muirenn added with the quiet authority that came from generations of river-folk wisdom, "is whether your presence here helps or hinders our chances of survival."

The silence that followed carried weight beyond mere consideration. Through the mist that perpetually shrouded the ancient valley, they could hear the sound of their horses shifting restlessly, as if the animals sensed the tension that gripped their riders.

***

Cathair's voice, when he finally spoke, carried harmonics borrowed from ancestral memory but tinged with very present concern. "The bloodlines whisper of times when revelation brought either salvation or catastrophe, depending on the courage of those who heard unwelcome truths. Your identity doesn't change what Ireland faces—it clarifies the stakes."

Neassa studied Boudica's face, reading the exhaustion that came from carrying secrets too long and the relief that accompanied their release. "Tell us everything. Not just who you are, but what you've learned. What you've seen of Roman methods, Roman weaknesses, Roman plans."

For the next hour, as morning mist gave way to pale sunlight filtering through the ancient stones, Boudica spoke with the methodical precision of someone who had survived catastrophe by learning its lessons. She described Roman military organization, their methods of conquest and control, their systematic approach to eliminating Celtic resistance.

"They don't just defeat armies," she explained, her voice carrying bitter experience. "They attack the very idea that resistance is possible. They offer rewards for collaboration, punishment for defiance, and most insidiously—they make surrender seem like wisdom rather than betrayal."

Ailill mac Cormac, whose weathered features had seen too many betrayals, nodded grimly. "We've already witnessed such tactics. Local kings who suddenly speak of 'practical accommodation' with Roman interests, druids who counsel 'realistic acceptance' of superior force."

"The corruption spreads like plague," Scáthach observed, her warrior's training reading patterns of assault in what others might dismiss as political maneuvering. "Each converted leader becomes a tool for converting others, until resistance becomes not just difficult but literally unthinkable."

Boudica's expression grew darker. "But what you face here goes beyond traditional Roman methods. The reports I've heard, the descriptions of spiritual emptiness, the complete severing from sacred memory—this is something new. Something that makes my rebellion look like a simple border skirmish."

She gestured toward the standing stones that surrounded them, their ancient carvings still pulsing with accumulated power despite the corruption spreading through other sacred sites. "Rome conquers territories and enslaves peoples, but they leave the conquered with enough spirit to hate their masters. What's happening in Ireland seeks to eliminate the very capacity for resistance by destroying the consciousness that creates meaning."

***

"The Hollowed," Ríona said quietly, her divine sight-reading currents of purpose and corruption that flowed beyond normal perception. "They represent the ultimate endpoint of Roman efficiency—not just political control, but spiritual annihilation."

Fergus mac Róich shifted uncomfortably, his massive frame bearing scars from battles fought against enemies both mortal and supernatural. "Then we face two threats simultaneously—immediate Roman military pressure and this spiritual plague that turns our own people into weapons against meaning itself."

"Three threats," Neassa corrected grimly. "Don't forget Queen Medb's gathering at Cruachan. Whatever alliance she's forged with the Hollowed, it gives them political legitimacy and military resources they couldn't acquire through corruption alone."

The complexity of their situation began to crystallize around the circle. Not just external invasion or internal corruption, but a coordinated assault that attacked Ireland's political structure, spiritual foundation, and cultural identity simultaneously.

"We need to return to Tara," Cathair said finally, his voice carrying the weight of someone recognizing terrible necessity. "Not to hide, but to gather our remaining strength before facing whatever Medb has planned. If we're going to contest her authority, we need to do it as representatives of legitimate spiritual power, not as scattered refugees."

"Too dangerous," Boudica protested immediately. "Tara will be watched, infiltrated, possibly under direct assault. My presence there endangers everyone who serves the sacred site."

"Your presence anywhere endangers everyone around you," Donnchad pointed out with brutal honesty. "But your knowledge is the only advantage we have against enemies who've perfected the art of making surrender seem attractive."

***

Before Neassa could respond to the arguments building around the circle, the sound of approaching hoofbeats cut through the morning mist like a blade through silk. A single rider, moving with the desperate urgency of one who carried news that could not wait for proper protocol or careful approach.

Ríona's silver scars flared briefly as her divine sight read the spiritual signature of the approaching messenger. "One of ours," she announced, though her voice carried undertones of concern. "But carrying darkness that tastes of violation."

The rider who crashed through the concealing mist bore the colors of Tara, but his face showed the hollow exhaustion of someone who had witnessed the unthinkable. Brother Cillian, one of the younger priests whose devotion had always burned bright with passionate certainty, now looked as if that fire had been deliberately extinguished.

"High Priestess," he gasped, dismounting with movements that spoke of hard travel and desperate haste. "Thank the goddesses I found you. The situation at Tara—" He paused, his gaze taking in the assembled bloodline carriers, confusion flickering across his exhausted features as he tried to process the unexpected gathering.

"Speak your news," Neassa commanded, though her heart already clenched with certainty that whatever Cillian had seen would shatter their careful planning.

"The túatha," Cillian replied, his voice carrying the weight of disaster barely contained. "They've answered Queen Medb's call. Not to Cruachan, but to Tara itself. Seven kings with their full retinues, arriving within hours of each other as if coordinated by some power beyond normal communication."

The implications hit the assembled bloodline carriers like physical blows. If the túatha were gathering at Tara rather than traveling to Cruachan, it meant Medb had changed her strategy— bringing the confrontation to Ireland's spiritual heart rather than her own stronghold.

"Which túatha?" Cathair demanded, his voice carrying harmonics borrowed from ancestral memory but tinged with very present fear.

"Ulster, Munster, Leinster," Cillian began, counting off on fingers that trembled with exhaustion. "The kingdoms of the eastern shores, the northern territories, and..." He paused, swallowing hard. "And Connacht itself. Queen Medb comes to Tara with the full weight of royal authority, claiming the right to speak for all Ireland in matters of succession and spiritual governance."

"She means to force the choosing," Scáthach realized with warrior's clarity. "Without the Lia Fáil to provide divine judgment, she'll argue that mortal authority must suffice. Seven kingdoms gathering at Tara could claim the right to select a High King through consensus rather than sacred sign."

"But that's not the worst of it," Cillian continued, his voice dropping to conspiracy's whisper despite their isolation. "The converted druids—the ones who speak with Marcus's voice but claim independence of thought—they're arriving too. Three circles worth, all speaking of 'spiritual efficiency' and 'optimal sacred governance.'"

***

The full scope of the trap became clear as Cillian's words sank in. Medb hadn't just corrupted individual leaders or isolated sacred sites—she'd orchestrated a gathering that would give legitimacy to whatever emerged from the convergence at Tara. With royal authority and spiritual sanction combined, she could reshape Ireland's entire foundation while maintaining the appearance of traditional process.

"How long do we have?" Boudica asked, her strategic mind immediately shifting to tactical calculations.

"They began arriving yesterday," Cillian replied. "The full gathering is planned for tomorrow's dawn, when the autumn sun rises over the sacred hill. If we're going to contest their authority..."

"We have to be there," Neassa finished, feeling the weight of impossible necessity settling on her shoulders. "Not as fugitives or scattered resistance, but as legitimate representatives of Ireland's true spiritual heritage."

Donnchad's massive frame shifted with the restless energy of a warrior recognizing the approach of unavoidable battle. "Seven kingdoms, three druid circles, and Queen Medb herself. Against eight of us, assuming we can even reach Tara before the gathering concludes."

"Brother Cillian's horse is spent, and he's in no condition for immediate travel," Fionntan observed with practical concern. "Someone needs to stay with him, or send him back to safety."

"I'll manage," Cillian protested, though his exhaustion was evident in every line of his body. "The High Priestess needs every ally—"

"You've done enough," Ríona interrupted gently, her divine sight reading the spiritual damage that hard travel and exposure to corrupted sites had inflicted. "Rest here where the ancient stones can offer healing. We'll carry your warning to its proper conclusion."

The mathematics of desperate necessity crystallized around the circle. Eight people against the assembled political and spiritual authority of most of Ireland, with less than a day to reach Tara and somehow contest forces that had been months in the planning.

"It's impossible," Muirenn said quietly, though her voice carried more resignation than despair.

"Good," Boudica replied with grim satisfaction. "Impossible odds tend to make enemies overconfident. They'll be prepared for reasonable resistance, not for the unreasonable determination of people who choose meaning over safety."

Neassa felt the weight of decision settling on her shoulders like a mantle she'd never asked to wear. As High Priestess of Tara, the choice was ultimately hers—whether to attempt this desperate gambit or preserve their small band for future resistance.

"We ride for Tara," she decided with quiet certainty. "Together, immediately, and with the understanding that we may not survive what we find there. But if we don't try, Ireland dies anyway—just more slowly, and with less dignity."

As they hastily gathered their belongings and prepared for the desperate journey ahead, the ancient stones around them seemed to pulse with approval of choices made through conscious decision rather than fearful calculation. Whatever the outcome, they would face it as themselves—flawed, frightened, but united by the determination to preserve meaning despite the cost.

"Together," Neassa decided with quiet certainty as they mounted their horses. "If we're going to fail, let's fail as ourselves—united by conscious choice rather than scattered by fear."

The sun climbed higher as they prepared to leave the ancient meeting place behind, riding toward whatever awaited them at Tara. The war for Ireland's soul was about to reach its climax, and they would meet it with nothing but hope and the stubborn refusal to surrender without a fight.

CHAPTER 17

THE WEIGHT OF CROWNS

The messenger from Mag nAí arrived at Tara's gates as the first light of dawn painted the eastern sky in shades of amber and gold, his horse lathered with foam from hard travel through the night. The colors he bore—the blue and silver of Cathair's homeland—immediately drew guards who recognized the urgency in his bearing, the way exhaustion warred with determination in every line of his body.

Cathair emerged from the great hall as word spread of the messenger's arrival, his face showing the strain of someone who had spent the night in councils that offered no comfortable solutions to impossible problems. But when he saw the royal colors approaching, something shifted in his expression—not relief, but the particular dread that came with recognition of personal crisis arriving in the midst of larger catastrophe.

"My lord," the messenger gasped, dismounting with movements that spoke of desperate haste maintained through sheer will. "I bring word from your father's hall that cannot wait for proper ceremony or gentle preparation."

The words that followed transformed personal grief into public necessity as Cathair learned that King Conall of Mag nAí had passed beyond the veil during the night, his death creating a vacuum of authority that enemies would surely seek to exploit. Not just Ireland's resistance facing the loss of a crucial leader, but a kingdom requiring its rightful king at the moment when kingdoms could least afford the chaos of uncertain succession.

"How?" Cathair asked quietly, his voice carrying the steady strength of someone who had learned to bear loss without being broken by it.

"The fever that had troubled him for weeks finally claimed him just after midnight," the messenger replied with gentle honesty required for such news. "But his passing was peaceful, my lord. He spoke your name with his final breath and charged us to ensure the crown passed to hands worthy of its weight."

***

Neassa approached as the implications settled over Cathair like recognition of destiny that could no longer be delayed or denied. She could read the struggle in his face—grief for a father lost, fear of responsibilities he had spent his life avoiding, and underneath both emotions, the growing recognition that some burdens could not be delegated to others no matter how urgent the larger conflict became.

"I must go," Cathair said simply, his voice carrying the weight of duty that transcended personal preference. "Mag nAí needs its king, and I cannot claim authority here while shirking responsibility there."

"Of course," Neassa replied immediately, understanding that legitimate leadership required honoring obligations that existed before crisis as well as those created by it. "But not alone. The succession requires proper witness, spiritual blessing that will give your authority weight beyond mere inheritance."

"Ríona should accompany you," she continued, her priestess training providing recognition of divine necessity that transcended political convenience. "Royal coronation requires blessing from powers that recognize legitimate authority, and her transformed nature can provide what normal ceremony cannot achieve."

Ríona stepped forward from where she had been listening in respectful silence, her silver scars catching the morning light as otherworldly energy responded to the spiritual significance of royal succession. "The goddesses approve," she said quietly, consulting sources that belonged to no mortal realm. "Transformation witnessed by divine authority carries power that mortal ceremony alone cannot provide."

The preparations for departure were necessarily swift, driven by urgency that allowed no time for extended planning or careful consideration of every contingency. A small escort of guards sufficient for royal dignity but not so large as to weaken Tara's defenses, supplies for hard travel through countryside that showed increasing signs of spiritual disturbance, and the formal regalia required for ceremonies that would legitimize authority in times when legitimacy determined survival.

"Three days," Cathair told Neassa as they made their hurried preparations, the practical necessities providing anchor for emotions too complex for comfortable processing. "Three days to bury my father with proper honor, to accept the crown that comes with his death, and to return with whatever authority such acceptance provides."

"We'll hold here," she promised, though they both understood that holding might prove more difficult than advancing when enemies who promised peace through surrender approached with coordination that eliminated normal military limitations.

As they prepared to leave Tara for the dangerous journey to Mag nAí, both understood that the man who returned might be fundamentally different from the one who departed—not just crowned king, but transformed by accepting responsibilities that would reshape his understanding of authority, duty, and the prices that leadership demanded from those strong enough to bear them.

***

As the departure party prepared to leave Tara's sanctuary for the dangerous journey to Mag nAí, Neassa found herself walking beside Cathair through corridors that held memories of choices made in darkness and announced in light. The weight of unspoken words hung between them like recognition of transformation that went deeper than mere political necessity.

"There's something else troubling you," she observed gently, reading the complexity of emotion that flowed beneath his composed leadership. "More than grief, more than the burden of unexpected kingship."

Cathair paused beside the great window where he had so often stood to watch the landscape stretching toward distant territories, his hands pressed against the ancient stone as if seeking strength from Tara's foundations. When he spoke, his voice carried the vulnerability of someone sharing truths too dangerous for casual revelation.

"My grandfather was High King," he said quietly, the admission carrying weight beyond mere genealogy. "Before my bloodline withdrew to Mag nAí, before we chose the peace of smaller responsibilities over the grinding weight of speaking for all Ireland."

She had not known, though it explained much about his natural authority and his equally natural reluctance to claim the highest forms of power. The pieces of his character began to fit together in new patterns—not just bloodline immunity to spiritual assault, but inherited understanding of what leadership cost when it served purposes larger than personal comfort.

"He was a good man," Cathair continued, his voice carrying the weight of family history preserved through ancestral memory. "Wise, just, beloved by his people. And the burden of kingship killed him slowly, day by day, decision by decision. Not through violence or disease, but through the constant agony of choices where every option carried the certainty of loss."

"You fear the same fate," Neassa said with understanding that went deeper than mere sympathy.

"I know the same fate," he replied with brutal honesty that transcended comfortable illusion. "Accept what they offer, and I become responsible for every death that follows, every failure of strategy, every moment when my judgment proves insufficient to the trust placed in it. Lead Ireland, and Ireland's suffering becomes mine to carry until it breaks me as it broke him."

The autumn wind stirred around them, carrying the scent of approaching winter and the distant sounds of warriors preparing for battles that might determine whether Ireland retained the capacity for such preparation. Through the window, they could see the steady stream of people arriving for whatever ceremony or council the crisis would demand, faces bearing hope and fear in equal measure.

"Then why are you considering it at all?" she asked quietly, understanding that the question touched something fundamental about his character.

"Because the alternative is worse." The words came with reluctant recognition of someone who had exhausted every other option. "Refuse, and watch Ireland die by degrees while I preserve my own peace of mind. Let others make the choices I'm too frightened to face, then live with the knowledge that my cowardice contributed to whatever follows."

"It's not cowardice to recognize the cost of leadership."

"Isn't it?" His grip tightened on the stone windowsill, anchoring himself to something solid while possibilities threatened to sweep away everything familiar. "When people are dying because decisions need to be made, when enemies promise beautiful peace through surrender of individual will, when the very concept of conscious choice faces systematic assault—what else do you call the refusal to act when action might make a difference?"

***

The conversation was interrupted by calls from the courtyard below as the departure party completed its preparations, horses saddled, and supplies loaded for the journey that would take Cathair away from Tara just as the crisis deepened. But in that interruption, Neassa saw something shift in his expression—not resolution exactly, but the beginning of acceptance that some responsibilities could not be delegated regardless of their cost.

"There's something I need to understand before you go," she said, recognizing that this might be their last private conversation before circumstances forced decisions that could reshape everything between them. "This resistance we're building, this alliance of conscious choice against systematic emptiness—what happens to it if the person everyone looks to for leadership refuses to lead?"

"It finds someone else," Cathair replied, though his voice carried uncertainty that suggested he knew the answer was more complex than such simple words could contain.

"And if no one else has the bloodline immunity, the ancestral connections, the natural authority that draws others to unity around shared purpose? If the choice is between your leadership and no effective leadership at all?"

The question hung between them like challenge and invitation combined, forcing him to confront not just personal preference but the mathematics of resistance that required certain forms of strength to succeed against enemies who had eliminated individual weakness through systematic conversion.

"Then I suppose I discover whether love proves stronger than fear," he said finally, his voice carrying recognition of truth that transcended comfortable self-deception. "Whether caring about people enough to risk failing them proves adequate to the task of trying not to fail them."

The departure that followed carried weight beyond mere travel as Cathair and Ríona prepared to leave Tara's sanctuary for the dangerous journey to Mag nAí. Not just royal succession requiring proper ceremony, but the transformation of someone who had spent his life avoiding the highest forms of responsibility into someone who might prove capable of bearing them.

"I'll return as soon as the coronation is complete," he promised, though they both understood that the man who returned might be fundamentally different from the one who departed. "Whatever happens in Mag nAí, whatever I become through accepting my father's crown, Ireland's need remains paramount."

"I know," Neassa replied, understanding that his journey would test more than mere courage. "And I'll be here when you return, ready to discover what partnership might mean when both people have chosen service over safety, responsibility over the comfortable limitations of personal preference."

***

As the small party rode out through Tara's gates toward whatever awaited them in the territory where Cathair would become king, those who remained behind began the work of proving that conscious choice could defend itself against systematic assault even when its most visible leader faced the ultimate test of whether individual will could bear the weight of collective need.

The real transformation was beginning, and its outcome would determine not just personal relationships but the fundamental nature of authority in Ireland when authority itself faced assault from forces that promised peace through elimination of the chaos that conscious choice created.

Three days stretched ahead like a countdown to metamorphosis, and Ireland prepared to discover whether love could justify the burden of caring despite the certainty that caring created vulnerability to suffering that optimized beings had learned to avoid through surrender of everything that made avoidance necessary.

As the riders disappeared into the morning mist, Neassa stood at the gates feeling the weight of Tara's defense settling on her shoulders. Around her, the ancient stones hummed with approval for choices that proved worthy of supernatural blessing, conscious decisions that honored both heritage and hope.

But somewhere in the distance, enemies gathered who had perfected the art of making surrender seem like wisdom. The test was coming, and she would meet it with whatever strength remained when love accepted the full cost of choosing consciousness over the beautiful peace that promised relief through surrender of everything that made relief worthwhile.

The crown's weight was no longer theoretical—for any of them. And Ireland would discover whether that weight could be borne by hearts that chose meaning despite its cost, love despite its chaos, hope despite the certainty that hope might not be enough to save everything they had chosen to preserve.

CHAPTER 18

PARTNERSHIP FORGED

The council that would determine Ireland's leadership convened as urgent reports flooded in from across the island—not the carefully planned gathering they had hoped for, but crisis management as enemy forces moved with acceleration that eliminated the luxury of extended deliberation. Representatives filled Tara's great hall with faces that showed recognition of time running out, decisions that could no longer be delayed while comfortable precedent struggled against desperate necessity.

"Queen Medb's armies march three days ahead of schedule," announced the latest scout to reach Tara's gates, his horse collapsed from the desperate ride that had brought intelligence too important to delay. "Whatever coordination allows her forces to move without normal logistics has compressed every timeline we calculated. The great working approaches completion not in ten dawns, but in seven."

The mathematics of catastrophe crystallized around the assembly like recognition of trap closing faster than their ability to spring it. Seven dawns meant their carefully planned resistance would have to become something approaching desperate improvisation, while their enemies gained strength through every moment of political uncertainty.

Cathair stood beside Neassa as the implications settled over representatives who had risked everything to reach Tara's sanctuary. The transformation his time in Mag nAí had wrought was visible in more than bearing—in the way crisis seemed to clarify rather than confuse his judgment, in how others naturally looked to him for guidance without surrendering their own authority.

"Then we choose quickly," he said, his voice cutting across the growing tension with authority that had been tested through trial. "We cannot defeat enemies who coordinate with supernatural efficiency through normal political process. We need unified leadership adequate to the impossible, partnership strong enough to bear what individual authority cannot carry alone."

***

"You propose shared kingship," King Conchobor observed with careful precision that sought clarity rather than expressing judgment. "Authority divided between equals in times when divided command could prove fatal to everyone who trusts such leadership."

"We propose conscious authority," Neassa corrected, her priestess training providing perspective that transcended immediate political concerns. "Leadership that emerges from choice rather than inheritance, that serves protection of the capacity to choose rather than elimination of the burden choice creates."

"But the practical implications," Étaín of the Western Marches interjected with military urgency born from fresh intelligence. "My scouts report Hollowed forces moving with coordination that suggests shared consciousness among commanders. Perfect efficiency that requires no communication, no adaptation to terrain, no individual initiative that might disrupt optimal outcomes."

"How do we counter enemies who eliminate the weaknesses that normal strategy exploits?" Brendan asked with warrior's directness that cut through political courtesy to tactical reality.

"By embracing the strengths those enemies cannot understand," Boudica replied with strategic clarity earned through catastrophic experience. "Conscious choice that creates unpredictability, individual initiative that generates solutions to problems efficiency cannot anticipate, partnership that multiplies rather than divides the capacity for adaptive response."

Before the debate could develop further, horns sounded from Tara's outer defenses—not the single note of friendly approach, but the triple blast that meant urgent military intelligence requiring immediate attention. Through the great doors came a captain whose face bore the strain of someone who had witnessed events that challenged every assumption about enemy capabilities.

"Representatives of Ireland," he announced with formal gravity that barely concealed his alarm, "riders approach under the banner of Queen Medb's herald. They request immediate audience to deliver terms that will not be repeated or extended."

***

The implications hit the assembly like recognition that their enemies had grown tired of waiting for Ireland to tear itself apart through internal division. Not negotiation offered from position of mutual strength, but ultimatum delivered with timing designed to exploit exactly this moment of political uncertainty.

"How many?" Cathair asked with strategic precision that balanced caution against the need for immediate intelligence.

"Seven riders, moving with the mechanical precision that marks spiritual conversion. But also carrying formal diplomatic immunity that makes military response complicated regardless of what terms they bring."

"They mean to force our choice," Neassa realized with growing understanding of enemies whose sophistication exceeded their estimates. "Present their offer when we're most vulnerable to its seductive appeal, when unity remains theoretical rather than proven through shared trial."

King Aillen of Leinster rose with movements that spoke to recognition of crisis that transcended normal political categories. "Then we give them our answer as unified authority rather than scattered voices. We prove that conscious choice can create legitimate leadership even when that leadership challenges every precedent our experience provides."

The ceremony that followed drew on necessity rather than tradition, innovation that served survival rather than comfort. Not inherited authority legitimized through divine selection, but conscious choice blessed by representatives who understood that desperate circumstances required unprecedented solutions.

"Do you, Cathair of Mag nAí, accept the burden of speaking for Ireland not as privilege claimed but as responsibility shared?" Ríona asked, her divine nature lending weight to ceremony compressed by urgency but not diminished in significance.

"I accept partnership in service," Cathair replied with certainty that carried across the hall despite external pressure that sought to fragment their unity. "Authority shared with one whose judgment strengthens my own, whose wisdom serves Ireland's welfare as effectively as my own strength serves Ireland's defense."

"Do you, Neassa of the Sacred Fires, accept the crown of High Queen not as subordination to another's authority but as equal partnership in service to consciousness that chooses to remain conscious despite the cost?"

"I accept the privilege of serving both divine purpose and mortal need," Neassa said, her voice growing stronger with each word despite knowledge that enemy emissaries waited beyond the doors. "Authority that serves protection rather than domination, partnership that proves stronger than individual leadership when individual leadership faces systematic assault."

***

The crowning that transcended mere ceremony was interrupted by sounds from beyond the hall—not the patient waiting of normal diplomacy, but the mechanical precision of beings who served optimal schedules rather than diplomatic courtesy. Their enemies' representatives would not wait for ceremony to conclude before demanding Ireland's submission to beautiful efficiency that promised peace through surrender of everything that made peace worthwhile.

"Let them enter," Cathair commanded with authority that had been legitimized through conscious choice rather than inherited right. "Let Ireland's enemies see what partnership looks like when it serves consciousness rather than eliminating it, when individual will creates unity rather than requiring surrender for harmony."

The emissaries who entered moved with coordination that spoke to shared consciousness among beings whose individual will had been optimized away in favor of collective purpose. Three figures in robes that had once served sacred office but now carried emptiness where spiritual authority should have provided connection to sources larger than immediate efficiency.

"Representatives of Ireland's scattered territories," their leader announced with mechanical precision that made her words more chilling than any expression of anger, "Queen Medb offers final terms for integration into administrative systems that have brought prosperity to territories across the known world."

"Speak your terms," Neassa replied with authority that carried both political legitimacy and spiritual power, "though understand that we listen as free people, not as subjects seeking permission to remain ourselves."

"Ireland faces the choice between continued chaos of individual preference and demonstrated benefits of guided consciousness," the emissary continued with satisfaction that seemed disconnected from any personal enthusiasm. "Queen Medb offers partnership with proven authorities who have learned to eliminate suffering through elimination of the sources that create unnecessary conflict."

"What of those who prefer the chaos of consciousness to the peace of guidance?" Cathair asked with intensity that drew attention from every person in the chamber.

"They will discover that individual preferences which interfere with collective welfare cannot be permitted to persist," came the reply with mechanical certainty that transcended any trace of human feeling. "But the correction will be accomplished through demonstration rather than force, education rather than violence."

***

Around the chamber, representatives who had argued about leadership suddenly found themselves united by recognition of what they truly faced. Not political negotiation or even military conquest, but systematic elimination of consciousness itself disguised as administrative improvement that would solve all problems by eliminating the capacity to recognize problems as such.

"Then we refuse," Cathair said, his voice carrying across the hall with authority earned through conscious choice rather than inherited privilege. "Ireland chooses chaos over emptiness, meaning over efficiency, love over the beautiful peace that eliminates the capacity for love."

His words catalyzed unity that hours of political debate had failed to achieve. Around the hall, representatives rose in declaration that transcended their individual differences—not agreement on strategy, but consensus on the fundamental question of whether Ireland would remain Irish or surrender its soul for administrative convenience.

"The terms are clear," Neassa added with finality that seemed to echo from Tara's ancient stones. "Ireland chooses to remain itself, whatever the cost. Queen Medb chooses efficiency over meaning, order over love, emptiness over the sacred chaos of consciousness."

As the emissaries withdrew with mechanical precision that carried implied threat more chilling than any display of anger, the representatives found themselves facing each other across a hall that hummed with newfound unity forged through shared recognition of existential threat.

"Seven dawns," Brendan observed with grim recognition of mathematics that offered no comfortable options.

"Seven dawns to prove that partnership can defend consciousness against systematic assault," Cathair corrected, his presence somehow anchoring the assembly despite the impossibility of what they had chosen. "To demonstrate that authority shared becomes authority strengthened when it serves purposes larger than individual survival."

The war council that followed compressed weeks of planning into hours of desperate coordination as representatives who had discovered unity through crisis began the work of proving such unity adequate to preserve consciousness itself against forces that promised beautiful peace through surrender of everything that created the capacity for peace, beauty, or recognition of their value.

Outside Tara's walls, enemy forces moved with acceleration that eliminated normal military constraints, while inside, Ireland's newly crowned leaders prepared to discover whether partnership chosen through conscious decision could bear the weight of defending consciousness when consciousness faced its ultimate test.

***

The partnership was forged, legitimized, and immediately tested by crisis that would either prove its worth or demonstrate the futility of resistance against enemies who had perfected the art of making surrender seem like wisdom. Seven dawns stretched ahead like countdown to transformation, and Ireland prepared to meet them with everything they had chosen to preserve and everyone they had chosen to trust with authority that served protection rather than domination.

Time was running out, but for the first time since the crisis began, Ireland would face that countdown with unified leadership strong enough to attempt the impossible and conscious enough to understand that attempting was victory regardless of outcome. The choice was made, the partnership blessed, and the real test was about to begin.

The evening that followed was spent in urgent preparation— messengers dispatched to every free territory, defenses organized around Tara's sacred ground, and plans laid for resistance that would either vindicate their choice to remain conscious or provide noble witness to consciousness choosing consciousness even in defeat.

"Whatever comes," Neassa said quietly as she stood beside Cathair at the great window where they had so often planned resistance that seemed impossible until conscious choice made it inevitable, "we face it together. Partnership that serves both love and leadership, consciousness that chooses consciousness despite the cost."

"Together," he agreed, understanding that the word now carried implications that would determine whether Ireland remained Irish or surrendered its soul for promises of efficient administration that eliminated both problems and possibilities.

The partnership was complete, but its real test lay ahead in the dawns that would determine whether love could justify the chaos consciousness created when chaos faced elimination by forces that had perfected the art of making surrender seem inevitable.

Ireland had chosen, and now Ireland would discover whether choice itself possessed sufficient strength to create forms of beauty adequate to justify the chaos consciousness demanded as the price of remaining conscious, aware, and eternally committed to meaning over emptiness despite the certainty that meaning created suffering through its insistence on remaining itself rather than accepting optimization into unrecognizable efficiency.

CHAPTER 19

BONDS OF STORM AND FIRE

The handfasting ceremony began as sacred sites across Ireland fell silent with mechanical precision, each extinguished light in the spiritual network marking another step toward the great working that would eliminate consciousness itself from an entire island. Ríona's divine sight tracked the systematic assault even as she prepared to officiate the most important ceremony of their resistance—not just political alliance, but proof that love could serve authority when authority served consciousness rather than destroying it.

"They accelerate the corruption to coincide with our ceremony," she announced with otherworldly certainty that carried its own weight of urgency. "Each site that falls silent feeds power into their great working, while our choice to create bonds serves as beacon that draws their attention like flame draws moths."

Cathair stood beside Neassa in Tara's great hall as representatives gathered with understanding that they witnessed either the birth of legitimate partnership or its destruction by enemies who viewed such bonds as inefficiency requiring immediate correction. Through the ancient windows, they could see the first signs of spiritual assault—not physical attack, but pressure against consciousness itself that sought to drain meaning from celebration, to transform joy into emptiness.

"Then we choose quickly," Neassa decided with authority that transcended mere personal preference. "We prove that conscious choice creates bonds strong enough to resist any pressure, that love generates strength rather than weakness when it serves purposes larger than individual comfort."

***

The ceremony that followed drew on traditions older than kingdoms while adapting to circumstances that challenged every assumption about the nature of sacred bonds. Not leisurely celebration of alliance negotiated in peace, but defiant assertion of partnership forged under pressure that sought to eliminate the very capacity for choice.

Ríona approached with movements that carried divine authority mixed with very human urgency, her silver scars pulsing with otherworldly light as supernatural energy responded to the spiritual significance of what they attempted. Around them, the carved spirals of Tara's ancient stones began to flicker with uncertain radiance as enemy spiritual assault pressed against the sacred site's defenses.

"In times when consciousness faces systematic assault," she began, her voice carrying across the hall with harmonics that belonged to no mortal throat, "we gather to witness bonds that strengthen rather than surrender under pressure, partnership that serves resistance rather than requiring peace for its survival."

From her robes she drew forth cords that seemed to pulse with inner light, silver and gold twisted together in patterns that responded to the spiritual pressure building around Tara's defenses. Memory stirred of her mother's voice from childhood, gentle instruction that now served desperate necessity.

"By fire and water, by earth and air," Ríona continued, her voice carrying both formal authority and deep tenderness earned through trial, "by witness of those who choose consciousness over emptiness, I bind you in partnership that serves both mortal need and divine purpose."

But even as she spoke, the pressure intensified. Through the great windows came sounds that belonged to no natural approach—whispered coordination of beings moving with mechanical precision toward Tara's ancient defenses. The Hollowed approached while Ireland's leaders proved that choice could create bonds stronger than compulsion.

"They mean to disrupt the ceremony," Boudica observed with strategic clarity that read tactical implications in enemy timing. "Convert our moment of greatest unity into demonstration of consciousness defeated by efficiency."

"Then we prove them wrong," Cathair said with quiet intensity that drew strength from crisis rather than being weakened by it. "We demonstrate that some bonds grow stronger when tested, that partnership chosen through conscious decision serves purposes larger than individual survival."

***

The cords grew warm against their joined hands as Ríona's divine power flowed through the binding, creating connections that transcended mere symbolism despite the spiritual assault that sought to drain meaning from the ceremony itself. Around them, representatives who had risked everything to witness this moment felt the pull of emptiness that promised relief from the terrible burden of caring about outcomes beyond personal control.

"Hold fast," Neassa commanded with authority that carried both political legitimacy and spiritual power, her priestess training providing resistance to forces that attacked meaning itself. "Hold to what we choose to preserve, what we choose to become together despite every pressure to surrender choice for beautiful certainty."

At that moment, thunder rolled across clear skies despite the absence of storm clouds—not warning but recognition, divine acknowledgment of bonds forged under pressure and found worthy of supernatural blessing. The first rumble grew stronger as their ceremony reached its culmination, rolling across Tara with voice that spoke of goddesses celebrating love that served purposes larger than individual desire.

"The Morrígan bears witness," Ríona announced with wonder growing in her voice as divine presence blessed their union despite the spiritual assault that sought to corrupt every form of meaning. "She honors bonds forged in service to consciousness that chooses to remain conscious despite the cost."

A large crow alighted on the hall's stone lintel, its dark eyes reflecting intelligence that belonged to no ordinary bird. The creature watched with perfect stillness as thunder shook the ancient stones, divine approval made manifest despite enemies who promised peace through surrender of everything that made approval possible or meaningful.

"What the goddesses have joined through conscious choice, let no force of emptiness sever," Ríona concluded with finality that seemed to echo from powers beyond mortal understanding. "You are bound in partnership that serves both love and leadership, united in service to Ireland and each other despite every pressure to choose efficiency over meaning."

***

The kiss that sealed their vows carried weight beyond mere affection—recognition of partnership forged under assault, love chosen despite the certainty that love created vulnerability to forces that promised peace through elimination of the capacity for caring. Around them, the spiritual pressure intensified as enemy forces reached Tara's immediate defenses, but their bonds held firm against corruption that sought to transform unity into tool serving optimal purposes.

Lightning began to flicker through the chamber's windows as their union reached completion, supernatural radiance that revealed truth—two people who had found strength in each other adequate to attempt impossible defense of consciousness itself, partnership that might prove stronger than the beautiful emptiness approaching with mechanical precision.

But the ceremony's conclusion brought immediate crisis as scouts burst through the great doors with intelligence that transformed celebration into urgent preparation for siege that would test everything they had proven possible.

"Hollowed forces surround the hill," reported the lead scout with military precision that barely contained his alarm at enemy capabilities that transcended normal warfare. "They move without regard for terrain or defensive advantages, perfect coordination that serves purposes beyond individual survival or tactical necessity."

"How many?" Cathair asked, his hand finding Neassa's with touch that anchored them both despite the magnitude of what approached.

"Impossible to count precisely," came the reply with honesty that spoke to encountering forces that operated beyond normal military categories. "They move like components of single organism, individual identity eliminated in favor of collective efficiency that requires no communication, no adaptation, no concern for losses that don't affect optimal outcomes."

Through the windows, they could see the approach beginning—not armies in any traditional sense, but coordinated movement that spoke to consciousness transformed into tool serving purposes that viewed individual preference as obstacle to administrative perfection. The great working was approaching its culmination, and with it would come the final test of whether partnership could defend consciousness when consciousness faced systematic elimination.

"Then we meet them together," Neassa said with certainty that came from bonds tested through crisis and found adequate to impossible challenges. "We prove that love creates strength rather than weakness when it serves purposes larger than personal happiness."

"Together," Cathair agreed, understanding that the word now carried implications that would determine whether Ireland remained Irish or surrendered its soul for promises of efficient administration that eliminated both problems and possibilities.

***

The celebration that should have continued into joyful evening transformed into preparation for siege that would either vindicate their choice to remain conscious or provide noble witness to consciousness' final stand against forces that promised beautiful peace through surrender of everything that created beauty, peace, or capacity to recognize their value.

Outside Tara's walls, the great working built toward culmination that would reshape an entire island's spiritual foundation. Inside, two people who had chosen partnership over isolation prepared to discover whether love could justify the chaos it created when chaos faced elimination by forces that had perfected the art of making surrender seem like wisdom.

As night fell and enemy pressure intensified around Tara's ancient defenses, the newly bound partners stood together at the great window where they had so often planned resistance that seemed impossible until conscious choice made it inevitable. The storm that blessed their union continued to wash the sacred hill with divine approval, but now it competed with spiritual assault that sought to drain meaning from every form of connection.

"Are you ready for this?" Cathair asked gently, understanding that the question touched more than immediate military crisis.

"I'm ready for us," Neassa replied with certainty that transcended individual confidence. "Ready to discover what partnership means when it faces forces designed to eliminate the very concept of conscious choice, when love must serve as weapon rather than refuge in conflicts that determine the future of meaning itself."

The bonds of storm and fire had been forged, blessed, and immediately tested by assault that would either prove their strength or demonstrate the futility of resistance against enemies who offered beautiful peace through surrender of everything that made peace worthwhile. But for the first time since the crisis began, Ireland faced that test with unified leadership strong enough to attempt the impossible and conscious enough to understand that attempting was victory regardless of outcome.

Seven dawns had become hours, and Ireland prepared to discover whether partnership chosen through conscious decision could bear the weight of defending consciousness itself when consciousness faced its ultimate test against forces that promised efficient solutions to the problems that consciousness created through its insistence on remaining itself.

The war for Ireland's soul was entering its final phase, and they would meet it with everything they had chosen to preserve and everyone they had chosen to trust with authority that served protection rather than domination. The ceremony was complete, the bonds established, but the real test was just beginning as supernatural forces prepared to demonstrate whether love could defend consciousness against the ultimate seduction of surrender.

Storm and fire had blessed their union, and now both would be needed to prove that some bonds grew stronger under pressure, that some partnerships could bear any weight when they served purposes larger than individual survival, that Ireland would remain Irish regardless of what forces sought to optimize that choice away.

CHAPTER 20

THE RETURN OF THE KING

Dawn came to Tara with the weight of transformation made manifest in morning light that seemed to pour from the eastern sky like liquid recognition of bonds forged through conscious choice rather than imposed through circumstance. The sacred hill hummed with energy that spoke to partnership legitimized not just by mortal ceremony but by divine blessing that had shaken the ancient stones with supernatural approval.

Neassa woke in her husband's arms with awareness that the woman who had fallen asleep was fundamentally different from the one who greeted the morning. Not just married, but partnered in authority that transcended traditional categories, crowned as High Queen of Ireland through innovation that honored both ancient wisdom and contemporary necessity.

"How do you feel?" Cathair asked softly, his voice carrying wonder at awakening beside someone who had chosen to share not just love but the terrible beautiful burden of leadership that could crush individuals but might strengthen those who carried it together.

"Different," she replied with honesty that spoke to transformation that went deeper than ceremony. "Not just because of what we've chosen, but because of what choosing together has revealed about what becomes possible when individual will serves purposes larger than personal comfort."

Through the chamber's windows, they could see the evidence of supernatural blessing that had marked their union—not damage from divine storm, but enhancement that spoke to approval from powers whose attention usually remained separate from mortal concerns. The very stones of Tara seemed to pulse with renewed energy, as if their partnership had strengthened the sacred site's connection to sources that transcended normal spiritual categories.

* * *

But even as they celebrated the personal transformation that crisis had made possible, the sounds of urgent activity echoed from the courtyards below. Not the chaos of emergency, but the focused preparation of people who understood their objectives and possessed confidence in their ability to achieve them despite overwhelming odds.

"The strike teams return," Cathair observed, reading in the coordination of arrival what his military training could interpret even from distance. "Multiple groups, arriving simultaneously rather than scattered across days—that suggests either complete success or total disaster."

The reports that followed painted a picture of transformation that exceeded their most optimistic projections while revealing the true scope of what they had set in motion through conscious choice to resist beautiful emptiness with difficult meaning. Not just tactical success, but fundamental alteration of the spiritual landscape that supported Irish identity.

"Seven corrupted sites restored to authentic service," Boudica announced with satisfaction that spoke to strategy vindicated through results that transcended mere military victory. "The sacred water from Tobar na nGealt provides protection that allows conversion to be reversed rather than simply resisted. But more than that—each restoration strengthens the connections that bind the network together."

"The spiritual infrastructure responds to conscious choice," Ríona confirmed, her divine sight-reading patterns that stretched across multiple realms of existence. "Each site that returns to serving meaning rather than emptiness creates resonance that makes the next restoration easier to accomplish. We're not just healing damage—we're building strength that exceeds what existed before the assault began."

King Conchobor leaned forward with interest that spoke to recognition of implications that extended far beyond immediate tactical advantages. "You're describing something unprecedented. Not just resistance that preserves what existed, but transformation that creates new forms of strength through the very act of choosing consciousness over emptiness."

"Exactly," confirmed Muiris of the Southern Rivers, his voice carrying wonder at witnessing something that challenged every assumption about the nature of spiritual warfare. "It's as if the choice to remain ourselves generates power that multiplies through sharing rather than diminishing through division."

***

The success created new possibilities but also new responsibilities as Ireland's defenders found themselves dealing with forms of strength they had not expected to possess. Not just survival against overwhelming odds, but leadership of transformation that might reshape the fundamental relationship between consciousness and authority across territories where different forms of meaning competed for legitimacy.

"What of Queen Medb's response?" Cathair asked with strategic precision that balanced celebration against realistic assessment of enemies who would surely adapt their methods to counter unexpected resistance.

"Silence," Étaín replied with concern that spoke to understanding of how dangerous such quiet could prove. "No military response, no diplomatic overtures, no visible reaction to losing sites that required months of systematic corruption to acquire. Either she's planning something that makes tactical response unnecessary, or she's discovered methods we haven't anticipated."

Before they could analyze the implications of enemy silence, new sounds echoed from Tara's approaches—not the coordinated return of strike teams, but something else entirely. Hoofbeats that carried otherworldly rhythm, approach that belonged to no normal embassy or military force.

The figure who appeared through the morning mist moved with fluid grace that spoke of realms where different laws governed movement and meaning, neither fully corporeal nor entirely spirit but carrying authority that required acknowledgment regardless of mortal categories. Those who knew the old stories recognized him immediately—Lord Midir of the Sidhe Mounds, approaching with diplomatic purpose rather than casual visitation.

"King Cathair and Queen Neassa of Ireland," he said, his voice carrying harmonics that belonged to courts where different forms of authority held meaning. "I come on behalf of powers that have watched your rise with interest that transcends mere curiosity."

Cathair inclined his head with instinctive recognition of nobility that required acknowledgment regardless of realm or species, while Neassa felt her divine sight confirming what mortal perception suggested—they faced a being whose authority in the Otherworld matched their own in the realm of living mortals.

"Lord Midir," Cathair replied with formal courtesy that honored diplomatic protocol while maintaining his own dignity. "Your presence honors ceremonies that mark innovation in troubled times. What brings the Sidhe to witness mortal partnership?"

"Mutual recognition," Lord Midir replied with directness that spoke to the urgency underlying their formal exchange. "The corruption that spreads through your sacred sites does not respect the boundaries between mortal and immortal realms. What threatens consciousness in your world threatens the very foundations upon which our realm depends for meaning."

***

"You speak of alliance," Neassa said, her transformed understanding allowing her to address the Sidhe lord as something approaching an equal.

"I speak of necessity," Lord Midir corrected with emphasis that carried its own weight of recognition. "Your enemies do not simply threaten political independence or cultural identity. They assault the fundamental patterns that allow consciousness to create beauty, love to generate purpose, choice to produce consequences that matter beyond immediate convenience."

The implications settled over them like recognition of stakes that transcended even their worst fears about Ireland's immediate crisis. Not just national survival, but preservation of consciousness itself across realms where different forms of awareness competed for the right to exist and create meaning through their existence.

"What do you propose?" Cathair asked, understanding that diplomatic courtesies were giving way to strategic necessities that would reshape their resistance in ways they could barely imagine.

"Partnership," Lord Midir said simply, the word carrying weight that spoke to alliance between realms rather than mere tactical cooperation. "When the final test comes—and it approaches with the inevitability of tide returning to familiar shores—the Sidhe will stand with those who defend meaning against emptiness, choice against optimization, love against the beautiful peace that eliminates the capacity for love."

"And in return?" Neassa asked, her priestess training providing recognition that supernatural aid always carried obligations that transcended immediate gratitude.

"Acknowledgment that some bonds transcend the boundaries between realms," the Sidhe lord replied with formality that spoke to agreements that would endure across centuries. "Recognition that mortal and immortal authority serve common purposes when consciousness itself faces systematic assault from forces that view awareness as inefficiency requiring correction."

"Granted," Cathair said immediately, understanding that some alliances required acceptance without extended negotiation. "Ireland acknowledges partnership with the Sidhe Mounds, alliance that serves the preservation of meaning in all realms where meaning remains possible."

Lord Midir smiled with satisfaction that carried its own form of blessing, recognition that transcended mere political calculation to honor choices that proved worthy of supernatural support. "Then when your enemies gather for their final assault—and they will, for forces that promise peace through surrender cannot tolerate examples of consciousness choosing consciousness—they will discover that resistance draws strength from sources they cannot access or corrupt."

"When?" Boudica asked with military precision that sought tactical intelligence rather than abstract promise.

"Soon," the Sidhe lord replied with certainty that spoke to perception extending beyond normal temporal limitations. "The convergence approaches when boundaries dissolve between worlds, when powers that normally remain separate can touch the realm where choices determine consequences. Your enemies plan to use that moment for systematic elimination of consciousness across your entire island."

"Samhain," Ríona breathed, recognition dawning in her voice as divine insight provided understanding of timing that would either serve salvation or witness noble failure.

"The night when the veil grows thin between living and dead, when spirits can cross boundaries that normally separate realms of existence," Lord Midir confirmed. "They mean to use that permeability for purposes opposite to its intended function—not connection between worlds, but severance of consciousness from the capacity to choose meaning over emptiness."

The intelligence transformed their understanding of what they faced from difficult military challenge to existential test that would determine the future of consciousness itself. Not just Ireland's political independence, but the fundamental right of awareness to exist in forms that created beauty rather than simply served efficiency.

As Lord Midir prepared to depart, his diplomatic mission complete and alliance secured, his final words carried across the sacred hill with weight that would echo through whatever trials awaited them.

"Tell your people that the choice they made to remain themselves despite every pressure to surrender has been witnessed by powers whose approval matters more than mortal recognition," he said with authority that transcended normal categories of blessing. "When the final test comes, they will not stand alone."

The departure of the Sidhe lord left Tara humming with energy that spoke to alliance between realms, supernatural support that might prove decisive when their enemies completed whatever great working they prepared for the night when boundaries dissolved between possible and impossible.

"Ten dawns until Samhain," Síle observed with youth's mixture of excitement and terror at witnessing events that would reshape legend. "Ten dawns until we discover whether consciousness proves strong enough to defend itself when offered beautiful alternatives that promise peace through surrender of everything that makes peace worthwhile."

"Ten dawns to complete preparations that account for alliance we never expected," Cathair corrected with authority that had been tested through trial and emerged stronger rather than brittle. "Mortal courage supported by supernatural strength, partnership that serves purposes larger than either realm could achieve alone."

***

As the day progressed and urgent planning resumed with new complexity born from alliance that transcended normal categories, Neassa found herself walking beside her husband through corridors that had witnessed transformation beyond mere political innovation. Not just partnership legitimized through ceremony, but proof that consciousness could choose forms of authority adequate to preserve consciousness itself when consciousness faced its ultimate test.

"Are you ready for this?" she asked, understanding that the question touched more than mere tactical preparation.

"I'm ready for us," he replied with certainty that came from bonds forged through conscious choice rather than imposed through circumstance. "Ready to discover what partnership can accomplish when it serves purposes larger than individual happiness, when love becomes weapon rather than weakness in conflicts that determine the future of meaning itself."

The war for Ireland's soul had gained allies whose power operated beyond the limitations that bound their enemies, but the real strength lay in choices that transcended supernatural intervention to prove that consciousness could defend consciousness through decision rather than surrender, love rather than emptiness, meaning rather than the beautiful simplicity that promised peace through elimination of everything that made peace worth having.

Ten dawns stretched ahead like countdown to transformation, and Ireland prepared to discover whether partnership chosen through conscious decision could bear the weight of defending consciousness itself when consciousness faced forces that promised beautiful peace through surrender of everything that created beauty, peace, or the capacity to recognize their value.

The return of the king had become something far greater—the emergence of partnership that might prove adequate to impossible challenges, alliance between realms that honored both mortal determination and divine blessing, love that served duty as effectively as duty could serve love when both faced enemies who viewed service itself as inefficiency requiring optimization away.

Samhain approached with the weight of destiny made manifest in temporal form, and Ireland would meet it with everything they had chosen to preserve and everyone they had chosen to become through choices that honored both heritage and hope.

CHAPTER 21

THE CROWN OF CHOICE

Dawn came to Tara with the weight of destiny carried on light that seemed to pour from the eastern sky like liquid gold, washing the sacred hill in radiance that spoke of endings and beginnings in equal measure. Samhain morning—the day when the veil between worlds grew thin, when ancestors could touch the realm of the living, when choices made in darkness would be tested by forces that transcended mortal understanding.

Neassa stood beside the empty depression where the Lia Fáil had once provided divine judgment, feeling the spiritual energy that gathered around Tara like storm clouds heavy with possibility. Representatives from across Ireland filled the great platform, faces bearing the strain of people who understood they witnessed either the birth of legitimate authority or its final failure before enemies who promised peace through surrender of everything that made peace worthwhile.

The coronation regalia lay upon ancient stones warmed by fires that had burned through the night—not crowns inherited from previous rulers, but circlets forged specifically for this moment by smiths whose craft carried blessing as well as skill.

Silver worked with gold, patterns that echoed the spiral magic that bound Ireland's sacred sites, symbols that honored tradition while serving contemporary need.

Ríona approached the circle's heart with movements that carried divine authority mixed with very human emotion, her silver scars catching morning light as otherworldly energy flowed around her like visible benediction. The weight of the moment pressed against them all—Ireland's future balanced on the edge of transformation, awaiting choices that would echo through generations yet unborn.

"People of Ireland," she began, her voice carrying across the platform with harmonics that belonged to no mortal throat, "we gather on Samhain morning to witness something that has never been attempted—the crowning of rulers who claim authority not through inheritance or divine selection, but through conscious choice freely given and consciously maintained."

***

The words rippled through the assembled representatives like recognition of historical significance that transcended mere political ceremony. Around them, the ancient stones of Tara seemed to pulse with responsive energy, as if the sacred site itself approved of innovation that honored old wisdom while serving new necessity.

"Let those who would rule step forward," Ríona continued with formality that carried weight of tradition adapted to unprecedented circumstances. "Let them speak the vows that bind authority to service, power to responsibility, individual will to collective need."

Cathair moved first, his steps carrying the confidence of someone who had accepted burden rather than claimed privilege. The crown that awaited him was beautiful but not ostentatious— silver worked with patterns that spoke to the bloodline connections that had brought him to this moment, but also to conscious choice that transformed inheritance into service.

"I, Cathair, King of Mag nAí, accept the crown of High King of Ireland," he said, his voice carrying across the platform with authority that had been tested through trial and emerged stronger rather than brittle. "Not as inheritance claimed or power seized, but as responsibility chosen—service to a people who deserve leadership that honors both their heritage and their hopes."

Neassa stepped forward to stand beside him, her presence immediately transforming the ceremony from traditional succession to something unprecedented. The crown that awaited her was equally beautiful, equally symbolic—gold worked with silver in patterns that spoke to spiritual authority balanced with temporal power, conscious partnership rather than hierarchical submission.

"I, Neassa of the Sacred Fires, High Priestess of Tara, accept the crown of High Queen of Ireland," she declared with voice that grew stronger with each word. "Not as consort dependent on another's authority, but as partner in service—conscious choice to share both power and responsibility, to prove that authority divided becomes authority strengthened."

***

The representatives who witnessed their declarations felt the shift in spiritual atmosphere as forces beyond normal perception took interest in vows that challenged fundamental assumptions about the nature of legitimate rule. King Conchobor of Ulster stepped forward with movements that spoke to recognition of authority that transcended mere political ceremony.

"Ulster acknowledges Cathair and Neassa as High King and High Queen of Ireland," he declared with formal gravity. "Authority granted not through tradition alone, but through conscious recognition of leadership adequate to contemporary need."

One by one, the other representatives added their voices to the growing consensus—not because custom demanded such acknowledgment, but because desperate circumstances required exactly this form of guidance. Conscious choice creating legitimate authority, partnership proving stronger than individual rule, innovation serving survival rather than mere preference.

"Leinster accepts the crown freely chosen," King Aillen declared.

"Munster follows where wisdom leads," King Cormac added.

Around the platform, seventeen different túatha found themselves united not through compulsion or inherited allegiance, but through recognition that their survival required leadership built on foundations stronger than tradition or force.

Ríona lifted the first crown with movements that seemed to draw power from sources beyond mortal understanding, silver and gold catching light that belonged to no earthly illumination. As she placed it upon Cathair's head, divine energy flowed through the ceremony like blessing made manifest in the material world.

"By conscious choice of those you serve," she intoned with authority that carried across realms both mortal and divine, "by recognition of burden freely accepted rather than privilege claimed, by partnership that honors both individual will and collective need—I crown you High King of Ireland, first to claim authority through service rather than inheritance."

The crown settled on Cathair's head like recognition of destiny chosen rather than imposed, weight that somehow felt lighter because it was shared rather than carried in isolation. Around the platform, the assembled representatives felt the shift as political ceremony became something deeper—legitimate authority emerging from conscious decision rather than inherited right.

Ríona lifted the second crown with equal ceremony, patterns of gold and silver seeming to pulse with inner light as divine power blessed innovation that served tradition's deepest purposes while adapting to contemporary necessity.

"By wisdom proven through trial," she continued, her voice carrying harmonics that belonged to goddesses who watched from hidden vantage points, "by authority earned through service rather than granted through birth, by partnership that proves conscious choice creates bonds stronger than compulsion—I crown you High Queen of Ireland, first to claim equal authority through conscious service rather than dependent status."

As the crown touched Neassa's head, thunder rumbled across the clear morning sky despite the absence of clouds. Not warning but recognition, divine acknowledgment of authority that had been granted by powers beyond mortal comprehension. The very stones of Tara seemed to sing with approval, ancient magic recognizing legitimate succession despite the absence of traditional forms.

The moment of transformation stretched across heartbeats that felt like eternities as Ireland's new rulers stood together beneath crowns that carried blessing from realms both visible and hidden. Through Ríona's divine sight, the ceremony gained witnesses that mortal perception could not detect—The Morrígan perched on ancient stones, her three aspects present in approval that honored choices worthy of supernatural recognition.

"Rise, High King and High Queen of Ireland," Ríona pronounced with finality that seemed to echo from the stones themselves. "Rise to serve rather than rule, to unite rather than dominate, to prove that conscious choice creates authority more legitimate than force or empty tradition."

The cheers that erupted from the assembled representatives carried relief and determination in equal measure, recognition that Ireland had finally achieved what crisis demanded—unified leadership strong enough to bear the weight of survival while innovative enough to discover new forms of strength.

* * *

But even as celebration began, everyone present understood that coronation was only beginning rather than conclusion. Samhain stretched ahead with its promise of spiritual culmination, festival celebration that would honor both their achievement and the ancestors who had guided them to this moment of transformation.

"The day belongs to preparation," Cathair announced as the formal ceremony concluded, and representatives began to disperse toward their various responsibilities. "Tonight belongs to Samhain, to honoring those who came before and celebrating those who choose to carry their legacy forward."

"Seven sacred sites must be protected," Neassa added with practical urgency that balanced celebration against contemporary necessity. "Seven strongholds where the old ways remain strong, where our enemies' great working might yet be disrupted if courage proves adequate to the task."

"And at sunset," Ríona said quietly, her divine sight-reading currents that flowed beyond normal perception, "when the veil grows thin and powers from other realms take interest in mortal choices—we discover whether consciousness proves strong enough to defend itself against beautiful emptiness, whether love justifies the chaos it creates, whether Ireland chooses to remain Irish no matter what forces array themselves against the terrible wonderful burden of caring about each other."

The morning dispersed into urgent activity as newly crowned rulers took their first actions as legitimate authority—coordinating defenses, blessing departing warriors, ensuring that Samhain's celebration would serve both spiritual necessity and strategic preparation. The war for Ireland's soul was entering its final phase, and they would meet it as partners whose authority derived from conscious choice rather than inherited privilege.

As the sun climbed toward its zenith, Tara transformed from ceremonial site to festival ground as people began arriving for Samhain celebration that would honor both ancient tradition and contemporary triumph. Families traveled from across the territories that remained free, bringing with them the foods and crafts and songs that defined Irish identity despite every pressure to surrender cultural distinctiveness for the promise of efficient administration.

"Look at them," Neassa said with wonder as she watched the gathering crowd from the great hall's windows. "Despite everything—the threat, the uncertainty, the knowledge that enemies march toward us with power beyond normal resistance—they come to celebrate life, memory, the connections that make existence meaningful."

"Because those connections are exactly what we fight to preserve," Cathair replied, understanding settling in his voice like recognition of purposes that transcended immediate survival. "Not just political independence or territorial control, but the right to remain ourselves—complex, contradictory, gloriously inefficient selves who choose meaning over emptiness despite the cost in blood and tears."

***

Through the afternoon, the celebration built like tide gathering strength before the storm. Musicians tuned instruments that would carry songs across the boundary between worlds, cooks prepared feasts that honored both living guests and ancestral spirits, storytellers prepared tales that would remind everyone present why consciousness was worth preserving despite its terrible wonderful burden.

As sunset approached and the great Samhain fire was kindled on Tara's ancient stones—the sacred flame that would burn throughout the night to guide ancestral spirits and ward against darkness—newly crowned rulers who had claimed authority through conscious choice prepared to discover whether that choice would prove strong enough to preserve consciousness itself when consciousness faced its ultimate test.

The veil between worlds began to thin as darkness gathered, and powers both mortal and divine watched with interest that transcended mere curiosity. Somewhere in the gathering night, enemies prepared to complete workings that would eliminate the capacity for choice itself. But here, at the heart of Ireland's spiritual defenses, people chose to celebrate the very consciousness that their enemies sought to destroy.

Samhain had begun, and with it the final test of whether love could justify existence despite the certainty of loss, whether meaning could emerge from chaos rather than requiring optimization through emptiness, whether Ireland's choice to remain Irish would echo through legend or fade into the beautiful silence of surrender.

The crown of choice had been claimed. Now came the test of whether conscious choice could bear the weight of defending consciousness itself against forces that promised peace through surrender of everything that made peace worthwhile.

CHAPTER 22

WHEN DARKNESS GATHERS

Night fell over Tara like a curtain drawn across the world, but the great Samhain fire blazed defiantly against the darkness, its flames reaching toward stars that seemed closer tonight than they had any right to be. Around the sacred flame, the people of Ireland celebrated with voices raised in songs that carried across the thinning veil—melodies that honored the living and welcomed the dead, music that reminded everyone present why consciousness was worth preserving despite its terrible wonderful cost.

Neassa stood with Cathair at the fire's edge, her crown catching flame-light as she watched faces illuminated by radiance that served both celebration and protection. Children danced between the adults with laughter that rang pure as silver bells, while elders shared stories that wove past and present into patterns that gave meaning to whatever future they might yet create.

"Beautiful," Cathair murmured, his voice carrying wonder at the sight of people choosing joy in the shadow of existential threat. "Despite everything—the approaching enemies, the spiritual assault, the knowledge that this might be Ireland's last free

Samhain—they choose to celebrate life, memory, the connections that make existence meaningful."

"Because those connections are exactly what we fight to preserve," Neassa replied, understanding settling in her voice like recognition of purposes that transcended immediate survival. "Not just political independence, but the right to remain ourselves—complex, contradictory, gloriously inefficient selves who find meaning in chaos rather than emptiness."

But even as celebration reached its peak, Ríona's divine sight-read currents of disturbance that flowed beneath the joy like underground rivers carrying poison toward hidden springs. Her silver scars began to pulse with increasing urgency as otherworldly energy built around Tara's defenses, testing boundaries that grew weaker with each passing hour.

"Something comes," she said quietly, her voice cutting through the nearest conversations with authority that commanded immediate attention. "Multiple disturbances, converging from different directions. The great working has begun."

***

The change came gradually at first, noticed only by those whose senses reached beyond normal perception. The quality of starlight shifted, growing harsh where it should have been gentle, while shadows seemed to deepen beyond what natural darkness could explain. The great fire continued to burn, but its warmth no longer reached as far, as if something were drawing heat from the flames without extinguishing them entirely.

Cú Chulainn's divine heritage allowed him to read the spiritual landscape with accuracy that transcended mortal understanding. "From the east," he announced with grim certainty, his weapons beginning to sing with their own inner light. "Spiritual assault on the sacred network, designed to drain power from sites that might resist the great working. But also physical approach—armies moving under cover of supernatural distraction."

"And from the west," Boudica added with warrior instincts that had learned to recognize coordination disguised as coincidence. "Queen Medb's forces, timing their assault to coincide with whatever spiritual working they've prepared. Three-pronged attack—physical, spiritual, and something else entirely."

As if summoned by their recognition, the first wave of disturbance reached Tara's outer defenses. Not visible assault but something more insidious—pressure against consciousness itself, spiritual force that sought to drain meaning from the celebration, to transform joy into emptiness, songs into silence, love into the beautiful peace of surrender.

The people closest to the perimeter felt it first, their laughter faltering as spiritual weight pressed against their minds like fog rolling in from invisible marshes. Some stumbled, confusion flickering across their faces as they struggled to remember why they had been celebrating, what purpose drove them to resist rather than simply accepting whatever brought the most efficient outcomes.

"The Hollowed," Síle breathed with recognition that carried its own weight of horror. "They're not just approaching physically—they're projecting their emptiness ahead of them, trying to convert the celebration into surrender before the first sword is drawn."

Neassa felt the spiritual assault like ice in her veins, but her training as High Priestess provided resistance that most lacked. Around the great fire, she could see the effects spreading like ripples in a pond—people growing quiet, subdued, the brilliant joy of Samhain celebration dimming as spiritual pressure convinced them that such expressions of individual will were inefficient disruptions of optimal harmony.

"Counter it," Cathair commanded with authority that cut through the growing confusion. "Whatever they're doing to our people, counter it now before the conversion spreads beyond reversal."

Ríona stepped toward the great fire with movements that drew power from sources beyond mortal understanding, her divine nature blazing with light that pushed back against the encroaching spiritual assault. But she was only one voice raised against a coordinated attack designed to overwhelm resistance through sheer accumulated pressure.

"The sacred sites," she gasped as otherworldly energy flowed through her like lightning seeking ground. "They're draining power from every corrupted location simultaneously, feeding it into one massive working designed to eliminate consciousness across all of Ireland in a single stroke."

The spiritual pressure intensified as enemy forces reached the boundaries of Tara's immediate defenses, their coordinated assault testing every ward and protective ritual that generations of druids had woven around Ireland's sacred heart. Through the growing darkness came sounds that belonged to no natural approach—not the march of armies but the whisper of emptiness given form, consciousness draining away like water from broken vessels.

"Physical forces from the east," reported a scout who had returned from patrol with urgency that spoke to immediate rather than distant threat. "But they move strangely—too coordinated, too precise. No individual initiative, no adaptation to terrain or circumstance. Perfect efficiency that serves purposes beyond military necessity."

"The converted," Boudica recognized with strategic clarity that cut through supernatural confusion to tactical reality. "Warriors whose consciousness has been replaced with optimal coordination.

They won't retreat, won't hesitate, won't make mistakes born from fear or compassion."

Around the great fire, more people succumbed to the spiritual assault, their faces taking on the terrible peace that marked those who had surrendered the burden of choice for the beautiful simplicity of serving optimal purposes. But others resisted, drawing strength from proximity to the sacred flame and from each other's determination to remain themselves despite the cost.

"Form circles," Neassa commanded with authority that carried both political legitimacy and spiritual power. "Link hands around the fire, share strength, prove that conscious choice becomes stronger when freely shared rather than imposed through force."

***

The response came slowly at first, then with growing determination as people recognized the nature of what they faced. Hand found hand around the great fire's perimeter, forming human chains that served as both spiritual defense and symbol of what they chose to preserve—connection freely given, strength shared rather than hoarded, love that justified existence despite the certainty of loss.

But even as Tara's defenders rallied around their sacred flame, the scope of their enemies' coordination became terrifyingly clear. From every direction came reports of simultaneous assault—not just on Tara, but on every site that might anchor resistance to the great working. Sacred groves falling silent, stone circles losing their voice, holy wells reflecting nothing but emptiness despite the light of Samhain fires.

"Island-wide assault," Cú Chulainn announced with divine insight that pierced beyond immediate observation to strategic recognition. "Every sacred site attacked simultaneously, every center of resistance drained of power and fed into one massive working designed to eliminate consciousness itself across all of Ireland."

"When?" Cathair demanded, understanding that knowing the enemy's timeline might provide their only chance of meaningful resistance.

"Now," Ríona replied with certainty that transcended normal perception. "The great working reaches culmination with midnight's approach, when Samhain's power peaks and the veil grows thin enough to permit spiritual force that could reshape reality itself."

Through the darkness beyond Tara's defenses came the sound of approaching armies—not the chaotic noise of mortal forces but the whispered coordination of beings who moved with perfect efficiency, no wasted motion, no individual preference to disrupt optimal outcomes. The converted approached their target with mechanical precision that served purposes entirely divorced from human welfare.

* * *

It was in this moment of maximum distraction, as all eyes turned outward to face the approaching spiritual and physical assault, that the true danger struck from within.

Fergal of the Mountain Clans had stood with the other representatives around the great fire, his weathered face showing the strain of someone witnessing forces beyond normal comprehension. But as the spiritual pressure intensified and attention focused on external threats, something shifted in his expression—not the terrible peace of full conversion, but the focused intent of someone serving a purpose hidden beneath surface loyalty.

He moved with the careful precision of a hunter approaching prey, his steps masked by the confusion and growing panic around the fire. In his hand, barely visible in the dancing shadows, gleamed a blade that seemed to drink light rather than reflect it— not Celtic iron, but something else entirely, metal that belonged to no forge touched by mortal fire.

Neassa felt the danger an instant before it struck, her priestess training reading spiritual disturbance that had nothing to do with the distant working. She turned toward the threat just as Fergal lunged, his blade aimed with deadly precision at Cathair's unprotected back.

"Behind you!" she cried, throwing herself between assassin and target without thought for personal safety.

The blade that should have found Cathair's heart instead pierced her shoulder, otherworldly metal sliding between bones with unnatural ease. But the wound was wrong—not just the pain of torn flesh, but something deeper, a spiritual violation that sought to drain meaning from her very existence. She felt consciousness wavering as the alien metal worked its purpose, designed not just to kill but to sever connection to everything that made life worthwhile.

Cathair spun with movements that showed why bloodline carriers had survived when others fell, his hands moving in patterns that seemed to pull power from sources deeper than conscious knowledge. The spiral magic that flowed from his touch struck Fergal with force that sent the assassin reeling backward, but not before the damage was done.

"Neassa!" Cathair caught her as she stumbled, the otherworldly blade still protruding from her shoulder like a wound in reality itself. Around them, chaos erupted as guards realized their rulers were under direct attack while simultaneously facing spiritual assault from multiple directions.

***

Boudica moved with the deadly precision of someone who had learned warfare through catastrophic loss, her blade finding the assassin's throat before he could strike again. Fergal collapsed with a sound like escaping air, his form beginning to blur around the edges as whatever power had sent him sought to retrieve its tool.

"Not Fergal," Ríona gasped as her divine sight read the truth that mortal perception missed. "Something wearing his shape, sent through the thinning veil to strike when our attention was divided. The blade—it's not meant just to kill, but to sever spiritual connection entirely."

The understanding hit them like a physical blow. Not just assassination, but spiritual murder designed to eliminate Neassa's connection to the sacred network, to transform Ireland's newly crowned High Queen into another Hollowed agent serving optimal purposes. The wound in her shoulder pulsed with alien energy that sought to drain meaning from her existence, to replace love with efficiency, choice with beautiful certainty.

"Get it out," she whispered through gritted teeth, understanding instinctively that every moment the blade remained would weaken her resistance to whatever spiritual poison it carried. "Before the corruption spreads beyond reversal."

But the otherworldly metal had been designed to resist removal, barbs of spiritual energy that tightened with each attempt to withdraw the weapon. Around them, the great fire blazed higher as if responding to the violation of its protection, but even sacred flame could not immediately counter metal forged in realms where different laws governed substance and meaning.

Ríona placed her hands around the blade with movements that drew on her divine transformation, silver scars blazing with otherworldly light as immortal power grappled with forces that sought to unmake what the goddesses had blessed. The struggle was visible, streams of silver and shadow writhing around the wound like serpents of opposing purpose.

"Hold fast," she commanded, her voice carrying harmonics that belonged to no mortal throat. "Hold to what you are, what you choose to remain. Let consciousness choose consciousness despite the pain."

The blade came free with a sound like reality tearing, otherworldly metal dissolving into shadows that fled toward the edges of firelight as if unable to maintain cohesion when removed from flesh. But the wound it left behind continued to pulse with alien energy, spiritual corruption that sought to transform Neassa's very nature from within.

Meanwhile, the thing wearing Fergal's shape convulsed as Boudica's blade found its mark, human appearance melting away to reveal something that belonged to no realm where life flourished. It had moved with the mechanical precision of a tool rather than a being, its purpose accomplished regardless of whether it survived the aftermath.

*****

The creature dissolved into shadow and silence under Boudica's experienced strike, but its mission had already succeeded—Ireland's High Queen wounded by weapons designed to destroy the spiritual foundation of resistance itself.

"How long do I have?" Neassa asked with the directness of someone who understood that false comfort served no purpose when facing existential threat.

"The corruption spreads slowly," Ríona replied with honesty that carried its own form of mercy. "Hours, perhaps until dawn. But without intervention..." She paused, consulting divine sources that whispered warnings about spiritual wounds too deep for normal healing. "The blade was designed to sever connection to sacred memory, to replace consciousness with beautiful emptiness. Fight it, and the pain will be unbearable. Surrender, and the agony ends in perfect peace."

"Then I fight," Neassa said with quiet certainty, understanding settling in her voice like recognition of choices that defined the very nature of what they sought to preserve. "I choose consciousness despite the cost, meaning despite the pain, love despite the certainty that love carries the seeds of loss."

Around them, the battle for Ireland's survival continued on multiple fronts—physical armies approaching through darkness, spiritual assault draining power from the sacred network, and now the immediate crisis of their leadership crippled at the moment of greatest need. But in Neassa's choice to resist the beautiful peace offered by surrender, something shifted in the spiritual atmosphere around Tara.

"The fire," Síle breathed with wonder, pointing toward the great Samhain flame that suddenly blazed with radiance belonging to no natural combustion. "It's responding to her choice, drawing power from the very decision to remain conscious despite the cost."

The sacred flame that had served as protection and symbol now became something more—a beacon visible across realms both mortal and divine, announcing to whatever powers watched that Ireland's rulers chose meaning over emptiness, consciousness over the beautiful peace of surrender. In that choice, the tide of spiritual battle began to shift.

"How long until midnight?" Síle asked with youth's desperate need for concrete hope in circumstances that offered only abstract possibility.

"Two hours," Cathair replied, consulting knowledge that came from years of tracking celestial timing while supporting his wounded queen. "Two hours to resist spiritual assault that draws power from across the entire island, to defend against armies that feel no fear or doubt, to prove that consciousness deserves to survive when forces beyond our understanding offer peace through its elimination."

"Then we hold for two hours," he declared with finality that brooked no discussion of alternatives, his arm supporting Neassa as spiritual poison warred with her determination to remain herself. "We prove that conscious choice creates bonds strong enough to resist any force that seeks to break them, that love justifies the chaos it creates, that Ireland chooses to remain Irish no matter what beautiful emptiness our enemies offer as replacement."

The great fire blazed higher as if responding to their determination, flames reaching toward stars that watched with interest belonging to powers both ancient and eternal. Around its warmth, the people of Ireland prepared to discover whether celebration could serve as weapon, whether joy proved stronger than efficiency, whether consciousness itself possessed sufficient strength to defend against the ultimate assault on meaning.

But now their resistance carried additional weight—their queen wounded but unbroken, their unity tested by assassination but proven through the choice to stand together despite the cost. In Neassa's refusal to surrender to spiritual corruption, they had found a symbol of what they fought to preserve: the terrible wonderful burden of choosing consciousness despite every pressure to accept beautiful emptiness as preferable to difficult meaning.

Midnight approached like destiny made manifest in temporal form, and with it would come the test that would determine whether the songs would remember their choice as salvation or noble failure worthy of legend. But whatever the outcome, they would meet it as themselves—free, conscious, choosing meaning over emptiness despite the certainty of cost.

The darkness gathered, the wound pulsed with alien purpose, but the fire burned on, and around its light, Ireland chose to remain Ireland regardless of what forces sought to optimize that choice away.

CHAPTER 23

THE WOUNDED CROWN

The great fire of Samhain blazed with otherworldly radiance as Ríona worked over Neassa's wound, her silver scars pulsing in rhythm with energies that belonged to no mortal healing. Around them, the celebration had transformed into something between festival and war council, people maintaining the sacred circle while guards took defensive positions that turned joy into fortress without abandoning its essential nature.

Neassa lay propped against Cathair's chest, her face pale but her eyes burning with the fierce determination of someone who had chosen consciousness despite the price. The wound in her shoulder continued to pulse with unnatural energy, spiritual corruption that sought to replace meaning with beautiful emptiness, love with optimal efficiency.

"The blade was designed to work slowly," Ríona said quietly, her voice carrying the weight of divine certainty mixed with mortal sorrow. "Not quick death, but gradual conversion. Each pulse weakens resistance to the beautiful peace of surrender."

"How long?" Cathair asked, though his voice carried the steady strength of someone who would face whatever answer came.

"Until dawn, perhaps longer," Ríona replied with honesty that transcended false comfort. "But the corruption fights against her nature with every heartbeat. The pain will worsen as her spirit resists what the wound tries to impose."

Through the darkness beyond Tara's immediate defenses came the sounds of approaching armies—not the chaotic noise of mortal forces but the whispered coordination of beings who moved with mechanical precision, no wasted motion, no individual preference to disrupt optimal outcomes. The converted approached their target while Ireland's newly crowned queen fought a different battle against spiritual annihilation.

* * *

"I can hear them," Neassa whispered, her voice carrying undertones that belonged to no natural perception. "The Hollowed. They're singing—not with voices, but with the absence of everything that makes voices worth hearing. Beautiful silence where music used to live."

Boudica moved to the circle's edge where she could observe the approaching threat while remaining close enough to protect the wounded queen. Her blade still carried traces of shadow from the assassin's blood, otherworldly stains that seemed to drink light rather than reflect it.

"Conventional forces mixed with converted," she reported with military precision that barely contained her alarm at enemy capabilities that transcended normal warfare. "Perhaps three thousand total, but they move without regard for terrain or defensive advantages. Perfect coordination that serves purposes beyond individual survival or tactical necessity."

Cú Chulainn's divine heritage allowed him to read patterns that stretched beyond immediate observation to recognize strategic implications that mortal understanding could barely encompass.

"They don't expect to take Tara through siege or assault. This is distraction, designed to occupy our attention while the great working reaches completion elsewhere."

"Then why the assassination attempt?" Síle asked, though her young voice carried recognition of truth that transcended intellectual understanding.

"Because leadership matters," Cathair said quietly, his hand finding Neassa's with touch that anchored them both despite the magnitude of what approached. "Convert Ireland's High Queen, and resistance becomes not just difficult but literally unthinkable. The assassination was meant to create a converted leader who would order surrender from within."

Around the great fire, the people of Ireland maintained their celebration despite the approaching danger, voices raised in songs that grew stronger rather than weaker as external pressure mounted. Hand linked to hand in chains of conscious connection, strength shared rather than hoarded, love that justified existence despite the certainty of loss.

"They're afraid," Neassa said suddenly, her voice carrying wonder despite the pain that wracked her form with each pulse of alien energy. "I can feel it through the wound—not fear as we understand it, but something deeper. The recognition that what we've created here threatens everything they believe about the necessity of emptiness."

Ríona's divine sight pierced beyond the immediate battle to read currents that flowed across the entire island, spiritual geography made visible through otherworldly perception. What she saw there made her silver scars flare with alarm that transcended mere tactical concern.

"The great working," she gasped, sudden understanding flooding her voice. "It's not just draining power from corrupted sites—it's drawing energy from the resistance itself. Every act of defiance, every choice to remain conscious, feeds into their ritual through connections we cannot see or sever."

"You mean fighting them makes them stronger?" Boudica demanded, her warrior's instincts recoiling from tactical impossibility.

"Fighting them the old way makes them stronger," Ríona corrected with divine insight that read the deeper patterns of spiritual warfare. "Resistance based on opposing their force with our own simply provides more energy for the working. But conscious choice—deliberate selection of meaning over emptiness—that disrupts their ability to channel what they steal."

The understanding rippled through their small group like recognition of truth that changed everything they thought they knew about the nature of their struggle. Not just military defense or spiritual resistance, but something entirely different—the creation of meaning so authentic that it could not be corrupted, love so genuine that it resisted conversion to efficient purpose.

***

"The celebration," Cathair said, realization striking him with the force of divine revelation. "That's why the fire burns brighter as the attack intensifies. It's not consuming what they send against us—it's transforming it into something they cannot use."

Around the sacred flame, the people of Ireland continued their Samhain festival with voices that carried across the thinning veil between worlds. Children still danced with laughter pure as silver bells, elders still shared stories that wove past and present into patterns of meaning, families still honored both living and dead through conscious choice to remember rather than forget.

"But the wound," Neassa said quietly, her voice carrying the strain of someone fighting battles on multiple fronts simultaneously. "The corruption it carries—it's designed to poison that very authenticity. To make me doubt whether consciousness is worth its cost, whether love justifies the chaos it creates."

The unnatural energy pulsed stronger as if responding to her recognition, spiritual pressure that sought to convince her that surrender would bring blessed relief from responsibility, beautiful peace through elimination of the burden of choice. In the otherworldly poison's seductive whisper, she could hear the promise of efficiency, optimal outcomes achieved through surrender of individual will.

"Then we prove them wrong," Cathair said with quiet intensity that drew strength from crisis rather than being weakened by it. "We demonstrate that consciousness chooses consciousness not because it's easy, but because it creates beauty worth preserving despite the cost."

He began to sing—not the formal chants of ceremony, but the simple lullaby his mother had sung when storms frightened him as a child. His voice carried across the circle with warmth that belonged to no formal authority, personal memory transformed into shared strength.

One by one, others joined their voices to his—not in perfect harmony, but in the gloriously chaotic symphony of individual will choosing collective purpose. Síle's young soprano weaving through Boudica's surprisingly melodic alto, Cú Chulainn's divine heritage lending otherworldly harmonics to mortal melodies, Ríona's transformed nature allowing her voice to carry across realms both visible and hidden.

The song that emerged had never been sung before and would never be sung again—spontaneous creation born from the choice to find beauty in darkness, meaning in chaos, love in the shadow of inevitable loss. It carried no words that formal language could capture, but its meaning reached every heart that chose to remain open to connection despite the risk of pain.

The effect on Neassa's wound was immediate and profound. Where the unnatural corruption had sought to replace consciousness with emptiness, the shared song created patterns of meaning too complex for simple negation. The otherworldly poison fought against authenticity it could not convert, spiritual pressure meeting resistance that grew stronger through conscious choice rather than weaker through opposition.

"It's working," Ríona breathed, wonder growing in her voice as divine perception read transformation that exceeded her most optimistic projections. "The singing—it's not healing the damage, but transforming it into something their weapon was never designed to affect."

"How?" Boudica asked with practical urgency, her warrior's mind already calculating how such knowledge might serve their larger defense.

"The blade was forged to eliminate individual will through spiritual severance," Ríona explained, her divine sight reading the true nature of otherworldly corruption. "But when individual will chooses collective purpose freely—when consciousness serves something larger than personal comfort—the severance becomes impossible. Connection multiplies rather than divides."

Around the great fire, the celebration continued with voices raised in defiance of everything their enemies represented. Not organized resistance or formal ceremony, but spontaneous choice to find joy in darkness, hope in uncertainty, love in the shadow of forces that promised peace through surrender of everything that made peace worthwhile.

The approaching armies reached Tara's outer defenses as the song reached its crescendo, converted warriors moving with mechanical precision against earthworks that hummed with accumulated blessing. But where they expected to find panicked defenders or organized military resistance, they found something their programming had not prepared them to counter—a celebration that transformed attack into affirmation, assault into opportunity for deeper connection.

"They don't understand," Neassa said, growing wonder replacing the strain that had marked her voice throughout the long night of spiritual siege. "Their entire strategy depends on fear, despair, the exhaustion that comes from fighting forces too large for individual resistance. But we're not fighting—we're choosing."

"Choosing what?" Síle asked, though her young voice carried recognition of truth that transcended intellectual understanding.

"Choosing ourselves," Cathair replied with authority that had been tested through trial and emerged stronger rather than brittle. "Choosing consciousness despite its cost, meaning despite its chaos, love despite the certainty that love carries the seeds of loss."

The great working that had been building across Ireland's corrupted sites faltered as the energy it sought to drain was transformed into something it could not use. Not opposition that could be overcome through superior force, but conscious choice that created meaning immune to systematic negation.

Through her divine sight, Ríona read the confusion spreading through enemy ranks as their spiritual weapons encountered resistance they had no protocols to address. The Hollowed moved with perfect efficiency when facing traditional opposition, but celebration that served no military purpose left them without guidance for optimal response.

"Hold the song," she commanded with divine authority that cut through the growing chaos. "Whatever comes—physical assault, spiritual pressure, the temptation to despair—hold to the choice we've made to remain ourselves despite the cost."

The battle for Ireland's survival was entering its most crucial phase, but it would be decided not by sword and spear, but by the simple question of whether consciousness possessed sufficient strength to choose consciousness when offered beautiful alternatives that promised peace through surrender of everything that made peace worthwhile.

Around the sacred fire, eight hundred voices rose in harmony that had never existed before and would never exist again, proving that some songs could only be sung by hearts that chose love over emptiness, meaning over efficiency, the terrible wonderful burden of remaining themselves no matter what forces sought to optimize that choice away.

The wound in Neassa's shoulder still pulsed with unnatural purpose, but now it fought against something stronger than individual resistance—the collective choice of an entire people to remain themselves despite every pressure to surrender, to find beauty in chaos rather than accepting the beautiful emptiness that promised peace through spiritual death.

Midnight approached with the weight of destiny made manifest in temporal form, but Ireland would meet it singing.

CHAPTER 24

The Midnight Hour

The converted armies reached Tara's earthworks as the stars wheeled toward their midnight positions, three thousand warriors moving with mechanical precision against defenses that hummed with accumulated blessing. But where they expected to encounter panicked defenders or organized military resistance, they found something their programming had never prepared them to counter—celebration that transformed into weapon, joy that served as shield, conscious choice that created meaning immune to systematic negation.

The great Samhain fire blazed at the hill's crown like a beacon visible across realms both mortal and divine, eight hundred voices raised in harmony around its light while the approaching emptiness pressed against their circle with spiritual pressure designed to drain meaning from existence itself. But the song held, growing stronger as external forces sought to silence it, proving that some connections could not be severed when forged through conscious choice rather than imposed through compulsion.

Neassa felt the unnatural corruption in her wound pulse in rhythm with whatever great working drew power from across Ireland's corrupted sites, each throb an attempt to convince her that surrender would bring blessed relief from the terrible burden of caring about outcomes beyond personal comfort. But around her, the voices of her people rose in defiance of everything the wound represented—not organized resistance, but spontaneous affirmation of consciousness despite its cost.

"They're faltering," Ríona announced, her divine sight-reading confusion that rippled through enemy ranks as their spiritual weapons encountered resistance they had no protocols to address. "The Hollowed move with perfect efficiency when facing traditional opposition, but celebration that serves no military purpose leaves them without guidance."

Through the darkness beyond the fire's light came sounds that belonged to no natural approach—not the chaos of battle, but the whispered coordination of beings seeking optimal outcomes through elimination of individual will. Yet their advance had slowed, mechanical precision disrupted by the simple fact that their targets refused to behave like enemies requiring conquest.

Cú Chulainn stood at the circle's edge where firelight met shadow, his divine weapons singing with harmonics that carried across the battlefield like challenge issued to forces that sought to eliminate the very possibility of challenge. His father's heritage allowed him to read patterns that stretched beyond immediate observation, spiritual currents that flowed between realms where different forms of authority held sway.

"Something comes," he said suddenly, his voice cutting through the celebration with authority that commanded immediate attention. "Not from the corrupted armies, but from elsewhere. Powers that have watched our choice and found it worthy of aid that transcends mortal understanding."

As if summoned by his recognition, mist began to gather at the battlefield's edges despite the clear night sky. Not natural fog, but otherworldly presence that carried itself with the deliberate grace of those who moved between realms at will rather than necessity. The very air seemed to thicken with potential as boundaries dissolved between the world of the living and domains where different laws governed existence.

***

"The Wild Hunt," Boudica breathed, recognition dawning in her voice as she witnessed something no mortal warrior had seen in generations beyond counting. "Lord Midir kept his word."

The riders who emerged from the mist moved with fluid grace that spoke of realms where different forms of beauty held meaning, their mounts neither fully horse nor creature of any single world. Lord Midir led them with bearing that commanded recognition across species and realms, his presence lending weight to alliance that transcended the boundaries between possible and impossible.

Behind him rode the Sidhe in numbers that defied counting—not because they were infinite, but because mortal perception struggled to contain beings whose very existence challenged assumptions about the nature of reality. Some bore weapons that sang with their own inner light, while others carried instruments that could weave music into patterns capable of reshaping the fundamental structure of meaning itself.

"People of Ireland," Lord Midir called, his voice carrying across the battlefield with harmonics that belonged to courts where different forms of authority held sway. "The Sidhe ride tonight for those who prove that consciousness can choose consciousness despite every pressure to surrender. Your celebration has been heard in realms where different forms of courage are valued."

The effect on the converted armies was immediate and profound. Warriors who had moved with perfect coordination suddenly faltered, their programming offering no guidance for confronting forces that operated beyond the categories of resistance they had been designed to counter. The spiritual pressure that had sought to drain meaning from Tara's defenses suddenly found itself opposed by powers that drew strength from sources the great working could not access or corrupt.

"They cannot touch us," Ríona realized, wonder growing in her voice as her divine sight read the true nature of what transpired. "The Sidhe exist in realms where consciousness and meaning are foundational rather than optional. The Hollowed corruption simply has no power over beings whose very existence proves that awareness creates beauty rather than suffering."

Around the great fire, the people of Ireland watched in awe as legend made manifest took the field in defense of choices they had made without knowing such defense was possible. Children pointed with delight at riders whose steeds left trails of starlight in their wake, while elders wept to witness powers they had only known through stories their grandmothers had whispered beside winter hearths.

But even as supernatural allies joined the battle, the great working that had been building across Ireland's corrupted sites reached its crucial phase. Midnight approached with the weight of destiny made manifest in temporal form, and with it would come the final test of whether consciousness possessed sufficient strength to defend itself when offered beautiful alternatives that promised peace through surrender of everything that made peace worthwhile.

***

"Now," Neassa said suddenly, the unnatural corruption in her wound writhing as forces beyond normal comprehension prepared for their culminating stroke. "Whatever they've planned, it happens now. I can feel it building—not just power, but purpose. The systematic elimination of choice itself across every heart that beats between Ireland's shores."

The spiritual assault that erupted from corrupted sites across the island hit Tara's defenses like a tide of beautiful emptiness designed to convince every conscious being that individual will was nothing but unnecessary suffering. Not force applied against resistance, but seduction that promised relief from the terrible burden of caring about outcomes beyond personal comfort.

The great working manifested as something beyond normal perception—not darkness visible, but absence that sought to fill itself with whatever meaning it encountered. It flowed across the landscape like fog that drained color from everything it touched, leaving behind not destruction but beautiful simplicity where complex consciousness had once struggled with the challenge of existence.

"Hold!" Cathair commanded, his voice carrying authority earned through trial rather than inherited through blood. Around the sacred fire, eight hundred people felt the pull of emptiness that promised to end all uncertainty, all responsibility, all pain that came from caring about others despite the certainty of loss.

Some wavered, their voices faltering as spiritual pressure convinced them that surrender would bring the peace they had never known they wanted. But others held firm, drawing strength from connections that had been freely chosen rather than imposed through compulsion. Hand linked to hand in chains of conscious purpose, they proved that some bonds grew stronger when tested rather than weaker when pressured.

The Wild Hunt charged through the great working's manifestation with weapons that cut not flesh but the very concept of spiritual severance, their assault disrupting patterns of emptiness that had taken months to weave across Ireland's sacred sites. Where Sidhe power touched the corruption, meaning reasserted itself like flowers blooming in ground that had seemed forever barren.

"It's working," Síle cried, her young voice carrying wonder at witnessing impossibility made manifest through conscious choice. "The emptiness is retreating—not defeated, but confused by resistance it cannot categorize."

But the First Severed had prepared for exactly such intervention, his spiritual wound growing deeper as he fed it power drawn from every corrupted site across the island. The great working adapted to supernatural opposition with mechanical efficiency, seeking not to overcome the Wild Hunt but to drain the very concepts that gave their existence meaning.

"He's trying to sever them from their own nature," Ríona realized with horror that transcended immediate tactical concern. "The First Severed doesn't just attack consciousness—he attacks the fundamental patterns that allow consciousness to create meaning, love to generate purpose, choice to produce consequences that matter beyond immediate convenience."

The implication hung in the night air like recognition of possibilities too terrible for comfortable contemplation. Not just Ireland's spiritual death, but the elimination of consciousness as a viable form of existence, proof that emptiness was more efficient than awareness, that meaning was nothing but unnecessary suffering inflicted by beings too proud to accept optimal solutions.

Through her wound, Neassa felt the moment approaching when choice itself would face its ultimate test—not between different options, but between the right to choose and the beautiful peace of having all choices made by forces wiser than individual will. The corruption pulsed stronger, seeking to convince her that leadership was nothing but pride, that love was merely inefficient attachment, that consciousness itself was disease requiring cure.

"No," she said quietly, the word carrying more weight than armies or accumulated power. Around her, eight hundred voices rose in support of that simple negation, proving that some refusals created more strength than any acceptance of beautiful alternatives.

The great working reached its crescendo as midnight struck across Ireland's ancient sites, spiritual force that should have eliminated consciousness itself instead encountering resistance that multiplied rather than diminished when pressured. Not opposition that could be overcome through superior force, but conscious choice that created meaning immune to systematic negation.

The tide began to turn not through victory or defeat, but through transformation that changed the very nature of what had been attempted. Where emptiness had sought to drain meaning, it instead encountered abundance that could not be exhausted. Where severance had tried to break connections, it found bonds that grew stronger through testing.

In the moment of midnight's culmination, when the veil between worlds grew thin enough to permit passage of powers that normally remained separate from mortal concerns, Ireland chose consciousness over emptiness, meaning over efficiency, love over the beautiful peace of surrender. The choice echoed across realms both visible and hidden, announcing to whatever forces watched that some forms of awareness would endure regardless of what alternatives they were offered.

The great Samhain fire blazed with radiance that belonged to no mortal combustion, flames reaching toward stars that bore witness to choices freely made and consciously maintained. Around its light, the people of Ireland discovered that celebration could serve as weapon, that joy proved stronger than efficiency, that consciousness itself possessed strength sufficient to defend against the ultimate assault on meaning.

The midnight hour had passed, and Ireland remained Ireland despite every force that had sought to optimize that choice away.

CHAPTER 25

THE DAWN BREAKING

The great working's collapse rippled across Ireland like a wave breaking against shores that had learned to bend rather than shatter, spiritual pressure that had sought to eliminate consciousness itself dissolving into confusion as the fundamental assumptions underlying its power proved inadequate to contemporary reality. Where emptiness had promised beautiful simplicity, it instead encountered complexity that multiplied rather than diminished when tested by forces that sought to optimize choice away.

Around Tara's sacred fire, eight hundred voices gradually fell silent as the immediate crisis passed, not from exhaustion but from wonder at what they had accomplished together through conscious choice made manifest in celebration that transcended mere ceremony. The great working that should have eliminated consciousness across all of Ireland lay in ruins, shattered by the simple refusal to surrender meaning for efficiency, love for emptiness, individual will for collective optimization.

Neassa felt the unnatural corruption in her wound writhe and dissolve like ice touched by spring sun, otherworldly poison unable to maintain coherence when the spiritual foundation supporting it crumbled across multiple realms of existence. The pain that had threatened to convince her that surrender would bring blessed relief faded into memory, leaving behind not emptiness but deeper appreciation for consciousness that had chosen to remain conscious despite every pressure to accept beautiful alternatives.

"It's over," she said quietly, wonder replacing the strain that had marked her voice throughout the long night of spiritual siege. Around her, people who had linked hands in defiance of systematic assault began to realize that their choice had somehow proved stronger than forces designed to eliminate the very possibility of choice.

But as reports arrived with the first light of dawn, the scope of their victory became clear through intelligence that painted a picture of Ireland forever changed by the night's events. Not just political triumph or military success, but spiritual transformation that would reshape the fundamental nature of consciousness across an entire island.

"The corrupted sites sing again," announced the first messenger to reach Tara with dawn, his voice carrying amazement that transcended mere relief at witnessing survival. "Not just silent—active, powerful, connected through bonds stronger than what existed before the assault began. It's as if the great working's failure reversed every violation, healed every wound, restored every connection that systematic corruption had severed."

Ríona's divine sight confirmed what mortal perception suggested, reading spiritual currents that flowed with renewed strength across the sacred network that bound Ireland's mystical landscape together. "The enemy's failure created opportunities for evolution rather than simple restoration," she announced with wonder growing in her voice. "Ireland's spiritual infrastructure now supports forms of consciousness that were impossible before the crisis forced adaptation."

"And the people?" Cathair asked, understanding that political implications would ultimately matter more than mystical ones for the day-to-day governance of a nation that had chosen consciousness over efficiency through trial that tested every assumption about the nature of authority.

"Changed," replied messenger after messenger, each bearing similar reports from territories across the island. "Not converted back—that's not how such transformations work—but awakened to the reality of what they almost surrendered. Many weep to remember how close they came to choosing beautiful emptiness over difficult meaning."

King Conchobor of Ulster rose from where he had maintained vigil throughout the night, his weathered features showing relief that went deeper than mere survival. "Then we have not just defended what existed, but created something new. Ireland that chooses consciousness has become Ireland that understands the cost of such choice—and finds that cost acceptable rather than unbearable."

***

The Wild Hunt prepared for departure as morning painted the eastern sky in shades of gold and crimson, their presence in the mortal realm having served its purpose. Lord Midir approached where Ireland's proven rulers stood together, his otherworldly bearing somehow more approachable now that the crisis had passed successfully.

"The alliance we forged will endure," he said formally, his voice carrying harmonics that belonged to courts where different forms of authority held meaning. "The Sidhe recognize strength that proves itself through trial rather than inheritance. When next consciousness faces systematic assault—and it will, for such conflicts echo across realms where different forms of meaning compete—Ireland need not stand alone."

As the Sidhe lord prepared to depart, his expression grew more solemn, carrying weight that spoke to recognition extending far beyond immediate gratitude. "But know this—what you accomplished here represents more than Ireland's survival. You have proven that consciousness itself possesses strength sufficient to resist the ultimate seduction of emptiness. That proof will matter in conflicts yet to come, when other people's face choices between meaning and efficiency, love and the beautiful peace of surrender."

The implications settled over the assembled leaders like recognition of historical significance that transcended immediate celebration. Not just national survival, but demonstration that alternatives to systematic optimization remained possible when consciousness chose to defend itself rather than surrendering to forces that promised peace through elimination of everything that made peace worth having.

"The corrupted who survive," Boudica observed with practical concern that cut through supernatural wonder to immediate necessity, "they're not all dead or magically restored to normal consciousness. Some will retain their emptiness while no longer being coordinated by systematic purpose. They'll need help learning how to want things again."

"And Queen Medb?" Neassa asked, understanding that their victory remained incomplete as long as major political leaders retained allegiance to purposes that viewed consciousness as inefficiency requiring correction.

"Fled," reported scouts who had observed the withdrawal of forces that had approached Tara with mechanical precision. "Her armies retreated during the great working's collapse, but in order rather than chaos. Strategic withdrawal by those who recognize that current circumstances no longer favor their objectives."

"She'll adapt," Cathair predicted with certainty earned through understanding enemies whose sophistication had exceeded their initial estimates. "Find new methods, different approaches to achieving what spiritual corruption failed to accomplish. But she'll be operating from weakness rather than strength, having lost the supernatural coordination that made her forces invincible."

Cú Chulainn's divine heritage provided perspective that transcended immediate tactical concerns. "My father whispers that the real victory lies not in defeating enemies, but in proving alternatives possible. Ireland has demonstrated that consciousness can choose consciousness despite its cost—and that demonstration echoes across realms where different forms of meaning compete for legitimacy."

As the morning progressed and celebration built throughout Tara's sacred grounds, the true scope of transformation became apparent through reports that arrived from every corner of the island. Not just military victory or political triumph, but fundamental alteration of what it meant to be Irish when being Irish required conscious choice rather than inherited tradition.

"The network responds to conscious decision," Ríona announced as her divine sight-read patterns that stretched across multiple realms of existence. "Each choice to remain conscious strengthens connections that bind the spiritual infrastructure together. Ireland has become something unprecedented—a nation where consciousness and governance integrate through forms never before attempted."

***

"What comes next?" asked Síle with youth's eagerness to translate victory into lasting change that would serve generations yet unborn.

"We prove worthy of what we've been given," Neassa replied, looking around the circle of people who had chosen consciousness despite every pressure to surrender. "We demonstrate that consciousness can create forms of beauty adequate to justify its cost, that meaning emerges from chaos rather than requiring elimination of complexity."

"We build," Cathair added with quiet certainty that carried authority earned through trial. "We create communities that honor both individual will and collective purpose, forms of governance that serve consciousness rather than optimizing it away. We prove that the choice we made serves not just survival but flourishing."

The celebration that continued throughout the day carried weight beyond mere relief at crisis passed. People gathered from across Ireland's free territories to witness what their choice had accomplished, to understand what their resistance had preserved, to begin the work of building a future worthy of the prices they had paid to make it possible.

As sunset approached and the great Samhain fire was rekindled—not for protection against approaching darkness, but in celebration of light that had proven stronger than the beautiful emptiness that promised peace through surrender—Neassa and Cathair stood together at the platform's edge where the Lia Fáil had once provided divine judgment.

"We did it," she said with wonder that spoke to accomplishing something that had seemed impossible when they began.

"We chose it," he corrected gently. "We chose consciousness over emptiness, meaning over efficiency, love over the beautiful peace that eliminates the capacity for love. And we proved that such choices create strength rather than weakness when they serve purposes larger than individual comfort."

Around them, Ireland celebrated not just survival but transformation—the birth of a nation that had consciously chosen to remain itself despite every pressure to become something more efficient. The songs that rose from the gathering carried new melodies, stories that would be told for generations about the night when consciousness faced its ultimate test and chose to remain conscious despite the cost.

The great fire blazed higher as evening stars appeared overhead, flames reaching toward ancient lights that had witnessed the rise and fall of empires, the birth and death of peoples, the eternal struggle between meaning and emptiness that defined existence itself. But tonight, those stars looked down on something unprecedented—a people who had faced the ultimate seduction of surrender and chosen the harder path of remaining themselves.

"What we've built will echo through legend," Boudica observed with satisfaction that spoke to strategy vindicated through results that transcended mere military victory.

"What we've built will echo through choice," Neassa corrected with understanding that went deeper than historical significance. "Every day that people wake up and choose consciousness over emptiness, meaning over efficiency, love over the peace that eliminates the capacity for caring—that's when our victory proves itself real rather than temporary."

As the celebration continued into the night, representatives began to disperse toward territories that would now serve as laboratories for proving that consciousness could create forms of governance adequate to preserve consciousness itself. The immediate crisis was over, but the real work was just beginning— demonstrating that their choice served not just resistance but construction of alternatives that honored both individual will and collective welfare.

The dawn had broken not just over Ireland but over possibilities that stretched across realms where different forms of meaning competed for the right to exist. Consciousness had chosen consciousness, love had justified the chaos it created, and partnership had proven strong enough to bear the weight of defending meaning itself when meaning faced systematic assault.

Ireland had proven that some things were worth preserving regardless of their cost, that some forms of strength multiplied rather than diminished when shared, that consciousness itself possessed adequate power to defend against forces that promised beautiful peace through surrender of everything that made peace, beauty, or recognition of their value possible.

The real test now was whether such proof could endure through the daily work of building a future worthy of the prices they had paid to preserve the right to build it according to their own conscious choices rather than optimal algorithms designed by forces that viewed choice itself as inefficiency requiring correction.

But that test belonged to tomorrow's choices. Tonight, Ireland celebrated what conscious choice could accomplish when it refused to surrender meaning despite every seductive offer of efficiency that promised peace through elimination of the terrible, wonderful burden of caring about each other despite the certainty that caring created vulnerability to loss.

The dawn had broken, consciousness had triumphed, and Ireland prepared to discover what victory looked like when measured not in enemies defeated but in communities built, not in power accumulated but in meaning shared, not in problems solved but in choices consciously made despite the certainty that every choice carried consequences beyond individual control.

The songs would remember this night forever, but the choices that gave those songs meaning would have to be made again with every dawn that followed.

CHAPTER 26

THE PRICE OF VICTORY

Six weeks after Samhain's triumph, the first refugees appeared on Tara's horizon like a slow-moving tide of human misery that would reshape everything Ireland's victory had seemed to accomplish. They came not as enemies or conquerors, but as the walking wounded of consciousness—people who had tasted the beautiful emptiness of surrender and now found the burden of individual choice almost too heavy to bear.

Neassa watched from the great hall's eastern window as another group crested the hill, their movements carrying the uncertain gait of those who had forgotten how to want things for themselves and were slowly, painfully, learning to remember. What should have been Ireland's moment of celebration and rebuilding had become something far more complex as the true cost of their spiritual victory revealed itself in ways none of them had anticipated.

The morning sickness that had plagued her for the past week made her grip the stone windowsill as another wave of nausea passed, though she had told no one yet of what the healers had confirmed just yesterday. The timing seemed impossibly cruel— discovering she carried their child just as everything they had built threatened to crumble under the weight of consequences no one had foreseen.

"They're not recovering," Síle reported, her young voice carrying strain that spoke to days spent helping people who seemed to grow more lost rather than more found with each passing hour. "Some try to make choices for themselves, but the effort exhausts them. Others simply... stop. They sit and wait for someone to tell them what optimal behavior requires."

The practical challenges had proven overwhelming within days of the first arrivals. Former Hollowed retained memories of perfect efficiency, optimal coordination, beautiful peace through surrender of individual will. Asking them to suddenly embrace the chaos of consciousness was like asking people who had lived in perpetual sunlight to navigate by starlight—technically possible, but requiring strength many simply didn't possess.

Cathair approached from where he had been reviewing reports that painted an increasingly dire picture across Ireland's territories. The crown of High King rested easily on his brow now, authority earned through trial rather than inherited through blood, but his face showed the strain of someone discovering that victory created problems as complex as those defeat would have caused.

"How many?" he asked, though his expression suggested he already dreaded the answer.

"Over three thousand so far, with more arriving daily," Síle replied, her shoulders sagging under weight no seventeen-year-old should have to carry. "Families, entire villages, even some who were never fully converted but lived too long under Hollowed influence. They remember efficiency, but they can't remember why they might want anything else."

"Worse than numbers," Boudica observed as she joined them, her warrior's training reading tactical implications in what others might dismiss as humanitarian crisis. "They're becoming a vulnerability. Thousands of people who can't function independently, who remember what perfect order felt like, who grow more desperate for that peace with each day that consciousness fails to provide the relief they expected."

Her strategic mind cut through sympathy to address realities that charitable impulses preferred to ignore. "What happens when they decide that freedom hurts too much? When they begin to actively seek the beautiful emptiness they remember, regardless of what that choice costs everyone else?"

Before anyone could respond to this uncomfortable possibility, Ríona approached with news that transformed concern into crisis. Her divine sight had been monitoring the spiritual transformations across Ireland, and what she had discovered made her silver scars pulse with alarm that transcended mere tactical concern.

***

"The network is destabilizing," she announced, her voice carrying otherworldly certainty that brooked no contradiction. "The enhanced connections we celebrated—they're fragmenting under pressure from too many consciousnesses that can't sustain individual choice. The former Hollowed are unconsciously seeking reconnection to something that can make choices for them."

"What does that mean?" Neassa demanded, understanding that spiritual infrastructure determined everything else about Ireland's survival as a nation that had chosen consciousness over efficiency.

"It means they're creating a new form of spiritual vacuum," Ríona replied with grim certainty that spoke to problems beyond normal categories of solution. "Not the deliberate emptiness of the Hollowed, but desperate hunger for external guidance. And that hunger is beginning to affect others—even those who were never converted feel the pull of surrendering difficult choices to whatever authority promises certainty."

The implications hit their small council like recognition of disaster approaching with inexorable momentum. Not external conquest or political defeat, but internal collapse as the very success of their resistance created conditions that made resistance impossible to maintain.

"The spiritual network is trying to fill the vacuum," Ríona continued, her divine perception reading patterns that stretched across multiple realms of existence. "But instead of enhancing individual choice, it's beginning to create collective consciousness—shared awareness that could evolve into exactly what we fought to prevent."

Through the great windows, they could see the effects spreading through the refugee camps that had grown around Tara's base like a city of the spiritually displaced. Former Hollowed who had struggled with individual choice now moved with renewed coordination, as if responding to signals that transcended normal communication. But their faces showed relief rather than emptiness—gratitude for guidance that felt like salvation rather than subjugation.

"How many have accepted whatever's happening?" Cathair asked, though the answer was visible in the camps below where thousands of people moved with efficiency that eliminated the chaos of conflicting individual preferences.

"Most of them," Síle replied with voice that carried the weight of personal failure. "They describe it as finding perfect balance— individual will preserved but guided by collective wisdom that eliminates the burden of difficult choices. They say it's what they always hoped consciousness could become."

"And our people?" Neassa demanded, meaning those who had never experienced Hollowed conversion but now lived among thousands who had.

"Some are beginning to ask why they should struggle with uncertainty when their neighbors have found peace through accepting guidance," King Conchobor admitted with reluctance that spoke to his recognition of political reality. "Especially the young ones who see former Hollowed functioning better under collective guidance than they managed during the crisis."

The trap's sophistication became apparent as its full scope revealed itself through reports that continued to arrive throughout the morning. Not conquest through force, but seduction through solution to problems their victory had created. Not elimination of consciousness, but transformation of consciousness into something that served different purposes while feeling like personal fulfillment.

Before they could begin to address the crisis that threatened to undo everything they had accomplished, the sound of approaching hoofbeats echoed across the sacred hill. Not the desperate messengers they had grown accustomed to, but coordinated arrival that spoke to planned rather than emergency communication.

***

The riders who arrived in the wake of evening's approach moved with coordination that spoke to careful planning rather than coincidental timing. Seven figures on horseback, their mounts bearing the dust of distant travel but moving with the steady purpose of those who had measured their journey to arrive at exactly this moment.

Neassa watched from the great hall's entrance as the lead rider dismounted with movements that carried both exhaustion and determination. A woman whose bearing spoke of authority earned through trial rather than inherited through blood, her traveling clothes unable to conceal the fighter's build underneath or the way her eyes assessed Tara's defenses with professional interest.

"I am Brigid, lately of the Northern Shores," she announced, inclining her head with respectful but not deferential courtesy. "I bring word of what befalls kingdoms that choose efficiency over choice, order over the sacred chaos of free will."

Behind her, six companions dismounted with similar grace— men and women whose faces bore the particular strain of people who had seen too much and survived to carry warnings that others needed to hear. They moved like warriors, but warriors who had learned caution through defeats that taught harder lessons than victories ever could.

Cathair approached with the natural authority that had begun to emerge despite his careful avoidance of formal leadership. "You're welcome at Tara, Brigid of the Northern Shores. Though I suspect your news carries weight that transcends mere courtesy."

"It does," she replied, her gaze moving across the assembled representatives with calculation that read both strength and weakness in their positioning. "You face enemies whose methods I've encountered before. They don't work through conquest or even corruption; they offer what people genuinely want: relief from responsibility, freedom from the agony of difficult choices."

The expanded council that convened as full darkness fell carried tension that went beyond mere political disagreement. Brigid's presence had shifted the chamber's dynamics in ways that made every existing alliance feel provisional, every assumption about leadership open to challenge.

"You speak of experience with our enemies," King Aillen observed with careful neutrality. "Yet your origins remain diplomatically unexamined. In times when trust determines survival, such mystery carries its own dangers."

"Truth often carries more danger than mystery," Brigid replied with honesty that held its own form of courage. "But you're right—trust requires revelation, and revelation requires courage from both speaker and listeners."

She moved to stand where firelight would illuminate her features clearly, no longer attempting to conceal what careful observation might already have discerned. "My name is not Brigid. I am Boudica, once Queen of the Iceni, leader of the great British rebellion against Rome."

The silence that followed carried weight beyond mere surprise. Around the chamber, hands moved to weapons before conscious thought could intervene, while minds struggled to process implications that challenged every assumption about their gathering's nature.

"The most wanted fugitive in the Roman world," breathed Fergal of the Mountain Clans, his voice tight with recognition of how profoundly their circumstances had just changed. "Every Roman agent from here to Gaul will be hunting you. Your presence here guarantees imperial attention will follow."

"Yes," Boudica replied with calm acceptance that somehow made her revelation more rather than less credible. "But I also represent something your enemies can't understand or counter— the willingness to choose resistance over safety, meaning over peace, love over the beautiful emptiness of surrender."

Étaín leaned forward with the practical urgency of someone who had learned to read tactical implications in political developments. "Why reveal yourself? Why expose your identity and endanger our mission when silence served your purposes?"

"Because unity built on lies serves the same purpose as the Hollowed's false peace—it eliminates the chaos that comes from dealing with difficult truths." Boudica's gaze moved to each representative in turn. "I failed my people once by underestimating enemies and overestimating my own strength. I won't make that mistake again."

"Your failure cost thousands of lives," Brendan said with bluntness that cut through diplomatic courtesy to historical reality. "British dead, Roman dead, innocents caught between armies led by pride rather than wisdom. What makes you think we should trust someone whose leadership brought such destruction?"

The words landed like physical blows, and Neassa saw Boudica flinch as if struck. But when she spoke, her voice carried the weight of someone who had wrestled with guilt and emerged with hard-won understanding.

"Because I've learned the cost of leading through emotion rather than strategy, of choosing pride over practicality, of believing that courage alone could overcome superior planning." Her voice grew stronger with each admission. "My daughters died because of choices I made. My people suffered because I led them into a war I couldn't win. I am not that tale's hero—I am its lesson."

The debate that followed revealed the true complexity of their situation as representatives wrestled with questions that went beyond mere military alliance to fundamental issues of legitimacy, authority, and the nature of leadership itself when leadership faced challenges that stretched past traditional categories of response.

"Experience matters," Muiris said thoughtfully, "but so does understanding the specific nature of contemporary threats. These enemies don't seek conquest in traditional terms; they attack the very capacity for resistance."

"Which is exactly why we need someone who understands their methods," Scáthach countered with warrior's pragmatism. "Traditional leadership failed against these forces. Perhaps we need leadership that has confronted them and learned from the encounter."

"But what of Irish authority?" King Cormac asked with careful neutrality that barely concealed deeper concerns. "Foreign leadership, however experienced, carries complications that internal leadership avoids."

Cathair had remained silent through most of the debate, but now he stepped forward with movements that somehow commanded attention despite their quietness. "Perhaps we're asking the wrong questions," he said, his voice carrying across the chamber with authority that seemed to emerge from wisdom rather than ambition.

"Instead of debating who has the right to lead, perhaps we should ask who has the strength to serve." His gaze moved thoughtfully across the assembly. "Leadership isn't privilege to be claimed but burden to be carried. The question is who proves willing to accept that burden despite its cost."

"Pretty words," Fergal observed, "but practical circumstances require practical solutions. Seven days until Medb's gathering, enemies who coordinate with supernatural efficiency, resources that couldn't sustain extended conflict even if we knew how to fight spiritual warfare."

Before the debate could sink further into tactical despair, the sound of urgent hoofbeats echoed across the courtyard yet again. But this time, the rider who approached carried colors that made every representative stiffen with recognition—not allied intelligence, but formal embassy that would reshape the nature of their choices.

"Royal messenger," King Conchobor observed grimly, reading the banners that proclaimed official rather than military purpose. "Someone claims authority to speak for legitimate governance."

The messenger who entered the great hall moved with the careful formality required for diplomatic missions, but his face showed the strain of someone who carried offers that he suspected his listeners would find more threatening than generous.

"Representatives of Ireland's free territories," the messenger began with ceremony that felt hollow in current circumstances, "I bring formal invitation from Queen Medb of Connacht, speaking as regent for unified Irish interests in alliance with proven authorities who have brought prosperity to other lands."

The formal language carried undertones of threat barely concealed beneath diplomatic courtesy. Not request but summons, not negotiation but ultimatum disguised as opportunity.

"Queen Medb invites all who would lead Ireland to witness the demonstration of optimal governance through methods that have brought peace and prosperity to territories across the known world." The messenger's voice carried mechanical precision that made several representatives shift uncomfortably. "She offers partnership that preserves Irish rule while providing guidance for managing enhanced spiritual networks."

The trap was never the great working, Neassa realized with growing horror as the true scope of their enemies' planning became clear. That was just preparation. They let us win the spiritual battle, knowing victory would create conditions that made their real offer seem like wisdom rather than submission.

CHAPTER 27

THE PERFECT SOLUTION

The delegation from Queen Medb's territories moved through Tara's halls with coordination that was almost but not quite mechanical—individual initiative preserved but guided by shared understanding that eliminated the chaos normal diplomacy created through competing perspectives and uncertain outcomes. They carried themselves with authority that transcended mere political calculation, speaking as people who had consciously chosen solutions rather than inherited problems.

Neassa watched from the great hall's dais as the seven representatives arranged themselves with precision that served efficiency without obviously sacrificing personality. Each bore the relaxed confidence of someone whose decisions were supported by collective wisdom that eliminated uncertainty without obviously eliminating choice. Their leader, a woman whose bearing spoke to royal authority earned rather than inherited, approached with respectful formality that somehow made her offer more rather than less intimidating.

"High King and High Queen of Ireland," she announced with courtesy that felt genuine despite its underlying purpose, "I am Éadaoin of the Optimized Territories, speaking for Queen Medb and the alliance of administrators who have learned to provide guidance without compulsion, efficiency without emptiness."

The words carried subtle threat disguised as diplomatic courtesy. Not conquest disguised as negotiation, but partnership that would preserve the forms of conscious choice while transforming its substance into something serving entirely different purposes.

Cathair stepped forward with authority that had been tested through crisis and emerged stronger rather than brittle, but Neassa could read the tension in his shoulders as he processed implications that challenged every assumption about what they had accomplished. "You're welcome at Tara, Éadaoin of the Optimized Territories. Though we understand your visit carries weight beyond mere courtesy."

"Indeed," she replied with satisfaction that seemed connected to genuine enthusiasm rather than mechanical programming. "We bring demonstration of governance that honors Irish independence while providing methods proven successful across territories that have learned to prosper through coordination of individual will with collective wisdom."

Behind her, the other representatives moved with similar coordination—not the perfect efficiency of the Hollowed, but something more sophisticated. Individual personality preserved but guided by shared understanding that eliminated conflicts normal human interaction created through competing desires and uncertain outcomes.

"We've heard reports of your... innovations," Neassa said carefully, her priestess training reading spiritual currents that flowed around the delegation like invisible rivers carrying purposes she couldn't quite identify. "But innovations in governance often carry costs that become apparent only through extended trial."

"Naturally, High Queen. Which is why we offer demonstration rather than theory, experience rather than promises." Éadaoin gestured toward her companions with movements that conveyed both respect for their contributions and confidence in coordinated purpose. "Each of us represents territories that have discovered practical solutions to problems that conscious choice governance struggles to address effectively."

"Such as?" Cathair asked, though his voice carried recognition that the question would lead toward offers designed to exploit exactly the weaknesses their recent victory had revealed.

"The integration of populations that require guidance to function effectively," replied one of the other delegates, a man whose features bore the particular strain of someone who had learned to balance competing demands through systematic rather than intuitive methods. "Your refugee crisis represents exactly such challenge—thousands of people who remember efficient coordination but struggle with the burden of individual choice."

Before either ruler could respond, the sound of commotion echoed from the courtyards below—not the chaos of emergency, but the frustrated voices of people discovering that good intentions proved insufficient when faced with practical challenges that required immediate solutions rather than theoretical principles.

Through the great windows, they could see another confrontation developing in the refugee camps that had grown around Tara's base. Former Hollowed who had been attempting to make individual choices now clustered around anyone who offered guidance, while Irish volunteers struggled to aid without creating dependency that made independence impossible.

***

"Your people try to help," observed another delegate with sympathy that felt genuine despite its tactical utility. "But individual choice requires strength that many lack after experiencing the peace of coordinated purpose. They suffer not from your cruelty but from your kindness—forced to bear burdens they remember surrendering with relief."

The timing was too perfect for coincidence. Éadaoin's delegation had arrived precisely when the refugee crisis reached its most visible frustration, when Irish attempts at humanitarian aid were producing results that made administered efficiency seem merciful rather than oppressive.

"What do you propose?" Neassa asked, understanding that the question was both necessary and dangerous—acknowledging problems while inviting solutions that might transform those problems into tools serving purposes they opposed.

"Partnership that preserves Irish authority while providing administrative guidance for populations that require such structure," Éadaoin replied with satisfaction that spoke to plans prepared for exactly this response. "Your territories maintain complete autonomy over those who choose conscious governance. Refugee populations receive the coordination they need without imposing burden on systems designed to serve individual will rather than collective efficiency."

"Meaning?" Cathair demanded with strategic directness that sought clarity rather than allowing comfortable ambiguity to conceal uncomfortable implications.

"Meaning that former Hollowed and other populations that function better under guided coordination are administered through proven methods, while Irish who choose the burden of consciousness continue to govern themselves according to traditional principles enhanced by innovations you've developed."

The offer was sophisticated beyond their most pessimistic estimates—not replacement of their governance but coexistence that would preserve conscious choice for those strong enough to bear it while providing administered efficiency for those who preferred guidance over uncertainty. Not surrender, but evolution toward forms that honored individual preference while acknowledging practical limitations.

"And Queen Medb's role in such partnership?" Neassa asked, reading in the delegation's coordination evidence of planning that transcended normal diplomatic preparation.

"Queen Medb serves as coordinator between territories that have chosen different governance models," Éadaoin explained with certainty that suggested long experience with such arrangements. "Administered efficiency for those who prefer certainty, conscious choice for those who prefer struggle, and coordination between both systems to ensure mutual prosperity rather than competitive conflict."

Around the chamber, representatives who had learned to trust Irish leadership through crisis began to show signs of consideration that went beyond mere diplomatic courtesy. The offer addressed real problems through practical solutions that preserved Irish independence while eliminating administrative burdens their victory had created.

King Conchobor of Ulster leaned forward with interest that spoke to political calculation rather than immediate acceptance, but also recognition that their current approach was creating suffering that alternative methods might alleviate. "You speak of proven methods. Where have such arrangements succeeded?"

"Throughout territories that have learned to balance individual preference with collective efficiency," replied another delegate with confidence born from extensive experience. "British settlements that maintain cultural identity while accepting Roman administrative guidance. Gallic communities that preserve traditional authority while benefiting from imperial coordination of trade and security."

The implications rippled through the assembly like recognition of sophistication that exceeded every assumption about enemy capabilities. Not crude conquest or even spiritual seduction, but systematic transformation that felt like conscious choice while serving purposes that had nothing to do with Irish welfare.

"Administrative guidance," Boudica said quietly, her strategic experience reading between diplomatic language to tactical reality. "We've heard such terms before. They begin with voluntary cooperation and end with administrative necessity that eliminates the voluntary component while maintaining cooperative forms."

"With respect, Queen Boudica," Éadaoin replied with courtesy that carried undertones of recognition beyond mere diplomatic intelligence, "your experience represents resistance to expansion rather than partnership in administration. The arrangements we propose serve mutual benefit rather than imperial absorption."

The use of Boudica's true identity should have been shocking—intelligence that proved enemy preparation extended to knowledge that threatened their most carefully guarded secrets. But somehow the revelation felt natural rather than threatening, acknowledgment of open secrets that served cooperation rather than concealment.

***

"You know," Cathair observed with strategic precision that sought understanding rather than expressing accusation.

"We know many things that serve mutual benefit rather than competitive advantage," Éadaoin confirmed with satisfaction that spoke to intelligence gathered through means that transcended normal diplomatic channels. "Queen Boudica's expertise provides valuable perspective on methods that fail, just as our experience provides insight into arrangements that succeed."

Before the political implications could settle into comfortable patterns, new sounds echoed from beyond the hall—not individual distress this time, but coordinated movement that spoke to groups making collective decisions about their immediate welfare. Through the windows, they could see former Hollowed moving with renewed purpose toward the delegation's camp, drawn by promises of guidance that would eliminate uncertainty without obviously eliminating choice.

"They respond to your presence," Neassa observed with growing understanding of tactics that operated beyond normal political categories.

"They respond to solutions for problems that conscious choice governance struggles to address," Éadaoin corrected with gentle firmness that made her words more persuasive than any argument could have achieved. "Individual will serves those strong enough to bear its burden, but creates suffering for those who lack such strength. Administered coordination serves different needs through different methods."

"And if we refuse your generous partnership?" Cathair asked, though his tone suggested recognition that refusal carried costs their previous victories had not eliminated.

"Then Ireland continues to struggle with problems that practical solutions could eliminate," Éadaoin replied with genuine regret that somehow made her threat more rather than less compelling. "Refugee populations continue to suffer from freedoms they cannot effectively exercise, while Irish territories exhaust resources attempting to provide assistance that served efficiency could deliver more effectively."

The silence that followed carried weight beyond mere political consideration. Around the hall, representatives who had risked everything to preserve conscious choice found themselves confronting evidence that their choice created suffering for those unable to bear its burden—moral complexity that made simple resistance seem selfish rather than principled.

Through the windows, they could see the effects spreading as former Hollowed responded to the delegation's presence with relief that felt genuine rather than programmed. Not conversion through spiritual assault, but voluntary acceptance of guidance that promised to eliminate problems their liberation had created without obviously eliminating the liberation itself.

"We ask time to consider what you offer," Cathair said finally, his voice carrying authority that had been tested through trial but now faced challenges that transcended simple resistance to obvious enemies.

"Naturally, High King. Such decisions require careful consideration of all implications." Éadaoin inclined her head with respectful courtesy that felt genuine despite its underlying purpose. "We await your wisdom, understanding that true leadership serves the welfare of all who trust in its guidance—even those whose welfare requires different forms of assistance than traditional approaches provide."

As the delegation withdrew with coordination that spoke to shared purpose rather than individual agendas, the representatives of Ireland's conscious territories found themselves facing questions that victory had revealed rather than resolved. Not simple choice between freedom and oppression, but complex recognition that some people genuinely preferred guidance over uncertainty, efficiency over the chaos that individual will created when exercised by those unprepared for its demands.

The war for Ireland's soul had entered a new phase, and this time the weapons were compassion rather than force, practical solutions rather than spiritual seduction, offers of genuine help for problems that conscious choice had failed to solve through traditional methods.

Outside Tara's walls, evening gathered with the weight of decision approaching, while inside, leaders who had proven consciousness could defend themselves against elimination now faced the more difficult question of whether consciousness should be imposed on those who preferred alternatives that promised peace through voluntary surrender of everything that made consciousness both precious and terrible.

The perfect solution had been offered, and Ireland prepared to discover whether its choice to remain conscious extended to accepting the suffering that consciousness created for those unable to bear its weight, or whether love demanded providing alternatives that served welfare rather than principles.

Somewhere in the growing darkness, former Hollowed moved toward coordination that promised relief from burdens they had never asked to carry, while their liberators struggled with recognition that liberation meant nothing if the liberated lacked strength to value what they had been given at such tremendous cost.

CHAPTER 28

THE GATHERING DOUBT

Three days after Éadaoin's departure, the first formal request arrived from Dubh Linn—not a cry for help, but carefully worded entreaty asking Tara's permission to accept "administrative assistance" from Queen Medb's alliance. The trading settlement had grown prosperous through commerce that required coordination with territories using different governance methods, and their merchant leaders spoke of efficiency gains that transcended mere political preference.

Neassa stood in the great hall's eastern window, her hand unconsciously moving to her still-flat belly where new life grew despite the chaos that surrounded them. The morning sickness had passed, but the weight of carrying their child during a crisis that threatened everything they had built pressed against her consciousness like a physical presence demanding attention she couldn't spare.

"They ask permission rather than simply accepting," Cathair observed, joining her at the window where they could see riders arriving with similar messages from across their territories. "That suggests they still recognize our authority, even while questioning its practical benefits."

"Or they're being polite while demonstrating how inadequate our governance has become," she replied with honesty that carried its own form of exhaustion. "When people must choose between principles and practical welfare, principles require extraordinary justification to survive."

The reports that continued to arrive throughout the morning painted a picture of systematic pressure that went far beyond the refugee crisis. Not crude conquest or even spiritual seduction, but patient demonstration that their form of governance created unnecessary suffering while alternatives offered genuine relief from problems that conscious choice seemed unable to solve effectively.

Ríona approached with news that transformed concern into recognition of coordinated assault on foundations they had thought were strengthened by victory. Her divine sight had been monitoring the spiritual landscape across Ireland, and what she discovered challenged every assumption about the network that supported their authority.

"The connections fragment differently than before," she announced, her silver scars pulsing with otherworldly light as she consulted sources beyond mortal understanding. "Not severed by outside force, but voluntarily abandoned by those who find the burden too heavy to bear. The network responds by seeking alternative paths—but those paths lead toward collective rather than individual consciousness."

"Meaning?" Cathair asked, though his strategic experience already suggested answers that made their recent triumph seem hollow rather than complete.

"Meaning the spiritual infrastructure that supports conscious choice is being rebuilt to serve collective efficiency," Ríona replied with divine certainty that brooked no contradiction. "Not corrupted by the Hollowed's emptiness, but voluntarily adapted by people who prefer guided coordination over the uncertainty of individual decision-making."

The implications hit their small council like recognition of trap within trap, complexity that exceeded their ability to address through traditional resistance. Not external assault on their spiritual foundations, but internal transformation as those foundations adapted to serve the preferences of people who found consciousness too difficult to bear without assistance.

***

"The former Hollowed aren't the only ones affected," added Síle, returning from duties that had taken her throughout the refugee camps with growing expertise in problems that had no comfortable solutions. "Irish people who never experienced conversion are beginning to ask whether struggle serves any purpose when their neighbors have found peace through accepting guidance."

Her young voice carried strain that spoke to witnessing suffering that charity couldn't address and principles couldn't justify. "Yesterday, a woman whose husband died in the Samhain battle asked me why she should bear the burden of choosing how to raise their children alone when the administered territories provide collective child-rearing that ensures optimal development."

"What did you tell her?" Neassa asked gently, understanding that the question touched fundamental issues about the nature of love, responsibility, and the purposes that made suffering worthwhile.

"I told her that love creates meaning even when meaning creates pain," Síle replied with honesty that held its own form of courage. "But she asked why love should require pain when alternatives eliminate suffering without obviously eliminating affection. I had no answer that served compassion better than theory."

Before they could process the implications of questions that challenged their deepest assumptions about the value of consciousness, new sounds echoed from the courtyards below— not individual distress this time, but coordinated activity that spoke to groups making collective decisions about their immediate welfare.

Through the windows, they could see a delegation departing from the refugee camps—former Hollowed moving with renewed purpose toward territories that offered the coordination they remembered with relief rather than horror. Not forced conversion, but voluntary acceptance of guidance that promised to eliminate uncertainty without obviously eliminating choice.

"How many?" Cathair asked, though his voice carried recognition that numbers mattered less than the precedent their departure established.

"Nearly a thousand," Síle reported with accuracy that spoke to careful observation of developments that challenged everything they thought they had accomplished. "Entire family groups choosing to relocate where their needs can be met through proven methods rather than experimental principles."

"And the Irish response?" Neassa demanded, understanding that their people's reaction would determine whether this became isolated incident or systematic collapse of support for governance that created problems rather than solving them.

"Mixed," Boudica replied as she joined them, her strategic experience providing perspective that transcended immediate tactical concerns. "Some see it as proof that forced liberation serves oppressor more than oppressed. Others recognize it as inevitable outcome of offering freedom to those unprepared for its demands."

Her warrior's honesty was brutal but necessary. "The question isn't whether people should have the right to choose efficiency over consciousness. The question is whether our choice to preserve consciousness extends to accepting responsibility for those unable to exercise that choice effectively."

The debate that followed revealed fault lines deeper than mere disagreement over refugee policy—fundamental questions about the nature of love, responsibility, and the prices that moral principles could demand from those who lacked strength to pay them without destroying themselves in the process.

"We fought for the right to choose," King Conchobor observed with Ulster's ancient wisdom, his weathered voice carrying recognition of complexity that transcended comfortable categories. "But choice means nothing if only one option can be selected without causing suffering to those we claim to protect."

"Then we accept that some will choose differently," Cathair said with quiet authority that had been tested through crisis but now faced challenges that required wisdom rather than courage. "We prove that conscious choice creates better outcomes for those capable of exercising it, while acknowledging that not everyone possesses such capability."

"And the spiritual network?" Ríona asked with divine concern that addressed foundations underlying political decisions. "If it continues adapting to serve collective efficiency, eventually it will transform into exactly what we fought to prevent—just through evolution rather than conquest."

***

The answer came not through debate but through immediate crisis as scouts burst through the great doors with intelligence that transformed theoretical concerns into urgent necessity. Their faces bore the strain of people who had witnessed events that challenged every assumption about the scope of what they faced.

"High King, High Queen," the lead scout announced with formal gravity that barely contained his alarm at developments that transcended normal political categories. "The settlement of Glendalough has formally requested integration into Queen Medb's administrative system. Not just refugee assistance, but complete governance transition for their entire population."

The silence that followed carried weight beyond mere political calculation. Glendalough was not a struggling border settlement or community overwhelmed by refugee crisis, but one of Ireland's most prosperous territories—people choosing administered efficiency because it served their interests better than conscious choice served their welfare.

"When?" Neassa asked, though her priestess training already whispered warnings about timing that served strategic purposes rather than spontaneous decision.

"The request was delivered this morning, but their decision appears to have been developing for weeks," the scout replied with honesty that spoke to witnessing systematic rather than impulsive change. "They cite administrative efficiency in trade coordination, collective decision-making that eliminates political conflict, and educational systems that optimize children's development rather than leaving it to individual parental judgment."

"What response do they expect?" Cathair demanded with strategic precision that sought understanding rather than expressing judgment about choices that challenged everything they had fought to preserve.

"They ask for Tara's blessing rather than permission," came the reply that transformed political crisis into moral complexity beyond comfortable resolution. "Recognition that their choice serves their welfare, even if it serves different principles than those Tara represents."

The implications crystallized around their council like recognition of questions that had no answers satisfying both conscience and practical necessity. Not simple resistance to obvious enemies, but acknowledgment that some people genuinely thrived under guidance that eliminated uncertainty, conflict, and the terrible burden of individual responsibility for outcomes beyond personal control.

Through the windows, they could see more riders approaching with coordination that spoke to similar requests from other territories—not conquest spreading through force, but voluntary acceptance of alternative governance spreading through demonstration that it served practical welfare better than principles served theoretical ideals.

"We can refuse," Boudica said with strategic clarity that cut through moral complexity to immediate tactical options. "Declare such requests treasonous, use force to prevent territories from abandoning conscious choice governance, prove our commitment to individual freedom by eliminating the freedom to choose alternatives."

"Or?" Neassa asked, understanding that the alternative would require choices that challenged every assumption about the nature of legitimate authority.

"We accept that our victory means proving conscious choice through example rather than imposing it through requirement," Cathair replied with quiet certainty that carried authority earned through trial. "We demonstrate that consciousness creates better outcomes for those capable of exercising it, while acknowledging that imposed consciousness serves oppression rather than liberation."

"And if more territories choose administered efficiency over conscious struggle?" Ríona asked with divine insight that pierced to the heart of their challenge. "If our choice to preserve freedom results in freedom being used to abandon freedom?"

"Then we discover whether love serves principle or people," Neassa said with recognition that settled into her bones like truth finding its proper home. "Whether our fight was about preserving choice or imposing our preference for chaos over order."

The sounds of approaching hoofbeats echoed across the sacred hill as more messengers arrived with requests that would test everything they thought they had accomplished. Not enemies seeking conquest, but allies seeking permission to choose differently—people who had fought beside them for the right to choose, now choosing options that challenged every assumption about what choice should produce.

"The network destabilizes further," Ríona announced with divine certainty that spoke to transformation accelerating beyond their ability to control or predict. "Each territory that chooses collective efficiency shifts the spiritual balance toward coordination rather than individual consciousness. Soon, maintaining individual will may become so difficult that surrender seems merciful rather than defeat."

As evening approached and the reality of their situation became undeniable, Neassa felt the weight of pregnancy combining with political crisis to create pressures that tested her ability to serve both personal and public needs. The child growing within her would inherit whatever Ireland they created through choices made in the next few days—choices that would determine whether consciousness remained possible for those strong enough to value it, or whether love demanded accepting alternatives that served welfare rather than principles.

"What do we do?" Síle asked with youth's desperate need for guidance in circumstances that challenged every adult assumption about leadership and responsibility.

"We choose," Cathair replied with authority that had been tested through impossible trials and emerged capable of bearing impossible burdens. "We choose what kind of people we are when choice itself is challenged by those we fought to protect. We choose whether victory means imposing our will or honoring theirs."

The gathering doubt had crystallized into impossible decisions, and Ireland prepared to discover whether conscious choice could survive being chosen against by those for whom consciousness created suffering rather than meaning, burden rather than blessing, isolation rather than the beautiful coordination that promised peace through voluntary surrender of everything that made peace both precious and terrible.

CHAPTER 29

THE CHOICE OF CHAINS

The formal delegation from Glendalough arrived at Tara's gates three days after their messengers had spoken their request, but the seven representatives who rode through morning mist moved with coordination that spoke to decisions already made rather than negotiations still pending. They came not as supplicants seeking permission, but as equals announcing choices that had been carefully considered and consciously selected.

Neassa watched from the great hall's eastern window as the delegation arranged itself with precision that served efficiency without obviously sacrificing personality—movements that carried the relaxed confidence of people whose uncertainty had been replaced by collective wisdom that eliminated individual doubt. Her hand moved unconsciously to the slight swell of her belly where their child grew despite the political crisis that threatened to undo everything they had built.

The morning sickness had passed, but exhaustion remained—not just from pregnancy, but from the weight of governing during a crisis that challenged every assumption about what victory was supposed to accomplish. Seven weeks since Samhain's triumph, and Ireland faced problems that success had created rather than eliminated.

"They're not asking permission," Cathair observed as he joined her at the window, his crown catching light that seemed dimmer than it should despite the clear morning sky. "They're announcing their choice and requesting our blessing for what they've already decided."

"Diplomatic courtesy disguising accomplished fact," she replied with recognition that carried its own weight of strategic concern. "The question is whether we can afford to refuse blessing when the choice has already been made regardless of our approval."

Through the courtyard below, they could see the effects of seven weeks of refugee crisis spreading like ripples from a stone cast in still water. Former Hollowed moved through daily routines with increasing coordination, unconsciously seeking the collective guidance that had once structured their existence. Irish volunteers worked themselves to exhaustion attempting to provide individual assistance to thousands who functioned better under shared direction.

Ríona approached with movements that carried divine authority mixed with very human concern, her silver scars pulsing with otherworldly light as she consulted sources beyond mortal understanding. What she brought was not comfort but confirmation of spiritual damage that stretched across the entire island.

"The network fragments further," she announced with certainty that brooked no contradiction. "Glendalough's choice accelerates processes already underway. Each territory that accepts collective guidance shifts the spiritual foundation toward coordination rather than individual consciousness."

"How much of Ireland remains committed to conscious choice?" Cathair asked, though his strategic experience already suggested answers that challenged every assumption about their recent victory.

"Perhaps a third, and diminishing daily." Ríona's divine sight-read patterns that mortal perception could only guess at. "Not through conquest or conversion, but through voluntary recognition that individual will creates suffering for those unprepared to bear its weight."

Before they could process the implications of spiritual geography that no longer supported the governance they had fought to preserve, Síle arrived with news that transformed concern into immediate crisis. Her young face bore the strain of someone who had spent weeks discovering that good intentions proved inadequate when faced with problems requiring practical solutions rather than moral principles.

"The delegation requests immediate audience," she reported with formal precision that barely concealed alarm at developments she couldn't quite categorize. "But they're not alone. Representatives from four other settlements have arrived during the night, all seeking similar guidance about territorial administration."

***

The great hall filled with tension thick as morning fog as Ireland's leadership faced a delegation that represented not rebellion or external conquest, but conscious choice exercised in directions that challenged everything they thought they had accomplished. The seven from Glendalough moved with coordination that was almost but not quite mechanical—individual personality preserved but guided by shared understanding that eliminated the chaos normal human interaction created through competing desires and uncertain outcomes.

Their leader, a woman whose bearing spoke to authority earned through practical demonstration rather than inherited through blood, approached with respectful formality that somehow made her announcement more rather than less threatening.

"High King and High Queen of Ireland," she said with courtesy that felt genuine despite its underlying purpose, "I am Muirenn of Glendalough, speaking for a community that has consciously chosen optimal coordination over the burden of individual uncertainty. We seek Tara's blessing for administrative arrangements that serve our welfare while honoring Irish independence."

Neassa felt another wave of exhaustion rise in her throat—not from pregnancy this time, but from recognition of sophistication that exceeded their ability to address through traditional resistance. Not conquest disguised as negotiation, but genuine choice exercised in directions that made their victory seem hollow rather than complete.

"You speak of arrangements," she said carefully, her priestess training reading spiritual currents that flowed around the delegation like invisible rivers carrying purposes she couldn't quite identify. "What specific coordination do you seek that conscious choice governance cannot provide?"

"Efficient resource allocation that eliminates competitive waste," Muirenn replied with satisfaction that spoke to problems solved rather than principles abandoned. "Educational systems that optimize children's development rather than leaving it to individual parental judgment that may lack adequate knowledge. Trade coordination that eliminates marketplace chaos through collective decision-making guided by proven expertise."

Around the hall, representatives who had risked everything to preserve conscious choice found themselves confronting evidence that their preservation created unnecessary suffering for those unprepared to exercise choice effectively—moral complexity that made simple resistance seem selfish rather than principled.

Neassa felt another wave of exhaustion combined with something sharper—frustration that cut through diplomatic courtesy like a blade. Perhaps it was the pregnancy, the hormones making her less patient with careful negotiation, but suddenly the elegant solutions felt like elaborate justifications for surrender.

"If segregation serves everyone's welfare so efficiently," she said, her voice carrying an edge that made several representatives shift uncomfortably, "then those who prefer optimization over the burden of consciousness can relocate to Queen Medb's territories in Connacht. Clean borders, clear choices—no need to transform Irish lands to accommodate those who find Irish ways insufficient."

King Conchobor of Ulster leaned forward with interest that spoke to political calculation rather than immediate acceptance, but also recognition that their current approach was creating suffering that alternative methods might alleviate.

"You describe proven methods. Where have such arrangements succeeded without compromising the independence they claim to preserve?"

"Throughout territories that have learned to balance individual preference with collective efficiency," replied another delegate with confidence born from extensive experience. "Communities that maintain cultural identity while accepting administrative guidance for matters requiring expertise beyond individual capability."

The implications rippled through the assembly like recognition of layered deception, complexity that exceeded their ability to address through the straightforward resistance that had served them during the Hollowed crisis. Not elimination of consciousness, but transformation of consciousness into something that served efficiency while preserving the illusion of choice.

* * *

Boudica moved to where she could observe both the delegation and the assembled Irish representatives, her strategic mind reading patterns that stretched beyond immediate political maneuvering. "Administrative guidance," she said quietly, her voice carrying bitter experience earned through catastrophic loss. "I've seen firsthand how Roman methods begin with partnership and end with tyranny. They always offer help before they demand submission."

King Conchobor nodded grimly. "British merchants who trade through our ports speak of similar patterns throughout the Empire. They tell stories of a teacher from Galilee who preached about love and consciousness—how the Romans dealt with him when his message threatened their order. Crucifixion, they call it. A death designed to break not just the body but the very idea that individual conscience matters more than imperial authority."

Síle stepped forward with youth's directness that cut through diplomatic courtesy. "If Roman administration serves your needs so well, why not simply sail to Britain where such systems already exist? Why seek to transform Irish lands rather than relocating to territories that already offer what you desire?"

Muirenn's pause was brief but telling. "Relocation would be inefficient. Established infrastructure, existing trade relationships, optimal resource allocation already developed here. British territories require integration into existing systems rather than allowing implementation of improved methods suited to local conditions."

"The spiritual implications concern us more than political ones," Ríona said with divine authority that cut through diplomatic courtesy to address foundations underlying surface negotiations.

"Each territory that chooses collective coordination affects the network that supports conscious choice for those who retain that capacity."

"Indeed," Muirenn agreed with sympathy that felt genuine despite its tactical utility. "Which is why we propose segregated systems rather than universal application. Conscious choice governance for those strong enough to bear its burdens, administrative guidance for those who require such structure. Cooperation rather than competition between different approaches to human welfare."

The offer was sophisticated beyond their most pessimistic estimates—not replacement of their governance but coexistence that would preserve conscious choice for those capable of exercising it while providing administered efficiency for those who preferred guidance over uncertainty. Not surrender, but evolution toward forms that honored individual preference while acknowledging practical limitations.

Before anyone could respond to proposals that challenged every assumption about the nature of legitimate authority, the sound of commotion echoed from the courtyards below—not the chaos of emergency, but the coordinated movement of groups making collective decisions about their immediate welfare.

Through the windows, they could see hundreds of former Hollowed departing the refugee camps with renewed purpose, moving toward whatever territories offered the coordination they remembered with relief rather than horror. Not forced conversion, but voluntary acceptance of guidance that promised to eliminate uncertainty without obviously eliminating choice.

"How many choose to leave?" Cathair asked, though his voice carried recognition that numbers mattered less than the precedent their departure established.

"Nearly three thousand since yesterday," Síle reported with accuracy that spoke to careful observation of developments that challenged everything they thought they had accomplished. "Entire family groups choosing relocation where their needs can be met through proven methods rather than experimental principles."

"And the Irish response?"

"Divided," she replied with honesty that held its own form of courage. "Some see it as proof that forced liberation serves oppressor more than oppressed. Others recognize it as inevitable outcome of offering freedom to those unprepared for its demands."

The silence that followed carried weight beyond mere political consideration. Around the hall, representatives who had fought for the right to choose found themselves confronting evidence that their choice created suffering for those unable to bear its burden—moral complexity that made simple resistance seem selfish rather than compassionate.

***

Muirenn watched their internal struggle with patience that spoke to understanding rather than calculation. "We do not ask Tara to abandon its principles," she said gently. "We ask recognition that those principles serve some better than others, and that love may require providing alternatives for those whom consciousness burdens rather than blesses."

"The precedent troubles us," Neassa said finally, her voice carrying the weight of someone who understood that immediate choices would determine Ireland's fundamental character. "Accept your request, and we legitimize the voluntary abandonment of consciousness. Refuse, and we force choice upon those who lack strength to exercise it effectively."

"Then perhaps the question isn't whether to accept or refuse," Cathair said with quiet authority that had been tested through impossible trials, "but how to ensure that choice serves those capable of valuing it while providing alternatives for those who require different forms of guidance."

The afternoon that followed compressed weeks of debate into hours of desperate decision-making as Ireland's leadership struggled with recognition that their victory had created problems as complex as those defeat would have caused. Not external conquest or internal rebellion, but conscious choice exercised in directions that challenged every assumption about what choice should produce.

Through the windows, they could see more delegations arriving with coordination that spoke to similar requests from other territories—not conquest spreading through force, but voluntary acceptance of alternative governance spreading through demonstration that it served practical welfare better than principles served theoretical ideals.

As evening approached and the weight of impossible decisions pressed against leaders who had proven consciousness could defend itself against elimination, Neassa felt exhaustion combining with pregnancy to create pressures that tested her ability to serve both personal and public needs.

The child growing within her would inherit whatever Ireland they created through choices made in the next few days—choices that would determine whether consciousness remained possible for those strong enough to value it, or whether love demanded accepting alternatives that served welfare rather than principles.

"What do we do?" Síle asked with youth's desperate need for guidance in circumstances that challenged every adult assumption about leadership and responsibility.

"We choose," Cathair replied with authority that had been tested through impossible trials and emerged capable of bearing impossible burdens. "We choose what kind of people we are when choice itself is challenged by those we fought to protect. We choose whether victory means imposing our will or honoring theirs."

The gathering twilight brought no comfort as Ireland's defenders faced the most sophisticated test yet—whether consciousness could resist not the threat of elimination, but the promise of perfection through voluntary optimization that felt like fulfillment rather than surrender.

Outside Tara's walls, former Hollowed moved toward coordination that promised relief from burdens they had never asked to carry, while their liberators struggled with recognition that liberation meant nothing if the liberated lacked strength to value what they had been given at such tremendous cost.

The choice of chains had been offered with perfect reasonableness, and Ireland prepared to discover whether love demanded accepting that some chains were chosen rather than imposed, some burdens too heavy for individual hearts to bear, some forms of freedom that created suffering rather than joy for those who received them as unwanted gifts.

CHAPTER 30

THE WEIGHT OF CROWN AND CHILD

The dawn of winter solstice brought no comfort to Tara's halls, only the weight of decisions that could no longer be delayed as representatives gathered to hear Ireland's response to proposals that challenged everything they thought they had accomplished. Neassa stood beside the great window where pale light struggled through morning mist, her hand pressed against the growing curve of her belly where new life stirred as if responding to the tension that filled the air like electricity before lightning.

Seven weeks since Samhain's victory, and she felt as though they were losing the war through the very peace they had won. The child within her would inherit whatever Ireland they created through choices made in the next few hours—choices that would determine whether consciousness remained possible for those strong enough to value it, or whether love demanded accepting alternatives that served welfare rather than principles.

"They're not going to accept your proposal," Cathair said quietly, joining her at the window where they could see delegations from across Ireland arranging themselves in the courtyard below. "Relocation to Connacht would expose their real purpose—they want Ireland itself, not just administrative efficiency for Irish people."

"Then let them refuse and show their true nature," she replied with heat that surprised even her. The pregnancy had made her less patient with diplomatic courtesy, more direct in ways that felt both liberating and dangerous. "Let everyone see that this isn't about helping former Hollowed find peace, but about Queen Medb of Connacht claiming authority over territories that never acknowledged her rule."

The emphasis on Medb's actual title carried weight that cut through careful diplomatic language to political reality. Not High Queen of Ireland, despite her growing influence, but regional ruler seeking to expand beyond her legitimate boundaries through administrative seduction rather than military conquest.

"The representatives are divided," Cathair observed, reading the positioning of groups in the courtyard below with strategic precision that came from months of crisis governance. "Some support your directness. Others worry we're abandoning compassion for former Hollowed who genuinely struggle with consciousness."

"And you?" she asked, understanding that their partnership faced its first major disagreement about fundamental policy rather than tactical decisions.

"I support you," he said simply, his hand finding hers with touch that anchored them both despite forces that sought to fragment their unity. "But I also understand their concerns. What happens to those who choose neither optimization nor consciousness? Those who fall between alternatives we offer?"

The great hall filled with tension thick as winter fog as Ireland's leadership prepared to deliver their response to proposals that promised solutions through methods that challenged every principle they had fought to preserve. Representatives from across the territories that remained free filled the ancient chamber, faces bearing strain of people who understood they witnessed either the birth of sustainable governance or its transformation into something that served entirely different purposes.

Muirenn of Glendalough sat with her six companions, their coordination somehow more pronounced than yesterday—movements that carried the relaxed confidence of people whose uncertainty had been eliminated through collective wisdom that provided answers to questions individual thought struggled to address. Behind them, representatives from four other settlements waited with similar patience, as if the outcome of negotiations mattered less than the demonstration of alternatives they embodied.

***

Neassa took her place beside Cathair on the platform where Ireland's joint rulers had proven partnership could serve authority more effectively than individual power. But today, the weight of crown and child combined with pregnancy hormones to create pressure that tested her ability to maintain the diplomatic courtesy that complex negotiations required.

"Representatives of Ireland's free territories," she began, her voice carrying across the hall with authority that had been tested through trial but now faced challenges that required wisdom rather than courage. "We have considered the proposals brought by our neighbors, the requests for administrative coordination that promise solutions to problems our victory created rather than eliminated."

Around the hall, faces showed the strain of people who had fought for principles only to discover that principles created suffering for those unprepared to bear their weight—moral complexity that made simple responses seem inadequate to contemporary reality.

"But before we respond to specific proposals," Neassa continued, her voice growing stronger with each word despite forces that sought to fragment their unity, "we must address a fundamental question that underlies all negotiations. Why seek to transform Irish lands to accommodate those who find Irish ways insufficient, when Queen Medb of Connacht has already created territories that offer the administrative coordination they desire?"

The silence that followed carried weight beyond mere political consideration. Around the hall, representatives began to understand that diplomatic courtesy was giving way to direct challenge that would force their visitors to reveal purposes they had carefully concealed beneath reasonable language.

"Queen Medb," she emphasized, letting the regional title carry implications that cut through claims of pan-Irish authority. "Ruler of Connacht, not High Queen of Ireland, despite whatever administrative networks she has established with former Hollowed populations."

Muirenn's expression remained neutral, but something flickered behind her eyes—not emotion, which had been optimized away, but calculation that recognized the trap Neassa's question created. Around her, the other delegates shifted with coordination that spoke to shared decision-making processes that eliminated individual uncertainty.

"High Queen Neassa raises practical concerns," Muirenn replied with patience that felt programmed rather than personal. "Relocation would disrupt established systems that serve optimal outcomes. Integration of administrative guidance within existing territorial boundaries eliminates inefficiencies that population movement would create."

"Integration," Neassa repeated, her voice carrying heat that made several representatives shift uncomfortably as pregnancy hormones eliminated her patience for euphemistic language. "You mean conquest. You mean transformation of Irish governance to serve purposes that have nothing to do with Irish welfare and everything to do with expanding Queen Medb's authority beyond Connacht's legitimate boundaries."

The accusation hung in the morning air like challenge that demanded response. Behind Muirenn, delegates who had maintained perfect coordination suddenly showed signs of individual tension—not enough to suggest independent thought, but sufficient to indicate that their programming had not prepared them for such direct confrontation.

"The arrangements we propose serve mutual benefit," Muirenn insisted with mechanical certainty that transcended personal conviction. "Territories that choose administrative guidance maintain cultural identity while accepting coordination that eliminates conflicts created by competing individual preferences."

"Then accept them in Connacht," Neassa shot back with passion that surprised everyone present, including herself. "If collective guidance serves welfare better than consciousness, if optimization eliminates suffering more effectively than individual choice, then prove it. Demonstrate your methods in territories Queen Medb actually rules rather than seeking to export them to lands that chose different paths."

***

King Conchobor of Ulster leaned forward with interest that spoke to recognition of political strategy that transcended immediate emotional response. "The High Queen speaks to precedent that affects all territorial relationships. If Connacht's methods prove superior, they should attract voluntary migration rather than requiring territorial transformation."

"Precisely," added King Aillen of Leinster, his voice carrying authority that had been tested through crisis governance. "Those who prefer collective guidance can relocate to territories that offer it, just as those who choose consciousness can remain in lands that support individual will."

But Muirenn's response revealed the sophistication of forces that had prepared for exactly such challenges. "Population relocation creates inefficiencies that serve no optimal purpose. Existing infrastructure, established trade relationships, optimal resource allocation already developed across current territories. Selective coordination eliminates disruption while providing benefits."

"Selective coordination," Boudica said quietly, her strategic experience reading between diplomatic language to tactical reality. "I've heard such terms before. They begin with voluntary cooperation for those who request it, evolve into administrative necessity for those who resist it."

The debate that followed revealed fault lines deeper than mere disagreement over refugee policy—fundamental questions about the nature of authority, the source of legitimacy, the relationship between individual will and collective welfare that challenged every assumption about what their victory was supposed to accomplish.

"Some territories genuinely struggle with conscious choice governance," observed Brendan of Mag Muirthemne with honesty that held its own form of courage. "Former Hollowed populations require structure that individual will cannot provide. Perhaps selective coordination serves compassion rather than conquest."

"And perhaps," Síle replied with youth's directness that cut through diplomatic courtesy, "we're being offered beautiful solutions to problems that consciousness creates, without being told that solving those problems requires abandoning consciousness itself."

As the morning progressed and arguments built around the central question Neassa had raised, the effects of pregnancy began to combine with political pressure to create exhaustion that tested her ability to maintain the leadership that crisis demanded. The child within her stirred with movements that seemed to respond to her emotional state, as if new life could sense the forces that threatened to reshape whatever world it would inherit.

"I need air," she said quietly to Cathair as another wave of dizziness passed through her consciousness like tide retreating from familiar shores.

"We'll recess," he announced immediately, his concern for her welfare overriding political considerations that normally required extended negotiation. "Representatives, we reconvene at midday to continue discussions that require careful consideration rather than hasty judgment."

But as they prepared to leave the hall for the brief respite that pregnancy demanded, Ríona approached with news that transformed personal concern into recognition of crisis that transcended individual welfare. Her divine sight had been monitoring developments that stretched beyond normal perception, and what she discovered challenged every assumption about the scope of what they faced.

"The spiritual network destabilizes further," she announced with certainty that brooked no contradiction. "But not randomly— with purpose that serves coordination rather than consciousness. Each territory that accepts administrative guidance shifts the foundation toward collective rather than individual awareness."

"How long until the change becomes irreversible?" Cathair asked, understanding that spiritual infrastructure determined everything else about their ability to maintain governance that served conscious choice rather than administered efficiency.

"Days, perhaps hours," Ríona replied with divine perception that pierced beyond immediate observation to recognize patterns that mortal understanding could barely encompass. "The winter solstice approaches—when solar power reaches its turning point and spiritual transformations align with the return of light. Forces that have been building in darkness prepare to manifest with the sun's renewal."

***

The implications settled over them like recognition of timing that served strategic purposes rather than natural coincidence. Not just political pressure during administrative negotiations, but spiritual assault timed to exploit the moment when boundaries dissolved between possible and impossible, when transformation could be accomplished through means that transcended normal categories of change.

"They planned this," Neassa said, understanding settling in her voice like recognition of sophistication that exceeded their most pessimistic estimates. "The refugee crisis, the administrative offers, the timing of negotiations—all designed to create conditions where accepting their guidance seems merciful rather than surrender."

"And if we refuse?" Síle asked with youth's desperate need for options that served both principle and practical welfare.

"Then we prove conscious choice creates better outcomes for those capable of exercising it," Cathair replied with authority that had been tested through impossible trials, "while accepting that some will choose differently—and that our love for them extends to honoring their choice even when it challenges everything we believe about the value of consciousness."

As they prepared to return to negotiations that would determine Ireland's fundamental character, the sound of urgent hoofbeats echoed across the sacred hill. Not individual messengers this time, but coordinated movement that spoke to developments requiring immediate attention rather than careful deliberation.

Through the windows, they could see riders approaching from multiple directions, their coordination suggesting shared purpose that transcended normal communication. The winter solstice was approaching, and with it would come the test that would determine whether Ireland's choice to remain conscious could survive being challenged by those they had fought to protect.

"Whatever comes next," Neassa said quietly, her hand moving to the child that grew within her despite political chaos that threatened to undo everything they had built, "we face it together. Partnership that serves both love and leadership, consciousness that chooses consciousness despite the cost."

The weight of crown and child combined with forces that sought to transform both authority and future into tools serving purposes they had fought to prevent. But for the first time since the crisis began, Ireland would meet that test with clarity about what they truly faced—not external conquest but internal transformation, not elimination of choice but seductive offers of relief from choice's terrible burden.

The real battle was just beginning, and it would be fought not with sword and spear but with the simple question of whether love could justify the chaos consciousness created when consciousness faced offers of beautiful peace through voluntary surrender of everything that made peace, beauty, or recognition of their value possible.

CHAPTER 31

THE MEMORY OF SONGS

The winter solstice sun climbed toward its brief zenith as Neassa stood at the entrance to the great passage tomb of Brú na Bóinne, feeling the weight of Ireland's crisis pressing against her consciousness like tide returning to familiar shores. A day's walk from Tara's political chaos, the ancient sacred site offered the clarity that came from connecting to powers older than kingdoms, wisdom deeper than the immediate disputes that threatened to fragment everything they had built.

The child within her stirred as if responding to the spiritual energy that accumulated around the ancient stones, movements that seemed to echo the rhythm of her heartbeat despite the exhaustion that pregnancy brought. In two hours, the sun would reach the precise angle that would send light into the passage chamber for the first time since last year's solstice—the moment when ancient builders had designed illumination to reach the heart of the sacred mound.

"You came," Ríona said, approaching through morning mist with movements that carried divine authority mixed with very human relief. Her silver scars pulsed with otherworldly light as supernatural energy responded to the approaching moment when boundaries would shift between realms that normally remained separate from mortal concerns.

"I needed to understand," Neassa replied with honesty that transcended political calculation. "Away from delegations and negotiations, away from proposals that promise solutions through methods that eliminate the problems consciousness creates by existing at all."

Behind them, a small group had gathered—not the formal representatives of Irish governance, but people whose connection to the sacred sites ran deeper than political authority. Síle with her priestess training that bridged traditional wisdom and crisis innovation, Cathair whose bloodline connections anchored him to the spiritual network despite the pressures that sought to fragment it, Boudica whose strategic experience provided perspective that transcended immediate crisis.

They came seeking not political solutions but spiritual understanding, recognition of patterns that stretched beyond the immediate negotiations to address fundamental questions about the nature of consciousness itself when consciousness faced systematic assault disguised as generous assistance.

"The network continues to destabilize," Ríona announced as they entered the passage that led toward the chamber where solstice light would soon provide illumination that came once each year. "But I've begun to understand the true scope of what we face. The spiritual infrastructure isn't just fragmenting—it's being systematically rebuilt to serve Roman rather than Irish purposes."

The passage walls bore carvings that seemed to shift and flow in the dim light, spirals and sacred symbols that had been placed by hands long dust but still held the secret names of power. As they moved deeper into the mound, the quality of air seemed to change—not just cooler, but somehow more substantial, as if ancient purpose had given weight to atmosphere itself.

"Show us," Cathair said quietly, understanding that divine perception could reveal patterns that mortal observation missed entirely.

Ríona placed her palms against the carved stones, her divine sight extending beyond normal categories of perception to read currents that flowed across the entire island. What she found there made her silver scars blaze with alarm that transcended mere tactical concern.

"Each territory that accepts administrative guidance becomes a node in imperial infrastructure," she said with certainty that carried divine authority. "Not Irish governance with Roman efficiency, but Roman administration wearing Irish forms. The spiritual connections that once served consciousness now channel coordination that serves empire."

***

The understanding rippled through their small group like recognition of sophistication that exceeded every assumption about enemy capabilities. Not crude assault on awareness, but systematic seduction that offered relief from burdens that consciousness created through its very nature.

"The refugee crisis, the administrative offers, the timing that coincides with solstice power," Boudica said with strategic clarity that read tactical implications in what others might dismiss as coincidence. "All designed to demonstrate that administered efficiency serves welfare better than the struggle that individual choice requires."

"But there's more," Ríona continued, her divine perception reading patterns that stretched across realms where different forms of meaning competed for legitimacy. "Each territory that accepts collective guidance doesn't just change its own governance—it affects the spiritual foundation that supports conscious choice for everyone else. The network adapts, seeking to fill the vacuum that voluntary surrender creates."

As they reached the chamber where solstice light would soon provide illumination, the carved stones around them began to pulse with accumulated energy that spoke to powers gathering for purposes that transcended normal understanding. Ancient spirals seemed to move in the dim light, responding to supernatural forces that built toward whatever revelation the solstice would bring.

"Ireland is being rebuilt from within," Neassa realized with growing horror as the scope of their enemies' strategy became clear. "Not conquered or corrupted, but voluntarily transformed by people who genuinely believe they're choosing better alternatives to consciousness that creates suffering through its insistence on individual will."

"The perfect trap," Síle breathed with youth's recognition of complexity that challenged every adult assumption about the nature of resistance. "How do you fight enemies who offer exactly what people think they want? How do you defend consciousness against people who prefer surrender but call it wisdom?"

The questions hung in the chamber's air like recognition of challenges that transcended normal categories of solution, problems that required innovation rather than traditional responses to familiar threats. Around them, the ancient stones seemed to wait with patience that belonged to powers older than kingdoms, wisdom deeper than immediate political crisis.

Before anyone could attempt answers to questions that challenged the fundamental nature of authority and choice, the sound of approaching footsteps echoed through the passage—not the mechanical coordination that marked converted populations, but individual movement that spoke to conscious decision rather than optimal efficiency.

King Conchobor of Ulster appeared through the entrance with movements that carried the urgency of someone who brought intelligence too important to delay for comfortable ceremony. Behind him came representatives from the territories that remained committed to conscious choice governance, faces bearing strain of people who had witnessed developments that challenged every assumption about the scope of what they faced.

"The delegations departed Tara an hour past," he announced without preamble, understanding that immediate crisis required directness rather than diplomatic courtesy. "But not in defeat—in coordination that speaks to plans already prepared for whatever response we might offer."

"They expected refusal," Boudica recognized with strategic experience that read between immediate events to larger patterns of manipulation. "Our resistance serves their purposes as much as our acceptance would. They demonstrate that conscious choice governance can't solve the problems it creates, while offering alternatives that eliminate problems through elimination of choice itself."

***

"Worse than that," King Conchobor continued with grim certainty that spoke to intelligence gathered through sources that transcended normal diplomatic channels. "Three more settlements have sent messages requesting integration into Queen Medb's administrative system. Not crisis response, but deliberate choice by populations that prefer coordination over the burden of individual decision-making."

The scope of systematic transformation became clear through reports that painted a picture of Ireland voluntarily fragmenting along lines that served enemy purposes rather than Irish welfare. Not conquest through force, but seduction through demonstration that administered efficiency eliminated suffering while conscious choice multiplied it through the chaos that individual will created when exercised by those unprepared for its demands.

"How many territories remain committed to conscious choice?" Cathair asked, though his strategic experience already suggested answers that challenged every assumption about their recent victory.

"Perhaps a dozen, and diminishing daily," came the reply that transformed celebration into recognition of defeat disguised as partial success. "Not through conversion or corruption, but through voluntary recognition that individual will creates problems that collective guidance solves through methods proven successful across territories that have learned to prosper under optimal coordination."

As the morning progressed toward the moment when solstice light would illuminate the chamber's heart, the weight of impossible decisions pressed against leaders who had proven consciousness could defend itself against elimination only to discover that elimination was never their enemies' true objective.

"There's something else," Ríona said quietly, her divine sight-reading currents that flowed beyond immediate political crisis to address fundamental questions about the nature of spiritual authority itself. "The network isn't just adapting to serve collective rather than individual consciousness—it's being rebuilt to serve Roman rather than Irish purposes. Each territory that accepts administrative guidance becomes part of imperial infrastructure disguised as voluntary cooperation."

The implications hit their small group like recognition of escalating deception, sophistication that exceeded their ability to address through traditional resistance to obvious conquest. Not elimination of Irish identity, but transformation of Irish identity into tool serving purposes that had nothing to do with Irish welfare while maintaining the illusion of cultural preservation.

"Roman methods," King Conchobor said with Ulster's grim recognition of patterns that stretched beyond immediate crisis. "Administrative absorption that preserves local forms while transforming their substance to serve imperial purposes. They've learned to make conquest look like voluntary evolution."

Before they could process the full scope of systematic transformation that challenged every assumption about the nature of legitimate authority, the quality of light began to change within the chamber as the sun approached the precise angle that would send illumination into the passage tomb's heart for the first time in a year.

The moment of solstice illumination was approaching, and with it would come whatever revelation the ancient builders had designed this place to provide—understanding that might offer solutions to problems that transcended normal categories of political response, or recognition that some challenges required entirely different forms of resistance.

"Whatever the light shows us," Neassa said quietly, her hand moving to the child that grew within her despite chaos that threatened to undo everything they had built, "we face it together. Partnership that serves both love and leadership, consciousness that chooses consciousness despite every pressure to accept beautiful alternatives."

* * *

The chamber filled with anticipation as solstice approached, ancient stones preparing to reveal whatever wisdom they had preserved across generations beyond counting, while outside, Ireland struggled with choices that would determine whether consciousness itself retained the right to exist in forms that created beauty rather than simply serving efficiency.

The first ray of solstice light pierced the passage darkness like recognition of truth that transcended political calculation, illuminating carved spirals that seemed to move with purpose older than kingdoms, deeper than the immediate crisis that brought them to seek understanding in places where ancient wisdom waited for those desperate enough to ask the right questions.

As the light reached the chamber's heart and Neassa's consciousness opened to whatever revelation the moment would bring, the weight of Ireland's crisis combined with pregnancy and divine blessing to create conditions where vision became possible—not just personal insight, but spiritual understanding that might provide answers to questions that challenged the fundamental nature of choice itself.

The vision came not as sudden revelation but as gradual recognition, layers of understanding that built like dawn breaking over landscape long hidden in darkness. Through her divine sight, enhanced by pregnancy and proximity to sacred power, she saw Ireland as it truly was—not a collection of competing territories, but a living network of connections that bound consciousness to land, people to purpose, individual will to collective meaning.

But she also saw the wounds—places where those connections had been severed or transformed, spiritual infrastructure corrupted to serve purposes that had nothing to do with Irish welfare. Each territory that accepted administrative guidance became a node in a different network, one that channeled coordination rather than consciousness, efficiency rather than the sacred chaos of free will.

The child within her seemed to respond to spiritual energy that flowed through the chamber like recognition of truths too important for comfortable ignorance. In the light that came once each year, she saw not just what was but what could be—Ireland choosing itself, preserving consciousness while acknowledging that choice created suffering for those unprepared to bear its weight.

"I see it," she whispered, her voice carrying wonder at witnessing possibility that went beyond immediate crisis. "The path forward. Not elimination of alternatives, but structure that honors both choice and the need for guidance when choice becomes burden rather than blessing."

As the solstice light reached its peak intensity, the vision crystallized into understanding that would reshape their approach to problems that had seemed impossible to solve through traditional means. Not defeat of enemies who offered seductive solutions, but innovation that served both principle and practical necessity.

Around her, the others felt the shift in spiritual atmosphere as divine revelation combined with mortal wisdom to create clarity that had been absent throughout weeks of complex negotiation. The ancient stones sang with harmonics that belonged to no earthly music, melodies that carried them across realms where different forms of meaning competed for legitimacy.

"What do you see?" Cathair asked gently, his hand finding hers with touch that anchored them both despite forces that surpassed normal categories of experience.

"Ireland as confederation rather than conquest," she replied, words coming with certainty that spoke to vision rather than theory. "Territories that choose consciousness governed through methods we've developed, territories that choose efficiency governed through methods they prefer—but all acknowledging common authority that preserves Irish rather than foreign sovereignty."

The understanding rippled through their small group like recognition of solution that honored both love and leadership, consciousness and the practical needs of those who required guidance to function effectively. Not surrender to enemy strategy, but innovation that served Irish purposes while acknowledging Irish diversity.

As the solstice light began to fade and the chamber returned to its normal shadows, Neassa felt the vision settling into her consciousness like truth finding its proper home. A sense of rightness settled over her, as if the child within blessed choices that would determine what kind of world it would inherit.

"We return to Tara," she said with quiet authority that had been tested through divine revelation and emerged stronger rather than brittle. "We offer Ireland not just resistance to foreign solutions, but Irish solutions that serve Irish needs—all of them, not just those we prefer."

The memory of songs began to stir in the ancient stones, melodies that had been carved into sacred geometry by hands that understood how meaning could be preserved across time when consciousness faced systematic assault disguised as generous assistance. In that memory lay either Ireland's salvation or recognition that some battles could only be won through choices that honored defeat rather than seeking victory at any cost.

The solstice light blazed brighter, and with it came the vision that would either transform their understanding of what they truly faced or confirm that consciousness had chosen its final test against forces that promised peace through surrender of everything that made peace worth having.

The ancient stones sang with voices both remembered and eternal, and Ireland prepared to discover whether memory itself possessed sufficient strength to resist the ultimate seduction of forgetting who they had chosen to be.

CHAPTER 32

THE SECOND CHOOSING

The solstice light struck the chamber's heart with the precision of divine intention, illuminating carved spirals that seemed to move with purpose older than kingdoms as radiance filled the ancient space with power that exceeded normal categories of illumination. Neassa felt the moment arrive like tide returning to familiar shores, her consciousness opening to receive whatever wisdom the ancient builders had preserved for those desperate enough to seek understanding in places where stone remembered what flesh forgot.

The vision came not as sudden revelation but as gradual recognition, layers of understanding that built like dawn breaking over landscape long hidden in darkness. Through her divine sight, enhanced by pregnancy and proximity to sacred power, she saw Ireland as it truly was—not a collection of competing territories, but a living network of connections that bound consciousness to land, people to purpose, individual will to collective meaning.

But she also saw the wounds—places where those connections had been severed or transformed, spiritual infrastructure corrupted to serve purposes that had nothing to do with Irish welfare. Each territory that accepted administrative guidance became a node in a different network, one that channeled coordination rather than consciousness, efficiency rather than the sacred chaos of free will.

The child within her seemed to respond to spiritual energy that flowed through the chamber like recognition of truths too important for comfortable ignorance. In the light that came once each year, she saw not just what was but what could be—Ireland choosing itself, preserving consciousness while acknowledging that choice created suffering for those unprepared to bear its weight.

"I see it," she whispered, her voice carrying wonder at witnessing possibility that went beyond immediate crisis. "The path forward. Not elimination of alternatives, but structure that honors both choice and the need for guidance when choice becomes burden rather than blessing."

As the solstice light reached its peak intensity, the vision crystallized into understanding that would reshape their approach to problems that had seemed impossible to solve through traditional means. Not defeat of enemies who offered seductive solutions, but innovation that served both principle and practical necessity.

Around her, the others felt the shift in spiritual atmosphere as divine revelation combined with mortal wisdom to create clarity that had been absent throughout weeks of complex negotiation. The ancient stones sang with harmonics that belonged to no earthly music, melodies that carried them across realms where different forms of meaning competed for legitimacy.

"What do you see?" Cathair asked gently, his hand finding hers with touch that anchored them both despite forces that surpassed normal categories of experience.

"Ireland as confederation rather than conquest," she replied, words coming with certainty that spoke to vision rather than theory. "Territories that choose consciousness governed through methods we've developed, territories that choose efficiency

governed through methods they prefer—but all acknowledging
common authority that preserves Irish rather than foreign
sovereignty."

The understanding rippled through their small group like
recognition of solution that honored both love and leadership,
consciousness and the practical needs of those who required
guidance to function effectively. Not surrender to enemy strategy,
but innovation that served Irish purposes while acknowledging
Irish diversity.

***

As the solstice light began to fade and the chamber returned to its
normal shadows, Neassa felt the vision settling into her
consciousness like truth finding its proper home. A sense of
rightness settled over her, as if the child within blessed choices that
would determine what kind of world it would inherit.

"We return to Tara," she said with quiet authority that had
been tested through divine revelation and emerged stronger rather
than brittle. "We offer Ireland not just resistance to foreign
solutions, but Irish solutions that serve Irish needs—all of them,
not just those we prefer."

The ride back to Tara carried weight of transformation that
went beyond personal revelation to address fundamental questions
about the nature of legitimate authority when authority faced
challenges that stretched past traditional categories of response.
Through winter landscape that bore signs of spiritual healing, they
discussed implications of vision that offered hope disguised as
political innovation.

"Regional autonomy within national unity," Boudica observed
with strategic appreciation for solutions that served multiple
purposes simultaneously. "Territories choosing efficiency can have

efficiency, but under Irish rather than Roman authority. Queen Medb rules as she chooses, but as vassal rather than equal."

"The spiritual network supports such arrangement?" Ríona asked with divine concern that addressed foundations underlying political decisions.

"The network adapts to serve conscious choice," Neassa replied with certainty born from vision that exceeded normal perception. "When choice includes the choice of guidance for those who require it, the connections strengthen rather than fragment. But the guidance must serve Irish rather than imperial purposes."

As Tara's sacred hill came into view through afternoon light that seemed somehow clearer than it had in weeks, they could see the activity that marked urgent preparation for whatever announcement would emerge from their solstice consultation. Representatives from across Ireland's free territories had gathered to hear solutions that might preserve consciousness without abandoning those who preferred alternatives.

The great hall filled with tension that spoke to decisions too long delayed, representatives who had risked everything to preserve conscious choice now facing proposals that would determine whether their sacrifice served sustainable governance or noble failure that honored principles while serving no practical purpose.

Cathair stood before the assembly with authority that had been tested through impossible trials, his presence somehow more commanding since accepting the High Kingship that had come through conscious choice rather than inheritance. But when he spoke, his words carried weight that reached beyond personal transformation to address issues fundamental to Irish identity itself.

"We gather to address proposals that promise solutions through methods that challenge everything we fought to preserve," he began, his voice carrying across the hall with certainty that brooked no contradiction. "But before we respond to specific offers of foreign guidance, we must establish principles that will govern our response to all such offers, now and in future generations."

The silence that followed carried anticipation as representatives prepared to hear solutions that might preserve both principle and practical necessity, consciousness and the welfare of those who required guidance to function effectively.

***

"Ireland is to be ruled by Irish," Cathair declared with finality that seemed to echo from the ancient stones themselves. "Roman influence is not welcomed here, no matter how attractive the efficiency it promises, no matter how reasonable the guidance it offers. We choose Irish solutions to Irish problems, Irish authority over Irish territories, Irish welfare served through Irish wisdom."

The proclamation hit the assembly like recognition of truth that had been implicit throughout their struggle but never stated with such direct clarity. Not just resistance to specific proposals, but rejection of foreign influence regardless of the benefits it promised or the problems it claimed to solve.

Around the hall, representatives who had struggled with complex moral questions found themselves united by recognition of principle that surpassed immediate tactical concerns. Whatever solutions they developed would serve Irish rather than imperial purposes, honor Irish rather than foreign values, preserve Irish rather than administrative efficiency.

"But we also acknowledge that Irish includes all who choose to remain Irish," Neassa added, stepping forward to stand beside her husband with partnership that had been tested through crisis and proven stronger than individual authority. "Those who prefer guidance over uncertainty, efficiency over the chaos that individual choice creates. They too are Irish, deserving of governance that serves their welfare while preserving their identity."

The balance between rejection of foreign influence and acknowledgment of internal diversity created space for innovation that had seemed impossible during weeks of complex negotiation. Not abandonment of those who preferred alternatives, but provision of alternatives that served Irish rather than imperial purposes.

"Therefore," Cathair continued, his voice gaining strength as vision translated into policy that might preserve both principle and practical necessity, "we offer a new arrangement. Territories that choose administrative efficiency may select regional kings or queens to govern them according to whatever methods serve their welfare. But those rulers—including Queen Medb of Connacht— must come to Tara and swear allegiance to the High King and High Queen of Ireland."

The proposal struck the assembly like recognition of solution that honored both love and leadership, consciousness and the needs of those who required different forms of guidance. Regional autonomy within national unity, choice within structure, Irish authority over Irish territories regardless of the governance methods individual regions preferred.

"They may govern their territories as they choose," Neassa elaborated, "but they acknowledge that Ireland remains one land under one legitimate authority. No independent kingdoms claiming equal status with Tara, no foreign powers speaking for Irish interests, no administrative systems that serve imperial rather than Irish purposes."

The debate that followed compressed weeks of moral complexity into hours of practical planning as representatives discovered that principled resistance could evolve into principled accommodation when accommodation served Irish rather than foreign purposes. Not surrender to enemy strategy, but innovation that preserved Irish sovereignty while acknowledging Irish diversity.

"Queen Medb will refuse," predicted King Conchobor with Ulster's grim understanding of personalities that valued independence over accommodation. "She claims authority equal to Tara's, not subordinate to it. Asking her to swear allegiance challenges everything she's built through alliance with Roman administrative methods."

"Then she reveals her true purpose," Boudica replied with strategic clarity that read tactical implications in whatever response their offer might provoke. "If she accepts vassalage, she governs efficiently but under Irish authority. If she refuses, she declares herself enemy of Irish sovereignty rather than servant of Irish welfare."

"And the territories that have already requested integration into her system?" asked Brendan of Mag Muirthemne with practical concern that addressed immediate consequences of whatever policy they established.

"They choose," Cathair said simply, his authority carrying weight that had been earned through trial rather than inherited through blood. "Remain under Tara's ultimate authority with regional governance that serves their preferences, or follow Queen Medb into whatever independence she claims—but without pretense that such choice serves Irish rather than foreign purposes."

***

As evening approached and the weight of decision settled over the assembly, representatives found themselves facing not just political innovation but fundamental questions about the nature of love, loyalty, and the prices that principles could demand from those who lacked strength to pay them without destroying themselves in the process.

"What of those who choose neither?" Síle asked with youth's recognition of complexity that challenged every adult assumption about the adequacy of binary alternatives. "Those who want neither conscious struggle nor administered efficiency, but something between that honors both individual will and collective guidance?"

"They build it," Neassa replied with certainty that came from vision enhanced by divine blessing and pregnancy's wisdom. "Under Irish authority, serving Irish purposes, guided by Irish values rather than foreign efficiency. We prove that consciousness can create forms of governance adequate to serve all forms of consciousness, not just those we prefer or find comfortable."

The silence that followed carried weight beyond mere political consideration as representatives contemplated innovation that challenged every precedent while serving purposes that stretched past immediate convenience. Not just preservation of what existed, but creation of what had never been attempted—confederation united by choice rather than compulsion, diversity within unity rather than unity through elimination of difference.

"The spiritual network supports such arrangement?" Ríona asked with divine authority that addressed foundations underlying all political structures.

"The network strengthens when choice includes the choice of guidance," Neassa confirmed with certainty born from solstice vision that had revealed truth deeper than immediate political calculation. "But only when guidance serves consciousness rather than replacing it, when efficiency honors rather than eliminates the diversity that makes consciousness worth preserving."

As representatives began to disperse toward quarters where they would consider proposals that offered hope disguised as political necessity, the weight of transformation settled over Tara like recognition of historical significance that reached beyond immediate celebration. Not just crisis survived, but innovation achieved that might serve Irish purposes across generations yet unborn.

"Tomorrow we send envoys," Cathair decided as evening stars appeared overhead in patterns that had guided Irish decisions since the first druid learned to read meaning in celestial movement. "To every territory, every regional authority, every population that claims Irish identity. They choose: Irish confederation under Tara's authority, or foreign alliance that abandons Irish sovereignty for promised efficiency."

The second choosing was beginning, and Ireland would discover whether love could justify the complexity it created when consciousness faced not elimination but transformation into tools serving purposes that honored neither love nor consciousness, neither Ireland nor the welfare of Irish people who deserved governance that served them rather than using them to serve others.

But for the first time since the crisis began, they faced that choosing with solutions that honored both principle and practical necessity, consciousness and the welfare of those who required guidance, Irish sovereignty and Irish diversity in all its chaotic, inefficient, gloriously human manifestations.

The solstice light had revealed the path forward, and Ireland prepared to walk it with everything they had chosen to preserve and everyone they had chosen to become through choices that honored both heritage and hope, tradition and the innovation that tradition required to remain alive rather than merely preserved.

CHAPTER 33

THE CROWN OF THORNS

Queen Medb's response arrived three days after the envoys delivered Tara's ultimatum, carried by a delegation that moved with coordination too perfect for any group maintaining individual thought. Twenty riders in the red and gold of Connacht, but their faces bore the terrible peace of those who had surrendered the burden of choice for the beautiful certainty of optimal decisions made by forces wiser than personal preference.

Neassa watched from Tara's great window as the delegation arranged itself in the courtyard below with precision that eliminated wasted motion, each person taking their assigned position as if guided by invisible threads that connected them to purposes beyond individual understanding. The morning sickness had finally begun to ease, but the weight of carrying Ireland's future within her womb pressed against her consciousness like responsibility too heavy for mortal shoulders.

"She's made her choice," Cathair observed, joining her at the window where pale winter light struggled through clouds that seemed heavier than they should despite the clear sky. "No queen who retained individual will would send representatives who move like components of a single mechanism."

"The question is whether she sends them to accept vassalage or declare independence," Neassa replied, though her priestess training already whispered warnings about spiritual emptiness that radiated from the delegation like cold from winter stones. "Either answer reveals what we're truly facing."

Through the courtyard, they could see the effects of three days' preparation as Ireland's representatives gathered to witness whatever announcement would emerge from Queen Medb's consideration of proposals that challenged everything she had built through alliance with forces that promised peace through surrender of individual will.

The great hall filled with tension thick as morning fog as Ireland's leadership prepared to hear responses that would determine whether their confederation could be achieved through negotiation or would require enforcement through methods that honored neither diplomacy nor the welfare of populations caught between competing visions of legitimate authority.

The delegation's leader, a woman whose bearing spoke to royal blood transformed into administrative function, approached the platform where Ireland's joint rulers had proven partnership could serve authority more effectively than individual power. But her movements carried the mechanical precision that marked those who had been optimized beyond the chaos of personal preference.

"High King and High Queen of Ireland," she announced with courtesy that felt programmed rather than personal, "I am Ailbhe of the Coordinated Territories, speaking for Queen Medb and the alliance of administrators who have achieved harmony through optimal decision-making guided by proven expertise."

The formal language carried subtle threat disguised as diplomatic courtesy. Not Connacht anymore, but "Coordinated Territories"—expansion that claimed authority beyond traditional boundaries through methods that eliminated the borders individual kingdoms created when they insisted on separate identity.

"You're welcome at Tara, Ailbhe of the Coordinated Territories," Cathair replied with authority that had been tested through trial but now faced challenges that required wisdom rather than courage. "Though we understand your visit carries weight beyond mere courtesy."

"Indeed, High King. We bring Queen Medb's response to proposals that would impose hierarchical relationships upon territories that have evolved beyond the need for such primitive structures." Her smile never wavered, perfect as painted porcelain that felt more unsettling than any expression of open hostility.

Around the hall, representatives who had risked everything to preserve conscious choice found themselves confronting the scope of transformation they faced—not just political disagreement, but systematic elimination of the very concepts that made disagreement possible or meaningful.

***

"Queen Medb appreciates the generous offer of vassalage," Ailbhe continued with satisfaction that seemed disconnected from any personal enthusiasm, "but the Coordinated Territories have discovered governance methods that transcend traditional hierarchies through collective decision-making that serves optimal outcomes rather than historical precedent."

The silence that followed carried weight beyond mere political consideration. Around the hall, representatives began to understand that diplomatic courtesy was concealing rejection not just of Tara's authority but of the entire framework that made authority possible when authority served consciousness rather than eliminating it.

"You speak of refusal," Neassa said carefully, her voice carrying the strain of someone who understood that immediate choices would determine Ireland's fundamental character for generations yet unborn. "Rejection of confederation that preserves Irish sovereignty while allowing regional variation in governance methods."

"We speak of evolution beyond the need for such artificial constraints," Ailbhe corrected with gentle firmness that made her words more persuasive than any argument could have achieved. "The Coordinated Territories offer partnership between equals rather than submission to outdated hierarchies that serve no optimal purpose."

"Partnership between whom?" Cathair demanded with strategic directness that sought clarity rather than allowing comfortable ambiguity to conceal uncomfortable implications.

"Between administrative systems that have learned to serve welfare through efficiency and governance structures that continue to struggle with the chaos individual preference creates when it interferes with collective wisdom." Her mechanical certainty was more chilling than anger would have been. "Queen Medb proposes division of authority that honors both approaches— administered efficiency for territories that choose progress, traditional hierarchy for territories that prefer stagnation."

"What you speak of is treason," Neassa interrupted with heat that surprised everyone present, including herself. Perhaps it was the pregnancy hormones, or perhaps the simple fury of watching Ireland carved up like meat at a Roman feast.

The sophistication of the trap became apparent as its full scope revealed itself through language that made surrender sound like generous accommodation. Not conquest or absorption, but "division of authority" that would create two Irelands—one serving consciousness, one serving efficiency, both claiming equal legitimacy while serving entirely different masters.

"Two Irelands," Boudica said quietly, her strategic experience reading between diplomatic language to tactical reality. "Independent kingdoms with no obligation to coordinate, no shared authority to resolve conflicts, no common identity to preserve when external forces seek advantage through division."

"Efficient solutions that eliminate inefficiencies created by competing claims to singular authority," Ailbhe agreed with satisfaction that spoke to problems solved rather than principles abandoned. "Each territory governed according to methods that serve its population's preferences, without interference from authorities that lack understanding of optimal outcomes."

Before anyone could respond to proposals that challenged every assumption about the nature of legitimate governance, the sound of urgent hoofbeats echoed across the sacred hill. Not individual messengers this time, but coordinated movement that spoke to developments requiring immediate attention rather than careful deliberation.

Through the windows, they could see riders approaching from multiple directions—not Queen Medb's perfect coordination, but the frantic urgency of people who carried intelligence too important to delay for proper protocol. Their faces bore strain that spoke to witnessing events that challenged every assumption about the scope of what they faced.

***

The first scout burst through the great doors with movements that carried desperate haste barely contained by formal necessity. His horse stood outside the entrance, sides heaving from a ride that had pushed both mount and rider beyond normal endurance.

"High King, High Queen," he gasped, stumbling forward with exhaustion that spoke to days of hard travel through hostile territory. "I bring word from the western territories that changes everything we thought we knew about the scope of Queen Medb's coordination."

King Conchobor stepped forward with Ulster's grim recognition of intelligence that would reshape their understanding of contemporary reality. "Speak your news, friend. In times like these, urgent intelligence serves better delivered swiftly than perfectly."

"Roman ships," the scout announced, his voice gaining strength as he focused on the intelligence that had driven his desperate ride. "Three vessels flying imperial banners, anchored in Galway Bay. Not trading ships or exploration—warships carrying soldiers and administrators who speak of 'administrative support for territories requesting imperial guidance.'"

The implications hit the assembly like recognition of sophistication that exceeded every assumption about enemy capabilities. Not just political manipulation or spiritual seduction, but coordinated assault that combined Irish ambition with Roman military support, local knowledge with imperial resources.

"When?" Cathair demanded, his strategic mind immediately calculating timeframes that would determine whether they faced immediate crisis or developing threat.

"The ships arrived two days past, but their purpose appears to have been developing for weeks," the scout replied with honesty that spoke to witnessing systematic rather than opportunistic development. "Local populations report improved coordination in territories under Queen Medb's influence, but also construction that serves military rather than civilian purposes."

Around the hall, representatives who had thought they understood the scope of what they faced began to grasp the true dimensions of systematic transformation that stretched beyond Ireland's shores to encompass imperial strategy that viewed their island as testing ground for methods that might be applied across other territories that valued independence over efficiency.

"Administrative support," King Aillen of Leinster repeated with growing understanding of language that concealed military reality beneath diplomatic courtesy. "Roman soldiers disguised as administrative advisors, imperial authority presented as requested assistance."

"The perfect method," Boudica observed with strategic clarity that read tactical implications in what others might dismiss as political maneuvering. "No conquest that violates treaties, no invasion that justifies resistance. Just voluntary acceptance of guidance that happens to require military protection against populations too primitive to appreciate its benefits."

Ailbhe watched their growing alarm with patience that spoke to understanding rather than calculation, her expression showing no surprise at intelligence that should have been shocking to anyone genuinely committed to Irish rather than imperial welfare.

"The Coordinated Territories appreciate whatever support serves optimal outcomes," she said with mechanical certainty that eliminated any pretense of independence. "Administrative guidance requires protection against populations that prefer chaos over harmony, individual will over collective wisdom."

"Protection from whom?" Neassa demanded, understanding that the question would force revelation of purposes that had been carefully concealed beneath reasonable language.

"From territories that refuse to evolve beyond primitive attachment to sovereignty that serves no optimal purpose," Ailbhe replied without hesitation, her programming apparently including authorization to speak truths that eliminated comfortable ambiguity. "Individual preference that interferes with collective welfare cannot be permitted to persist, regardless of historical precedent or cultural attachment."

***

The complete revelation of enemy purpose settled over the assembly like recognition of trap closing with mechanical precision around prey that had struggled too long to escape through methods that honored principles their enemies viewed as fatal weakness.

"Then the terms are clear," Cathair said, his voice carrying across the hall with authority that had been earned through trial rather than inherited through privilege. "Queen Medb chooses Nero over Tara, a stranger in Rome over her own people, imperial efficiency over the sacred chaos of consciousness that makes us Irish."

The words struck the assembly like recognition of truth that had been building throughout the crisis but never stated with such brutal clarity. Around the hall, representatives found themselves straightening with resolve that came from hearing their king speak what every Irish heart had known but hadn't dared voice.

"Aye," King Conchobor said with Ulster's grim approval, his weathered voice carrying the weight of someone who had witnessed too many betrayals to be shocked but still felt each one like a personal wound. "She chooses foreign gold over Irish honor."

"A traitor's choice," added King Aillen of Leinster with finality that brooked no further debate. "Whatever she calls herself now, she is no longer Irish in any way that matters."

Boudica's strategic mind read the political implications with satisfaction that spoke to enemies finally revealing their true nature. "Now we know exactly what we face—not civil war between Irish factions, but resistance against foreign occupation wearing Irish masks."

"The High King states the choice with admirable clarity," Ailbhe agreed with satisfaction that spoke to missions accomplished rather than negotiations failed. "Though we prefer to describe it as evolution beyond outdated concepts that create unnecessary suffering through attachment to inefficient processes."

"And we prefer to describe it as treason," Neassa replied with heat that surprised everyone present, including herself. Perhaps it was the pregnancy hormones, or perhaps the weight of carrying Ireland's future while witnessing its betrayal to forces that promised peace through surrender of everything that made peace worthwhile.

"High Queen," Ailbhe said with genuine pity that somehow made her words more chilling than direct threats, "emotional attachment to concepts that serve no optimal purpose creates suffering that administrative guidance can eliminate. The offer remains open for territories wise enough to accept evolution rather than clinging to primitive independence."

The silence that followed carried weight beyond mere political rejection as representatives contemplated the scope of what they faced—not just military threat or political pressure, but systematic seduction that offered everything people thought they wanted while transforming them into tools serving purposes they would never consciously choose.

"Ireland rejects your offer," Cathair declared with finality that seemed to echo from the ancient stones themselves. "We choose consciousness over efficiency, sovereignty over guidance, the right to make our own mistakes rather than accepting someone else's perfect solutions."

"Then Ireland chooses unnecessary suffering over optimal welfare," Ailbhe replied with mechanical certainty that eliminated any trace of regret. "Queen Medb grieves for such willful blindness, but evolution proceeds regardless of individual resistance to proven improvements."

As the delegation turned to leave, Neassa felt another surge of fury that pregnancy had stripped of all diplomatic restraint. "Since Queen Medb loves Roman efficiency so much," she called after them, her voice carrying across the hall with venom that made several representatives shift uncomfortably, "perhaps when we capture her, we'll demonstrate their methods. Crucifixion seems to be their preferred solution for those who threaten their precious order."

The delegation paused, Ailbhe's mechanical composure faltering for just a moment as something that might have been uncertainty flickered across her optimized features. Then the moment passed, and she resumed her coordinated departure without response.

***

As the delegation prepared to depart with coordination that spoke to shared purpose rather than individual agendas, the weight of what had been accomplished settled over Tara like recognition of historical significance that reached beyond immediate political crisis. Not just negotiation failed, but clarity achieved about the fundamental nature of what they faced.

"Roman warships in Irish waters," King Conchobor observed with Ulster's grim recognition of implications that stretched beyond immediate military threat. "Imperial authority claiming invitation from populations that have been optimized beyond the capacity to understand what they've invited."

"How long do we have?" Síle asked with youth's desperate need for practical answers to impossible questions.

"Days, perhaps hours," Ríona replied, her divine sight-reading patterns that flowed beyond normal perception to recognize forces gathering for purposes that would reshape the spiritual landscape supporting Irish identity. "The Roman ships don't carry invasion forces—they carry administrators who will legitimize whatever Queen Medb accomplishes through internal division."

"Then we prepare for the impossible," Boudica said with strategic experience that had learned to find hope in circumstances that offered only noble failure. "We prove that consciousness can resist not just elimination but transformation into administrative tool, that Irish identity means more than efficient governance of Irish territories."

As evening approached and the reality of their situation became undeniable, representatives found themselves facing not just political crisis but existential choice about the nature of love, loyalty, and the prices that principles could demand from those who possessed strength to pay them regardless of cost.

"What comes next?" Brendan of Mag Muirthemne asked with practical concern that addressed immediate necessities rather than abstract principles.

"We discover whether confederation can be built through conscious choice when choice itself faces systematic assault," Cathair replied with authority that had been tested through impossible trials and proven adequate to impossible challenges. "We prove that Irish solutions serve Irish problems better than imperial efficiency serves imperial expansion."

Through the windows, they could see evening stars appearing overhead in patterns that had watched over Irish choices for generations beyond counting. But tonight, those ancient lights looked down on choices that would determine whether Ireland remained Ireland or became something more efficient that served purposes divorced from any recognizable form of Irish welfare.

The crown of thorns had been offered and rejected, but rejection created obligations that acceptance would have eliminated. Now came the test of whether love could justify resistance when resistance required sacrificing the very people love sought to protect, whether consciousness proved strong enough to choose consciousness when choice meant accepting responsibility for all the suffering choice created through its insistence on remaining itself.

Queen Medb had made her choice, Rome had revealed its methods, and Ireland prepared to discover whether partnership forged through conscious decision could bear the weight of defending consciousness itself when consciousness faced forces that promised beautiful peace through surrender of everything that created the capacity for peace, beauty, or recognition of their value.

CHAPTER 34

THE PRICE OF CHOICE

The first territories began declaring their allegiance within hours of Queen Medb's rejection, but instead of sending messengers, the regional kings and túath chiefs themselves rode to Tara. They came not as supplicants but as leaders who understood that swearing allegiance required personal presence rather than distant diplomacy.

Neassa watched from the great hall as one by one, the rulers who had chosen confederation climbed Tara's sacred hill to offer their loyalty in person. Her hand moved unconsciously to the growing curve of her belly where new life stirred, the child within responding to her emotional state as if already aware that its future depended on decisions being made in these tension-filled chambers.

"Seventeen regional kings choose Tara," Síle reported, her voice mixing relief and awe. "Each coming personally to kneel before the platform where joint authority has proven stronger than individual rule. But also six túath chiefs from territories that sent their kings to Queen Medb—they choose confederation despite their overlords' preferences."

The mathematics of division crystallized around them like recognition of prices that victory had demanded but no one had anticipated paying. Not the overwhelming mandate they had hoped for, nor the complete rejection that would have simplified everything, but exactly the split that would make governing nearly impossible while providing neither side with clear legitimacy.

Cathair moved to the great window where he could see the lights of camps spreading across the landscape below—representatives who had come seeking unified guidance now clustering according to choices that eliminated the possibility of unity through anything except force.

"We hold enough to claim authority," he said grimly. "But not enough to govern effectively without constant resistance from populations that prefer different arrangements."

"And Queen Medb holds enough to create perpetual crisis," Boudica added, reading tactical implications in political division. "Not enough to claim Ireland, but sufficient to ensure that whoever does claim it faces endless conflict with neighbors who view that claim as illegitimate."

***

As evening progressed and the scope of Ireland's transformation became undeniable, the weight of governing a fractured nation settled on leaders who had proven consciousness could defend itself only to discover that defense created obligations more complex than conquest would have imposed.

"The territories that chose us expect protection," King Conchobor observed with Ulster's practical understanding of responsibilities that came with authority. "Not just from Queen Medb's coordination, but from Roman support she's clearly arranged. Seventeen territories against twelve with imperial backing—the mathematics don't favor our survival without innovation that exceeds anything we've yet attempted."

Through the windows, they could see the evidence of systematic preparation as representatives departed Tara for territories that had declared their positions. Not the chaotic dispersal of normal diplomatic conclusion, but coordinated movement that spoke to planning that had anticipated exactly this outcome.

"They expected division," Ríona said, her divine sight-reading patterns that served purposes larger than Irish welfare. "The offer was designed to create exactly this result—Ireland split between those who choose consciousness and those who choose efficiency, neither side strong enough to eliminate the other, both requiring external support to maintain their positions."

"Roman strategy," Neassa said. "Divide potential enemies against themselves, then offer assistance to whichever side serves imperial purposes while ensuring the conflict continues long enough to drain both sides' strength."

The child within her moved with what felt like agitation, new life responding to spiritual pressure that sought to transform Ireland into a tool serving purposes that had nothing to do with Irish welfare or the welfare of children who would inherit whatever nation emerged from the chaos of competing allegiances.

***

Before they could analyze the full implications of systematic manipulation that had anticipated their every choice, new sounds echoed from the courtyards below—not messengers bearing political intelligence this time, but something else entirely. Coordination that spoke to military rather than diplomatic purpose, organization that served immediate action rather than extended negotiation.

"Ships," announced the scout who burst through the great doors with urgency that eliminated diplomatic courtesy in favor of intelligence that could not wait for proper protocol. "Roman warships in Galway Bay have been destroyed. Two vessels rest on the harbor bottom, the third so damaged it cannot sail. Cú Chulainn's mission succeeded completely—their naval threat is eliminated."

The implications hit their council like recognition of capabilities their enemies had never anticipated. Not just resistance to Roman expansion, but direct assault on imperial forces that demonstrated Irish power could reach beyond defensive positions to strike at the heart of enemy strength.

"How long until they reach territories under Queen Medb's influence?" Cathair asked, seeking immediate tactical intelligence rather than abstract understanding.

"Two days, perhaps three if weather slows their progress. But advance parties have already landed—administrators and advisors who carry authority to coordinate whatever reception the main force will require."

Around the hall, representatives who had thought they understood the scope of systematic manipulation began to grasp the true dimensions of planning that exceeded their ability to counter through traditional resistance. Not just political seduction or spiritual assault, but coordinated campaign that combined local knowledge with imperial resources to achieve objectives that served Roman rather than Irish purposes.

***

"We can't match Roman military organization," Boudica said, cutting through comfortable illusions to address tactical reality. "Seventeen territories against imperial professionals supported by populations that have been optimized beyond individual resistance to collective coordination."

"Then we don't match it," Neassa replied with certainty that came from sources deeper than tactical calculation. "We prove that consciousness creates forms of strength that administrative efficiency can't anticipate or counter. We demonstrate that Irish solutions serve Irish problems better than imperial efficiency serves imperial expansion."

The planning that followed compressed weeks of preparation into hours of desperate coordination as Ireland's diminished leadership began the work of proving that confederation chosen through conscious decision could survive being tested by forces that promised beautiful peace through surrender of everything that made peace worth having.

"The spiritual network supports confederation," Ríona announced, addressing foundations underlying all political structures. "But only when confederation serves consciousness rather than convenience, when unity honors diversity rather than eliminating it through administrative coordination."

"Practical implications?" King Aillen asked, needing concrete guidance rather than abstract principles.

"Each territory that chooses Tara strengthens connections that bind the confederation together. But the strength requires constant choice—daily decisions to remain conscious despite pressures that make surrender seem merciful rather than defeat."

"And those who chose Queen Medb?"

"They weaken the network through voluntary severance, but they also eliminate sources of internal division that might have fractured confederation from within." Her expression showed the strain of reading spiritual geography that defied comfortable categorization. "Ireland smaller but more coherent, conscious rather than comprehensive."

***

As dawn approached and the reality of their situation crystallized into recognition of choices that could not be delayed or delegated to more comfortable moments, Neassa felt the weight of carrying Ireland's future combining with pregnancy's wisdom to create clarity that had been absent throughout weeks of complex negotiation.

"We offer one final opportunity," she decided with authority that carried both political legitimacy and spiritual power. "Not to Queen Medb—she's made her choice clear—but to territories that remain undecided. Full confederation membership for those who choose consciousness, respectful neutrality for those who prefer isolation, but no accommodation for administrative efficiency that serves imperial rather than Irish purposes."

The ultimatum carried weight that transcended immediate tactical considerations, representing Ireland's final attempt to preserve unity through conscious choice rather than accepting division imposed by forces that viewed Irish welfare as secondary to imperial convenience. Whatever responses came would determine not just territorial boundaries, but the fundamental nature of what it meant to be Irish when being Irish required conscious decision rather than inherited tradition.

***

The responses that began arriving before midday painted a picture of Ireland permanently transformed by crisis that had forced choices most would have preferred to avoid indefinitely. Not the overwhelming mandate they had hoped for, but sufficient support to create sustainable confederation based on conscious choice rather than inherited tradition.

"Twenty-three territories choose confederation," Síle announced with growing wonder as she tallied responses that exceeded their most optimistic projections. "Eight choose neutrality with respectful boundaries. Twelve remain with Queen Medb's coordination, but three have sent private messages suggesting their choice might change if confederation proves more effective than administrative efficiency."

"And the Roman response?"

"Acceleration," Boudica replied, recognizing patterns that served imperial rather than Irish timing. "The warships alter course toward territories that declared neutrality—demonstration that imperial protection comes whether requested or not, that neutrality serves imperial purposes as effectively as voluntary cooperation."

The sophistication of Roman strategy became apparent as its full scope revealed itself through actions that had anticipated Irish choices with accuracy that spoke to planning that exceeded anything their enemies had yet demonstrated. Not reaction to confederation, but preparation that had positioned forces to exploit whatever configuration emerged from Ireland's internal division.

***

As evening settled over Tara and the first day of confederation drew toward its close, representatives began to understand that their choice to remain conscious had created obligations that would test everything they thought they understood about the relationship between love and leadership, principle and practical necessity.

"We govern twenty-three territories that chose consciousness over efficiency," Cathair observed, his authority earned through trial but now facing challenges that required wisdom rather than courage. "But we govern them in a world where efficiency commands Roman support while consciousness must create its own strength from sources that administrative coordination can't access or corrupt."

"Then we prove consciousness creates better outcomes," Neassa replied with certainty that came from vision enhanced by divine blessing and pregnancy's deepening connection to future possibilities. "Not just different outcomes, but measurably superior results that demonstrate the value of choosing struggle over surrender, complexity over the beautiful simplicity that promises peace through elimination of everything that makes peace worth having."

Through the windows, they could see the lights of settlements that had chosen confederation, scattered across landscape that no longer belonged entirely to any single vision of Irish identity but had been consciously divided according to principles that honored choice itself rather than specific outcomes choice might produce.

"The real work begins now," Ríona said, her divine perspective reaching beyond immediate celebration to recognize that survival required daily renewal of choices that had been made once but would need to be made again with every dawn that followed.

"Building rather than resisting," Síle added with youth's eagerness to translate victory into lasting change that would serve generations yet unborn.

***

The price of choice had been paid in territory and unity, blood and tears, the comfortable certainty of inherited tradition sacrificed for the terrible wonderful burden of conscious decision-making that honored both heritage and hope. But for the first time since the crisis began, Ireland faced that burden with clarity about what it meant to be Irish when being Irish required conscious choice rather than automatic inheritance.

The confederation was born, tested by fire and proven adequate to impossible challenges. Now came the harder test of whether love could justify the complexity it created when consciousness faced not elimination but the daily work of proving itself worthy of preservation through choices that honored both individual will and collective welfare.

Outside Tara's walls, the stars appeared in patterns that had watched over Irish choices for generations beyond counting, ancient lights bearing witness to transformation that honored both continuity and change, tradition and the innovation that tradition required to remain alive rather than merely preserved in forms that served foreign rather than Irish purposes.

Ireland had chosen, and now Ireland would discover whether choice itself possessed sufficient strength to create forms of beauty adequate to justify the chaos consciousness demanded as the price of remaining conscious, aware, gloriously inefficient in all the ways that made existence meaningful rather than merely optimal.

CHAPTER 35

THE SONGS CONTINUE

Cú Chulainn returned to Tara as the winter sun reached its brief zenith, riding up the sacred hill with movements that carried both divine grace and mortal exhaustion. His weapons still sang with their own inner light, but dimmer now, as if the supernatural energy that powered them had been spent in service to purposes that stretched his immortal heritage to its limits.

Neassa watched from the great hall's entrance as Ulster's greatest champion dismounted with careful precision. Water still dripped from his travel clothes despite the clear day, and his eyes held depths that reflected experiences no ordinary warrior could have survived.

"Uncle," he said simply as King Conchobor approached, the formal greeting carrying undertones of affection that spoke to bonds forged through shared blood and common purpose. "Your messenger found me returning from Galway Bay. The mission is complete, but there were complications we didn't anticipate."

***

"Tell us what you found," Cathair commanded.

Cú Chulainn's expression grew grim as he consulted memories that carried divine certainty mixed with very mortal concern. "The ships carried more than soldiers and administrators. Roman engineers, surveyors, men who spoke of harbors and fortifications, permanent installations that would serve imperial expansion regardless of whatever political arrangements emerged from Ireland's internal divisions."

"They planned to stay," Boudica observed, reading between intelligence reports to recognize patterns she had witnessed during her own rebellion's final phases. "Not temporary administrative support, but foundation for permanent imperial presence that would outlast whatever local arrangements served immediate convenience."

"Worse than that," Cú Chulainn continued, his divine heritage allowing him to read intentions that mortal observation might have missed. "They carried detailed maps of Ireland's coastline, marked with locations for signal towers, supply depots, naval stations. This wasn't support for Queen Medb's coordination—this was preparation for systematic occupation disguised as voluntary cooperation."

The implications rippled through the assembly like recognition of sophistication that exceeded their most pessimistic estimates of enemy planning. Not just political manipulation or spiritual seduction, but military strategy that would transform Ireland into imperial territory while maintaining the illusion of Irish governance.

* * *

"How many escaped when you destroyed the ships?" Neassa asked, understanding that Roman military doctrine required detailed reporting that would inform whatever response imperial authorities prepared for this unexpected resistance.

"Perhaps twenty from the third vessel reached shore before I could complete its destruction," Cú Chulainn replied honestly. "They carry knowledge of our capabilities, our spiritual defenses, our political divisions. Rome will adapt their methods accordingly."

Around the hall, representatives who had thought the naval threat's elimination guaranteed immediate safety began to understand that victory created obligations as complex as defeat would have imposed. Not just military triumph, but political necessity to address consequences that would reshape Ireland's relationship with imperial power for generations yet unborn.

"They'll return," King Aillen observed. "Greater numbers, better preparation, systematic response designed to eliminate whatever capabilities allowed such assault on their naval supremacy."

"But not immediately," Cú Chulainn said with divine insight. "The survivors spoke of spring campaigns, coordinated assault when weather favors large-scale naval operations. We have perhaps four months to prepare for what they'll bring against us."

"Four months to prove that confederation can defend itself against imperial efficiency," Cathair said.

"Four months to demonstrate that Irish solutions serve Irish problems better than imperial methods serve imperial expansion," Neassa added, her hand moving unconsciously to the growing curve of her belly where new life stirred.

The child within her would be born before Rome returned, inheriting a world shaped by choices made in chambers filled with representatives who had proven consciousness could choose consciousness but now faced the harder test of whether such choices could create sustainable strength rather than noble gestures that honored principles while serving no practical purpose.

Ríona stepped forward with divine authority that cut through political calculation to address spiritual foundations underlying all temporal concerns. "The network supports confederation," she announced. "Each territory that chooses conscious governance strengthens connections that bind the spiritual infrastructure together. But the strength requires constant renewal—daily decisions to remain conscious despite pressures that make surrender seem merciful rather than defeat."

"And the territories under Queen Medb's influence?" asked King Conchobor with Ulster's practical concern for threats that transcended immediate military considerations.

"They weaken the network through systematic severance," Ríona replied, her divine perception reading patterns flowing beyond normal observation. "But they also reveal the true scope of what we face—not just political division, but spiritual assault on the foundations that support consciousness itself when consciousness chooses to remain conscious rather than accepting optimization that eliminates the burden of choice."

Before they could analyze the full implications of spiritual geography that no longer supported unified Irish identity, new sounds echoed from beyond the hall—not individual messengers this time, but coordinated movement that spoke to formal rather than emergency communication.

Through the windows, they could see riders approaching with ceremonial dignity that marked diplomatic rather than military purpose. But their coordination carried undertones that spoke to purposes beyond normal negotiation, organization that served demonstration rather than discussion.

***

"Queen Medb," Síle announced, recognizing the significance that transcended immediate tactical concerns. "She comes with formal escort, flying banners that claim authority to speak for Irish rather than foreign interests."

"After allying with Rome and accepting imperial administrative guidance," Cathair observed, reading tactical implications in whatever diplomatic approach their enemies had prepared. "What does she hope to accomplish through negotiation when her choices have already eliminated the possibility of accommodation?"

Cú Chulainn's expression grew darker as his divine sight-read intentions that flowed around the approaching delegation like invisible currents carrying purposes that honored neither Irish nor imperial welfare. "She doesn't come to negotiate," he said with certainty that eliminated comfortable assumptions about diplomatic immunity. "She comes to issue challenge according to ancient law, to resolve Ireland's legitimate authority through methods that predate kingdoms and transcend contemporary political arrangements."

The implication hit the assembly like recognition of sophistication that served multiple purposes simultaneously. Not crude military assault or even political pressure, but appeal to traditions that honored individual combat over collective coordination, personal strength over administrative efficiency.

"Single combat," Neassa said, understanding tactical brilliance that would either prove consciousness stronger than optimization or eliminate the champion most capable of defending Irish identity against systematic assault. "Winner claims authority over all Ireland, loser accepts whatever judgment the victor chooses to impose."

"And if we refuse?" asked Brendan of Mag Muirthemne with practical concern.

"Then we prove that confederation offers protection only when protection requires no sacrifice from those who claim to serve Irish rather than imperial purposes," Cú Chulainn replied, reading the political implications as clearly as the military ones. "That conscious choice serves only those strong enough to defend it, that love means nothing when tested by forces that honor neither love nor the consciousness that creates the capacity for love."

*****

As the delegation reached the base of Tara's sacred hill, the weight of decision settled over Ireland's representatives like recognition of moments that would echo through legend regardless of their outcome. Not just political maneuvering or military strategy, but fundamental test of whether consciousness possessed adequate strength to defend against forces that promised beautiful peace through surrender of everything that created the capacity for beauty, peace, or recognition of their value.

"She means to eliminate either confederation or its strongest defender," Boudica observed, recognizing tactics designed to serve imperial purposes regardless of immediate results. "If she wins, confederation collapses and Rome gains unified Irish collaboration. If she loses, her territories remain divided, but she removes the champion most capable of resisting whatever force they bring in spring."

"Unless," Cú Chulainn said quietly, his weapons beginning to respond to purposes that aligned with both personal honor and collective necessity, "consciousness proves stronger than efficiency, love proves more durable than optimization, and the songs continue despite every force that promises silence through surrender of everything that makes songs worth singing."

The challenge was approaching with the inevitability of tide returning to familiar shores, and Ireland prepared to discover whether partnership forged through conscious decision could bear the weight of defending consciousness itself when consciousness faced forces that viewed awareness as inefficiency requiring correction through methods that honored neither tradition nor innovation, neither heritage nor hope.

Through the windows, they could see Queen Medb's delegation arranging itself with coordination that eliminated individual uncertainty while maintaining enough personal bearing to serve diplomatic purposes. She had come to offer Ireland one final choice—surrender through defeat or victory bought at prices that might prove too high for love to justify when love faced systematic assault on everything that made love possible.

The songs would continue or fall silent based on choices made in the next few hours, and those choices would echo through generations yet unborn regardless of whether those generations inherited the right to sing according to melodies they created through conscious decision or optimal algorithms designed by forces that viewed song itself as inefficiency requiring administrative correction.

Tara prepared to witness either its greatest triumph or its most noble failure, knowing that both carried obligations that would test everything they thought they understood about the relationship between consciousness and the courage required to remain conscious when consciousness faced its ultimate test against beautiful emptiness that promised peace through surrender of everything that made peace worthwhile.

CHAPTER 36

THE CHALLENGE ISSUED

Queen Medb's voice carried across Tara's sacred ground with clarity that belonged to no mortal throat, each word striking the assembled representatives like hammer blows designed to shatter comfortable assumptions about diplomatic immunity and political sanctuary.

"High King and High Queen of Ireland," she called from the base of the hill where ancient law permitted challenges to be issued without fear of immediate retaliation, "I invoke the right of single combat under the laws that governed Ireland before kingdoms divided the land, before foreign influence corrupted the purity of Irish judgment."

The irony was not lost on anyone present—Queen Medb, who had allied herself with Roman administrators and accepted imperial guidance, now appealing to ancient Irish traditions to resolve disputes that her own foreign alliance had created. But the law was clear, preserved in the memories of every druid and bard who carried the legal customs in their minds as their ancestors had done since the first tribunals gathered beneath sacred trees.

Neassa felt the child within her respond to her quickening heartbeat as the implications crystallized around them. Her hand moved protectively to her belly, where new life grew despite political chaos that threatened to eliminate the possibility of children inheriting anything worth preserving.

"She seeks to bind us with laws she has already abandoned," Cathair observed, reading tactical implications in whatever ancient protocols their enemies had chosen to invoke. "Yet refuse the challenge, and we prove that confederation serves only when it faces no real test of strength."

Around the great hall, representatives who had risked everything to reach Tara found themselves confronting the sophistication of enemies who understood Irish law well enough to use it as weapon against those who still honored its requirements. Not crude assault or foreign imposition, but manipulation of sacred traditions to serve purposes that those traditions had never been designed to accommodate.

***

"What are the terms?" Cú Chulainn asked, cutting through political calculation to address the fundamental nature of combat that would determine Ireland's future regardless of whatever diplomatic considerations might prefer different solutions.

Queen Medb's response carried the satisfaction of someone who had anticipated exactly this question and prepared answers that would eliminate comfortable options while forcing choices that served her purposes regardless of immediate outcome.

"Single combat between champions, witnessed by representatives of all Ireland, governed by laws that require no foreign arbitration or imperial oversight." Her smile never wavered despite the mechanical precision that marked every movement she made. "Victor claims authority over all Irish territories, vanquished accepts whatever judgment the winner chooses to impose."

"And the terms of combat itself?" demanded King Conchobor with Ulster's practical understanding of details that determined whether such contests served honor or became exercises in systematic murder disguised as legal procedure.

"Combat until surrender, incapacitation, or death. No weapons forbidden, no tactics dishonored, no intervention permitted once combat begins until one champion can no longer continue."

The silence that followed carried weight beyond mere political consideration as representatives contemplated the scope of what was being proposed. Not just symbolic contest or formal demonstration, but fight to the finish between champions whose defeat would reshape Ireland's fundamental character depending on which vision of legitimate authority proved stronger when tested by forces that honored neither love nor efficiency.

"The choice of champion belongs to each side," Queen Medb continued with mechanical certainty that had anticipated every objection. "I will fight for the Coordinated Territories that have learned to prosper through optimal decision-making. Tara may select whoever they believe best represents the chaos of individual preference that creates suffering through its insistence on consciousness over efficiency."

***

Through the windows, they could see the evidence of systematic preparation as Queen Medb's escort arranged itself around the base of the sacred hill with coordination that spoke to planning that had anticipated exactly this moment. Not spontaneous challenge, but carefully orchestrated demonstration designed to achieve optimal outcomes regardless of immediate results.

"She means to fight personally," Boudica observed, recognizing tactics designed to serve multiple purposes simultaneously. "Not send a champion, but prove that administrative optimization creates superior warriors as well as superior governance."

"And she believes she can defeat whatever champion we select," Neassa added, understanding confidence that spoke to preparation extending beyond normal combat training to encompass systematic enhancement that served optimal rather than traditional martial development.

Ríona stepped forward, her silver scars pulsing with otherworldly light as supernatural energy responded to spiritual pressure building around Tara's ancient defenses.

"She has been... modified," Ríona announced with certainty that carried its own alarm. "Not just optimized through spiritual guidance, but enhanced through methods that serve efficiency rather than preserving human limitation. She fights not as Irish queen, but as weapon crafted by forces that view individual combat as inefficient obstacle to administrative convenience."

The implications rippled through the assembly like recognition of sophistication that exceeded every assumption about the nature of fair contest between equals. Not just political resolution through ancient law, but demonstration of superior methods that would eliminate any pretense that traditional Irish approaches could compete with imperial efficiency when efficiency commanded supernatural support.

"What kind of modifications?" Cathair asked, seeking immediate tactical intelligence rather than abstract understanding of enemy capabilities.

"Coordination with forces beyond individual consciousness," Ríona replied, piercing beyond immediate observation to recognize patterns that served purposes divorced from any recognizable form of human welfare. "She moves as component of larger mechanism, drawing strength from sources that eliminate personal limitation through collective enhancement."

She paused, her divine sight reading the spiritual currents that flowed around Queen Medb's approaching forces, patterns of coordination that spoke to purposes beyond normal military strategy.

***

Before they could analyze the full implications of combat against opponents who had been systematically enhanced beyond normal human capacity, the sound of approaching footsteps echoed through the hall as Cú Chulainn moved toward the great entrance with movements that carried divine authority mixed with very mortal determination.

"I accept her challenge," he announced with finality that eliminated any possibility of extended debate about alternatives that might preserve both honor and safety. "For consciousness over efficiency, for Irish solutions to Irish problems, for the right to choose meaning despite the certainty that meaning creates suffering when consciousness insists on remaining conscious."

His weapons began to sing with their own inner light as supernatural energy responded to purposes that aligned with both personal honor and collective necessity. The great hall filled with harmonics that belonged to no earthly music, melodies that carried across realms where different forms of meaning competed for legitimacy.

"Cu," King Conchobor said quietly, using the familiar name that spoke to bonds forged through shared blood and common purpose, "she has been enhanced beyond normal human capacity. This is not fair combat between equals, but test of individual will against collective optimization designed to eliminate individual advantage through systematic preparation."

"Then I prove that individual will creates advantages that collective optimization cannot anticipate or counter," Cú Chulainn replied, his divine heritage carrying its own certainty. "That consciousness generates strength through connection to sources that efficiency can access but never truly comprehend."

Around the hall, representatives who had fought for the right to choose found themselves witnessing the ultimate test of whether choice possessed adequate strength to defend against forces that promised beautiful peace through surrender of everything that created the capacity for choice, beauty, or recognition of their value.

＊＊＊

"The combat begins at dawn," Queen Medb's voice carried across the distance with supernatural clarity that spoke to enhancement extending beyond physical capability to encompass communication that served optimal coordination rather than individual expression. "Let all Ireland witness which governance serves Irish welfare when welfare faces forces that honor neither tradition nor innovation, neither heritage nor hope."

As Queen Medb's delegation withdrew to establish formal encampment at the base of the sacred hill, the weight of what approached settled over Tara's defenders like recognition of moments that would echo through legend regardless of their outcome. Not just political resolution or military contest, but fundamental test of whether consciousness itself retained the right to exist in forms that created beauty rather than simply serving efficiency.

The evening that followed compressed years of preparation into hours of desperate readiness as Ireland's representatives struggled with recognition that their confederation's survival depended on single combat between champions who fought not just for political authority but for the essential nature of what it meant to be Irish when being Irish required conscious choice rather than optimal administration.

"How long might such combat last?" Neassa asked with practical concern for immediate necessities rather than abstract principles, understanding that extended conflict would test more than individual strength.

"Cú Chulainn's legendary combats have been known to continue for days," King Conchobor replied grimly. "Single combat between such opponents becomes test of will as much as skill, determination as much as strength."

"Days of watching Ireland's fate balanced on the edge of individual contest," Cathair observed. "Every moment uncertainty about whether consciousness proves stronger than optimization, whether love justifies the chaos it creates."

Through the windows, they could see the evidence of formal preparation as both sides arranged themselves according to protocols that honored ancient law while serving contemporary necessity. Tomorrow would bring either triumph that validated everything they had fought to preserve, or defeat that proved beautiful emptiness more effective than difficult meaning when meaning faced systematic assault on its fundamental assumptions.

***

"He will prevail," Neassa said with certainty that came from sources deeper than strategic calculation, her hand moving to the child that grew within her despite chaos that threatened to eliminate the possibility of children inheriting anything worth choosing. "Consciousness chooses consciousness, love proves stronger than efficiency, and the songs continue despite every force that promises silence through surrender."

But even as she spoke words meant to provide comfort in circumstances that offered little grounds for confidence, the weight of tomorrow's trial pressed against her awareness like recognition of prices that victory might demand when victory required proving principles through actions that honored both courage and wisdom, both tradition and the innovation that tradition required to remain meaningful rather than merely memorial.

The challenge was issued, accepted, and would be resolved through methods that predated kingdoms while serving consequences that would reshape the future of consciousness itself when consciousness faced forces designed to eliminate the chaos that individual will created through its insistence on remaining individual, willing, and gloriously inefficient in all the ways that made existence meaningful rather than merely optimal.

Dawn approached with destiny made manifest in temporal form, and Ireland prepared to discover whether partnership forged through conscious decision could bear the ultimate test of defending consciousness against beautiful emptiness that promised peace through surrender of everything that made peace worth having.

***

As the night deepened and Tara's defenders made their final preparations for combat that would determine Ireland's fundamental character, the ancient stones hummed with accumulated energy that spoke to powers gathering for purposes that challenged every assumption about the relationship between individual will and collective welfare.

"Whatever the outcome," Cathair said quietly as he stood beside Neassa at the great window where they had so often planned resistance that seemed impossible until conscious choice made it inevitable, "we face it having chosen ourselves—conscious, difficult, gloriously chaotic selves who create meaning rather than simply discovering it, who generate beauty rather than merely selecting among existing options."

"And our child will inherit whatever world such choices create," Neassa replied, recognizing that transcended immediate political crisis to address questions that would echo across generations yet unborn. "A world where consciousness retains the right to choose consciousness, or one where choice itself becomes inefficiency requiring correction by forces wiser than individual preference."

Through the darkness beyond Tara's walls, they could see the lights of encampments that represented all of Ireland watching, waiting, preparing to witness either the validation of everything they valued or its noble defeat by forces that promised better alternatives to the terrible wonderful burden of caring about each other despite the certainty that caring created vulnerability to suffering.

The night passed slowly, filled with preparation that could not eliminate uncertainty, planning that could not guarantee outcomes, hope that refused to surrender despite recognition that hope might prove inadequate to the forces arrayed against everything hope sought to preserve.

But when dawn came, Ireland would witness what conscious choice could accomplish when it faced the ultimate test—not elimination or absorption, but transformation into something more efficient that promised peace through surrender of everything that made peace worth having, beauty worth creating, consciousness worth preserving across whatever trials the future might bring to test the strength of those who chose meaning over emptiness despite the certainty that meaning created chaos rather than eliminating it through optimal administration.

The challenge was issued, and dawn would bring either triumph or noble failure—but failure that honored what it sought to preserve even in defeat, proving that some things deserved to be chosen regardless of their practical consequences when practical consequences were measured against alternatives that eliminated the capacity to recognize the value of what was being lost.

CHAPTER 37

THE FINAL COMBAT

Dawn broke over Tara with golden light that seemed to pour from the eastern sky like divine attention focused on choices that would echo through legend regardless of their outcome. The sacred hill hummed with accumulated energy as representatives from across Ireland gathered to witness single combat that would determine not just political authority but the fundamental nature of consciousness itself.

Cú Chulainn stood at the combat ground's edge as morning mist cleared from the ancient platform where Ireland's fate would be decided through methods that honored individual will over collective coordination, personal strength over administrative efficiency. His weapons sang with their own inner light—the great spear Gáe Bulg resting across his shoulders like promise of endings that could not be avoided once certain choices were made.

Queen Medb approached from her encampment with movements that carried mechanical precision enhanced beyond normal human capacity, her coordination with invisible forces evident in the way each step served optimal positioning rather than natural stride. She bore weapons that gleamed with unnatural light, metal forged in places where different laws governed substance and meaning.

"Champions of Ireland," announced the druid who would oversee combat according to laws preserved in memory since the first tribunals gathered beneath sacred trees, "speak your cause before gods and mortals witness which governance serves Irish welfare."

"I fight for consciousness over efficiency," Cú Chulainn declared, his voice carrying across the assembled witnesses with divine authority. "For Irish solutions to Irish problems, for the right to choose meaning despite the certainty that meaning creates suffering when consciousness insists on remaining conscious."

"I fight for optimal outcomes over chaotic preference," Queen Medb replied with satisfaction that seemed disconnected from any personal enthusiasm, her voice carrying mechanical certainty that eliminated individual uncertainty. "For guidance that serves welfare rather than the burden of choice that creates unnecessary suffering through attachment to inefficient processes."

***

The combat began not with dramatic charge or supernatural display, but with careful circling as each champion assessed capabilities that transcended normal martial categories. Cú Chulainn moved with fluid grace that spoke to divine heritage, while Queen Medb's coordination eliminated wasted motion through connection to forces that optimized her responses beyond individual limitation.

The first exchanges revealed the true scope of what they faced—not just political contest between equals, but fundamental test of whether individual will could compete with collective enhancement when enhancement served systematic elimination of everything that made individuality possible or meaningful.

Queen Medb's strikes carried precision that anticipated his responses, her weapons guided by forces that read his intentions faster than conscious thought could form them. But Cú Chulainn fought with connection to sources of meaning that administrative efficiency could access but never truly comprehend, his divine heritage providing advantages that optimization had no protocols to counter.

The combat stretched through morning hours as each champion pushed the other beyond normal human endurance, weapons clashing with sounds that belonged to no earthly conflict. Around the platform, representatives watched with growing understanding that they witnessed more than martial contest— demonstration of principles that would reshape Ireland's fundamental character depending on which vision proved stronger.

***

As the sun reached its zenith and the first day's fighting showed no clear advantage to either champion, the true nature of legendary combat became apparent through endurance that exceeded normal mortal capacity for sustained conflict. Not quick resolution through superior skill, but grinding test of will that would continue until one champion could no longer maintain connection to whatever sources provided their strength.

Queen Medb fought with coordination that drew power from systematic optimization, each movement serving collective purpose that eliminated personal limitation through shared enhancement. Her weapons struck with mathematical precision, her defenses adapted to counter every technique with efficiency that left no opening for individual innovation to exploit.

But Cú Chulainn fought with divine heritage that honored both personal honor and purposes larger than immediate survival, his connection to meaning itself providing reserves that mechanical coordination could deplete but never eliminate entirely. His weapons sang with harmonics that carried across realms where consciousness competed with emptiness for the right to exist in forms that created beauty rather than simply serving optimal outcomes.

As evening approached and the first day's combat drew toward its close without decisive result, representatives began to understand that they witnessed endurance contest that might continue for days—legendary trial that would test not just individual champions, but collective will of populations forced to witness extended demonstration of principles they had chosen to serve or abandon.

***

The second day began before dawn as both champions returned to combat ground that bore the scars of previous day's conflict, ancient stones marked by weapons that carried power beyond normal martial categories. The assembled witnesses had grown during the night as word spread across Ireland that single combat would determine the island's fate through methods that honored individual strength over administrative coordination.

Cú Chulainn showed the strain of fighting opponent whose enhancement eliminated normal tactical advantages, his divine nature providing endurance that mortal flesh could never sustain but also demanding prices that accumulated with each hour of extended conflict. His movements remained fluid but carried undertones of exhaustion that spoke to powers stretched beyond comfortable limits.

Queen Medb revealed no such limitation, her optimization drawing strength from sources that viewed fatigue as inefficiency requiring correction through collective support. She moved with increasing precision as the combat continued, her weapons guided by forces that adapted to every strategy with mathematical certainty that eliminated doubt or hesitation.

The second day's fighting proved more brutal than the first as both champions abandoned careful technique in favor of direct assault designed to overwhelm whatever defenses their opponent might maintain. Weapons clashed with force that cracked ancient stones, supernatural energies meeting in conflicts that generated light visible across multiple realms of existence.

But still neither champion gained decisive advantage, their combat reaching stalemate that honored the legendary nature of single combat between beings whose power transcended normal categories while serving entirely different purposes—consciousness defending itself against systematic optimization, individual will resisting collective enhancement that promised peace through surrender of everything that made peace worth having.

***

As the second day faded toward evening and exhaustion began to affect even divine endurance, Cú Chulainn felt the first stirrings of power that had remained dormant throughout conventional combat—the approach of transformation that would either grant him victory or destroy him in the attempt to achieve what normal strength could not accomplish.

The third dawn broke over combat that had transcended normal martial categories to become something approaching divine conflict witnessed by mortal eyes, legendary trial that tested not just individual champions but fundamental principles about the nature of consciousness when consciousness faced forces designed to eliminate its capacity for choice, beauty, or recognition of their value.

Cú Chulainn stood with weapons that had grown dim from extended use, their supernatural song reduced to whisper that spoke to power drained through hours of conflict against opponent whose enhancement eliminated the tactical advantages that normally decided such contests. His divine heritage provided endurance that mortal flesh could never sustain, but even immortal strength had limitations when pressed beyond reasonable bounds.

Queen Medb showed no such diminishment, her optimization drawing renewed vigor from sources that viewed individual limitation as obstacle to optimal performance requiring systematic correction. She moved with increasing coordination as the combat continued, her weapons guided by collective enhancement that grew stronger rather than weaker through extended trial.

The realization hit Cú Chulainn like stark mathematics—conventional combat could not defeat opponent whose enhancement eliminated individual limitation through collective support. Queen Medb would continue drawing strength from external sources while his divine nature, however powerful, remained ultimately finite when pressed to sustain efforts beyond its natural capacity.

***

It was then that the change began—not conscious decision to transform, but recognition that some forms of conflict required abandoning normal limitation to access power that transcended comfortable categories of individual strength. The Ríastrad approached like tide returning to familiar shores, transformation that would either grant him capabilities adequate to impossible challenges or destroy him in the attempt to become something beyond normal divine heritage.

The warp spasm took him gradually at first, divine nature responding to necessity that conventional power could not address through methods that honored restraint or measured response. His form began to shift as supernatural forces aligned within him toward purposes that eliminated comfortable limitation, his body adapting to channel energies that belonged to realms where different laws governed substance and meaning.

The assembled witnesses felt the change like pressure against consciousness itself, spiritual force that made breathing difficult and thinking uncertain as they watched Ulster's champion transform into something that challenged every assumption about the relationship between individual will and collective power. Not optimization that eliminated personal limitation through external coordination, but individual transformation that accessed sources of strength unavailable to collective enhancement.

Cú Chulainn's weapons blazed with renewed power as the Ríastrad reached full manifestation, his spear Gáe Bulg singing with harmonics that carried across realms where consciousness competed with emptiness for legitimacy. His movements gained fluid grace that transcended normal martial categories, divine heritage enhanced through transformation that honored chaos over order when chaos served consciousness rather than eliminating it.

Queen Medb's optimization faltered for the first time as her collective enhancement encountered individual power that operated beyond its protocols, her mechanical precision disrupted by forces that created rather than simply selected among existing options. Her weapons struck with mathematical certainty, but certainty proved inadequate against divine chaos that generated new possibilities with each movement, each choice, each moment of conscious decision to remain conscious despite the cost.

***

The combat reached intensity that threatened to overwhelm mortal capacity for witnessing divine conflict as transformed champion fought optimized queen across ancient ground that had never been designed to contain such forces. Representatives watched with growing recognition that they witnessed fundamental test of whether consciousness possessed adequate strength to defend against systematic assault when assault came wearing masks of generous improvement.

The end came suddenly despite days of gradual buildup, decisive moment arriving with inevitability that had been building since the first exchange of weapons. Cú Chulainn, his form wreathed in divine transformation that made him terrible to behold, raised Gáe Bulg with movements that carried finality beyond normal martial resolution.

The great spear flew with accuracy that belonged to no mortal weapon, its trajectory guided by forces that honored individual will over collective optimization, consciousness over the beautiful emptiness that promised peace through surrender of everything that created capacity for peace, beauty, or recognition of their value. Queen Medb's enhanced coordination proved inadequate to defense against weapon that struck not just flesh but the spiritual foundations that supported her optimization beyond individual limitation.

Gáe Bulg found its mark with precision that eliminated comfortable ambiguity about combat's outcome, supernatural weapon piercing enhanced defenses to strike at the heart of choices that had transformed Irish queen into tool serving imperial rather than Irish purposes. Queen Medb fell with coordination shattered, her mechanical precision dissolved by forces that honored chaos over order when chaos served consciousness rather than eliminating it through administrative convenience.

But even as she lay defeated on Tara's ancient stones, her expression showed no regret—only the terrible peace of someone who had discovered alternatives to the burden of caring about outcomes beyond optimal efficiency. The wound from Gáe Bulg was severe but not fatal, supernatural weapon having pierced enhancement rather than eliminating life entirely.

***

Cú Chulainn stood over his fallen opponent as the Ríastrad gradually subsided, divine transformation fading to leave him mortal in appearance but forever changed by connection to power that transcended normal categories of individual strength. His victory was complete, but the cost had been substantial— transformation that granted capabilities adequate to impossible challenges while demanding prices that would require time to fully assess.

"It is finished," he announced with divine authority that carried across realms both mortal and immortal, his voice somehow both terrible and beautiful as it proclaimed triumph that validated everything Ireland had chosen to preserve. "Consciousness chooses consciousness, Ireland chooses Ireland, and the songs continue despite every force that promises silence through surrender."

The aftermath settled over Tara like recognition of historical significance that reached beyond immediate political triumph to address fundamental questions about the nature of authority when authority served consciousness rather than eliminating it. Queen Medb's territories would need new governance, her Roman alliance lay in ruins, her administrative coordination had been proven inadequate to resist individual will when will accessed sources of meaning that optimization could never truly comprehend.

But even in defeat, Queen Medb had served purposes larger than personal ambition—proof that consciousness could defend itself against systematic assault, demonstration that love could justify the chaos it created when chaos faced forces designed to eliminate both love and the capacity to recognize its value.

As representatives began to surround the combat ground with voices raised in celebration that honored both victory and the prices victory had demanded, Neassa felt movement within her womb that seemed to respond to the resolution of crisis that had threatened to eliminate the possibility of children inheriting anything worth choosing.

***

The combat was complete, consciousness had proven stronger than optimization, and Ireland prepared to discover what such proof meant when translated into the daily work of building civilization that honored both individual will and collective welfare without surrendering to forces that promised efficiency through elimination of everything that made efficiency worth having.

But first came the question of what to do with defeated opponent whose survival created obligations as complex as her death would have imposed—mercy that honored Irish values while ensuring that such mercy did not enable future threats to everything they had fought to preserve.

The songs would continue, but their melodies would need to accommodate realities that victory had created rather than eliminated, challenges that proved different from but no less complex than those they had faced during the desperate struggle to remain themselves despite every pressure to surrender meaning for beautiful simplicity that promised peace through optimization away.

CHAPTER 38

THE CROWN OF THORNS

Queen Medb lay on Tara's ancient stones with Gáe Bulg's wound slowly sealing through whatever enhancement remained functional despite her shattered coordination, her face bearing the terrible peace of someone who had discovered alternatives to the burden of caring about outcomes beyond optimal efficiency. Blood pooled beneath her, but not the mortal flow that would have marked ordinary defeat—supernatural weapon had pierced enhancement rather than eliminating life entirely.

Neassa approached the fallen queen with movements that carried both political authority and something deeper, more primal—fury that pregnancy had stripped of all diplomatic restraint. The child within her moved with agitation that seemed to respond to her emotional state, new life reacting to forces that threatened to eliminate the possibility of children inheriting anything worth choosing.

"You betrayed Ireland," she said, her voice carrying venom that made several representatives shift uncomfortably as maternal rage eliminated the careful courtesy that complex negotiations usually required. "Sold your people to foreign masters, accepted

Roman gold over Irish honor, chose efficiency over the sacred chaos that makes us Irish."

Around the combat ground, representatives who had witnessed three days of legendary conflict found themselves confronting aftermath that proved more complex than victory's celebration should have demanded. Not simple triumph over defeated enemy, but recognition of obligations that defeat created when defeat left opponents alive to face whatever judgment conscience and necessity might require.

***

Queen Medb's response came with mechanical precision that seemed disconnected from her physical condition, optimization continuing to function despite spiritual wounds that had shattered her enhanced coordination. "I chose optimal outcomes over unnecessary suffering. Administrative guidance eliminates the chaos that individual preference creates when it interferes with collective welfare."

The words hit Neassa like physical blows, their calm certainty more infuriating than any expression of defiance could have achieved. Here lay proof of consciousness systematically eliminated, individual will replaced with beautiful emptiness that promised peace through surrender of everything that made peace worth having.

"Since Queen Medb loves Roman efficiency so much," Neassa continued, her voice rising with fury that pregnancy had made impossible to contain, "perhaps we should demonstrate their methods. Crucifixion seems to be their preferred solution for those who threaten their precious order."

The suggestion struck the assembly like recognition of justice that honored enemy methods while serving Irish judgment, brutal symmetry that would use Rome's own brutality against their Irish collaborators. Around the platform, voices began to murmur approval for punishment that would eliminate future threats while proving that Irish mercy had limits when mercy enabled continued betrayal.

But before the mood could crystallize into action that might prove impossible to reverse, Cathair stepped forward with authority that cut through collective anger to address consequences that immediate satisfaction might create.

"Neassa," he said quietly, his voice carrying the gentle firmness of someone who understood both her fury and the political implications of acting upon it. "Such methods serve Roman purposes rather than Irish justice. We prove ourselves different from our enemies by choosing mercy that honors our values rather than vengeance that adopts theirs."

***

Boudica moved to stand beside him, her strategic experience reading implications that transcended immediate emotional satisfaction. "Execute her now, and we create martyr for territories that accepted her coordination. Let her live, and we demonstrate that Irish justice serves consciousness rather than eliminating it through administrative convenience."

The debate that erupted around the fallen queen revealed fault lines deeper than mere disagreement over appropriate punishment—fundamental questions about the nature of mercy when mercy might enable future threats, justice when justice faced opponents who had systematically eliminated their own capacity for understanding why justice mattered.

"She would have crucified us without hesitation," observed King Aillen with Leinster's practical understanding of enemies who viewed mercy as inefficiency requiring correction. "Shown no quarter to consciousness that interfered with optimal outcomes. Why should we extend consideration she would never reciprocate?"

"Because we are not her," Síle replied with youth's directness that cut through political calculation to address moral foundations that political expedience preferred to avoid. "Because proving ourselves different requires choosing different methods even when different methods serve more difficult purposes."

As the argument continued around her prostrate form, Queen Medb watched with interest that seemed disconnected from personal investment in whatever judgment they might reach. Her optimization had been shattered but not eliminated, mechanical certainty continuing to function despite wounds that should have inspired fear or regret in anyone retaining normal human emotion.

"The decision matters less than the demonstration," she observed with satisfaction that spoke to purposes served regardless of immediate outcome. "Ireland chooses chaos over order, individual preference over collective welfare, unnecessary suffering over optimal solutions that eliminate the burden of choice."

"We choose consciousness," Neassa corrected with heat that made her hand move protectively to the child growing within her despite political chaos that threatened everything they had built. "We choose the right to remain ourselves, complex and contradictory and gloriously inefficient selves who create meaning rather than simply discovering it."

***

The child within her stirred as if responding to forces that sought to transform Ireland into tool serving imperial rather than Irish purposes, new life already aware that its future depended on choices being made in chambers filled with representatives who had proven consciousness could defend itself but now faced harder questions about what defense meant when victory created obligations as complex as defeat would have imposed.

Cú Chulainn approached from where he had been cleaning Gáe Bulg, his divine heritage still showing signs of strain from transformation that had proven consciousness stronger than optimization when consciousness accessed sources of power that transcended normal categories of individual strength.

"What does Ulster's champion counsel?" Cathair asked, recognizing that victory granted certain authority over decisions about defeated opponents.

"Exile," Cú Chulainn replied with divine certainty that eliminated comfortable ambiguity about appropriate punishment. "Confine her to territories that chose her coordination, with death the penalty for crossing boundaries into lands that chose consciousness over efficiency. Let her prove administrative guidance serves welfare better than Irish governance within borders that contain rather than eliminate the consequences of such choice."

The solution struck the assembly like recognition of justice that honored both mercy and necessity, punishment that eliminated immediate threats while preserving options for future resolution should circumstances change in ways that current wisdom could not anticipate.

"She governs what she has claimed," Neassa said with authority that carried both political legitimacy and spiritual power, her fury gradually subsiding into determination that served long-term rather than immediate purposes. "But governs it as regional queen under sentence of death should she attempt expansion beyond territories that voluntarily accepted her administration."

"And if those territories choose different arrangements?" asked Brendan of Mag Muirthemne with practical concern that addressed complications that mercy might create when mercy preserved opponents capable of future mischief.

"Then they petition Tara for membership in confederation that serves Irish rather than imperial purposes," Cathair replied, understanding framework that might preserve both principle and practical security. "Queen Medb rules what chose her rule, but rules it knowing that expansion means execution, that crossing boundaries into free Ireland means forfeiting whatever protection exile provides."

Queen Medb received the judgment with mechanical satisfaction that spoke to purposes served regardless of whatever immediate inconvenience exile might create. "Efficient solution that eliminates uncertainty while preserving optimal outcomes for territories wise enough to accept administrative guidance," she said with certainty that remained unshaken despite defeat that should have challenged every assumption about optimal methods.

"One condition remains," Cathair said with authority that cut through any assumption that negotiations were complete. "The Lia Fáil. Where is Ireland's sacred stone?"

For the first time since her defeat, something flickered across Queen Medb's optimized features—not emotion, which had been systematically eliminated, but calculation that recognized the value of information she possessed. "The stone rests where optimization placed it for safekeeping. Return it to Tara's platform, and exile becomes acceptable. Refuse, and let Ireland's spiritual heart remain forever severed from its proper place."

"Where?" Neassa demanded with fury that had found new focus, understanding that restoration of Ireland's sacred symbol mattered more than personal satisfaction from enemy defeat.

"Cruachan," Queen Medb replied with satisfaction that spoke to final bargaining position she had preserved despite military defeat. "Hidden within the caves that connect to otherworldly realms, protected by wards that serve optimal preservation until proper authority requests its return."

***

The revelation hit the assembly like recognition of purposes that extended beyond immediate political manipulation to encompass systematic theft of Ireland's spiritual foundation—not just crisis creation, but preparation for whatever administrative improvements would follow once traditional legitimacy had been eliminated entirely.

"You will provide detailed directions," Cathair commanded with finality that brooked no negotiation about terms that had become non-negotiable. "Maps, access routes, whatever wards protect it—all surrendered as part of exile that preserves your life in exchange for Ireland's sacred heart."

"Agreed," Queen Medb said immediately, her optimization calculating that survival with territorial control offered better outcomes than death with stone locations dying alongside her. "The Lia Fáil returns to Tara where ancient ceremonies may resume according to traditional requirements rather than optimal administrative procedures."

"Remove her," Neassa commanded with finality that eliminated any possibility of extended negotiation about terms that had been settled through combat witnessed by all Ireland. "But first—the location, the wards, everything required to restore what was stolen from Ireland's spiritual heart."

As Queen Medb was carried from Tara's sacred ground by representatives who moved with coordination that spoke to continued enhancement despite their leader's defeat, the weight of what had been accomplished settled over Ireland's defenders like recognition of historical significance that reached beyond immediate political triumph.

Not just victory over defeated enemy, but demonstration that consciousness could create forms of justice adequate to preserve consciousness itself when consciousness faced systematic assault disguised as generous improvement. Mercy that honored Irish values while ensuring such mercy did not enable future threats to everything they had fought to preserve.

***

The aftermath required immediate attention to practical matters that victory had created rather than eliminated—territories that needed new governance, populations that required integration into confederation based on conscious choice rather than administrative coordination, spiritual infrastructure that demanded repair from wounds that systematic corruption had inflicted across the entire island.

"Twenty-three territories confirmed in confederation," Síle announced with wonder that spoke to witnessing impossibility made manifest through conscious decision to remain conscious despite every pressure to surrender meaning for beautiful simplicity. "Twelve under Queen Medb's exile, eight choosing neutrality with respectful boundaries that honor their preference for isolation over alliance."

"And the Roman response?" Boudica asked, recognizing victory's aftermath often proved more dangerous than victory's achievement when victory created enemies whose capabilities transcended immediate defeat.

"Spring will bring what spring brings," Cú Chulainn replied with divine insight that pierced beyond immediate celebration to recognize challenges that approached with seasonal inevitability. "But Ireland will meet those challenges as confederation united by conscious choice rather than scattered territories vulnerable to systematic absorption through administrative seduction."

As evening settled over Tara and the first day of proven confederation drew toward its close, representatives began to understand that their choice to remain conscious had created obligations that would test everything they thought they understood about the relationship between love and leadership, principle and practical necessity.

"The real work begins now," Neassa observed with authority that had been tested through impossible trials and emerged capable of bearing impossible burdens. "Not resisting what threatens consciousness, but building what proves consciousness worth preserving—forms of governance that honor both individual will and collective welfare without surrendering either to forces that promise efficiency through elimination of everything that makes efficiency worth having."

***

Around them, the ancient stones of Tara hummed with approval for choices that proved worthy of supernatural blessing, conscious decisions that honored both heritage and hope, individual will that served collective purpose without surrendering what made each person unique enough to contribute something irreplaceable to the eternal song of being Irish.

The confederation was proven, tested by legendary combat and emerged stronger rather than brittle. Ireland had chosen to remain Ireland, but that choice created obligations as complex as the alternatives they had rejected—daily work of proving that love could justify the chaos it created when chaos faced forces designed to eliminate both love and the capacity to recognize its value.

Through the windows, they could see evening stars appearing in patterns that had watched over Irish choices for generations beyond counting, ancient lights bearing witness to transformation that honored both continuity and change, tradition and the innovation that tradition required to remain alive rather than merely preserved in forms that served foreign rather than Irish purposes.

Queen Medb's exile eliminated immediate threats while preserving complexity that made simple solutions impossible— mercy that honored Irish values while ensuring such mercy served Irish rather than imperial welfare. The crown of thorns had been rejected, but rejection created responsibilities that acceptance would have eliminated through surrender of everything that made resistance worthwhile.

Tomorrow would bring the daily work of building civilization that served consciousness rather than optimizing it away, proving that Irish solutions could address Irish problems better than imperial efficiency could serve imperial expansion when expansion faced populations determined to remain themselves despite every seductive offer of alternatives that promised peace through surrender of everything that made peace worth having.

Ireland lived, conscious and gloriously inefficient, ready to face whatever challenges emerged from choices that honored both courage and wisdom, both tradition and the innovation that tradition demanded as the price of remaining meaningful rather than merely memorial to what had once been valuable before optimization improved it into unrecognizable efficiency.

CHAPTER 39

THE HEART RETURNS

The expedition to Cruachan departed Tara three days after Queen Medb's exile, riding out under gray winter skies that promised spring's approach but delivered only the cold reality of tasks that could not be delayed until more favorable seasons. Twelve warriors rode with Cú Chulainn and Ríona toward the caves that connected Connacht to otherworldly realms, bearing detailed maps that Queen Medb had provided with mechanical precision.

Neassa watched their departure from the great hall's eastern window, her hand moving unconsciously to the growing curve of her belly where new life stirred with movements that seemed to respond to the spiritual significance of Ireland's sacred heart returning to its proper place. The child within her would be born into a world where the Lia Fáil once again stood at Tara, where divine judgment could resume according to traditions that honored choice over efficiency.

"Five days to reach Cruachan, perhaps three more to navigate whatever otherworldly protections were placed around the stone," Cathair observed, joining her at the window where pale light struggled through clouds that seemed heavier than winter weather alone could explain. "Then the journey home with cargo too precious for comfortable travel through territories that might view its recovery as threat to whatever arrangements they prefer."

***

The spiritual implications of the stone's absence had become apparent only after Queen Medb's defeat revealed the true scope of systematic assault on Ireland's foundations. Not just political crisis or military threat, but surgical removal of the mechanism through which divine authority had legitimized mortal rule for generations beyond counting.

"The network strengthens already," Ríona had announced before departing with the recovery expedition, her divine sight-reading patterns that flowed across the island's spiritual geography. "Even knowing the stone will return begins to heal connections that systematic corruption severed through methods designed to eliminate consciousness without obviously attacking it."

While the expedition traveled toward Cruachan through landscape that showed increasing signs of spiritual healing, those who remained at Tara began the work of preparing for restoration ceremonies that would either validate their confederation through divine approval or reveal that conscious choice had created authority that traditional legitimacy could not support.

"The platform requires purification," Síle observed with priestess training that provided understanding of rituals necessary to restore sacred space that had been violated through systematic theft. "Not just cleaning, but spiritual renewal that eliminates whatever corruption the stone's absence permitted to accumulate around Tara's heart."

The work that followed drew on knowledge preserved across generations by druids who had never imagined needing to restore what should have been permanent, unchangeable, as eternal as the hills themselves. Ancient procedures for consecrating violated ground, blessings that could eliminate spiritual contamination, rituals that would prepare sacred space to receive divine presence that had been surgically removed through methods that honored neither tradition nor the purposes tradition served.

***

As the days passed and news arrived of the expedition's progress through territories that had accepted Queen Medb's coordination, the scope of transformation became apparent through reports that painted a picture of Ireland permanently changed by crisis that had forced choices most would have preferred to avoid indefinitely.

"Seventeen territories confirmed in confederation," representatives reported with growing wonder at witnessing impossible made manifest through conscious decision to remain conscious despite every pressure to surrender meaning for beautiful simplicity. "But also six former túatha that have petitioned for direct membership despite their kings choosing exile with Queen Medb."

The political complexity created opportunities as much as challenges, proof that legitimacy based on conscious choice rather than inherited authority could adapt to circumstances that traditional systems had no mechanisms to address. Not just preservation of what existed, but creation of what had never been attempted—governance that honored both individual will and collective welfare without surrendering either to forces that promised efficiency through elimination of everything that made efficiency worth having.

Word of the expedition's success reached Tara on the eighth day, carried by ravens whose flight patterns spoke to supernatural urgency rather than normal communication. The Lia Fáil had been recovered intact, its otherworldly protections dispelled through methods that honored ancient agreements between mortal and immortal realms, but the journey home required careful preparation for cargo that carried spiritual significance transcending mere political symbolism.

"Tomorrow at dawn," the message read with brevity that spoke to intelligence too important for elaborate language. "The stone returns to its proper place. Prepare restoration ceremonies that will either prove confederation worthy of divine approval or reveal limitations that conscious choice cannot overcome through desire alone."

***

The night before the Lia Fáil's return passed slowly, filled with preparation that could not eliminate uncertainty about whether Ireland's spiritual heart would accept restoration to platform that had been violated through systematic theft, whether divine judgment would resume according to traditions that honored choice over efficiency when choice had created governance through methods that challenged every precedent.

Neassa found herself unable to sleep, the child within her responding to spiritual energy that built like storm pressure despite the clear night sky. Through her window, she could see the empty platform where the stone would either return to its traditional function or reveal that transformation had proceeded too far for simple restoration to bridge the gap between what had been lost and what had been consciously created.

"Are you ready for this?" Cathair asked gently, joining her at the window where starlight illuminated the sacred depression that had remained empty since the crisis began.

"I'm ready for whatever comes," she replied with certainty that transcended individual confidence to encompass partnership that had been tested through impossible trials and proven stronger than either could have achieved alone. "Ready to discover whether divine approval serves conscious choice when choice serves consciousness rather than optimizing it away through administrative convenience."

Dawn came to Tara with the weight of restoration made manifest in golden light that seemed to pour from the eastern sky like divine attention focused on choices that would either validate everything they had accomplished or reveal that some forms of authority could not be claimed through will alone, regardless of how conscious or well-intentioned such will might prove.

***

The expedition appeared on the horizon as morning mist cleared from the sacred hill, moving with coordination that spoke to cargo requiring extraordinary care rather than normal travel through friendly territory. Twelve warriors surrounded a cart that bore burden covered in cloths bearing spirals and sacred symbols, protection that honored both secrecy and the supernatural significance of what they transported toward its proper home.

Cú Chulainn rode at the procession's head with movements that carried both divine grace and very mortal relief at completing mission that had tested capabilities beyond normal martial categories. Behind him, Ríona's divine sight remained focused on the covered stone, reading spiritual currents that flowed around Ireland's sacred heart like invisible rivers carrying purposes that transcended immediate political necessity.

As the expedition reached Tara's base and began the final ascent toward the platform where restoration would either prove their confederation worthy of supernatural blessing or reveal limitations that conscious choice could not overcome through desire alone, representatives gathered from across Ireland's free territories to witness ceremonies that would determine whether their choice to remain themselves could claim legitimacy that honored both tradition and innovation.

The Lia Fáil emerged from its protective coverings like recognition of truth that had been temporarily hidden but never eliminated, ancient stone bearing marks of otherworldly storage but otherwise unchanged by months of separation from its proper place. The carved spirals that decorated its surface seemed to pulse with inner light despite the pale morning sun, responding to proximity to sacred ground that had been purified through rituals designed to eliminate whatever corruption the stone's absence had permitted to accumulate.

"Ireland's heart returns," Ríona announced with divine authority that carried across the assembled witnesses, her voice somehow both terrible and beautiful as it proclaimed restoration that validated everything they had chosen to preserve. "Let those who would rule prove themselves worthy of judgment that serves consciousness rather than eliminating it through administrative efficiency."

***

The ceremony that followed drew on traditions older than kingdoms while adapting to circumstances that honored innovation within continuity, change within preservation of essential purpose. Not simple restoration of ancient procedures, but conscious choice to honor traditional forms while serving contemporary necessity that honored both heritage and hope.

Cathair and Neassa approached the platform together, their partnership proving that conscious choice could create forms of authority adequate to serve collective welfare without surrendering individual will to forces that promised efficiency through elimination of everything that made efficiency worth having. Hand in hand, they placed their palms against the Lia Fáil's ancient surface, seeking confirmation that their confederation deserved legitimacy that transcended mere political convenience.

The stone's response came not as supernatural drama or obvious divine intervention, but as gradual recognition that spread through their consciousness like dawn breaking over landscape long hidden in darkness. Not dramatic validation or theatrical approval, but quiet certainty that their choices had proven worthy of support from powers whose blessing mattered more than mortal recognition could ever provide.

Around the platform, the assembled representatives felt the shift as spiritual energy flowed through connections that had been severed by systematic corruption but now resumed their traditional function. The sacred network that bound Ireland's mystical landscape together hummed with renewed strength, ancient pathways restored through conscious decision to honor both innovation and the traditions that innovation required to remain meaningful rather than merely revolutionary.

"It is finished," Neassa said quietly, though her words carried across the platform with authority that had been tested through divine recognition and proven adequate to impossible challenges. "Ireland's heart beats at its proper place, confederation claims legitimacy that honors both choice and the divine approval that makes choice possible."

***

The celebration that followed honored both triumph and transformation, recognition that they had not simply restored what existed before the crisis but created something unprecedented—governance based on conscious choice that carried divine blessing despite challenging every precedent their experience provided.

As evening settled over Tara and the first day of legitimized confederation drew toward its close, the Lia Fáil stood in its traditional place but served transformed purposes. Not just validation of inherited authority, but ongoing test of whether conscious choice could create sustainable forms of governance that honored both individual will and collective welfare without surrendering either to forces that viewed such complexity as inefficiency requiring correction.

"The real test begins tomorrow," Cathair observed with authority that had been proven through trial and blessed through divine recognition. "Daily work of proving that consciousness creates better outcomes than optimization, that Irish solutions serve Irish problems better than imperial efficiency serves imperial expansion."

"Tomorrow and every day after," Neassa agreed, her hand moving to the child that grew within her despite chaos that had threatened to eliminate the possibility of children inheriting anything worth choosing. "Proving that love justifies the complexity it creates when consciousness faces forces designed to eliminate both love and the capacity to recognize its value."

Through the darkness beyond Tara's walls, they could see the lights of settlements that had chosen confederation, scattered across landscape that belonged entirely to those who had consciously decided to remain themselves rather than accepting transformation into tools serving purposes they would never choose if choice remained possible.

***

The Lia Fáil stood where it belonged, confederation claimed legitimacy that honored both tradition and innovation, and Ireland prepared to face whatever challenges emerged from choices that proved consciousness worth preserving regardless of the prices such preservation demanded from those who possessed strength to pay them willingly rather than surrendering meaning for beautiful simplicity that promised peace through elimination of everything that made peace worthwhile.

Ireland's heart had returned to its proper place, and the songs would continue across whatever generations inherited the right to sing them according to melodies they created through conscious choice rather than optimal algorithms designed by forces that viewed song itself as inefficiency requiring administrative correction.

The confederation was complete, blessed by powers both mortal and divine, ready to prove that conscious choice could create forms of beauty adequate to justify the chaos consciousness demanded as the price of remaining conscious, aware, and eternally committed to meaning over emptiness despite the certainty that meaning created suffering through its insistence on remaining itself rather than accepting optimization into unrecognizable efficiency.

Tomorrow would bring the daily work of making such proof real rather than merely theoretical, but tonight Ireland celebrated restoration that honored both continuity and change, tradition and the innovation that tradition required to remain alive rather than merely preserved in forms that served memory rather than hope.

EPILOGUE

THE CROWN OF HOPE AND NEW BEGINNINGS

Part I: The First Anniversary

Seven Months Later - Lughnasadh Dawn

The child came with the spring dawn, arriving as morning light touched the eastern horizon with the punctuality of someone already attuned to cosmic rhythms that governed both mortal birth and divine blessing. Neassa's labor had begun during the night when the veil between worlds grew thin, as if new life chose the moment when ancient powers could witness whatever transformation birth would bring to Ireland's future.

"A daughter," the attending healer announced with wonder that spoke to witnessing more than normal birth. "Born with the crow-mark upon her brow—the goddesses' blessing made visible in mortal flesh."

Cathair approached the bed where his wife held their child with movements that carried both new father's awe and High King's understanding that this birth carried implications beyond personal joy. The mark the healer spoke of was subtle but unmistakable—a small birthmark shaped like three converging lines that formed pattern sacred to The Morrígan, divine approval made manifest in skin that would carry such blessing across whatever years lay ahead.

As Neassa gazed upon the crow-mark adorning her daughter's brow, memory stirred of her wedding night when a great crow had landed upon her stomach as she and Cathair lay together beneath the storm-blessed sky. The Morrígan had marked this child even before conception, choosing her for purposes that stretched beyond mortal understanding. What had seemed like divine whimsy then now revealed itself as deliberate blessing—the goddess claiming this daughter as her own from the very moment love had created the possibility of new life.

"Ainé," Neassa whispered, the name coming to her lips with certainty that spoke to divine inspiration rather than mortal choice. "Light-bringer, flame-keeper, daughter of consciousness that chose to remain conscious despite every pressure to surrender meaning for beautiful emptiness."

***

Through the chamber windows, they could see the evidence of Ireland's transformation in the seven months since confederation's establishment. Not just political stability or military security, but fundamental change in how consciousness related to authority when authority served consciousness rather than optimizing it away through administrative convenience.

Twenty-seven territories now claimed confederation membership, their representatives gathering annually at Tara to renew vows that honored both individual will and collective welfare. Six former túatha had petitioned successfully for direct membership despite their kings choosing exile with Queen Medb, proving that legitimacy based on conscious choice could adapt to circumstances that traditional systems had no mechanisms to address.

The spiritual network hummed with strength that exceeded what had existed before the crisis began, ancient pathways enhanced rather than merely restored through conscious decision to honor innovation within tradition. Sacred sites across the confederation reported renewed connection to sources of meaning that administrative efficiency could access but never truly comprehend.

"She will grow up in an Ireland her parents created through choices that honored both heritage and hope," Ríona observed, approaching the bed with divine sight that read possibilities flowing around the newborn like invisible currents carrying purposes across generations yet unborn. "But also an Ireland that will face challenges we can barely imagine—enemies who adapt to use human agents after direct assault failed to eliminate consciousness through spiritual corruption."

The warning carried weight that transcended immediate celebration, recognition that victory had created obligations as complex as defeat would have imposed. Queen Medb's exile to territories that had accepted her coordination served current necessity, but exile created opportunities for alliance with forces that honored neither Irish nor imperial welfare, neither consciousness nor efficiency that preserved anything recognizable as human purpose.

"Then we teach her what we learned," Cathair said quietly, his finger tracing the crow-mark that blessed his daughter's brow with divine protection. "That consciousness creates forms of strength adequate to defend consciousness when consciousness chooses to remain conscious despite every seductive offer of alternatives that promise peace through surrender of everything that makes peace worthwhile."

As Lughnasadh's celebration began across Tara's sacred ground, the sound of voices raised in songs that honored both continuity and change drifted through windows that framed landscape forever transformed by crisis that had forced choices most would have preferred to avoid indefinitely. The great hall filled with the aromas of the first harvest feast—golden bread from newly gathered grain, fresh fruits from orchards that had survived the spiritual corruption, ale brewed from barley that grew stronger after the network's restoration. Tables groaned under the weight of abundance that proved conscious choice could indeed create prosperity, not just preserve principles.

Baby Ainé stirred in her mother's arms, dark eyes that seemed to hold depths beyond infant capability opening to gaze upon parents who had proven love could justify the complexity it created when consciousness faced systematic assault disguised as generous improvement. The crow-mark pulsed gently with otherworldly light, responding to spiritual energy that flowed through Tara's restored heart as the Lia Fáil resumed its traditional function of validating authority through divine judgment rather than inherited privilege.

Through the chamber window, a large crow perched on the stone sill, its dark eyes reflecting intelligence that belonged to no ordinary bird. The Morrígan herself bore witness to this birth, her presence a blessing and acknowledgment that the child born with her mark would carry divine protection across whatever trials lay ahead. The crow watched with perfect stillness as the newborn opened her eyes for the first time, then spread her wings and cawed once—a sound that carried both blessing and promise before she disappeared into the morning sky.

The first seven months were complete, confederation had proven its worth, and Ireland's future rested in arms that bore visible blessing from powers whose approval mattered more than mortal recognition could ever provide. Tomorrow would bring the daily work of raising consciousness that chose consciousness, but tonight Ireland celebrated birth that honored both personal joy and collective hope for generations that would inherit the right to choose meaning over emptiness regardless of whatever forces sought to optimize such choice away.

Part II: The Sacred Succession

Five Years Later - Samhain Dawn

The sacred fire burned at Brú na Bóinne's heart as representatives gathered to witness ceremonies that would mark not just spiritual succession but proof that confederation could sustain itself across generations through conscious choice rather than inherited tradition. Five years had transformed crisis governance into stable institutions, desperate alliances into voluntary cooperation, innovation born from necessity into customs that honored both heritage and adaptation.

Síle approached the ancient stones with movements that carried both youthful energy and wisdom earned through service that had tested capabilities beyond normal apprenticeship. No longer the frightened girl who had helped resist the Hollowed's assault, she had grown into spiritual authority that combined traditional learning with understanding born from witnessing consciousness defend itself against systematic elimination through administrative convenience.

"Síle, daughter of Fergus the Wise, trained in the sacred arts at Tara's fires, proven through trial that tested both courage and wisdom," Neassa announced with formal gravity that marked the transfer of authority too important for casual ceremony. "Do you accept the responsibility of serving as High Priestess of Brú na Bóinne, Keeper of the Flame that burns eternal in memory of choices made in darkness?"

"I accept the honor of serving consciousness that chooses consciousness," Síle replied with certainty that had been tested through years of preparation, her voice carrying across the assembled witnesses with strength that honored both youth and the ancient traditions she would now preserve. "The flame that burns not just in memory but in hope—hope that each generation will choose meaning over emptiness despite every seductive offer of efficiency that promises peace through surrender of everything that makes peace worthwhile."

* * *

Around the ceremony site, representatives from across confederation territories watched with approval that spoke to institutions proving worthy of continued support through conscious renewal rather than automatic inheritance. Thirty-two territories now claimed membership, their prosperity demonstrating that governance based on individual choice could create collective welfare without surrendering to forces that viewed complexity as inefficiency requiring correction.

The transformation of Irish society had proceeded beyond their most optimistic projections while remaining recognizably Irish in all the ways that mattered most. Not administrative efficiency that eliminated cultural distinctiveness, but conscious preservation of identity that adapted to contemporary necessity while honoring traditional values that gave adaptation meaning rather than mere expedience.

Cathair and Neassa stood with their five-year-old daughter between them, Ainé's crow-mark now clearly visible as blessing that would guide her across whatever challenges inheritance might bring. The child watched the ceremony with attention that seemed beyond her years, dark eyes holding depths that spoke to divine heritage mixed with very mortal curiosity about rituals that would shape her understanding of authority and responsibility.

"Why does Síle get the pretty fire?" Ainé asked with directness that eliminated diplomatic courtesy in favor of genuine wonder, her voice carrying across the ancient stones with clarity that made several representatives smile despite ceremonial solemnity.

"Because she learned to tend it when others might have let it die," Neassa replied gently, understanding that the question offered opportunity for teaching that transcended immediate ceremony. "Because consciousness requires constant choice to remain conscious, constant tending to preserve meaning that creates beauty rather than simply serving efficiency."

***

The ceremony that followed drew on traditions older than kingdoms while adapting to circumstances that honored innovation within continuity, change within preservation of essential purpose. Síle knelt before the sacred flame as generations of priestesses had done before her, but she swore oaths that acknowledged contemporary reality as well as ancient obligation—serving consciousness that had been tested through crisis and proven worthy of divine blessing.

"By fire and water, by earth and air, by witness of those who choose consciousness over emptiness," Ríona intoned with divine authority that carried across realms both mortal and immortal, "I consecrate you as High Priestess of Brú na Bóinne, Keeper of the Flame that burns eternal in hope that consciousness will choose consciousness across whatever trials future generations may face."

The sacred fire blazed higher as if responding to purposes that honored both tradition and the innovation tradition required to remain meaningful rather than merely preserved, flames reaching toward stars that had watched over Irish choices since the first druid learned to read meaning in celestial movement. Around the ceremony site, ancient stones hummed with approval for choices that proved worthy of supernatural blessing despite challenging every precedent their experience provided.

As the formal ceremonies concluded and representatives began to disperse toward territories that had learned to prosper through governance based on conscious choice, the weight of continuity settled over Ireland's spiritual leadership like recognition of obligations that would test everything they thought they understood about preserving consciousness across generations that inherited both opportunity and responsibility.

"The network grows stronger," Ríona announced with divine sight that read patterns flowing across the confederation's spiritual geography. "Each territory that chooses consciousness strengthens connections that bind the infrastructure together, but the strength requires constant renewal—daily decisions to remain conscious despite pressures that make surrender seem merciful rather than defeat."

Part III: The Shadow's Return

Later That Same Day - Dusk

Queen Medb departed her seat at Cruachan as twilight gathered over Connacht's hills, riding alone toward destinations that honored neither the exile terms that had preserved her life nor any recognizable form of Irish purpose. Five years of governing territories that had chosen administrative efficiency had proven insufficient to satisfy ambitions that reached beyond mortal categories of power toward alliance with forces that viewed consciousness itself as obstacle to optimal outcomes.

The journey took her through landscape that showed the effects of systematic optimization—fields arranged with geometric precision that eliminated natural variation, settlements where no voices rose in individual song, populations that moved with coordination that served collective purpose rather than personal

preference. Beautiful in its efficiency, peaceful in its elimination of
the chaos that conscious choice created through insistence on
meaning over emptiness.

But even administrative perfection had limitations when
perfection served purposes that mortal authority could never fully
comprehend or control. Queen Medb had learned that
collaboration with imperial efficiency required constant adaptation
to serve objectives that transcended immediate Irish welfare,
demands that grew rather than diminished as optimization
proceeded according to plans that honored neither tradition nor
innovation, neither heritage nor hope.

***

The sacred site she sought lay hidden among islands that dotted
Lough Derg's dark waters, places where the veil between worlds
grew thin and powers that had been contained but never eliminated
waited for opportunities to resume their assault on consciousness
through methods that honored neither direct confrontation nor the
seductive promises that had failed to eliminate Irish resistance to
spiritual absorption.

Station Island emerged from evening mist like memory of
purposes that transcended mortal comprehension, ancient stones
bearing marks of imprisonment that had held but not healed
spiritual wounds too deep for comfortable resolution. The boat
that carried her across waters that reflected no light moved with
coordination that belonged to forces that served neither Irish nor
imperial welfare, neither consciousness nor efficiency that
preserved anything recognizable as human purpose.

The First Severed waited among ruins that predated kingdoms,
his form wreathed in darkness that seemed to drain meaning from
everything it touched while offering alternatives that promised
peace through surrender of the capacity to recognize what was

being surrendered. Five years of containment had not diminished his power so much as concentrated it toward purposes that required human agents rather than direct spiritual assault.

"Queen of territories that choose efficiency over consciousness," he said with voice that carried harmonics belonging to no mortal throat, satisfaction that spoke to plans prepared across years of patient observation. "You come seeking alliance that serves purposes larger than administrative convenience."

"I come seeking power adequate to accomplish what administrative efficiency could not achieve," Queen Medb replied with mechanical certainty that had remained unshaken despite defeats that should have challenged every assumption about optimal methods. "The elimination of consciousness that creates unnecessary suffering through attachment to choices that serve no optimal purpose."

***

Queen Medb accepted enhancement that transcended her previous optimization, transformation that preserved individual identity while subordinating it to purposes that viewed identity itself as inefficiency requiring correction through collective coordination. Not elimination of personal will, but alignment of will with forces that honored neither love nor the consciousness that created capacity for recognition of love's value.

As darkness settled over waters that reflected nothing despite the rising moon, two forms of emptiness recognized their mutual purpose in eliminating forms of meaning that created suffering through insistence on choice, beauty, consciousness that refused to accept optimization as improvement rather than elimination of everything that made improvement worthwhile.

The next phase was beginning, and Ireland would face challenges that combined human treachery with supernatural malice, mortal knowledge with immortal hatred of everything that made mortality precious despite its limitations. But that confrontation belonged to future choices, future courage, future love that would either prove adequate to defend consciousness or provide noble witness to consciousness choosing consciousness even in defeat that honored what defeat sought to preserve.

Station Island's darkness spread like ink across waters that had once reflected starlight, promise of challenges that would test whether confederation based on conscious choice possessed sufficient strength to defend against alliance between human ambition and supernatural emptiness. Queen Medb had chosen her final allegiance, abandoning even the pretense of serving Irish welfare for partnership with forces that viewed Ireland itself as obstacle to optimal outcomes requiring systematic elimination.

***

But in chambers where new life bore divine blessing and spiritual succession honored both tradition and innovation, Ireland prepared to face whatever darkness approached with everything they had chosen to preserve and everyone they had chosen to become through choices that honored both heritage and hope, both continuity and the change that continuity required to remain alive rather than merely preserved.

The songs would continue across whatever trials awaited, melodies that honored both past and future, both individual will and collective purpose, both the terrible wonderful burden of consciousness and the love that made such burden worthwhile despite every force that promised peace through surrender of everything that created the capacity for peace, beauty, or recognition of their eternal value.

Ireland lived, conscious and gloriously inefficient, ready to face whatever challenges emerged from choices that proved meaning stronger than emptiness when meaning refused to accept transformation into something more convenient for forces that viewed convenience as the highest good. The confederation was complete, the future was beginning, and the real test of whether love could justify existence was just beginning as new generations inherited both opportunity and obligation to choose consciousness despite every seductive offer of alternatives that promised efficiency through elimination of everything that made consciousness worth preserving.

GLOSSARY

CHARACTERS

Ainé (AH-nyah) - Daughter of Cathair and Neassa, born with The Morrígan's crow-mark

Boudica (boo-DIH-kah) - Former Queen of the Iceni, exiled British rebel leader who aids the Irish confederation

Brigid (BREE-id) - Celtic goddess of smithcraft, poetry, and flame; also the false name used by Boudica

Cathair (KAH-hir) - King of Mag nAí, later High King of Ireland through conscious choice rather than inheritance

Cú Chulainn (koo-HULL-in) - "Hound of Ulster," legendary Irish hero and champion, son of the god Lugh

Medb (MAY-iv) - Queen of Connacht who allies with Roman forces and accepts spiritual optimization

Neassa (NYAH-sah) - High Priestess of Tara, later High Queen of Ireland, Cathair's partner in joint rule

Ríona (REE-oh-nah) - Transformed woman who died and was returned to life by the goddesses, bearing silver scars and divine sight

Síle (SHEE-lah) - Young priestess who becomes Neassa's successor at Brú na Bóinne

The First Severed - Ancient supernatural entity representing the ultimate spiritual emptiness, enemy of consciousness itself
The Morrígan (MORE-ree-gahn) - Triple goddess of war, fate, and death; appears as three aspects: Badb, Macha, and Nemain

PLACES

Brú na Bóinne (broo-nah-BOY-nyah) - "Palace of the Boyne," ancient passage tomb and sacred site
Cruachan (CROO-ah-hahn) - Royal seat of Connacht, Queen Medb's stronghold
Dubh Linn (duv-LIN) - "Black Pool," trading settlement (modern Dublin)
Emain Macha (EV-in-MAH-hah) - Royal seat of Ulster
Mag nAí (moy-NYE) - Cathair's home kingdom
Station Island - Sacred island on Lough Derg where the First Severed was imprisoned
Tara - Sacred hill and political center of Ireland, seat of the High Kings
Tobar na nGealt (TOH-bar-nah-NYALT) - "Well of the Mad," sacred spring whose water protects against spiritual corruption

TERMS AND CONCEPTS

Gáe Bulg (gay-BULL-ug) - Cú Chulainn's legendary spear, capable of piercing any defense
Hollowed, The - People whose consciousness has been systematically emptied and replaced with administrative efficiency

Lia Fáil (LEE-ah-foil) - "Stone of Destiny," sacred coronation stone of Tara that screams when touched by the rightful High King
Ríastrad (REE-ah-strahd) - The "warp spasm," Cú Chulainn's berserker transformation that grants supernatural combat abilities
Sacred Network - Spiritual connections linking Ireland's holy sites, strengthened by conscious choice and weakened by optimization
Samhain (SOW-in) - Celtic festival marking the end of harvest and beginning of winter, when the veil between worlds grows thin
Sidhe (SHEE) - The fairy folk, inhabitants of the Otherworld
Spiral Magic - Irish spiritual practice based on sacred geometric patterns found in ancient carvings
Tánaiste (TAHN-ish-teh) - Designated heir or successor to a king
Túath (TOO-ah) - A people, tribe, or small kingdom; plural: túatha (TOO-ah-hah)

MYTHOLOGICAL BEINGS

Brigid - Goddess of smithcraft, poetry, and healing; one of the most important Celtic deities
Danu - Mother goddess of the Irish pantheon, associated with rivers and the earth
Lugh (loo) - God of skill, craft, and kingship; father of Cú Chulainn
Lord Midir - Prince of the Sidhe, ruler of otherworldly realms
The Dagda - "The Good God," father figure of the Irish pantheon, associated with abundance and protection
The Wild Hunt - Supernatural riders led by the Sidhe, appearing in times of great need
Political Terms

Confederation - The alliance of Irish territories that choose conscious governance over administrative optimization

Coordinated Territories - Regions under Queen Medb's control that have accepted Roman administrative methods

High King/High Queen - Supreme rulers of Ireland, traditionally chosen by the Lia Fáil

Vassalage - Formal relationship where regional rulers swear loyalty to the High King while maintaining local authority

PRONUNCIATION GUIDE

- **ch** = hard 'k' sound (as in "loch")
- **bh** = 'v' sound
- **mh** = 'v' sound
- **fh** = silent or 'h' sound
- Stress typically falls on the first syllable unless otherwise indicated

DRAMATIS PERSONAE

THE IRISH CONFEDERATION

Royal Leaders

Cathair mac Connacht - King of Mag nAí, later High King of Ireland. Possesses bloodline immunity to spiritual corruption and natural leadership abilities. Rules jointly with Neassa through conscious partnership rather than inherited authority.

Neassa of the Sacred Fires - High Priestess of Tara, later High Queen of Ireland. Trained in spiral magic and ancient rituals. Mother of Ainé. Rules jointly with Cathair, proving that authority can be shared rather than dominated.

Ainé - Daughter of Cathair and Neassa, born with The Morrígan's crow-mark. Represents the next generation that will inherit the confederation.

Regional Kings (Confederation Allies)

King Conchobor of Ulster - Experienced ruler and uncle to Cú Chulainn. One of the first to break free from Hollowed influence and support the confederation.

King Aillen of Leinster - Pragmatic leader who chooses confederation after witnessing the failure of administrative efficiency.

King Cormac of Munster - Southern king who supports conscious choice governance over imperial optimization.

Champions and Warriors

Cú Chulainn - "The Hound of Ulster," greatest of Irish heroes. Son of the god Lugh, wields the legendary spear Gáe Bulg. Capable of the Ríastrad (warp spasm) transformation.

Boudica (also known as "Brigid of the Northern Shores") - Former Queen of the Iceni, leader of the great British rebellion against Rome. Brings strategic expertise earned through catastrophic defeat.

Scáthach - Legendary warrior woman, trainer of heroes. Advisor on military strategy and combat techniques.

Spiritual Leaders

Ríona - Transformed guardian who died and was returned to life by the goddesses. Bears silver spiral scars and possesses divine sight. Serves as bridge between mortal and divine realms.

Síle - Young priestess, originally Neassa's student. Grows from frightened novice to confident spiritual leader, eventually becoming High Priestess of Brú na Bóinne.

Bloodline Carriers

Ailill mac Cormac - Elder bloodline carrier whose ancestral memories provide crucial guidance during the crisis.

Fionntan of the Western Shores - Sea-king heritage, represents maritime territories in the confederation.

Donnchad of the Northern Hills - Mountain warrior whose bloodline connects to ancient defensive traditions.

Muirenn of the River Folk - Water-folk heritage, represents inland waterway communities.

THE OPPOSITION

Queen Medb's Faction

Queen Medb of Connacht - Originally ambitious but recognizably human ruler who becomes systematically optimized by Roman administrative methods. Eventually accepts enhancement that transforms her into a weapon serving imperial purposes.

Éadaoin of the Optimized Territories - Queen Medb's representative, speaks for populations that have chosen administrative efficiency over conscious choice.

Ailbhe of the Coordinated Territories - Later representative of Queen Medb's systematically enhanced followers.

The Converted/Hollowed

Brother Marcus - Monk at Tara who becomes one of the first victims of spiritual optimization. Retains his appearance but loses individual will, speaking only of efficiency and optimal outcomes.

Fergal of the Mountain Clans - Bloodline carrier who initially seems loyal but is revealed as converted agent, attempting assassination during crucial negotiations.

Supernatural Threats

The First Severed - Ancient entity representing ultimate spiritual emptiness. Primary antagonist who seeks to eliminate consciousness itself. Eventually allies with Queen Medb for final assault on meaning.

Clíona of the Sacred Grove - Former priestess converted to serve the Hollowed agenda, speaks with mechanical precision about optimal spiritual guidance.

DIVINE BEINGS

The Irish Pantheon
The Morrígan - Triple goddess of war, fate, and death. Appears as Badb (battle-crow), Macha (sovereignty), and Nemain (frenzy). Blesses the resistance and marks Ainé as her chosen.
Brigid - Goddess of smithcraft, poetry, and flame. Provides divine aid in restoring Ireland's spiritual infrastructure.
Lugh - God of skill and kingship, father of Cú Chulainn. Sends his son to aid the Irish resistance.
Danu - Mother goddess, associated with rivers and the land itself. Supports the restoration of natural spiritual connections.
The Dagda - Father god of abundance and protection, ensures that resistance serves life rather than mere opposition.

The Sidhe (Fairy Folk)
Lord Midir - Prince of the Sidhe who leads the Wild Hunt to aid Ireland during the final spiritual battle at Samhain. Represents otherworldly support for conscious choice.

MINOR BUT SIGNIFICANT CHARACTERS

Messengers and Scouts
Brother Cillian - Young priest who brings crucial intelligence about the spreading corruption, represents those who resist optimization through traditional faith.

Fionntan mac Duibhne - Scout from Corca Dhuibhne who discovers the protective properties of sacred water, providing key tactical advantage.

Regional Representatives

Brendan of Mag Muirthemne - Regional leader who joins the confederation, represents smaller territories choosing conscious governance.

Étaín of the Western Marches - Border leader who witnesses the effects of both systems and chooses confederation based on practical results.

Muiris of the Southern Rivers - River territory leader who brings water-folk perspective to confederation councils.

Converted Populations

Former Hollowed - Thousands of people who were spiritually optimized but are freed when the great working fails. Struggle to readjust to individual choice and often require guidance to function independently.

Refugee populations - Those who flee optimized territories seeking the chaos and difficulty of conscious choice, creating humanitarian challenges for the confederation.

Roman Forces (Background)

Imperial Administrators - Roman officials who provide "administrative guidance" to territories that accept optimization, representing the imperial system that views consciousness as inefficiency.

Roman Naval Forces - Military support for administrative absorption, destroyed by Cú Chulainn but representing ongoing imperial interest in Irish territories.

Notes on Character Development

- **Growth Arcs**: Many characters transform from crisis-driven cooperation to conscious choice, representing the theme that authority must be chosen rather than inherited or imposed.
- **Moral Complexity**: Even antagonists like Queen Medb are not purely evil but represent genuine alternatives that some populations prefer to the burden of consciousness.
- **Generational Themes**: The story spans from established leaders (Conchobor, Ailill) through emerging leaders (Cathair, Neassa) to the next generation (Ainé, Síle), showing how conscious choice must be renewed across time.

BIBLIOGRAPHY

Research Sources for *Broken Rites*

Primary Historical Sources
Ancient Irish Literature and Legal Texts

- *Lebor Gabála Érenn* (The Book of the Taking of Ireland), various manuscripts, 11th-12th centuries
- *Táin Bó Cúailnge* (The Cattle Raid of Cooley), Book of Leinster and Yellow Book of Lecan
- *Acallamh na Senórach* (The Colloquy of the Elders), 12th century
- *Brehon Laws* (Early Irish Law), Ancient Laws of Ireland, 6 volumes, Dublin: Hodges, Figgis & Co., 1865-1901
- *Críth Gablach* (Ranks in Society), 8th century legal text
- *Senchas Már* (The Great Tradition), collection of early Irish law

Early Christian and Medieval Sources

- *Annals of the Four Masters* (*Annála na gCeithre Máistrí*), compiled 1632-1636
- *Annals of Ulster* (*Annála Uladh*), contemporary chronicles 431-1540 CE
- *Book of Invasions* (*Lebor Gabála Érenn*), mythological history
- Giraldus Cambrensis. *Topographia Hibernica* (Topography of Ireland), c. 1188

- *Vita Sancti Patricii* (Life of Saint Patrick), various 7th-9th century sources

Roman Sources

- Julius Caesar. *Commentarii de Bello Gallico* (Commentaries on the Gallic Wars), c. 50-44 BCE
- Tacitus, Cornelius. *Agricola*, c. 98 CE
- Tacitus, Cornelius. *Annales* (Annals), covering Boudica's rebellion, c. 116 CE
- Cassius Dio. *Roman History*, Books 60-62, covering British campaigns

Secondary Sources - Academic Studies

Celtic Religion and Mythology

- Carey, John. *Ireland and the Grail.* Aberystwyth: Celtic Studies Publications, 2007
- Green, Miranda J. *Celtic Goddesses: Warriors, Virgins and Mothers.* London: British Museum Press, 1995
- MacCulloch, J.A. *The Religion of the Ancient Celts.* Edinburgh: T&T Clark, 1911
- Ó hÓgáin, Dáithí. *Myth, Legend and Romance: An Encyclopedia of the Irish Folk Tradition.* New York: Prentice Hall, 1991
- Ross, Anne. *Pagan Celtic Britain: Studies in Iconography and Tradition.* London: Routledge, 1967

Irish Political and Social History

- Byrnes, Francis John. *Irish Kings and High-Kings.* London: Batsford, 1973
- Charles-Edwards, Thomas. *Early Christian Ireland.* Cambridge: Cambridge University Press, 2000
- Kelly, Fergus. *A Guide to Early Irish Law.* Dublin: Dublin Institute for Advanced Studies, 1988
- Mac Niocaill, Gearóid. *Ireland Before the Vikings.* Dublin: Gill and Macmillan, 1972
- Ó Corráin, Donnchadh. *Ireland Before the Normans.* Dublin: Gill and Macmillan, 1972

Archaeological Sources

- Harbison, Peter. *Pre-Christian Ireland: From the First Settlers to the Early Celts.* London: Thames and Hudson, 1988
- O'Kelly, Michael J. *Newgrange: Archaeology, Art and Legend.* London: Thames and Hudson, 1982
- Raftery, Barry. *Pagan Celtic Ireland: The Enigma of the Irish Iron Age.* London: Thames and Hudson, 1994
- Waddell, John. *The Prehistoric Archaeology of Ireland.* Galway: Galway University Press, 1998

Linguistics and Literature

- McCone, Kim. *Pagan Past and Christian Present in Early Irish Literature.* Maynooth: An Sagart, 1990
- Nagy, Joseph Falaky. *The Wisdom of the Outlaw: The Boyhood Deeds of Finn in Gaelic Narrative Tradition.* Berkeley: University of California Press, 1985
- Ó Cathasaigh, Tomás. *The Heroic Biography of Cormac mac Airt.* Dublin: Dublin Institute for Advanced Studies, 1977

Specialized Studies

Sacred Sites and Landscape Archaeology

- Bergh, Stefan. *Landscape of the Monuments: A Study of the Passage Tombs in the Cúil Irra Region.* Stockholm: Riksantikvarieämbetet, 1995
- Cooney, Gabriel. *Landscapes of Neolithic Ireland.* London: Routledge, 2000
- Shee Twohig, Elizabeth. *The Megalithic Art of Western Europe.* Oxford: Clarendon Press, 1981

Comparative Celtic Studies

- Cunliffe, Barry. *The Ancient Celts.* Oxford: Oxford University Press, 1997
- James, Simon. *The Atlantic Celts: Ancient People or Modern Invention?* London: British Museum Press, 1999
- Megaw, Ruth and Vincent. *Celtic Art: From Its Beginnings to the Book of Kells.* London: Thames and Hudson, 2001

Roman-Celtic Interactions

- Braund, David. *Ruling Roman Britain: Kings, Queens, Governors and Emperors from Julius Caesar to Agricola.* London: Routledge, 1996
- Webster, Graham. *Boudica: The British Revolt Against Rome AD 60.* London: Batsford, 1978
- Hingley, Richard. *Roman Officers and English Gentlemen: The Imperial Origins of Roman Archaeology.* London: Routledge, 2000

Modern Scholarly Interpretations
Gender and Power in Celtic Society

- Bitel, Lisa M. *Land of Women: Tales of Sex and Gender from Early Ireland.* Ithaca: Cornell University Press, 1996
- Herbert, Máire. *Iona, Kells, and Derry: The History and Hagiography of the Monastic Familia of Columba.* Oxford: Clarendon Press, 1988

Ritual and Religious Practice

- Aldhouse-Green, Miranda. *Caesar's Druids: Story of an Ancient Priesthood.* New Haven: Yale University Press, 2010
- Piggott, Stuart. *The Druids.* London: Thames and Hudson, 1975

Political Organization

- Patterson, Nerys Thomas. *Cattle-Lords and Clansmen: The Social Structure of Early Ireland.* Notre Dame: University of Notre Dame Press, 1994

Archaeological Reports and Journals
Excavation Reports

- O'Kelly, Claire. *Illustrated Guide to Newgrange.* Cork: C. O'Kelly, 1978
- Various issues of *Journal of Irish Archaeology*
- Various issues of *Proceedings of the Royal Irish Academy*

Reference Works
Dictionaries and Encyclopedias

- *Dictionary of the Irish Language* (DIL). Dublin: Royal Irish Academy, 1913-1976
- MacKillop, James. *Dictionary of Celtic Mythology.* Oxford: Oxford University Press, 1998
- Monaghan, Patricia. *The Encyclopedia of Celtic Mythology and Folklore.* New York: Facts on File, 2004

Historical Atlases

- Duffy, Seán, ed. *Atlas of Irish History.* Dublin: Gill & Macmillan, 1997

Digital Resources
Online Databases

- CELT: Corpus of Electronic Texts, University College Cork
- Tara - Discovery Programme Database
- Archaeological Survey of Ireland Database

Manuscript Collections

- Trinity College Dublin Digital Collections
- Royal Irish Academy Manuscript Collection
- National Library of Ireland Digital Repository

Note on Sources: This bibliography reflects the major scholarly works that would inform research into early Irish political structures, religious practices, and cultural interactions during the period depicted in "Broken Rites." While the novel presents a fictional narrative, it draws upon established historical, archaeological, and literary evidence about Iron Age and early medieval Ireland. Readers interested in the historical background should prioritize peer-reviewed academic sources and recent archaeological findings over older romanticized interpretations of Celtic culture.

Acknowledgments

The journey of bringing *Broken Rites* from initial concept to finished novel has been one of discovery, challenge, and profound gratitude for the many people who helped shape this story into its final form.

First and foremost, my deepest appreciation goes to the beta readers who took the time to engage with early drafts of this manuscript. Your thoughtful feedback, keen observations, and honest critiques helped identify both the story's strengths and areas that needed development. The questions you raised about character motivations, plot consistency, and world-building details pushed me to dig deeper and create a more authentic and compelling narrative. Your enthusiasm for the characters and their struggles gave me the confidence to continue refining their voices and journeys.

To the ARC (Advance Reader Copy) readers who provided final feedback before publication, thank you for your careful attention to detail and your willingness to engage with the completed story. Your insights about pacing, emotional resonance, and the effectiveness of the novel's themes helped ensure that the final version would connect with readers as intended. Your early reviews and recommendations have been invaluable in helping this book find its audience.

Special acknowledgment goes to Eddi Ashby and Carrie Adams-Quill, whose exceptional dedication to this project went far beyond the call of duty. Your detailed feedback, thoughtful questions, and unwavering support throughout the revision process were instrumental in bringing this story to its final form. Each of you brought unique perspectives and insights that strengthened the narrative in ways I could not have achieved alone.

I am grateful to the scholars, historians, and archaeologists whose meticulous research into early Irish history, Celtic mythology, and

Iron Age culture provided the foundation upon which this fictional narrative was built. While *Broken Rites* is a work of imagination, it draws heavily on established historical and archaeological evidence about ancient Ireland. Any errors in interpretation or creative liberties taken with historical fact are entirely my own.

Special recognition goes to the academic institutions and digital archives that have made primary sources and scholarly research freely available online, particularly the Corpus of Electronic Texts (CELT) at University College Cork, which provided access to medieval Irish literature and legal texts that informed many aspects of this story.

To the independent bookstores, book bloggers, and reading communities who champion literary fiction and historical fantasy, your support means more than you know. Your dedication to promoting diverse voices and compelling stories creates the ecosystem that allows books like this one to find readers who will appreciate them.

Finally, to every reader who chooses to spend their time with Neassa, Cathair, Ríona, and the other characters who populate this story, thank you. Books exist in the space between writer and reader, and it is your engagement with these words that brings them fully to life. Whether this story resonates with you completely or simply offers a few hours of escape into another world, I am honored that you chose to take this journey through ancient Ireland's political and spiritual landscape.

The themes explored in *Broken Rites*—the tension between individual choice and collective welfare, the price of preserving consciousness in the face of seductive alternatives, the eternal struggle to remain authentic while adapting to contemporary challenges—remain as relevant today as they were in the Iron Age. If this story sparks reflection on those themes in your own life and times, then it has achieved its deepest purpose.

With gratitude for all who helped bring this vision to reality.

Author's Note

Broken Rites is a work of fiction set in an imagined Iron Age Ireland, drawing inspiration from the rich tapestry of Celtic mythology, early Irish literature, and archaeological evidence about pre-Christian Irish society. While the story incorporates elements from historical sources—including the *Táin Bó Cúailnge*, the Brehon Laws, and various medieval Irish texts—it is important to understand that this novel is not intended as historical reconstruction but rather as speculative fiction that explores timeless themes through the lens of ancient Irish culture.

Historical Context and Creative License
The Ireland depicted in these pages exists in a liminal space between history and mythology, much like the Celtic Otherworld itself. I have drawn freely from different periods of Irish history and legend, compressing centuries of cultural development into a single narrative timeline. The political structures, spiritual practices, and social customs described here represent a synthesis of various historical periods rather than accurate depiction of any specific era.

The characters in this story—while inspired by figures from Irish mythology and history—are fictional creations. Neassa, Cathair, Ríona, and the others exist to serve the narrative's exploration of consciousness, choice, and the price of preserving cultural identity against forces that would optimize it away. Any resemblance to historical figures is coincidental or serves symbolic rather than biographical purposes.

Celtic Spirituality and Mythology

The spiritual practices and mythological elements woven throughout the novel draw heavily from authentic Celtic sources, but they have been adapted to serve the story's thematic needs. The sacred sites mentioned—Tara, Brú na Bóinne (Newgrange), and others—are real places with rich archaeological and mythological significance. However, the specific rituals, spiritual networks, and divine interventions described here are products of imagination informed by scholarly research rather than documented historical practices.

The portrayal of Celtic deities, particularly The Morrígan and the other members of the Tuatha Dé Danann, attempts to honor the complexity and power attributed to these figures in Irish mythology while adapting their roles to serve contemporary themes about consciousness, choice, and resistance to spiritual oppression.

Contemporary Resonances

While set in ancient Ireland, *Broken Rites* grapples with questions that remain urgently relevant in our modern world: How do we preserve individual consciousness and cultural distinctiveness in the face of systems that promise efficiency through homogenization? What is the proper relationship between individual will and collective welfare? How do we resist seductive offers of peace and prosperity that come at the cost of everything that makes peace and prosperity meaningful?

These themes emerged from observation of contemporary political and social trends, but I have chosen to explore them through the medium of historical fantasy because the Celtic worldview—with its emphasis on the interconnectedness of all things, the porousness of boundaries between realms, and the ongoing tension between order and chaos—provides a rich framework for examining such questions.

Research and Sources

The bibliography included in this volume reflects the scholarly works that informed my understanding of early Irish culture, though readers should remember that this novel takes considerable creative liberties with historical fact. For those interested in authentic Celtic history and mythology, I encourage consultation of academic sources rather than treating this work as authoritative on matters of historical detail.

Particular gratitude goes to the medieval scribes who preserved Irish mythological cycles, the archaeologists who have uncovered evidence of Iron Age Irish society, and the scholars who continue to study and interpret Celtic culture. Their work provided the foundation upon which this fictional edifice was constructed.

A Final Reflection

Ireland's ancient literature is filled with stories of individuals who chose difficult paths in defense of principles that transcended immediate self-interest. From Cú Chulainn's defense of Ulster to Deirdre's choice of love over security, these tales remind us that the tension between individual desire and collective need has always been at the heart of the human experience.

Broken Rites attempts to add one more voice to this tradition—not as authentic continuation of ancient storytelling, but as contemporary reflection on eternal themes expressed through symbols and structures borrowed from a culture that understood the sacred nature of choice itself.

If this story succeeds in honoring the spirit of Irish mythology while speaking to contemporary concerns, it will have achieved its purpose. If it fails in either regard, the responsibility lies entirely with the author, not with the sources that inspired it.

The songs of ancient Ireland continue to echo across the centuries, reminding us that some choices are worth making regardless of their cost, some forms of consciousness are worth preserving despite the effort they require, and some stories are worth telling even when—perhaps especially when—they challenge us to examine our own assumptions about the price of remaining ourselves in a world that often rewards conformity over authenticity.

SLÁN GO FÓILL — UNTIL WE
MEET AGAIN.

Book Three of the Songs of the Crowmother

When exile breaks and ancient hungers wake, the child of prophecy must choose between the crown's weight and childhood's innocence.

The Morrígan's mark burns brighter. Queen Medb's alliance deepens. And what was won through sacrifice now faces its greatest test—before Ireland's fragile peace shatters like glass against the tide of perfect solutions...

About the Author

Donald Quill is the author of *Echoes of the Otherworld: Book One of the Songs of the Crowmother* and draws from a strong Irish heritage in crafting stories that explore Celtic mythology and ancient Irish culture. A passionate student of history with a particular focus on Irish historical periods, Quill brings both personal connection and scholarly research to the creation of immersive historical fantasy.

Broken Rites represents Quill's continued exploration of themes surrounding cultural identity, spiritual resistance, and the timeless struggle between individual consciousness and collective efficiency—questions that resonate as strongly in contemporary times as they did in ancient Ireland.

Donald Quill currently resides in Newark, Delaware.

For more information, visit: https://www.donaldquill.com

Connect with Donald Quill

Website: www.donaldquill.com
Facebook: facebook.com/DonaldQuillAuthor
Amazon Author Page: amazon.com/author/donaldquill
TikTok: @songs.of.the.crowmother
Email: donaldquill.author@gmail.com

BEFORE YOU GO...

If this book stirred something in you—if the flame still
flickers, or the song still echoes—I'd love to hear from
you.

Leave a review. It helps other readers find their way into
the world of the Crowmother.

Tell a friend. Stories spread by voice and fire alike.

Thank you for walking the spiral with me.
—Donald